The Storyteller:

Live for Today and Look Toward the Future

David L. Schapira

ISBN-13: 9781494253172
ISBN-10: 1494253178

Acknowledgements

It is imperative that I thank my wife Karen, as she has been my soul mate and companion for over thirty years. Her excitement with my writing nearly equals mine.

Thank-you to my relatives and friends who have encouraged me to put my stories to pen, lo, these many years. A special thank-you to Mike, Rick, Jerry P., James F., Ruben, and Ralph, platoon members whom I`ve either visited or kept contact with since we`ve returned from Vietnam.

I have a special acknowledgement for James P., Jerry C., Jesus, and Larry, 2nd Platoon warriors who gave the ultimate sacrifice while in combat. These men are my true heroes and will never be forgotten.

Table of Contents

Prologue		vii
I	The Draft	1
II	A Basic Start	13
III	M.O.S.	27
IV	It`s a Learning Process	31
V	Three More Months at Polk	55
VI	Earning Sergeant Stripes	75
VII	Rules & Responsibilities	139
VIII	On the Job Training	153
IX	It Can Get Scary	189
X	Bring on the Enemy	221
XI	Life Can Hurt, Too	287
Epilogue		321

Prologue

Finding an enjoyable book is not so easy. For me, I enjoy humorous or action-packed books. My main focus when reading is to understand who the main characters are. I want to delve into the emotions of these people, so that I can appreciate important changes happening to them from the beginning to the end of their existence in the story.

The Storyteller: Live for Today and Look Toward the Future features ONE main character. He is put into unavoidable situations which seem completely alien to him. Abe is of the Jewish faith, but this is by no means a book about religion. He is a naïve fellow who tries to negotiate his way through military service, including a tour in Vietnam, at a time (1968-1970) of unrest in America. One dilemma after another confronts Abe, and he encounters unusual characters, and harrowing, pulse-raising situations that are inherent in any military experience. His being Jewish makes this story even more interesting as boys of the faith, that I knew back then, were not known for military prowess during the 60`s... lawyers and doctors, yes, soldiers, no.

This book is a fictional writing, but it is also loosely based on actual events. While in the service, Abe will discover much hilarity, great sorrow, happy moments, and terrifying adventure throughout the twenty-two and a half months of his commitment to America. **Enjoy this fast-moving novel.**

I

The Draft

Aging has always been confusing to me. The young dream of being older, while the old wish to be younger. A boy, in Iowa City, Iowa, during the 1960`s, looked forward to being 14 years old so he could get a driver`s permit. And at the miracle age of 16, that boy could get his driver`s license and be able to drive the streets on his own. All right, I AM that boy, and driving solo was a day I had looked forward to since I was ten.

My name is Abraham Dicker Stein, named after my maternal grandfather, who was the cantor of our town`s only synagogue. Abe wasn`t a common name in Iowa City, but I liked it.

Mine was a smallish, university town, and while growing up, I found many things to occupy my time, so I was never bored. Each new birthday brought a promise of new adventures, yet, I constantly found myself either looking forward to being even older, or regretting having to leave a younger, more innocent year behind me. For instance, when I turned ten I knew I could join Little League, a dream of mine since seven. But, while playing Little League, I dreamed of playing Babe Ruth with the older boys. However, when I DID get into Babe Ruth, I missed the much easier time of playing Little League, as competition got tougher the older I got.

Turning older, however, also meant advancing another year in school, and THAT meant harder homework with more studying. Since I didn`t like school work, I often wished I was back in earlier grades where there was more time to play. I was a late bloomer, so the lack of maturity was a constant challenge.

The age of thirteen was supposed to change me in a big way. I had my bar mitzvah, which was my becoming a man, according to the Jewish religion. Oy, was preparing for THAT occasion tough for me. I was supposed to be a man, but in reality, I was a lazy, hyper-active kid for years AFTER my bar mitzvah. I just never seemed satisfied with my age, no matter what age I got to be.

As I have mentioned, turning sixteen was a huge age for me…driving, playing high school baseball, and being allowed to go on dates were all good reasons for turning sixteen. However, it was age 16 when I developed a hyper-thyroid condition. To combat that disease I was treated with radioactive iodine, and placed in a six-year observation program. I mention SIX years because being in this study changed my future in a big way, as you will find out later.

With my medical condition under control, I went about life normally, but aging was still fascinating to me. Eighteen meant graduation, and turning twenty-one meant I could drink alcohol legally in Iowa. I wasn`t looking forward to turning thirty, however. For some reason there was a saying that nobody over thirty could be trusted. And turning fifty, well, talk about being old. I didn`t want to get to fifty very quickly because I was sure fun stopped and death couldn`t be too far behind. My grandparents were in their 60`s, and they seemed ancient. As a kid I could NEVER visualize myself turning 50 let alone 60. In those days nobody talked about `senior discounts` or Medicare, so aging was a major concern of mine.

Today I am 67 years of age, and my fears of being my grandparents` age has become a reality. As a young person I didn`t get injured much, and I played ALL the sports. I`d get bumps and bruises, but they healed quickly. At my current age, daily aches and pains are constant companions, and healing from REAL injury takes forever, though I eventually heal. It is the changes I see in my mental state that are bothersome to me. I watched my grandmother suffer from a debilitating mental problem. Toward the end of her life she couldn`t recognize anybody in my family, and had even reverted to speaking Russian or Yiddish. She could remember facts from her childhood, but couldn`t remember things she was told a mere fifteen minutes earlier. It broke my heart. I now find myself having trouble remembering some facts or statements from more recent occurrences. When I am reminded of these things, I usually respond, "I don`t remember that," and actually mean it. I`m getting a little worried about further slippage.

One of the ways that I use to fight memory loss is to tell stories. I LOVE telling stories. Recounting past events forces me to remember some of the smallest facts about things that I went through. I can remember details of events, as far back as age five, when I started talking. There are times I begin a story and see people getting bored rather quickly. Sadly for me, that does happen. But there are certain topics that DO seem to captivate listeners when I speak. One of the more interesting topics covers the years 1968-1970, the years I was in the military. Those years cover me from when I was twenty-two until twenty-four years of age, but I remember that time in my life clearly....well, for the most part. Let`s put my memory to the test, shall we?

Previously I mentioned being on a six-year observation program for a thyroid condition, which I developed at age sixteen. For two years I visited my Internal Medicine doctor, he would ask me questions, nod his approval at my progress, and I would carry on with my life. At age eighteen, however, I began to appreciate the fact that I was being observed, but for selfish reasons.

That was the year 1964, and in Iowa eighteen-year-old boys were obligated to register for the military draft. The United States had gotten involved in a war in Southeast Asia, Vietnam to be more specific. Since America`s involvement had intensified to the point where enlisted men weren`t enough to fill deployment quotas, all fifty states were being asked to send young men, who had registered with their draft boards.

In 1964 I really didn`t know anything about Vietnam, so it bothered me when I was told to report to Des Moines for a required physical, intended to see if I was draft worthy. I asked a few of my older friends if passing the tests automatically meant I would be headed into the army. One answer sounded good...if I was enrolled in school, I could get an educational deferment. I raced to the University of Iowa and signed up for a full class load WELL before I reported to Des Moines.

I had a Plan B, too, even though I knew I wouldn`t need it, being a student and all. When I would arrive for my physical, I would tell EVERYONE that I was not an outdoorsman, which is true. I camped out once in my life and couldn`t sleep. The ground was too hard. Couldn`t be a soldier if I had trouble sleeping on the hard ground, could I? Also, I had only fired a rifle one time in my life, and that was a BB gun. At 15, while in Texas visiting my birth father, I joined him hunting. He wanted to kill a deer, but I told him I had the Bambi Syndrome, and could NEVER kill anything. I agreed to carry a BB rifle, and then he asked me if I could shoot at cottonmouth snakes in a swamp. I don`t particularly care for snakes, so I agreed to go on the hunt. Never even came close to hitting a snake, though. Soldiers hunt people and kill them. I would let the military know I couldn`t really shoot at a person. Nope, I would let everybody know that I was NOT soldier material. Still, I was very nervous when we rolled into the Des Moines military facility.

I didn`t get a chance to tell anyone my sad tales about being a poor soldier prospect. The people in uniform were too busy yelling at us most of the time. "Move over there," and "Let`s keep this line moving," were popular phrases that were shouted incessantly. It started to get comical to me because much of the yelling was aimed at guys who looked hung-over, high, or were just plain malingerers. I didn`t take any of the shouting personally, but was a bit frustrated because I couldn`t find anyone who wanted to hear my reasons for not being a good draft choice. Suddenly, I was sent to a room to speak with a guy in a white coat. I assumed he was a doctor, so I was SURE he would listen to my sad stories, plus I would DEFINITELY tell him I had enrolled in school. "Mr. Stein," he began before I could open my mouth, "you will be classified 1-Y. Seems you are in a medical study on your thyroid. Is that correct?"

"Yes, doctor, since I have been sixteen. What does 1-Y mean?"

"Means you won`t be drafted. You have a medical deferment."

"So I won`t be eligible for the Draft as long as I`m 1-Y? The doctor nodded as a yes. "What classification would make me eligible to be drafted?" I asked.

"1-A," the doctor stated. "You will be called for physicals from time to time, but unless you get the 1-A designation, you won`t be drafted."

I was ecstatic and smiled all the way back to Iowa City. My thyroid observation program got me through THIS physical, and going to school for the next four years would keep me out, too. The army wasn`t going to get Abraham Dicker Stein!

I wasn`t a mature 18-year-old. I mean, believing I could get out of serving in the military by using camping and snake-hunting stories is something a 10-year-old would use. But I didn`t care. I was starting school and NOT being drafted. I wasn`t going to have to put my immaturity on display for real soldiers to see, at least not right away.

My freshman year in college was a mixed blessing. I had worked in a factory during the previous summer, so I could easily handle the tuition to school. Living at home helped a great deal, too. I joined a fraternity so my social life picked up drastically. However, GOING to school was different. I had a couple of classes a day, scheduled at various times, so it was my responsibility to get to them on time. Also, the workload was WAY more difficult than in high school, too. Sadly, I didn`t do well with either getting to my classes or doing my work. My immaturity was on full display during my freshman year of school, and I struggled mightily.

My mother comes into play during this part of my story. She was the biggest influence in my life. My father, Leib, passed away when I was thirteen years old. My mother, Miriam, took on three jobs to make ends meet in our family, and with me as the oldest child, I was expected to set the example for my two younger brothers and one sister. My mom was a master at Jewish guilt, and she gave me two pearls of wisdom to help me guide my life. She would say, "Do the best you can in anything you do," and "Don`t embarrass the family name." Doing my best was hard, but NOT too hard. Let me explain. I played sports every chance I got, and I thought I was pretty good at most of them. I enjoyed athletics so I worked

VERY hard at getting better. My school work was the problem. High school classroom work wasn`t all that difficult. I considered it relatively easy, therefore I was smart enough to get decent grades without doing much homework. If I brought home an average grade, my mom would ask if that was the best I could do, and I would say it was. Since I was too lazy to do homework, and waited until the last moment to get things done, it really WAS the best I could do. So, from my way of looking at it, I wasn`t technically lying to her. I didn`t embarrass the family name, either. Oh, I would do some silly things, like making crank phone calls to teachers I didn`t like, but nothing was so dastardly it could be classified a serious criminal act.

Freshman year, however, brought things to a head. I had a great time in my fraternity, especially socializing with my fraternity brothers, but I didn't put in the time studying like the other guys, so my grades slipped badly. I was in a Jewish fraternity, whose traditional academic work ethics allowed us to become successful adults. My fraternity had the highest grade-point average amongst all the fraternities, but I found ways to play instead of doing the required work for good grades. My mom was so busy working, she assumed I was doing what needed to be done, so she let me alone. When she found out I was lagging in my schoolwork effort, she was upset. I PROMISED her I would turn around my grades during my second year at Iowa. I worked another summer in a factory, and then promised MYSELF, as I had my mother, that I would turn things around in the classroom my second year. I couldn`t do it, though, so a couple of weeks into that second year, I quit school.

My mother had a rule for her kids. We could live in her house as long as we were either full-time students, or had a full-time job. When I told her I left school, and that I didn`t want to get a job right away, she told me it was time for me to leave the nest. It was a house rule, and I knew I would have to leave, but I was nervous about it.

I wasn`t without a `move out` strategy, however. I had a friend from high school who had moved out of HIS house at eighteen, worked his way to Europe on a cargo ship, and traveled throughout the continent for over a year. His parents had a lot of money, though, so he didn`t have to worry about working, or where his next meal would come from. All I had heard about his trip was that he had lots of fun, and I felt it should be my turn to see what he had been talking about. Since I worked the previous two summers in a factory, I had saved, what I thought, was a lot of money. So I bought a one-way ticket to New York City, and bid my family a fond adieu.

I left my home town as a bushy-tailed, bright-eyed dreamer, with expectations of fun and adventure. Within three weeks I found out New York was MUCH more expensive than I had figured it to be, and the people weren`t as friendly as folks I knew back in Iowa. With my money supply dwindling quickly, my hopes for getting to Europe faded at the same rate. I was NOT going to admit the mistakes I made to anyone, so I got out of New York and started a twenty-month odyssey throughout the United States, Canada, with a short stint in Mexico, too. It would take another book to cover those travels, so suffice it to know that I returned to Iowa City thinking of myself as a more mature and responsible person. My mom welcomed me back home and, in August of 1967, I re-enrolled in the University of Iowa.

School still proved to be a challenge for me. Though my grades would be slightly better, I was NOT ready to be a serious student. However, an event happened at the start of the year that would change my life. I met a girl and fell in love. Jill Simons was a freshman from Lincoln, Nebraska, and I met her at a fraternity function in September. We were inseparable, and even made plans to get married in September of 1968. Then came a monkey wrench. With Jill back in Lincoln planning the wedding with her mother, I received a letter in the mail indicating I was to report to Des Moines for another military physical. I was confident that I still fell under the six-year thyroid observation program, so I expected a 1-Y classification again, at least that is what I told Jill when I called her to let her know about my trip to Des Moines. So, in mid-August of 1968, I went through my physical and was finally called into the doctor`s office.

“Mr. Stein, you have been classified 1-A, and we will be notifying your draft board immediately,” the doctor said with absolutely NO emotion. But I got emotional.

"That can`t be, doctor," I said with a certain amount of panic in my voice. "I am still within the six-year observation program of a thyroid study. The six years aren`t up yet."

"Actually," the doctor said calmly, "we have a letter from the Internal Medicine physician in charge of your program, and he tells the army that, as far as he is concerned, you are healthy enough to serve your country."

I was stunned and in shock. I don`t even remember the bus ride back to Iowa City. Sleep that night was impossible, but I knew I had to talk to MY draft board as soon as I could. The next morning I arrived at the post office, where the board`s office was located, an hour before anyone would be there to speak to me. Finally, Mrs. Martin, secretary for the board, and a person I had known since I was quite young, sat before me with an interesting report.

"You have nothing to worry about, Abe," I heard her say. "At least I`m pretty confident that you don`t. The Iowa City board just finished filling its August quota, and it is highly unusual for the army to ask us for additional men once the monthly quota has been filled."

"Oh, thank the Lord, and thank-you for telling me that, Mrs. Martin. I`m planning on getting married in ten days, and getting drafted would stop that for sure."

"Well," Mrs. Martin said hesitantly, "I said I was PRETTY confident about not being asked for additional men. But, two months ago the army required that we send them one more person."

"Where does that leave me?" I inquired.

"Right now, because of your age, you are right at the top of our list. You stand number two to be drafted. You`re a student, too, right? Once you start school this year, you will simply apply for a 1-SC deferment which will allow you to continue schooling one year at a time, as long as you are a full-time student.

I felt pretty good as I left the draft board office. I had it all worked out. The August quota had been filled for the year, and it is seldom that the army would return to ask for more people. Even if they did I was number two on the list, and the most they asked for in the past was one new body. Once school started in September, I would be allowed to apply for a school deferment, one year at a time, through my Master`s and PHD degrees. I was CERTAIN the big, bad army wasn`t going to get Abe Stein.

Still, I hadn`t mentioned my going for a physical to Jill, let alone tell her about my 1-A classification, or going to the draft board. Calling my fiancé to discuss the situation became a priority of mine, too, since I had already talked to my mother about everything. My mom`s advice was to postpone the wedding until AFTER I was sure that being in school would keep me out of the military. Her rationale seemed solid. The wedding would be taking place in Jill`s parent`s home, and a small reception would follow at the Lincoln Golf Country Club, where her family were members. I felt certain that the reception could be re-scheduled with very little problem. To me, delaying the wedding date would be the best move.

Jill was the youngest child in her family, and to say she was spoiled would be an understatement. She wanted WHAT she wanted WHEN she wanted it, and that was always the bottom line. My phone call to her went relatively well. I told her about my trip to Des Moines, being declared 1-A, and about my up-lifting visit to the draft board. But, when I mentioned that perhaps we ought to delay our nuptials until AFTER I got a deferment, Jill simply informed me that she had the wedding plans finalized and we weren`t changing anything. I then asked her to tell her parents, who were in the room during my call, about what we were facing, and get their opinions on the matter. Jill muffled the phone so I couldn`t hear their conversation, and after several minutes she got back on the phone to tell me that the wedding was going on as planned. I only found out AFTER the marriage that Jill`s parents felt the same way as my mom, but, like I previously mentioned, Jill was spoiled and ALWAYS got her way. Ten days later we were married.

The wedding was small but beautiful. The reception had more people than I expected, but it was beautiful, too. I don`t remember too much about either event. I was just happy to have Jill as my wife. I was twenty-two and Jill was only nineteen, but I just knew this marriage was going to last for eternity. The honeymoon was pure bliss and both Jill and I were excited about going back to school as Mr. and Mrs. Stein. Jill was so impressed with the Jewish religion that she had converted to Judaism prior to our wedding. She worked hard on that, too, so I was impressed. However, we both agreed to a non-sectarian wedding for her family`s sake, and my mom was ok with that, too.

I was a happy man when we returned from our Florida honeymoon. I checked the accumulated mail we had gotten when we were away, and saw a very official-looking letter in the pile. I opened it and my heart slammed against my Adam`s Apple when I saw the first word…. "Greetings." I was being drafted! The first chance I got, I went to the university to apply for a 1-SC deferment. Since classes hadn`t officially started, the deferment was my only chance of eluding this dilemma. I was told by the university registrar, that since I hadn`t attended continuously for the four previous years, I was too late to apply for a 1-SC. Bottom line…I was screwed.

The worst scenario had occurred. The day I had gone to Lincoln for my wedding the army had come back to my draft board for TWO extra men to serve. Mrs. Martin had tried to get in touch with me. She thought she could inform me of the situation BEFORE I got married, but she had no way of reaching me in Lincoln. She apologized for even mentioning that I might be safe for August, but the dye was cast. I would have to report to Des Moines, within the month, to raise my hand and step forward. Both my mom and Jill`s parents were upset at the news, but understood that I was going away for two years. My mom had been a W.A.V.E. during WWII and Jill`s mother and father seemed genuinely proud that their daughter`s husband was going to serve his country. Jill, on the other hand, was irate at the news, and wondered if there were ways to NOT have to serve in the military. There were only two options that I knew, which I found out through guys who were trying to dodge the draft. One way was to leave the country, and that was the choice of most draft dodgers. But I loved America, and that was NEVER going to be an option for me. The second choice was to serve two years in jail. Not only would THAT embarrass the family name, but try to get a good job after being in prison. I rejected both options. With my mind made up to go through with my decision to become a soldier, Jill started to openly hate the military.

In 1968 the conflict in Vietnam was being escalated, and people were beginning to protest mightily against our country`s involvement there. We hadn`t declared war on North Vietnam, but The United States seemed compelled, for some reason, to stopping the spread of Communism into the southern part of Vietnam. First, our country played the role of being advisors to our friends. (so I was told) Then, apparently, we decided that we had to take aggressive action to halt the Communists. Whatever the political agendas, the bottom result was that more of our young people were being sent to the war-torn country. And more and more of these people were dying. I wasn`t for war, but I didn`t protest against it, either. I did have a friend who enlisted in the service right out of high school. He was sent to Vietnam and was killed. Then, just before I was to fly to Basic Training I ran into another friend, and HE had just returned from Vietnam, but he had lost one of his legs in combat over there. There were also a lot of students burning their draft cards, but the fact remained....I was going to be in the army, so I declined to join Jill when she went to campus to join protest groups. Instead of protesting, I watched the news. All the network evening news covered peace talks SOMEWHERE amongst the combatants, though they weren`t going too well, so I prayed for a ceasefire. I thought I heard that Congress was trying to find a way to curb our combat involvement in the war. (though, I now believe that was wishful thinking on my part) And I also saw in the news that protests were springing up on many more campus sites daily, which showed a growing resentment in America`s involvement in Asian politics. Yes, I was trying to persuade myself that I may be going into the army for two years, but I wasn`t absolutely certain that I would be going to Vietnam. I also tried desperately to explain to Jill that I would do everything I possibly could to stay in the United States, but she would pretend not to listen. She just believed that I didn`t love her anymore, based on my decision to BE a soldier. I spent my last few weeks telling her that the time would fly by and we would be back together in short order. I even told her I was going to petition to get out early so that I could start back into school. But, I just couldn`t say anything to reach her.

I had two sad faces staring at me at the bus depot the morning I departed. My mom looked grief-stricken and worried. My wife looked unhappy and sad. I kissed them both good-bye, and told both I loved them. I held my wife close and told her I would miss her very much. She whispered in my ear that she loved me very much. I smiled at her, then **with a tear in my eye I boarded the bus, but I was also terrified about what lay before me.**

II

A Basic Start

The bus ride wasn`t memorable except for two things. One, the trip seemed to only take a few minutes, though Des Moines was usually an hour and a half ride by car. Secondly, I recognized someone from my high school also on the bus. I didn`t know Jimmy Wardlaw very well, as we hadn`t been in any academic classes together. He wasn`t exactly a loner, as many classmates seemed to know him. But his behavior was a bit odd on occasion, which led a lot of people (me included) to think he may have had a screw loose in his head. The only weird event that I actually witnessed happened in study hall during our senior year. One day, our monitor teacher had gone out into the hall to converse with another teacher. It was chilly outside, and there were three wasps on the window sills walking about in very lethargic states. No students felt in danger, even those sitting next to the windows. However, as soon as the monitor left the room, Jimmy raced to the wasps. I thought he might crack open the windows and shoo the insects outside, but instead he took a small knife from his pocket and cut the heads off each one. One girl let out a loud 'Oooooo' which prompted the teacher to scurry back into study hall.

"Mr. Wardlaw," the monitor blurted out, "what are you doing? Is that a knife you have? Report to Mr.Piersol immediately." It is worth noting that Mr. Piersol was the assistant principal, and his primary role in school was to dole out punishment to misbehaving students.

Jimmy walked to the classroom door, turned toward the class, scrunched up his eyebrows, and with his best impression of Jimmy Durante said, "Ha cha cha cha cha," and left the room. OK, so the incident wasn`t a big deal, just a strange one. But that is how I remember Wardlaw. I sat next to him on the bus ride to Des Moines, but we didn`t talk much. About the only thing I remember us saying was him telling me he was #1 on the draft list, and I told him I was #2.

Arriving at the induction center seemed hectic to me. Uniformed men yelled at us constantly to move here or there. One positive did come of the turmoil, however, as six of us decided to buddy up. We hung together and when we were ordered somewhere, we all went together. Two fellows were from Newton, Iowa, two from Des Moines, and then there was Jimmy and me. Word came to us that most of us would be headed to Ft. Polk, Louisiana for basic training. One of the uniformed soldiers from the center decided to scare us. He told everyone within earshot that Polk was the training center for soldiers being sent to Vietnam, and the base had a fitting nickname…the sewer of America. Yep, he scared me, and made me very nervous, too. I`m sure that is what he had in mind, but what made it particularly cruel was that he was laughing while giving us that delightful information.

Suddenly, we were all ushered into a room. The six of us stayed close together for support. We raised our hands and gave an oath of allegiance, then we stepped forward for a reason unknown to me, and finally we were told that we had just become members of the United States military. Everything was fast and efficient, and when it was over five of us new 'friends' decided that we could get through basic training if we stayed strong as a group. Yes, I said five. After the oath, Jimmy Wardlaw looked at the rest of us and said, "I`m not going to that stinking Vietnam." He pulled an envelope from his suitcase, flashed it at us, then pivoted around and demanded to talk to somebody in charge. I knew that Jimmy`s father had some kind of clout in Iowa City, so I guessed that his father would, somehow, get his son a cushy job anywhere but Asia. We discussed, briefly, why that guy even came to Des Moines in the first place, then waited until the last moment to present a letter from his dad. The other four looked at me for an answer, like Wardlaw and I had been friends for many years. I just said, "That`s Jimmy. He`s a weird egg." Then we were all told to exit the door and head to the busses.

We lined up single-file and walked toward the door. We were to stop and give our name to a soldier, who was sitting at the exit with a box of papers. Those papers were orders for our basic training companies. Once outside we were to head to designated busses and board. However, the first six fellas lining up were quickly ushered through the door WITHOUT orders. A marine could be seen gathering them up and they headed in a direction away from our busses. I was ninth in line, so I got a clear view of what took place. "What just happened?" the guy in front of me asked the soldier giving us orders.

"Give me your name and keep moving. That had nothing to do with the rest of you," was the answer we got. But the rumor mill seemed certain that those six soldiers were going to be marines. All I could think about was that the marine stopped at six men, and didn`t continue to nine. I considered that my first close call in the military.

Once the five of us got our orders, we compared them. Four of us were assigned to the same basic training unit. But Chuck Harrington, one of the Des Moines draftees, was assigned to North Fort Polk, while the rest of us 'buddies' would do basic in South Polk.

We flew from Des Moines to Dallas, and had to switch planes. From there we were to fly to South Fort Polk. That second plane was small, really small. In fact, there were only nine seats on the mosquito-sized plane. We had to run to get onto the plane, and we got soaked to the skin. There had suddenly developed a driving rain storm in the Dallas area. We taxied to take-off position, and sat there….for over an hour. No one on board said a word the entire time. Suddenly, the pilot came onto the intercom and said, "The rain seems to be letting up somewhat, and we think we see a hole in the clouds. We`re going to try and make it through the clouds."

All right, several thoughts crossed my mind at that very instant. First, he COULD have turned around to talk to us. That was a very small plane, and we were all sitting within feet of his compartment. Second, the rain did NOT seem to be letting up. I couldn`t see the end of the wing on my side of the plane, for crying out loud.

Finally, he told us he was 'going to try' to get us through a hole in the clouds… TRY? I started praying like I had never prayed before. I just couldn`t believe it. I was in the army just a few hours, but I was sure that I was going to die on my first day. The plane taxied a short distance and, suddenly, we were roaring down the runway just as fast as the plane`s two propellers could move us. We lifted off the ground and tumbled through the clouds. The flight wasn`t long, but very turbulent. Many of us felt a little queasy once we landed. The rain hadn`t let up one bit during the entire flight, and once we were on the ground, and the side exit door was open, there was still a torrential downpour in progress. We nine new inductees each had one suitcase on board with us, but we certainly didn`t want to de-plane. The rain would ruin our luggage in short order. The pilot turned to us and told us we needed to get off immediately as he had to return to Dallas. We moved down the stairs into the teeming torrent. The plane moved away and I finally got a look at where we were…on a landing strip in the middle of nowhere. There were no shelters to stand under, no buildings to run to, there wasn`t a bench to sit on even if anyone wished to sit in the driving rain. Just one little road was spotted leading up to the strip. Otherwise we were just standing in an empty field.

By my NOT waterproof watch it was 2:00 a.m. With no one there to pick us up and get us somewhere out of the rain, the nine of us huddled silently together, and watched our suitcases getting destroyed by the non-stop rain. No one spoke. It was kind of cold, and we were very tired. But, mostly, we just stood around kind of in shock, wondering what was next.

An hour and a half passed, when someone yelled, "Look, headlights." Within minutes a small army bus was roaring up next to us, a door opened, and a guy in uniform, who turned out to be a corporal but thought he was a general, yelled at us, "Get in here right now, you morons. What are you doing standing in the rain?"

I couldn`t believe that guy. There wasn`t a shelter in visible sight, and he wanted to know why we were standing in the constant rain. Now THAT was a stupid question, and I had to wonder who the real moron was. But again, here was a guy in uniform YELLING at us….at three-thirty in the morning! I just hoped that the yelling wasn`t going to be a constant thing with the soldiers at this training facility. But, as it turned out, yelling was the one constant they all had in common.

The ride was a mere 15 or 20 minutes long then we turned into an area which had barracks everywhere. The bus and the rain stopped simultaneously, which made me happy. I just wanted to quietly get into my barracks, while we were in a dry moment, and sleep for maybe five or six hours. I was starting to get a pretty bad headache. The idiot driver stood and faced us, and then he roared, "We do NOT want to disturb the rest of the company recruits, who arrived earlier today. They are in the barracks sleeping, so y`all are going to be sleeping in the testing hall. Now quietly dismount my vehicle and enter the doors straight in front of you." We, the newest recruits, quickly and silently hustled off the bus and headed through the doors of our sleeping quarters for the evening.

There was nothing in the room…just tables and chairs. The building was stark but we were all exhausted. I headed to the furthest table in the room, placed my destroyed, rain-soaked suitcase on the ground, and lay down using my folded arms as a pillow. I had to try to get rid of my splitting headache, but more than that, I was bemoaning the fact that this was just the FIRST day of my army life. I began wondering how I would survive for two years having days like this.

It seemed like I had just closed my eyes, however, when I was awakened by some of the loudest yelling I had ever heard. The sound in the testing room seemed to be ricocheting from wall to wall, and my head started pounding again. I looked at my watch, and it was 5:00 in the morning, and I tried to focus on where the noise originated. A sergeant, wearing a Smokey the Bear hat, had entered the room, and he didn`t appear happy to be in there with us. "Get up, you lazy vermin," he shouted. "Leave your belongings right where they are, and get your asses out to formation. You have thirty seconds, so move it, move it, MOVE it."

All nine of us ran outside, though I kind of staggered outside, I was so tired. We stood shoulder to shoulder. 'Smokey' stood in front of us and glared. Men from the other buildings were running outside, too, but they were organizing into four groups in front a building that didn`t look like a barracks. The sergeant, who was with us, bellowed, "If your LAST names begin with A through F, get your butts over there," and he pointed to one of the groups. "If your last names begin with G through L, that is your group. Last names from M through R get over there. And the rest of you numbnuts belong to me, so get to that last group. Now MOVE!"

A 19-year-old named Jackson Williams, a fellow Iowa draftee from Newton, Iowa, joined me in running to the 4th platoon. I knew him as Willie. A third Iowa draftee, Charles 'Skip' Lonnegan, ran to the 2nd platoon. Thomas 'Rock' Rockland, the final member of our Iowa draftee group, hustled to the 3rd platoon. I was glad that I knew someone in my barracks from the start. In fact, Willie and I made a pact. We would occupy one of the bunk beds in the middle of our barracks, be as quiet as possible while doing what we were told to do, and get through our nine weeks of basic training as quickly and easily as we could.

Once in the platoon, everyone shifted around until we had eleven men in three lines. The first line, though, had twelve men. 'Smokey,' or rather our drill sergeant, watched us intently as we formed our four lines. The sergeant didn`t have an imposing physical appearance, as he was short and slightly built. But his military bearing was outstanding. He stood ramrod straight with his shoulders back and chest jutting forward, and each move he made was crisp and exact. He also had a stare that appeared to drill holes through any person who was displeasing him. Finally, he spoke in a loud voice. "My name is Staff Sergeant Moreno. You will address me simply as Sgt. Moreno, not sir. Is that understood?"

While most of us answered 'yes, sergeant,' there were a couple of 'yeah, sergeant,' and one numbskull who answered, 'ok.' To say Moreno was upset with our responses would be an understatement. He jumped on one inductee after another, berating their answers or the intensity of the responses, and even the looks on their faces. I was spared any individual harassment, but my head was, once again, throbbing with pain, and all I could think about was how much I hated the military at that moment.

Finally, after many in the platoon were straightened out on how to address a drill instructor, including the proper volume of voice, and we practiced a few more 'yes sergeant' responses, Moreno had just one more question. "Has anybody here had any R.O.T.C. training, either in high school or college?" Five guys raised their hands, and Moreno started pointing, "You are the squad leader of the first squad, you the second, you the third, you the fourth, and you are the platoon leader. What`s your name, platoon leader?"

"Michael Vinson," was the weak response.

"How are you supposed to address me, Vinson? And answer like you have a pair," Moreno roared.

"Michael Vinson, Sgt. Moreno," the inductee yelled back.

"Get in front of the platoon, Vinson, and whenever I tell you to do something, or the company commander tells the company to do something, you will repeat it to the platoon. Is that understood?" Moreno said in a more mellow voice.

"Yes, Sgt. Moreno," Vinson answered strongly, but his was a somewhat shaky voice.

"And you, 4th Platoon, will do whatever Platoon Leader Vinson tells you to do, isn`t that right?"

"Yes, Sgt. Moreno," we all answered in unison and with volume.

The answer of why we had 45 men instead of 44 was solved. Our platoon would have a leader, and the four squads would consist of eleven men.

While my platoon was going through its trial and tribulations, of Moreno giving orders and Vinson repeating them, the other three platoons seemed to be doing the exact same thing. Finally, everybody was given the order to stand at ease. The door to the command building opened in front of us, and out came a rather tall man, who walked with a haughty gait to the edge of the porch. At once, all four drill instructors roared, "ATTENTION," and the four newly appointed platoon leaders parroted the command.

."At ease," said the first lieutenant, who was our company commander. Again the platoon leaders repeated the command.

He scanned all the platoons with an arrogance meant to show us his superior station in the army. "I am 1st Lieutenant Carlton J. Garman II. I was shot in the heart in Vietnam, but that didn`t kill me. The army sent me here where I find myself standing in front of all the dregs they could find. My mission is to turn you sniveling, momma`s boys into tough soldiers like your cadre and I are. We WILL do that." He quickly scanned the troops again then said, "Are there any college grad-u-eights here?" He seemed please with himself for sounding out each individual syllable for the word.

About twelve or thirteen guys raised their hands, including Skip Lonnegan, who had actually graduated from law school, and was preparing to pass the Bar for the state of Iowa, but was drafted before that could happen. "You, Boy," Garmin said while pointing at one of the inductees with his hand in the air, "get me a cup of coffee from the mess hall, with two sugars…NOW!" The lieutenant continued to babble, but my headache made it difficult to really listen for anything important. Finally, he finished his coffee, turned away from us, and like a pompous peacock, he strutted back inside his command building. As he turned, the drill sergeants called us to attention, and when he disappeared, we were sent to have breakfast.

After we ate, we were given some time to go to our various barracks, and get to know one another. I took three aspirin, then Willie and I talked to one or two other guys near our bunk. A very short time later, we were called to a second formation. We were informed that we had three objectives that morning: get military haircuts, get inoculated for any possible overseas assignments, and gather up our army clothing from supply. It was when we were marching from our camp that I FINALLY realized that my civilian life was in the rearview mirror. I had to accept that I had become a soldier in the United States Army.

In order to get from one place to another, without the use of trucks, soldiers marched. Trudging along in any ramshackle way is not acceptable for the military. Before we left camp, we were given a brief description of how a soldier is expected to march. There was a proper length of stride, a certain distance of arm swing, a good posture format, etc., but we DIDN`T practice marching around the compound very long. We had a schedule to keep, so it was expected that everyone could march correctly in short order. That wasn`t the case. Almost immediately after leaving our grounds, the drill sergeants began yelling at many of the recruits. Some of the soldiers, apparently, couldn`t tell their right feet from their left. Some of the guys couldn`t keep up the pace, so they scurried with small steps to stay with the group. THAT really upset the sergeants, as it totally ruined the uniformity of footwork on which the army makes demands. Some of the fellas just plain couldn`t figure out what was being shouted at them, and then there were a few who seemed to WANT to screw up, for whatever reason. Still headachy and tired from a terrible first day, I was in a daze, but didn`t find it too hard to remember what we had learned. Marching was not a problem for me and I was thankful. I didn`t want any shouting aimed my way.

About a mile from camp, the yelling abated quite a bit. Suddenly, one of the drill instructors started to chant some words, which had a definite rhythm intended to keep the recruits moving along in step. Everybody`s arms and legs magically began moving uniformly when the chants started. We found out later that these ditties were called Jody songs. Jody was, supposedly, this guy back home, who was stealing soldiers` girls during training. The intent of the lyrics was to entertain, but the practicality was to get soldiers to be synchronized by having everyone stepping on the left foot at the same time, then the right foot, as we marched from place to place. First, the sergeant would chant a stanza, followed by the soldiers repeating the words. Then another stanza and a repeating of those words. Here is an example of a Jody song. The sergeant would sing, "Ain`t no reason looking down." The rest of us would repeat the words in the same song delivery. "Ain`t no discharge on the ground," followed by our repeat. "Jody`s got your girl, that`s true," (repeated by troops) "There`s not a thing that you can do." (again a repeat.) "Am I right or wrong?" (now, troops say 'you`re right,' while landing on their right feet) "Tell me if I`m wrong." ('you`re right') "Sound off," would be the drill instructor`s next commands, while staying in rhythm, followed by a "One, two," by the troops. The sergeant repeated, "Sound off," followed by the marchers, "Three, four." Then we had the big finish with the chanting sergeant saying, "Bring it on down." And the troops would finish, "One, two three, four, one, two…three, four." The last two words are said quickly on top of each other (after a very short delay in chanting) in order to keep the correct timing of the right and left feet. We enjoyed when people started chanting Jody songs. They were not only entertaining, but the distance we marched seemed shorter and more bearable. It helped the slower learners get into step more quickly and be able to keep up with the pace better, too. Some of the guys didn`t like the inference of a man who might be stealing their girls. I wasn`t one of them. I was confident that Jill would be waiting for me, with open arms, when I was finished with my two years in the service.

Sometimes the marching turned into jogging. This was called 'double time' and was used to expedite our movement because of the distance we had to cover, a timetable that we had fallen behind, or to increase our endurance in order to get us in better physical shape. At these times, Jody chants ceased, and the platoons became elongated and chaotic. Men started falling back and started walking during these periods of jogging, too, which enabled the drill sergeants to exercise their vocal chords to the maximum. Judging by our first double time experience, there were a LOT of poorly-conditioned recruits in our company.

Our first destination was a military barber shop. Once we arrived, we stayed in formation while being allowed to be at ease. We stood there for a long time. It was known that the army would hurry up to a location, then wait for instructions to be given. I blamed the lack of conditioning for that. I reasoned that if every one of us was in shape, then we wouldn`t have to double time, which meant we could MARCH up to our destinations just in time for the instruction to begin. Anyway, we ALWAYS seemed to hurry up then wait. We waited at that barber shop for nearly an hour, on our feet, without being allowed to speak to anyone. Inductees, who were caught whispering to the man next him, were ordered by a cadre member to 'get down and give me ten.' The soldier would then drop to the ground and execute ten push-ups. Waiting was pure torture to me.

At last, a sergeant came outside and scanned our company. Then, what was becoming the all too usual and irritating loud yelling that every sergeant seemed comfortable doing, he pointed to two recruits and barked, "You and you, front and center." A very tall kid and a fairly short kid moved quickly to the sergeant. Other than the whimsical appearance of the one soldier rising just inches above the second soldier`s waist, I thought nothing of seeing them standing side by side. Both did have longish hair, but long hair was a fashionable look for males in the late sixties. The tall recruit had a pitch-black Afro that was a full six inches in length. The shorter guy came out of my platoon. His name was Vandersant and he claimed to be a guitarist in a rock band from somewhere in Georgia. His hair was straight and shiny and it stretched nearly to his butt.

Both inductees were taken into the shop, but when they exited, they made quite a sight. The barber had taken the taller kid and shaved, what looked like a runway, right down the center of his head. On either side of the three-inch scalping, the Afro remained the same as before. To me his haircut had the same look as that of the tv character, Bozo the Clown. The Georgia soldier had the sides of his head shaved, exposing only a three-inch swath of hair from his forehead all the way down to his back. This poor little guy also had the misfortune of ears that jutted out in a Dumbo-like fashion. There they stood in front of us, one guy with a Bozo look and the other with a skunk-like Mohawk. I was on the verge of laughing but stopped short. Then the sergeant ordered these two poor guys to hook their arms together and start skipping around the area. The company exploded in laughter, including me.

Suddenly, sergeants were in the faces of laughers. "You think laughing at your buddies is fun?" is the comment I heard Sgt. Moreno use as he berated the 4th platoon. "Get down and start knocking out push-ups," Suddenly, all laughing soldiers were on the ground. "You will continue doing push-ups until you stop laughing," was the battle cry of every drill instructor.

I figured out later that the haircut/push-up scenario was the first attempt by our cadre to try to unify all the recruits. They were trying for a one-for-all-all-for-one goal, trying to get us to become one unified mean, green, fighting machine. Getting us to lose our individual personalities and become one cohesive unit was essential to the sergeants. But, like I said, I didn`t figure that out until after we arrived back at camp. Meanwhile, seeing these two guys skip around the barber area was hilarious to me, and I was having trouble stopping my laughter. After I completed 30 or 40 push-ups, I noticed that the laughing had subsided considerably. In fact, I was so tired that I made myself stop, too, and popped to my feet. As soon as I saw the weird combo, still skipping, back on the ground I went. Soon I was the last man down. Then Moreno was on me like a wet hen, and I did another 40 push-ups before I about collapsed from exhaustion. Too tired to laugh anymore, I rose to my feet, and the skipping stopped. Sgt. Moreno just glared at me before returning to the front of our platoon.

Led by the two 'skippers,' all the inductees were sent into the barber shop, one by one. Once a recruit was inside, he sat in a chair. The barber held a long-toothed electric razor. That instrument looked like it would be better suited for the sheering of sheep, not for giving haircuts to men. The barber would start at the front of the head and give three long sweeps from front to back, clearing the tops of the skull completely of hair. Then, after a series of short swipes around the base of the head, the barber was finished and told the seated soldier to exit the building. The haircut I got took less than a minute....I swear. My hair wasn`t particularly long to begin with, but when I got out of the chair, bald as a cue ball. I felt like my head was filled with helium. I actually felt several pounds lighter, too. When the last recruit exited the shop, and every one of us had received the army`s Type-A haircut, I actually understood the reason for all the yelling and push-ups beforehand. One hundred and eighty of us were bald. It was difficult to tell who was a pretty boy, or a rich kid, or a farmer. Civilian clothing DID give some indication of who was what, but 'civies' would be eliminated by day`s end.

After another short march and a long wait at the base infirmary, we were told to prepare for four injections....two in each arm. A few guys grumbled about getting shots, some even admitted being afraid of needles. To my recollection, the worst a shot could feel to a man would be like a small pinch. So seeing soldiers acting nervous, or squeamish about a little prick was annoying to me....all right, four pricks. I just wanted to get the inoculations over with so we could move on. I was about to fall asleep standing up. That`s how tired I was beginning to feel.

"O.K., girls," a drill sergeant said, "Get in a single line. And when you get your shots, try to act like men. No crying." I kind of smirked when I got into line.

There were four medical assistants at the head of the line, two on either side of the troops. As I got closer to the front I didn`t notice any of the technicians holding needles. They actually looked like they were holding weapons. Each of these objects had a stubby snout, with a huge dispenser of liquid attached underneath. There was also a trigger on the contraption, and when an inductee stood in front of a technician, the snout was pressed hard against the arm, and the trigger was pulled. A sound of 'whooop' was heard and grimaces appeared on each soldier`s face. A medical corpsman would say 'next' and all of us would move up in line. I admit that I had expected four little pricks from needles, not going through a gauntlet of gun-toting, trigger-happy pricks.

Some of the recruits were anticipating the trigger being pulled, and would flinch ever so slightly. This caused bleeding and cursing, followed by yelling from the drill instructors. Damn that yelling! I was bound and determined NOT to make any kind of fuss. The first shot I received was in my right arm….'whooop.' It hurt. Then came the left arm, another right, then left again. I`m not sure how thick the serum was, but when I tried to put my shirt back on, I struggled. The push-ups at the barber shop made my arms feel weak, but add the shots, and I could barely raise my limbs above my waist.

The injection experience went rather quickly. When all the recruits were finished, we were ordered to do ten push-ups. Normally, that would be no problem for most of the men, but with arms feeling like lead, ANY movement of the arms was a chore. A lot of the guys struggled to get the push-ups finished, which led to a lot more yelling, which brought back the intensity of my headache. "Was this day never going to end," I kept asking myself…and it was still mid-morning. With everyone finally on his feet, the order to 'shake it out' was given. We were told that the post-shot exercise was intended to get the injected serums moving throughout the body. That may be true, but my whole body was hurting, especially the arms I was shaking.

Our last march was to the base supply building. We got into a single-file, and moved forward, kind of like being on an assembly line. The first supply person gave each soldier a quick glance, handed him two or three pair (forgot exactly how many) of olive-green uniforms, which were taken from the small, medium, or large bins. Then the inductee moved forward to the next supply member. There were three really large recruits in our company. Their uniforms were taken from a stack of uniforms that looked like Omar, the Tent Maker sewed them. But, generally, everyone`s uniforms fit rather well. Several pairs of socks were then distributed, along with some underwear, and a belt. Holding on to the accumulating items was becoming cumbersome, and beginning to feel exceptionally heavy, too, especially with sore arms. Fortunately, we picked up a foot locker right after the clothing. While it may have helped reduce the clumsiness of carrying so many items, the locker was also heavy. Add bulkiness to the equation, and many of my fellow inductees struggled while trying to move forward. This, of course, induced more yelling. There were a few more military-related items given to each of us, and we ended our supply adventure by being issued a pair of boots. All soldiers were asked for a shoe size. There were no half sizes available. I wore an eleven and a half shoe normally, so I was given the next larger size....a twelve. I had to wear double socks just to keep the blistering to a minimum.

Once we had our supplies, we placed our lockers on top of our right shoulders and began the march back to our company area. The distance wasn`t too far, but one of the more sadistic sergeants decided it would be fun to have us double time much of the way. After formation, we were dismissed in order to get the lockers into the barracks. Everyone was exhausted, and I took a couple more aspirin. THEN we were called to formation so we could go to lunch. Yep, it was noon. Our day was only half over.

The rest of the day was spent with us being restricted to our barracks.... thankfully. There was no more marching OR yelling....also, thankfully. We WERE given instructions on how to correctly set up our foot lockers, how to make our bunks the military way, how to polish boots and brass. Sgt. Moreno gave us a roster for nighttime guard duty, but Willie and my squad weren`t assigned that task the first night. I remember the lights being turned out, then nothing until morning. My first full day in the service had come mercifully to an end.

III

M.O.S.

My best friend in high school was Isaac Rutkowski. Ike had been drafted one month before I was. We had talked briefly about him having to go to a war zone, but neither of us was too worried about that happening. He was a smart guy, almost a nerd, and had a serious commitment to academics. I admired his willingness to try sporting endeavors, but his physical skill level was not that of most athletes at City High School. He was, as I mentioned, very bright, By the time Ike was drafted, he already had a college degree in psychology, so we were pretty certain that the army would use him in a support capacity instead of putting him behind a rifle in the jungle somewhere. Actually, given Ike`s poor eyesight, he likely wouldn`t be able to see what he was shooting at, let alone hit a target, especially if he was missing his glasses. He was tested at 20/200 in his right eye, and 20/impossible in the left. Not that men with poor eyesight COULDN`T serve on the front lines, so to speak, but Ike`s chance of ending up a fighting soldier was very remote. So, when I was drafted, the two of us concentrated on ME not being put into the infantry.

During the first week of Basic, all inductees are given a battery of tests designed to show strengths and weaknesses for possible military job assignments…. aptitude tests, if you will. Once these guidelines are established, each soldier is given an m.o.s. designation. This referred to the military occupation service, where the army used a man`s test score results in an attempt to BEST assign him to a job, based on his unique qualifications.

Ike, being the college psychology major that he was, informed me that some of the questions on the test could be quite tricky. His skill at answering the awkward questions was evident and he received a social service designation out of basic training. He worked in counseling departments his entire two years, and never left the United States. Here is an example of a tricky question. See how you would have done answering it.

If you (inductee) have a beautiful autumn afternoon day to spend with your girlfriend, (or wife) which of the following events would you choose for the two of you:

A) Take her to see your favorite football team in action?
B) Take her to the Redwood Forest for a picnic and a hike
C) Sit around and compose love poems to one another?

Before Ike forewarned me about this kind of question, I likely would have chosen going to a football game. In fact, that would have been a no-brainer for me, as sporting events were what I loved to be around when I was growing up.

Ike DID warn me, however, that had I chosen football, the answer might have indicated that I had a certain amount of aggressive behavior, which would fit perfectly in the infantry mentality. Choosing the picnic answer would show that a fella had an affinity for the outdoors. That is a perfect trait to have for any infantryman. Picking the writing of poems could indicate a lack of toughness, so the army would likely NOT consider choosing that person to be in the infantry. Still, in 1968 the United States was escalating the number of troops being sent to Vietnam, so NO answer could absolutely be a safe one. I wanted to make it perfectly clear that I wasn`t interested in being placed in the infantry, so any answers on that test, showing effeminate tendencies, or dealing with indoor interests, I chose. I was desperately trying to be selected as a Jewish chaplain`s assistant, where I`d stay in the United States for two years, and drive the REAL chaplain to services on Saturday mornings. I would, naturally, do his clerical work, and any other errands required for an assistant, too. Hey, I had to dream, didn`t I?

Ike was, in fact, doing HIS basic training in South Polk, too. Every Saturday morning he and I would be excused from our companies to attend Jewish services at the base chapel. That was sweet, as we both got out of a little 'camp beautification' (cleaning the camp grounds) while we were attending to our religious needs. Finally, Ike had to leave basic training. He informed me of his m.o.s. in social services, and that he would be reporting for duty at a re-hab facility, at Ft. Huachucha, Arizona, where he would also be getting further training in his field. I was sad to see him go, but happy for him, too.

In order to strengthen my chances of working in my 'dream' m.o.s. I had written to the rabbi of my Iowa City synagogue, and asked him to send a letter to my commanding officer. The letter would state that I had attended seven years of Hebrew school, and been bar mitzvahed. The rabbi could embellish as much as he might want, though I doubted that would be much since I didn`t attend weekend services regularly. In fact, I went only when my Orthodox Jewish grandparents told me I had to attend. I DID, however, go to all holiday services. I was at least THAT Jewish. The rabbi was to then ask Lieutenant Garman to forward the letter to the committee making the m.o.s. decisions.

I also asked the base chaplain to write a letter, on my behalf, indicating my constant attendance on Saturdays. I eventually mustered up enough chutzpah to ask Lt. Garman to write one for me, too. That didn`t happen until after I had been in basic training for five weeks. I felt the need to show that I was becoming a squared-away troop before asking HIM for help. I was hoping he would have some kind of clout which might help me.

The lieutenant said he`d think about writing, but I didn`t hear real commitment in his voice.

Somehow, and I don`t remember exactly WHEN either, I learned that my infantry m.o.s. score was 80, perhaps the lowest in the company. A base score of 100 was supposedly required to qualify for ANY m.o.s. I also heard that my clerical scores were high enough to be considered for an office job, perhaps being a chaplain assistant, or so I hoped. When we marched to Beagle Hall, one week before the end of our basic training, to actually find out what our jobs would be, I wasn`t too nervous. I did pray, however, that I would be assigned to ANY m.o.s. other than infantry.

I heard my name, then the designation 11-Bravo. Instantly I went into shock. Infantry I was to be in the infantry. I had answered my questions specifically to avert being assigned 11-Bravo. I had regularly attended religious services on Saturdays. I had asked for several letters to support my efforts to become a Jewish chaplain assistant. I scored well on tests to be anything BUT a foot soldier. When the announcement was made, I didn`t want to believe it, but I heard it loud and clear....Abraham Stein, 11-Bravo. I`m sitting here now, typing the story, and I am still in shock. Where did it go wrong? In actuality, 97% of the company was assigned 11-Bravo, and that included all but ONE draftee....Skip Lonnegan. The enlisted guys were in shock, too. Comments of "I didn`t sign up to get shot," and "wait `til I see my enlistment officer," were very common. It was just a bad day for most of us.

As for Skip`s assignment, it seemed that the current company clerk was due to be released from the army, and Lonnegan was the perfect replacement. He was a law school graduate, with an understanding of paperwork. He would learn everything he needed to know in no time. I was jealous. The good news is that Skip would never leave that company in South Ft. Polk. The bad news is that Skip wound never leave that company. He would never get the opportunity of being assigned to a foreign country. The lucky bastard. I never heard from him again, but I want to believe that he got to be bored out of his mind. Willie and Thomas were assigned 11-Bravo, too. There were just the three of us, from the original Des Moines six, remaining together. Half of us were gone within the first ten weeks of our being inducted.

IV

It`s a Learning Process

Before moving beyond the basic training experience, I would like to tell you about the ENTIRE nine weeks, not just the beginning and my job placement. There was a mixed-bag of events sprinkled throughout those weeks.

I, personally, had EVERYTHING to learn. The entire military lifestyle was foreign to me. I was truly a blank sheet, and I knew I had to learn fast....very fast. When we marched to the various venues, and the instructor would start his class with, "If you don`t learn what I am instructing today, you will die in Vietnam," I paid particular attention.

Many, MANY instructors indicated death, and it didn`t matter that I was trying for a NON-infantry m.o.s., I felt the urgency to learn. I really did find weaponry classes very interesting, however, so learning was fun. The second reason for my paying attention, however, came as a surprise to me. During the middle of the third week in basic training, I became a leader in my platoon. With the responsibility of leadership I felt I should learn as much as I could, as quickly as I could, in order to help those who were just as green in the service as I was. Becoming a leader, though, changed the whole outlook of my role in the military.

Almost since the start of Basic Training, 4th Platoon had developed the reputation of being the worst platoon in the company. We DID have several guys who seemed to have two left feet when it came to marching. We had several guys who were slow learners in the classes. But, every platoon had some of those soldiers. Every platoon had a couple of trouble-makers, too. Our platoon, however, had five really hard-core problem inductees, who proved to be contrary to most everything that the platoon was trying to accomplish. They shirked their work assignments, mocked our platoon leader, Mike Vinson, and were just generally loud and stand-offish. They let it be known that they didn`t appreciate anyone putting his nose in their business. Four of these rabble-rousers were bad news, and I stayed out of their way. But the fifth member of this group, named Samuel Whitman, was kind of a friend of mine. During the second, or third day (I forget which day exactly) Sam and I were given kitchen patrol together. We peeled potatoes, washed dishes, scrubbed walls, and just about every other lowly kitchen detail imaginable, together. We got a whole day to get to know one another. He was from Chicago and was a big Bears football fan. Though I came from Iowa, I loved the Bears, too. He loved the Cubs….so did I. Those two teams alone kept us busy talking for hours, about statistics and prospects for the next year. He said he was the eldest of five siblings, and the only male in the family. I told him I was the eldest in my family, but I had two brothers and one sister. We both liked being the oldest child. Neither of us had much recollection of having a father figure around the house. My dad was always working, and he died when I was thirteen. His dad just left for parts unknown when Sam was a toddler. I think he enjoyed my company that day as much as I enjoyed his.

Sam, however, was a definite member of the behavioral misfits. In fact, he was their leader. He was a big guy, and quite intimidating physically, and he told everyone in the platoon that they were to refer to him as Mr. Whitman, and that included me. Sam had turned surly, but I never forgot that he had a softer side. One day I saw Sam standing alone near his bunk. He had his back to me as I walked up to him and said, "How`d the Bears do this past weekend?" The big man whirled around with a snarl on his face, ready to rip into the speaker. But, when he saw it was me, and that we were the only two people in the barracks, we had a short, pleasant conversation. In fact, he and I had several nice talks during Basic Training, but they were always short. He NEVER wanted his cronies to see him being friendly to another member of the platoon. I respected his reputation of being a rough and tough individual. I even called him Mr. Whitman. Still, I felt confident that if I ever needed Sam`s help with anything, he`d come through.

These five mal-contents would do whatever the company cadre told them to do, though much of the time it was done grudgingly. But they hated Vinson telling them what to do, and their squad leaders had to practically beg them to help with assigned chores around the barracks. They just didn`t like taking orders, and that`s the bottom line.

Physical Training tests were designed to measure a man`s fitness. Since many inductees came into the service in various stages of fitness, the army worked at getting its soldiers into combat-readiness shape. To do this, companies would march their recruits, several times in nine weeks, to the base`s p.t. course where physical improvement could be measured.

During the 3rd week, my company was returning to camp, from our second p.t. testing, when Sgt. Moreno yelled out, "Is that Jewish personnel here?" Normally Moreno would either march along side, or just in front of our platoon. When he shouted this question out, however, he was behind and to the side of us, which confused me a little when I tried to locate his position. Once I established where he was, and being the only Jewish soldier in the entire company, I knew he wished to see me. I double-timed to his position.

"Private Stein reporting, Sergeant Moreno," I said.

"When we get back to the camp, do you think you could take over as platoon leader?"

"Private Vinson isn`t doing a great job," I started to answer.

"I DIDN`T ask you to comment on Vinson," Moreno barked. "I asked if YOU could run this platoon as soon as we return to base."

"I can, Sgt. Moreno," I blurted out without thinking about what I was saying.

When I was sent back into formation to finish our return march, I was mentally chastising myself. After all, didn`t Willie and I make a pact to stay quietly in the middle of the barracks and just do what we were told to do? Wasn`t getting through Basic Training, as unobtrusively as possible, the final objective? Now, in just my third week in the military, I was being elevated to a position where I was to become the 4th platoon whipping boy for Sgt. Moreno, Lt. Garman, and all other company cadre. I also believed that it was going to become MY responsibility to turn around our platoon`s terrible reputation. That meant I had to get Sam Whitman, and his band of miscreants, to work WITH the platoon. I had NO idea how I was going to accomplish that feat.

As soon as we returned to base, the four platoons got into the usual lunch-time formation, and waited to be dismissed. All platoons were to stay in the area until individually called for lunch. Fourth Platoon was to be the first to lineup for the meal, but Sgt. Moreno kept us in formation when Lt. Garman ordered the company to be excused. With no fanfare, Moreno said, "I want Vinson and Stein to switch places." Vinson was at my side before I could take my first step toward the front of the platoon. He still looked like a scared, nervous wreck, but he also looked relieved to NOT be in charge. I scampered to the front. "Private Stein is your new platoon leader," Sgt. Moreno said curtly. "All right, platoon leader, take your men to lunch." Then our drill sergeant walked away.

During meals, the platoon leader`s job was considered fairly simple, just monitor the men as they go through a set of monkey bars, located on the way to the mess hall, then keep the men orderly as they entered to eat. Each soldier was to stand at ease, and be a good meter behind the man in front of him. This assured a straight, respectful entrance into the hall, and also assuring there was no jamming at the front of the line. The leader than ate after his platoon was through the line, and the next platoon leader had taken HIS place. The first two weeks worked very well. The camp cadre would watch the platoon leaders, though, to ensure peaceful lines. With the start of the third week, however, the drill sergeants had no more supervision duties, and with raw barrack platoon leaders in charge of the line, things started to change for the worse. Since there were no windows along the waiting line wall, and with inductee leaders in charge of lunch entry, one group of soldiers decided to push the envelope of decorum. Before discussing the disturbances that occurred in meal lines, I feel obligated to talk about race. If there are people who will take offense at, or are sensitive to the talk about a person`s color, then I urge you to skip the next twelve paragraphs, or so. It will be easy for you to tell when I have re-joined my story.

I grew up in Iowa City, Iowa, a small town, which also happens to be the home to the University of Iowa. To me, it was an idyllic town in which to grow up. The only real problems I remember were those of immature kids involved in childish pranks....peeing on hot school radiators on winter days, as one example. There was a joy-riding ring of junior high students during my time in school, but that was pretty much the extent of any kind of crime involving students. There were a few Black children and Brown children, but most of the school population was White. To my friends and me, kids were kids, and I never heard a single racial slur toward anyone, or any negative comment based on a person`s religious preference. There WERE cliques based on common interests, but there wasn`t any animosity between any groups, per se. Certainly, there were some kids that didn`t like other kids, but that was usually based on the fact that these children had already met each other and friction developed from there. There was never any pre-judgement based on any global halo effect. Yes, Iowa City was a safe and rather harmonious place in the 50`s and 60`s, as far as I could tell.

I didn`t experience any prejudice until I turned nineteen, and decided to travel around the U.S.A., on my own, for nearly two years. In New York City I had to walk blocks out of my way to avoid gangs on the various street corners. People I met in New York had told me that strangers weren`t welcome in certain areas, so I didn`t question, or challenge, those statements. I was very naïve, and thought that if these gangs of kids met me, they might like me enough for us to get along. But I was NEVER looking for trouble, so I rejected that urge. I noticed that most gangs, in NYC, Miami, and Los Angeles, were composed of Black or Hispanic kids, who didn`t like each other, but the hatred of White people was a shared factor. The fact that I might be hated for my color bothered me. Also, during my traveling, I made a stop in Raleigh, North Carolina. The first night I was there, I decided to drink beers in a bar, where nineteen was the legal age. I watched, with surprise, when a Black marine was warned NOT to stay for a drink. I questioned the bar tender, whom I befriended earlier in the day, why a marine was threatened. He told me that Blacks and Jews were hated in that area. I sat quietly for a few minutes, then left. I didn`t see the need to tell him I was Jewish.

I could never really understand most prejudices. To be honest, however, I AM prejudice against attitudes. If a person shows me a negative or hateful attitude, I usually move away and go about my business. But color, religion, and social status have no bearing on how I feel toward anyone. Let me meet a person and talk awhile, then I will form an opinion. I will know rather quickly if that is a person I want to be around. I do not pre-judge, even in today`s world. I was raised that way.

Basic Training didn`t change my attitudes on prejudice, either, though at times by beliefs were challenged. On the surface, Sam Whitman displayed a terribly negative attitude. But, when he and I talked one-on-one we got along just fine. I DID avoid his cronies in the 4th platoon, and, yes, they were all black in color. Those four guys didn`t like anybody, so I dealt with them as little as possible throughout Basic. Truth be known, 4th Platoon had eleven Black men, including my friend Willie. I seriously disliked being around Sam`s buddies because of their poor attitudes in general, including Sam when he was with them.

My first REAL encounter with racial overtones, aimed specifically at me, occurred during my first responsibility as lunch monitor. And it happened right after my appointment as platoon leader. There were twelve or fourteen Black soldiers in our company, who decided it was their right to move to the front of the meal lines any time they felt like it. That included Sam and his followers from the 4th Platoon. We had no behavior problem when the company cadre was watching the line. But, when the recruit platoon sergeants became the ONLY monitors, this group of Black soldiers would stroll to the front of the lines as they pleased.... every meal. Other soldiers in line, especially the ones already standing near the entrance of the mess, would object and complain to the platoon leaders. As a group, however, this Black gang would begin giving bullying behaviors. Their harsh stares would lead to challenges to the complainers, and even threats. I remember the first time Vinson was left alone to monitor the line, and the cutting to the front became HIS problem. He walked down the platoon and said, "Just let them go. We don`t want any trouble. We`ll be inside soon enough." The other leaders were just as perplexed as to what should be done. Fortunately, these bully tactics had only happened for two days prior to my taking over as platoon leader, but when I DID take over, I faced the same dilemma. Since our platoon was first to eat, I didn`t want any trouble, either. We kind of accepted that Sam and his four pals would move to the front, and while I didn`t think that was fair to the rest of the guys, it was my first time monitoring, so I just wanted to get through the meal without making Sam my enemy.

However, when the next platoon lined up behind us, and some of Sam`s friends came forward to join him, I got a little nervous. Also, many Black soldiers in our company, had adopted a hand-shaking ritual that was rather bizarre. When they would greet, they would go through a series of hand-fluttering, finger intertwining, and body gyrations, that was not only weird to watch, but worse than that, it took a minute or more to complete. I, generally, had no problem with the greetings. A group of Blacks could take a good ten minutes or more of handshaking each time they got together, and that was fine with me….in the company area. I just went about whatever I was doing, and wasn`t affected, or offended, by this strange way of getting together. But in the front of a line headed inside for a meal, that behavior was ridiculous. Everyone in line would be forced to wait until ALL of Sam`s group had finished the ritual and moved inside, before we could eat. I felt, on my first duty, that I had to stop the behavior before it got started.

As the other platoons started lining up behind ours, Sam`s buddies started moving toward the front of the line. "Where are you guys going?" I asked as a couple of them were getting closer to Sam.

"Goin` up here with the rest of the Brothas," one of them answered.

"No, you`re not," I said quickly and firmly. "You will not be cutting in front of my platoon. Now move back to your own squads."

"Why you White mother…ker," one of them retorted, "What are you going to do about it if we don`t?"

"I`m not going to do anything," I explained. "But I will let Sgt. Moreno decide what HE is going to do about it. I will let him know who you are, and that you`ve been cutting the line every meal for the last couple of days. What do YOU think he is going to do with that news?"

The gaggle of disgruntled soldiers slowly retreated to their platoons while muttering obscene language and issuing threats my way. I was getting nasty stares from Sam and his crew, too, but the rest of the 4th platoon members had smiles on their faces. Then the line began moving into the mess hall for lunch.

Word got out about my confrontation and the cutting in front of meal lines just ceased. Seemed like nobody wanted the drill instructors to get involved. Also, none of the threats, that were hurled my way during that lunch, came to fruition. I`m pretty sure Sam had something to do with that.

A couple of days after my altercation, I asked Willie why it was that only the Black militant inductees, like Sam, felt the need to be disrespectful and inconsiderate to everybody else by thinking they had the right to cut lines. Willie told me that he thought many of them may be trying to prove they were equal to Whites, and could be superior if they wanted to be. He got to talking about slavery and equality through Civil Right proposals, and I stopped him. "Willie," I said, "I don`t feel that any of these guys have ever been slaves. Likely never met one, either. I`ve always thought that all men should be treated equally. It seems that these goof-balls are hiding behind racism in order to be bullies, and why would anybody like to be around bullies? It`s just not acceptable in today`s society. I know their ancestors were slaves for hundreds of years, but that problem was dealt with and resolved one hundred and fifty years ago. There is no slavery today in America. I`m thinking that if acting out with poor behavior is an allowable act for descendants of enslaved relatives, and Blacks were slaves for a couple hundred years, what kind of behavior should be expected from me? My Jewish ancestors were slaves for five or six THOUSAND years. You didn`t cut in the lines, Willie, and I think that is because your parents did a great job teaching you right from wrong. I have seen you trying those feeble handshakes, but you don`t particularly seem to enjoy doing them. And you are DEFINITELY not a rude or uncivilized Black man. What makes those guys so different? I don`t get it."

"No, you likely don`t, Abe." Willie answered. "But, I`ve felt hate aimed at ME because of the color of my skin, even in Iowa. I have, however, chosen to try harder to fit in, and not become a rabble-rouser. My parents have instilled in my brothers, sisters, and me that fighting is the last resort. So, I usually just bite my tongue when I feel hate coming my way. I don`t know what the situations were for Sam or any of that group. They must have seen plenty of hate in their home towns, though. But you`re right, I`m not like them, and I don`t think I ever will be."

Willie and I remained very good friends, and I think I became more sensitive to those around me who might have been victims of racial prejudice. As an aside, to this day I have never shown prejudice against anyone because of color, religious difference, or social standing. But, I never will appreciate being around people with poor attitudes or who act like bullies.

I wish to welcome back those of you who didn`t want to hear stories or thoughts about prejudice. I still have, however, three more note-worthy stories to tell you from my basic training.

Drill instructors had a common goal, not only in our company, but in EVERY company in Basic Training, to develop soldiers. The transforming of 180 eclectic individuals into military clones was hard work. From the very start of our arrival, drill sergeants did lots of yelling, recruits did lots of repetitions, and the physical exercise seemed non-stop. But I have to admit, that after nine weeks, our company was looking, sounding, and acting just like real soldiers.

There was one private, sadly, who wouldn`t get with the program. His name was Harrison Johnson, a draftee from Baton Rouge, Louisiana. The facts were, however, that he conformed to MOST of the military guidelines. He marched correctly, polished his boots and brass beautifully, and he never complained when he was given kitchen duty. But Harry, as the rest of us called him, declared himself a conscientious objector. He told anyone and everyone, who would listen, that he loved America, and he would serve in Vietnam if he was ordered. He even bragged about how all the men in his family were military men. His dad and two uncles fought in WWII. His older brother had served with the army in Korea. His two cousins had both enlisted as marines, and both had returned from tours in Vietnam. What made Harry different than ANY of them was the fact that he refused to carry a weapon. He wouldn`t pick up a rifle, pistol, bayonet, ammunition of any kind, not even a smoke grenade, which wasn`t a weapon at all, but rather a device used to mark the position of people who were out in the wilderness. Harry DID want to let our company cadre know that he was a peaceful person, but he also wanted them to know that he didn`t want to get drummed out of the military for his views. Even though he was drafted, and did not enlist, Harry had told his dad that he would try to serve as a radio operator, or as a medic, but he wouldn`t fire upon the enemy under any circumstances. His father was apparently okay with his son`s decision to be a pacifist. According to Harry, getting kicked out of the service would be even more embarrassing for his father to accept than not fighting. So Harry worked hard at being a soldier…. just not a fighting soldier.

However, his drill instructor took it as a challenge to get Harry to handle weapons, while making the trainee miserable along the way. He shamed and insulted Harry, had him do many extra k.p. stints, gave him more push-ups than any two other soldiers had to do, and had him running in place many more hours than any other soldier in the company….by far. Harry took it all. Then the sergeant started punishing the entire platoon because of Harry`s objector stand. This caused his platoon to want to give the objector a blanket party, which meant his barracks mates would wait until Harry went to sleep one night, throw a blanket over him, then while holding him down, those brave soldiers would pummel his body with hard objects, including fists. My Iowa friend, Skip Lonnegan, who had become Harry`s squad leader by that time, stopped the beating. Somehow, Skip got word to Lt. Garman, anonymously, about the impending trouble. The 2nd platoon drill sergeant was told, by the lieutenant, in no uncertain terms that NO blanket parties would be tolerated. So, the sergeant gave EXTRA work to the entire platoon because HE had been humiliated. That whole platoon was a mess by the fifth week of training, and it was only because we had Sam and his royal pains that we STILL had the worst reputation in the company through the first six weeks.

Harry`s problems first surfaced on the day that the inductees were introduced to the M-16 rifle. Everybody else in the company was eager to learn about this weapon. It was a newer weapon in the army arsenal, and lighter than rifles that were previously used. We had instruction on how to assemble and disassemble the rifle, and how to clean and take care of it in all kinds of weather. Lt. Garman had told us how fortunate we were to be training with the M-16, as many other companies still had to train with the much heavier and more awkward M-1. The

M-16 had become the main rifle being used in Vietnam, and the gun enthusiasts and hunters in our company were quite anxious to compare the handling of this weapon with the ones they had at home. I wanted to see what kind of marksman I would become, since I had only handled a BB gun in the past. I actually enjoyed learning all about the M-16. However, since I was planning on becoming a chaplain`s assistant, I didn`t feel I would ever need to fire it again, or any other weapon, for that matter. But I was also very competitive, so being a top marksman in the company was something I strived to be. I paid very close attention to all the instruction.

The yelling began when Harrison refused to pass a rifle to another inductee. He simply refused to touch the weapon, plain and simple. A drill instructor was in Harry`s face immediately, yelling at the top of his lungs. The bellowing was performed with such intensity that the sergeant`s face turned beet red. Harry just calmly took all the screaming. Finally, the draftee was escorted from the training session, and the weapons class continued. We did NOT get to fire the M-16 that day, however. I was a little disappointed.

When we returned to base the company was dismissed....all but Harry Johnson. His drill instructor and another cadre member were ripping into him. Harry did push-ups until his arms collapsed. He ran in place and low-crawled for at least an hour. But Harry didn`t complain. No one in my platoon had much to say on Johnson`s situation. In fact, most of the guys were relieved that the sergeants weren`t yelling at any of us.

Individual M-16s were issued the day after we were given our instruction on it. Harry was issued a broom, and he gladly accepted it. While the rest of the company practiced marching in formation with weapons, Harry practiced with his broom. When the rest of us were given time to clean and care for the weapon, Harry was doing exercises, which were aggressively monitored by any available company cadre. The same scene was played out whenever we were given instruction on any weapon. Harrison Johnson had become a laughing stock.

For the most part, 1st, 3rd and 4th Platoons didn`t really care about the abuse Johnson was getting, and the consensus was that he brought it upon himself.

We DID care one morning, however, when everyone was re-issued rifles one morning, and informed that we were going to be marching with our weapons out of the company area. Harry was issued his customary broom, and 2nd Platoon members appeared a bit restless when Lt. Garman exited his office door. Even before we were called to attention, the lieutenant noticed the uneasiness of Johnson`s platoon, and asked the platoon leader if there was a problem. "Yes, Sir, there is," the leader (whose name I can`t remember at this time) said. "Would it be possible to leave Private Johnson here when we march outside the camp area?"

"Company," Garman said with some indignation in his voice, "I`ve been asked if I can grant a special favor to a member of 2nd Platoon. It`s true that Private Johnson has, indeed, brought disgrace upon this company with his conscientious objector crap. But, we do not stop OUR training, or alter it in any way because we have a screwball in our midst. You must all try harder to convince this private of the errors of his way, especially you, 2nd Platoon, as you all live with him twenty-four hours a day. Now, drill sergeants, let`s prepare to move." With that we were snapped to attention, and marching away from our protective company cocoon. It was very embarrassing to see soldiers stopping what they were doing to stare at us, and to hear the snickering. But there he was, marching with a broom and making our company look silly....Private Harrison Johnson.

It should be noted that the 'blanket party' for Harry was going to occur the night of our first march off company grounds. Skip was right to get it stopped, but we marched a couple more times with weapons, and each time Johnson and his broom brought embarrassment to our company. The truth is that nothing, not shame, insults, constant yelling, or non-stop physical exercise, could persuade Harry from his conviction, and for that he probably should be commended. He took everything handed out to him, and I can`t think of one single soldier who befriended him. Looking back, it might have been in the interest of the army to just let Harry march with nothing, as opposed to having him carry a broom. That thing was much longer than our rifles, and stuck out like a sore thumb. In the end, however, Harrison Johnson got his just desserts....an 11-Bravo m.o.s. I wonder if he survived Vietnam.

Harry did take a LOT of drill instructor time away from the rest of us. But he was by no means the only soldier who was yelled at. No platoon, no individual, was immune from cadre wrath. If the company objective was for the privates to hate company personnel, then the plan worked well. I must admit, though, that yelling served a purpose. If an inductee was doing something, ANYTHING incorrectly, a drill sergeant would yell out what the mistake was. The yelling would get the attention of all the soldiers nearby. In this way, the error was pointed out AND the solution given. This eliminated the individualistic approach to learning, which saved a lot of time, and that was good because there was SO much to learn in nine weeks. Still, constant yelling had a definite affect on company morale, which was very low most of the time. No matter how hard the privates worked to do the RIGHT things, they received very, VERY little positive re-enforcement. Lt. Garman once said, "There`s SOME improvement being made around here, but you clowns have a long, LONG way to go." If that was his way of commending us after we strove to improve ourselves, then getting a warm and fuzzy feeling was never going to be accomplished.

Finally, on the Friday of our seventh week, the platoons were given an opportunity to have a positive moment. Lt. Garman must have gotten word on how bad morale had sunk. He, therefore, decided to have all the barracks cleaned that Friday morning, which wasn`t unusual. But he also said that when the cadre held the barracks inspection that afternoon, the platoon deemed having the cleanest building would get a reward. There would be a two-day furlough issued to the whole platoon. He would allow every member of the winning platoon the opportunity to go into Leesville, Louisiana for the weekend. The furlough would start at 1700 hours that Friday evening, (military for five in the afternoon) with the directive that everyone must ALSO be back on grounds no later than 1200 hours Sunday. (noon) Two things to note here…Leesville had a reputation as a terrible town in which to spend a weekend, and secondly, the 4th platoon had been judged filthiest barracks on almost EVERY inspection since we had started training. The latter was, to no one`s surprise, due to the lack of effort by Sam and his cohorts. Let`s face it, if a barracks is given three hours to make things shine, and five members are either doing nothing, or doing things poorly, NO barracks could have a chance of looking its best. The fact was, that OUR barracks was always held up to be an example of what a barracks SHOULDN`T look like. The lieutenant even allowed the other three platoons to walk through our barracks, one day, to see how poor we were. I`m not kidding. I had no better luck than Vinson when it came to getting the five malcontents to work in the barracks. So, when Lt. Garman told the company that we would have FOUR hours, not three, to make the barracks glisten, I had no grand allusion of us winning. The instructions seemed simple enough. All the platoons would have from eight in the morning until noon to do their best jobs of cleaning. The drill instructors would march us off to an afternoon class after lunch while the rest of the company cadre inspected each barracks. After returning from that class, we would have a short formation and the winning platoon would be announced.

When Garman excused the company, and all the soldiers returned to their respective barracks to work for that furlough, Sgt. Moreno asked to see me. He looked at me with his steely eyes narrowing to a squint to show a more stern gaze than usual, then he said, "Get the job done." That was it. Those few words, but said with conviction, and he disappeared, leaving me to wonder what in the hell I was going to do.

Usually, when I gave the squad leaders their assigned duties for barracks clean-up, it was left up to them to motivate their troops. Sam`s boys, naturally, didn`t pay attention to any squad leader, and they didn`t care if I saw them lounging, either. Their only concern was getting caught by Moreno. Those five guys would just go through the motions until one of them noticed our drill instructor headed to the barracks. Then all five would look busy as could be. Sgt. Moreno was not fooled by their tactics, however, but he said little to them. He was just happy if they did ANYTHING to improve the platoon image. He left things up to me, for the most part, and, like I said, getting Sam, et al, to put in the effort, was something like pulling teeth…difficult, and painful.

I knew that this barrack`s cleaning had to turn out differently. I was certain that Sgt. Moreno was NOT going to drift by to see how things were going. Drill instructors had been instructed by Lt. Garman to stay out of the contest. But, more importantly, this cleaning had a goal, something for the guys to work toward, and I knew I had to use that as motivation. In addition, I needed to try a technique that my grandmother used effectively in my family. She was an expert at putting Jewish guilt on people when she wanted to get things done. I thought that I might give that mystique a shot, too. Still, I was nervous while going back to the barracks.

I was pleasantly surprised, however, when I arrived. The guys were in GOOD moods, and there was a lot of talking. Pete Tuttle was a local Leesville soldier, and he was the center of attention. "What they got to do in your little town, Tuttle?" one of the fellas asked.

"Well, lots of stuff. They got a bowling alley, a golf course, some restaurants, lots of bars, and a whorehouse," was his immediate answer. "I don`t think prostitution is legal," he continued, "but that`s where soldiers go to get laid. Nobody`s ever been arrested that I know of." Soldiers were looking at one another, smiling, and nodding. "Don`t confuse Leesville with Las Vegas, though, especially the whorehouse. I ain`t never been in there, but my cousin has. He says our town whores are nasty. Vegas is supposed to have classy whores." I even saw Sam and his crew listening in while trying NOT to be paying attention. I knew I had only four hours to get things done, so I had to, reluctantly, cut Pete off.

"All right, let me have your attention for a couple of minutes," I started. "Sounds like you guys might want to get off this stinking base for a couple of nights. Anybody want to stay here this whole weekend?"

"Come on, Abe," I heard someone in the back of the group say. "you know we wanna get out of here, and you do, too."

"Most of us want to get into Leesville, but I want to know if EVERYBODY here wants to." I continued. "Willie, do you?"

"I`m going to be with you, numbnuts," Willie retorted.

"How about you, Sam," I said, looking directly at Whitman, who was standing with his group of problem soldiers. "Do you think you and your buddies can find something to do in that little town for a weekend?"

With his crew nodding approvingly, Sam said, "Yeah, that might be cool." All right, it wasn`t a loud and forceful show of support, but it was the first time that any of these five guys ever acknowledged that they agreed with the rest of the platoon on ANYTHING!

A couple of the soldiers that usually do the clean-up work started to smile and they, too, began to nod approvingly. Then I knew it was up to me. I had to instill a confidence in everybody that 4th Platoon could go from worst to first, and I had to show that I believed in what I was saying. "Fine, then," I began. It`s no secret that the rest of the company considers us a non-threat in this contest, and let`s face it, we haven`t done a good job at cleaning the barracks since we`ve been in Basic. We probably deserve our rotten reputation. But, that`s our ace in the hole....no one expects anything from us. We have four hours to do the impossible, and show that we can do whatever we set our minds to do. If we are to move from chumps to champs, it is going to take EVERYBODY`S effort, and that means giving a 100%. We will start with the usual places we clean, then find places we don`t usually clean, and work in those areas. If you have finished an assigned area, then ask your squad leaders where you can work NEXT. You may be asked to help a buddy or yours, or someone you don`t particularly get along with. Don`t question the assignment, just help. Keep thinking about the weekend furlough to motivate yourselves. We will polish things so shiny that the cadre will be able to see their reflections. We will dust so well that Sgt. Moreno can use those white gloves of his to check the surfaces, than pick up his food with the same gloves, and not worry about his sandwich having any dirt on it. No one is going to be hawking anyone else. The only person who knows that he HASN`T given it his all is that person alone. But, I am confident, that if each and every one of us gives 100% effort, then there is no way in hell that 4th Platoon can lose this contest. I`ve got to ask you to all to do me, and yourselves, a favor. When we go to lunch, knowing we have done everything we can possibly do to clean this place, don`t tell ANYONE what we did here. Let others continue to believe that we are the underdog platoon. But you and I will know differently. And when we return from our morning instruction, and it is announced after lunch that THIS platoon has earned the company`s first two-night furlough, well then, the rest of the platoons can kiss our asses. Now, without raising our voices so that someone outside might hear us, do YOU think we can do this? Can we win that weekend pass?"

With some guys having gritted teeth, and others having clenched fists, and almost every soldier having a determined look on his face, the one unified sound I heard was, "Yeah!" I looked right as Sam Whitman, and he gave me another affirmative nod, though still not a smile to let me know he was in it all the way. "Fine," I said, finishing up, "then let`s do this thing, not just talk about it."

For the next four hours the squad leaders took over and not a soul rested. I could hardly believe those were the same people I had lived with for seven weeks. With just minutes before we were called to lunch, the leaders and I finished our inspection. It seemed like every inch of the barracks had been attended to. Each soldier`s bunk could have passed as the epitome of how a military bed should be made. Even Sam`s bunk was impeccable, which REALLY pleased me, as he usually had the droopiest bed on the floor. Every opened footlocker was identical to the one beside it, with all contents perfectly placed inside. Spacing between the lockers and bunks was nearly perfect. The latrine sparkled, and there was no dust to be found anywhere. I was so proud of the guys I could hardly contain my emotions, and I felt compelled to speak. "This place looks GREAT!" I started. "All of you worked your butts off with a superior effort. No other barracks will look this good, and I feel confident about that. I know we will win that weekend pass, but if, for some unknown reason we don`t, I want all of you to know that I KNOW that the top platoon in this company is standing right here in front of me. I couldn`t be prouder of us, and you should feel the same way." Just as I was fighting off the urge to hug everybody, the call to lunch was made. "Remember, though," I continued, "not a word to anyone. We will win this reward, `cause we are the best platoon, and now WE know it. This afternoon everybody else will discover that, too. Let`s go eat."

The afternoon class was informative, at least I think it was. But I was looking around at all the soldiers, who were supposed to be listening to the instructor. Most of them seemed as fidgety as I was. It EVENTUALLY hit me that we weren`t the only platoon excited about getting off base, and I also forced myself to realize that the other three barracks must have looked great, too. I was very nervous. Truth be told, the class may have been informative, but all I remember hearing the instructor say was, "If you didn`t learn what I taught you today, there is a good chance you could be killed in Vietnam." Then the class was over.

As we marched back to camp, I could sense a change in the company`s demeanor. The marching seemed crisper and the echoing of the 'Jody' chants were louder and clearer. Every platoon was truly trying to shine, and I figured that each one was confident in winning that 2-day furlough. I knew we did everything WE could do to present our barracks as the top entry, but it only seemed fair to assume that the other three platoons had gone the extra mile, too.

Once back in the company area each platoon got quickly into formation. All cadre disappeared inside the command building, but the inductees remained calm. Our patience was apparently being tested, too. Finally, Lt. Garman and the sergeants exited and the lt. decided to torture us with some general company announcements. He hemmed and hawed around a little, and tried to tell a joke. That guy was being a jackass, as he held the furlough carrot dangling in front of us. FINALLY, he stopped yammering, and scanned the company from left to right, then back again. Then with a small, wry smile on his face he said, "Congratulations to the winner of the weekend pass ....4th Platoon."

There wasn`t a big build-up. It wasn`t said with exaggerated expressiveness. It was a short, simple, rather quiet announcement, but the whole camp had explosive reactions. Moans, groans and cursing came instantly from members of the other three platoons, and I really couldn`t blame them for being upset. I would have had the same ugly comments if we hadn`t won....but we DID win. Our platoon went nuts. We were screaming with joy while hugging one another. It was a great feeling to be named the winner. All four drill instructors started screaming for the platoons to come to attention, then we platoon leaders started parroting the commands, until FINALLY all four groups of soldiers were standing, at attention, and being absolutely quiet. The other three platoons were quickly released back to their respective barracks, but Sgt. Moreno held us at attention until the yard was clear.

Most of us weren`t expecting him to give us a heart-warming, congratulatory speech. We knew he wasn`t that sort of person. He paraded in front of us for a few moments, then stopped in front of me. He scanned the entire platoon with his omnipresent glaring frown, then he said in a voice loud enough for the whole company to hear, "That`s the way it should be done!" Then in a softer, yet still strong tone he continued. "You are required to leave this company area by 1700 hours today. If you are still here, at that time, you will be restricted to base like the rest of the losers. Is that understood?"

"Yes, Sergeant," was the extremely loud response.

"You are required to be BACK in camp no later that 1200 hours, two days from now. Is THAT understood?"

We again responded, "Yes, Sergeant," with just as much vigor.

"Any man wandering in here after that time will be given kitchen patrol for a week, and you don`t have to say you understand that because that WILL happen. Platoon dismissed." He pivoted and left the area within seconds.

All right, it wasn`t a strong, congratulatory speech, but Moreno actually seemed a little excited, as well as a little surprised, that we won. The 45 members of our platoon knew how hard we worked, so we were VERY excited to be able to leave Ft. Polk. By 1650 hours, there wasn`t a soul from 4th Platoon remaining on company grounds.

Descriptions of what happened to all of us in Leesville is really insignificant. I`m guessing that most of the stories were a pack of lies anyway. There were the usual prostitute stories, and certainly there were many, many 'getting drunk' stories. When I asked Simmons, the youngest member of our platoon, at seventeen years of age, how he got hold of all the booze he claimed to have drunk, he said, "I had my ways." It didn`t matter who was telling the truth or who wasn`t. Everybody just seemed happy to have gotten away from the base for two nights. All Willie and I did was go bowling on Friday evening, rent clubs and played nine holes of golf Saturday morning, then bought a six-pack of beer to watch football on tv that Saturday afternoon. It was the first time we had seen tv in over seven weeks. By Saturday night we were exhausted, so we went to bed early and slept in until after nine on Sunday morning. After a great breakfast we headed back to the company area. We didn`t see a single member of our platoon the entire two days, and that was fine with us.

At 1200 hours that Sunday, even though not a man in 4th Platoon was happy to be standing in formation, we all stood a little taller. I even had a near smile on my face. We all knew that the rest of the company was jealous of us, and we loved it.

The last two weeks of Basic was a simple return to the first seven weeks. No private was safe from the tongue-lashings from company cadre. Harrison Johnson continued to get more than his share of abuse. I personally want to thank Harry for sticking to his guns, so to speak. By refusing to even touch any weapon, that soldier seemed to have kitchen patrol every, single day. That took a daily slot away from the rest of us, so we ended up having less k.p. than most inductees around Polk. If you are reading this, Harry, thanks for the k.p. relief.

Toward the end of the 8th week of training, the company had an athletic carnival. Platoons competed against one another in a number of events. These included: the three-legged race, the wheel-barrel race, the two-man egg toss, and the bat race. The bat race was funny to watch. Each platoon had a separate lane to run. Located 50 yards from the start was a chalked, four-foot diameter circle. There was a softball bat inside the circles.

When the race began, the first member of the respective platoons, raced to his circle, put his hands on top of the bat, his head on top of his hands, then circled around the bat ten times. His head was NOT to be lifted from his hands, while the other end of the bat wasn`t allowed to be lifted off the ground. When he got finished spinning, each runner dropped the bat and raced back to his platoon to slap the hand of the next man in line. The second runner would sprint the 50 yards, then start HIS spinning. It didn`t matter if a runner spun quickly or slowly, everybody looked drunk trying to return to his platoon. Guys falling to the ground, or running sideways for many yards, often with bats still in hands for a short distance, was the cause of great laughter. The whole athletic event was a huge morale-builder for all of us. In fact, talk began spreading amongst several soldiers that there might be ANOTHER 2-day furlough for the carnival`s top-performing platoon.

Who knew that 4th Platoon had so many athletic types, and Sam Whitman was a star in every event. WE were declared the winning platoon, but there was NO furlough offered. We received two 'rewards,' however. The first was pretty great. Our platoon had the privilege of being first in line for the next six meals. The second wasn`t so great. We were ordered to clean-up the egg shells, and other garbage, which resulted from the carnival. It had become abundantly clear to us that our platoon evolved into the elite platoon in the company. We hoped that Sgt. Moreno might have been proud of our accomplishments like we were, but as he held us in formation before being released to clean, all he said was, "All right….good job. Now, Platoon Leader Stein, get these grounds spotless," then he disappeared. The disappointment at not being recognized by our drill instructor, for our outstanding effort, was evident in the faces of the guys. The squad leaders grudgingly moved to their assigned clean-up areas, and it should be noted that Sam and his cronies refused to help….not even a little bit.

Other than finding out our m.o.s. classifications during the final week, the only other incident occurred when our company went to our last physical training evaluation. I saw my fellow Iowa City draftee, Jimmy Wardlaw, there.

When we arrived at the p.t. field we saw two other companies there, too. All Basic Training graduates were required to get final physical assessments during graduation week. One company was finishing up their testing as we approached, while the third company was marching in from the opposite direction of our arrival.

The mile run is always the last discipline tested. That was my least favorite skill because to get the maximum high score, a man had to run the mile in six minutes or less….in combat boots. My endurance was NOT the best, so I worked hard, every time, to beat that six-minute limit. Anyway, while the two arriving company drill instructors were devising a skill schedule for our companies, we privates were allowed to watch the end of the mile, which was being run by the company already present. I headed to the backstretch near the first turn of the quarter-mile track, and there he came. Jimmy Wardlaw was on his last lap, and not looking like he was having a good time. I wanted to be sarcastic and ask him how his fight to stay out of the army was going, but with obvious pain showing on his face, I decided to be encouraging instead. "Go get `em, Jimmy," I hollered. Wardlaw never broke step as he passed my position on the fence. Never looked my way, either. He simply gave me the middle-finger salute, up by his right temple, and ran to the finish. I wondered if that was Jimmy`s normal reaction to hearing his name during ANY army exercise. I just laughed and then our company was called to formation. I ran into Jimmy years later, back in Iowa City, and he told me he never left the States, but he never stayed at a rank higher than private for long, either. Seems like he and the army butted heads often, so any promotion he got was lost quickly.

The usual scenario for inductees with the infantry m.o.s. included a second nine weeks of training in an advanced infantry company, then off to Vietnam. Willie, Thomas, and I happened upon a way to delay our journey to Asia. We got orders to be enrolled into a class promoting leadership, called Leadership Preparation Class. That would be a two-week assignment, then we would be sent to an Advanced Infantry Training company for our nine weeks. However, having completed the L.P.C. course we would also become automatic squad leaders or platoon leaders at our A.I.T company.

Skip Lonnegan went home for a two-week leave following our graduation from Basic Training. After his return, he took over the clerking duties for Lt. Garman`s company. We three had wanted to tease Lonnegan about being Garman`s whipping boy for the next class of misfits, but in our hearts we were all just plain jealous of him. No amount of harassment by Garman, or ANY of the company cadre, would be as scary as ending up going to a war zone. Skip had somehow gotten on-the-job instruction by the out-going clerk as we got closer to graduation. With his background as a lawyer, Lonnegan became a quick study, so his stepping into the clerk`s slot was a no-brainer. Garman knew what he was doing by grabbing Skip. As it turned out, the company clerk had one more week remaining in the army, after Lonnegan`s return from leave. That one week was all the time Skip needed to become acclimated to all the clerking procedures....the lucky bastard. I didn`t know companies could just have a new clerk with only nine weeks in the army, but that is what happened to Skip, and we future infantrymen were happy for him.

There`s not much to tell about the graduation ceremony itself. There weren`t too many family members in attendance. That seemed reasonable enough, since many of us had to report to our next duty assignments shortly after commencement was over. There were several National Guard members in our company, however, including three in our platoon. The mousy Private Vinson was one of them. The Weekend Warriors, as they were affectionately called by the cadre, treated the ceremony much like school kids treated high school graduations. They were hugging each other, slapping one another on the back, and generally laughing way too loudly for my liking. They let all of us know that the worst of their military career was over....surviving Basic Training. None of THEM would have to serve overseas. They were all headed back to their families, jobs, schools, or maybe just to the enjoyment of a beer while watching Saturday football. The enlisted men, and we draftees were continuing our military training. While the guardsmen contemplated going home to their real world, most of the rest of us knew that we had to turn into serious soldiers in a hurry. The eventuality of being sent to Vietnam was quickly becoming our reality, so graduation wasn`t a laughing matter to Willie, Thomas, or me.

Harry Johnson marched in our graduation ceremony. At least we didn`t carry weapons, so he didn`t have to carry a broom. A couple of guys from his platoon talked about beating on him after the service, anyway, but cooler heads knew disciplinary action would follow, so they settled for some simple harassing catcalls. I wasn`t in the 2nd platoon, so I couldn`t possibly be privy to all the extra yelling they endured as a result of Johnson`s refusal to touch weapons. He DID cause laughter for our whole company when we marched with the M-16`s, so nobody in other platoons liked him either. But, he also got us less k.p. duty, so I stayed out of the jibes he took. I don`t know if he went to Nam, but if he was as dedicated at being a radioman, or medic, as he was stubbornly against carrying weapons, maybe things worked out for him. All I know is that I never wanted to be around him, or anyone like him, again. By 1300 hours, on graduation day, Willie, Thomas, and I had our duffle bags packed, and we were headed to the Leadership Preparation Course, which was located in a different section of South Ft. Polk.

V

Three More Months at Polk

My two weeks at L.P.C. are hazy, but I do remember spending most of the time in classes, not the field. The Military Code of Justice handbook was hammered into our heads. We learned the particulars of many, many more weapons than we saw in Basic. Most importantly we worked in situations where leadership needed to be demonstrated. There WAS yelling, so it wasn`t a picnic. But compared to what we had been exposed to in our first nine weeks, this training was like a vacation. Our company only had 50 soldiers, and we were called candidates, not momma`s boys or other derogatory names. Most of the fellas in our company were enlisted men. They were young high school graduates, who were interested in making the army a career, but they didn`t have the credentials for becoming officers. The L.P.C. class was setting them up as potential candidates for the Non-Commissioned Officers Academy, a program which graduated instant sergeants. The three of us, from Iowa, decided that the N.C.O. instruction was something good for us, too, after our Advanced Infantry Training stint was over. To me, the longer I could stay in the United States, the better the chances that I could avoid being sent to Asia.

L.P.C. had a 90% graduation rate, and ALL of the graduates were given permission to get orders for the N.C.O. Academy. We had to successfully serve as leaders in our A.I.T. units first, however, before getting those orders. Willie, Thomas, and I got lucky in another way, too. We asked for, and received, assignments for the same Advanced Infantry Training unit.

We reported to our A.I.T. unit two days before the nine-week session was to begin. Then we were sent to our platoons, with mine again being the 4th platoon, and we got to meet our tactical non-commissioned officers. In Basic Training the sergeants were called drill instructors, since the troops were constantly drilled in marching and other 'basic' necessities. In A.I.T. sergeants gave mostly practical instruction on survival in a war zone, therefore, each instructor was referred to as a tactical n.c.o. I was very interested in knowing more about the four platoon tactical sergeants, and discovered that only one had the rank of E-6 staff sergeant.(all four drill sergeants in Basic were E-6) This E-6 had gotten his rank by putting in a lot of time as an E-5 buck sergeant. The other three sergeants were E-5, but got THEIR rank by simply graduating from the N.C.O. Academy. Following their nine-week stint in A.I.T., all three of the E-5`s were going to be headed to Vietnam. Graduates of the Academy were known as shake-and-bake sergeants, since none of them had combat experience. So essentially, our company was going to be training with very few soldiers having any knowledge of actual war exposure. This made me nervous, and when Willie and I reported to our alphabetically assigned barracks for a talk with our E-5 leader, I was sure I was older than the tac. sergeant. I later found out he was 22 years of age, (I was 23 at the time) but he had the face of a 16-year-old.

"I see that I have two L.P.C. graduates in my platoon," he began the conversation. "Either of you have any experience as a leader in your Basic Training company, as well as L.P.C.?"

"I was platoon leader for a little over six weeks," I commented.

"Good, you will be MY platoon leader in this platoon. You are Stein, right?" he said looking at the name tag on my fatigue shirt. "And you, Williams," he said to Willie, "You will be 1st Squad`s leader. I am Sergeant Huffington, and I know we will have a great nine weeks together. I am relying on you two to really help me by being my eyes and ears within the platoon. The troops arrive tonight and tomorrow. We start training in two days. Get familiar with the company layout, and if you have any questions, my quarters are in that building." And he pointed somewhere outside. We didn`t really see where exactly, then he disappeared. This sergeant, whom Willie and I called 'baby-face' when he wasn`t around, was a 180 degree different sergeant than Moreno. Moreno was hard-core, and self-reliant. Huffington seemed un-sure and needy. I hoped that this guy would be a take-charge soldier if we had any difficulty in our barracks.

Speaking of barracks, this barracks had a separate room for the platoon leader, which was the same setup we had in Basic Training. In fact, having my own room was a MAJOR perk for me wanting to be platoon leader, though if anything awful happened in Basic concerning my platoon….let`s just say that Moreno had me in that little room, with the doors closed, reading me the riot act about things that the platoon had screwed up. His yelling could definitely be heard in the bay area. My feeling was that Moreno saw the tongue-lashing as being more of a private thrashing if he couldn`t see anybody else around. I really wasn`t expecting that Huffington would be there much, so I was happy to again have my own room and NOT sleep in the same bay area with the other soldiers. Enjoying a little privacy, when I needed it, kept me sane, too, I believe.

Thomas Rockland sauntered into our barracks a few minutes after Huffington left and immediately declared, "Kind of got us a strange tac. in 3rd Platoon. He doesn`t know if he should be buddies with us or ignore us. Wouldn`t make eye contact. Seems like a bookworm to me. I got Patterson, from L.P.C., in the platoon with me. Pat has his shit together so when we were asked which one of us could be the platoon leader, I said 'he could.' I`m the squad leader for 1st Squad."

"Me, too," chimed Willie, then the three of us headed out to familiarize ourselves with the new company layout. New arrivals were signing in as we explored, and by the next day, we had the full compliment of soldiers for our Advanced Infantry Training company.

It was evident almost from our first formation that we had vastly different sorts of soldiers with us than we had in Basic Training. A few major groups stuck out. We had the gung-ho types. These soldiers consisted of mostly enlisted fellas, who thought that the army was wasting everybody`s time by giving another nine weeks of training. They loved to talk about going to Nam and killing gooks, which was a derogatory term one of the guys had heard from his older brother, a Vietnam veteran. Although these guys were angry more than I thought they should be, they were good troops, and they did what they were asked to do by platoon leaders and squad leaders. They were, however, the kind of soldiers who didn`t listen well, therefore, they would rush through exercises without thinking about what they were doing. This caused them to screw up a lot in the field. I believe most of them joined the military right out of high school. I thought this not only because they were young-looking but also because most of their discussions in the barracks centered around girls they had known from some wild high school parties back home. I also knew I could count on any of them if I ever I needed something to get done, so I was glad that I had several 'gung-ho' soldiers in my platoon.

The company had some groups of soldiers I classified as trouble-makers. While Basic Training mainly had the agitating Black Brotherhood, led by Sam Whitman, there were other groups of trouble-makers in A.I.T. who could equal Sam`s buddies when it came to being ornery. For sure, we had a rather sizable number of Black soldiers in our A.I.T. company, too, but they didn`t cause any MAJOR problems. They were loud a lot of the time, however, especially while doing those obnoxious, time-consuming handshakes. They seemed to enjoy talking about all the women they wanted to 'bag,' including each other`s sisters, cousins, and girlfriends. That kind of talk usually enhanced the shouting to another level of loudness, but no particular problems ever came from it. Those guys just seemed bent on getting under each other`s skin. Pushing and shoving occurred, yes, fighting, no. They also liked to brag about the trouble they got into back in the `hoods. To hear them, it sounded like each soldier should have been in jail for fifty years. Whenever I heard some of THAT bragging, I had to kind of snicker to myself. I couldn`t believe ANYONE could get into all the trouble they said they did. But, then again, I was still a rather naïve kid from Iowa, who DIDN`T get into much trouble. Many of those soldiers had enlisted into the military, so staying OUT of trouble was a goal most of them strived to achieve. Since Sam and his group had all been drafted and didn`t want to be in the army, they were just down-right belligerent much of the time. They actually enjoyed showing contempt toward 'the Man,'(Sam`s term) which seemed to represent authority figures, especially White authority. The A.I.T. Black enlistees worked well with the gung-ho soldiers, for the most part, but like

I had mentioned before, they liked to be left alone in their off time. That was fine by me, I wanted to be left alone, too.

One group of particularly difficult soldiers, called themselves Southern Rebels. There were twenty of them in our company, and I believe they considered themselves modern day Confederate soldiers. They referred to anyone that disagreed with them as Yankees, and at least three of them had Confederate flags amongst their personal belongings. They knew that slavery was no longer around, but Willie had two, of our platoon`s three, Rebels in his squad for the first two weeks. He had trouble getting them to do anything, and we finally had to switch them to another squad following one nasty encounter.

Willie`s squad had latrine duty on that day. He asked the two Rebels to clean the urinals, and they refused. I was nearby when Willie gave the job to those two rednecks, so I heard clearly the conversation that followed. "We don`t clean pissers or crappers," one of them said.

"If you don`t clean the urinals, who do you think should clean them?" Willie asked.

"Him," was the retort, and he pointed at a Black soldier who was cleaning a toilet at the time, and fortunately neither heard nor saw what was going on.

Willie kept his cool, and I joined him to assist if he needed any help convincing those two yahoos to get to work. Without raising his voice, Willie said, "Everyone will do all the jobs during our nine weeks here. Today is your turn to clean the urinals. So, quit complaining and get the job done." I was very impressed with Willie`s cool manner.

The two Southern soldiers proceeded to the urinals, but one of them mumbled under his breath, "My great-granddaddy wouldn`t have taken that order." Then, the same idiot turned and looked right at Willie and said, "I don`t like your kind," then he looked at me and said, "or your kind either." They got the job done, but I convinced another squad leader to switch two of his tougher soldiers for Willie`s two trouble-makers, which worked out better for both squads. Willie and

I talked later about the comments 'don`t like your kind,' and 'your kind, either,' We humorously decided that he was referring to us as being two good-looking guys, not a Black and a Jew.

The Black soldiers and the Southern Rebels avoided each other as much as possible, and surprisingly both groups did the jobs asked of them….eventually. That was good.

However, it was another group of mal-contents that gave ALL of us the most problems. Those were the guys who were hoping for a different m.o.s. but received an infantry classification instead. Some of them were enlisted personnel, but most of them were draftees. They didn`t want to have anything to do with more training being geared toward fighting in the jungle. They didn`t want to work around the barracks, either, even shirking their duties entirely when they were in really nasty moods. If the squad leaders or platoon leaders threatened to turn them over to the cadre, the usual response was, "What are they going to do, send me to Vietnam?' Thankfully, this was a rather small group, fifteen at most, but their behavior was detrimental to all four platoons. Their negativism ended up costing us weekend passes until the fourth week, and that was only because the worst of these offenders was removed from the company during the fourth week. That guy was a pain-in-the-ass to everyone, and that included our company commander, Lt. Aaron.

This lieutenant wasn`t as arrogant as Lt. Garman, and he seemed more interested in producing men who could be competent as soldiers than did our Basic commander. For the first three and a half weeks, Aaron seemed to be hoping that the men would conform to his notion of discipline. He gave heart-to-heart talks to the company, then commanded the tac.`s to do the same to each platoon. Most of us wanted to make it through A.I.T. without too many problems. But the agitating group, a.k.a. the disappointed m.o.s. soldiers, would say, or do, things that couldn`t be tolerated, and that caused bad feelings throughout the company. I remember one that sticks out.

It was during the fourth week when the lieutenant had to prove he had more than just words to back up his threats of discipline action. The 1st platoon had a fella that I considered the biggest agitator in the company. He convinced other agitators to be sluggards, whiners, or just plain anti-everything. We were getting ready to head out for a field exercise, and Lt. Aaron was giving last-minute instructions to the company. That was when this trouble-maker, we`ll call him jerk #1, (can`t remember his name) decided to push one of the gung-ho soldiers. The lieutenant saw the push and yelled, "Soldier, you just bought your platoon extra p.t. after we return from the field."

"That`s bullshit," yelled jerk #1 right back. The 1st platoon tac. sergeant raced to that guy, grabbed him by the scruff of the neck, and hauled him away.

"You will NOT be seeing that man again," Aaron said. "Is there anyone else who has a comment?" When we returned from training, jerk #1 WAS gone, and 1st Platoon had a half hour extra physical training. During our next company formation, the lieutenant simply said, "I am a man of my word, and I am telling you now. If there is anyone else here wanting to display insubordination, just act out like that loudmouth this morning. I can tell you now, that I know of a few alternatives to you being here, but you won`t like any of them, and ALL of them can affect your future outside the army, as well. Do what you are told, and we will get through the next five weeks just fine." Guesses of court martial, or being drummed out of the army with a dishonorable discharge, were the two consequences that most of us felt was the result of jerk #1`s disappearance from our company. But that was just speculation. We didn`t care what happened to him. The company was rid of a real problem child.

The expulsion of the do-nothing agitator was on Wednesday, and on Thursday Lt. Aaron did his best to encourage the company to conform to A.I.T. living. He didn`t have to do that, as his warning from the previous day convinced most of us that he wasn`t putting up with anybody who was going to be a top-notch problem. He DID mention that there would be one and two-day passes available for individuals or platoons showing worthiness. In fact, on the Friday afternoon, of that very week, it was announced that the entire 1st platoon would have a 24-hour pass. It was to start at 1200 hours the next day. Hey, didn`t 1st Platoon have the company`s worst do-nothing jerk in their platoon? Of course, he was no longer with them, but they also didn`t do anything special to earn the pass. I guessed the furlough was given for two reasons. First, the tactical n.c.o. of that platoon was the experienced E-6 sergeant, and he may have asked for a favor from Aaron. After all, he WAS the only combat veteran in our company, so maybe he figured his platoon should be allowed the first company privilege. Secondly, I guessed that this sergeant figured by giving a reward to the rest of his platoon, he could better mold them for the remainder of our training. I never saw any improvement in them, however.

Sergeant Huffington tried a rah-rah speech with us when we returned from the lieutenant`s 'encouragement' speech. That was kind of funny since he rarely had anything to do with us other than to be with us for training classes. Every platoon had its Black hand-shakers, Southern Rebels, gung-ho types, and do-nothing agitators, and, sadly, we never got that company pride that every leader looks for in his troops. The answer there was simple, most everybody was convinced that this was the last training they would get before heading to Vietnam. And, for the most part, they were right. Our tac. never tried that kind of speech again. So, I figured it was up to me to get things done around the barracks. I did my best at trying to convince the soldiers of 4th Platoon to work in positive ways. My grandmother`s Jewish guilt didn`t work very well, however, especially with headstrong soldiers having their own agendas. And getting the barracks cleaned was ALWAYS a cuss-filled endeavor.

Here I must give another reader alert. The use of obscene language in A.I.T. was MANY more times prevalent than it was in Basic Training, and I feel the need to address the issue. Again, if you don`t wish to hear my thoughts on cursing, it will be easy enough to find where my story picks up. It will be, however, in about seven or eight paragraphs.

While growing up in Iowa City, Iowa, I don`t remember hearing a single curse word until I was ten years old. A kid in my neighborhood said a word one day that I didn`t understand. When I asked him what that strange word meant, he explained it. Then he translated all the rest of the offensive language that he knew. In my town, in the 1950`s, and even in the early 1960`s, swearing was considered rude and basically used by the un-educated. If a boy was heard cussing, by his mom, he was threatened with having his mouth washed out with soap. A dad would threaten a boy with a belt. I NEVER heard a girl use foul language, not even in high school.

Even the words 'damn' and 'hell' were considered offensive. Not only did I never hear my mom use any curse words, I never heard any of my relatives cuss, and I had some tough cousins who lived in Chicago.

Through my teen years, swearing in public was frowned upon by most of the people I knew. There was a sense of disrespect associated with people who cussed, too. It`s even possible that people in my town may have thought that cursing was a trait of the poor, or done in homes where children didn`t have proper up-bringing. While I did hear men, who worked construction and other manual labor jobs, curse every now and then, I NEVER heard a man in a tie and coat cuss. I`m not sure how poor parenting or low financial standing contributed to the use of foul language. I considered my family poorer than most of my friends` families. That only meant we didn`t have a lot of money to spend, not that we should be labeled as socially misfit kids. My neighbor, the kid who taught me all the swear words he knew, was the son of a doctor, and his family had much more money than we did. The fact was, he talked back to his mom AND dad, which was kind of taboo in the fifties, too. My mom worked all the time, and had three jobs when my dad passed away in 1959. We kids hardly ever got to see her, but right after my dad passed she said something to me that I have always remembered, "Don`t embarrass the family name. I wouldn`t want to have people think I can`t raise my children to be normal." My mom had had a fairly hard life herself, so I listened when she spoke to me.

In today`s world, obscene language seems to be the norm. It is hard to find a movie that doesn`t have foul language peppered throughout. Young people liberally use curse words in everyday conversation. It`s almost like they can`t make their point clear without cussing. Boys, girls, rich, poor, young kids, and especially teenagers, seem to have lost the art of having, for lack of a better term, a 'civilized' conversation. To many of us older folks, hearing such language, ESPECIALLY from young people, is still shocking. Like drinking and smoking, the use of obscene language seems to be a way that rebellious youngsters try to prove that they have grown up. I recently read about a town in the Northeast, whose residents had heard so much public cursing from its teenagers, that a petition had been passed around, trying to get a new city law where the youthful offenders would receive fines for foul language. I doubt that will ever happened, however, what with 1st Amendment rights and all.

Let`s face it, today`s society accepts foul language as ordinary. It still sounds offensive to my ears when I hear young people swearing. Just yesterday I was standing in line, waiting to be let into a wrestling tournament, and the four cheerleader-type girls behind me were having an animated social conversation about a party they had attended the night before. EVERY single girl used the f-word as adjectives…like nobody could hear them, for crying out loud. We could ALL hear them, and that included grandparents going in to the gymnasium to see their grandchildren wrestle. The cursing wasn`t really loud, but loud enough that the thirty, or so, people standing near the girls could hear it. The f-words didn`t even stop when I stared at them and shook my head with a disgusted look on my face. They ignored me. I couldn`t help wonder if they spoke like that in front of their parents. Yep, cursing in public is still a rude, offensive, disrespectful act, in my opinion.

However, when I was in the service, especially after having left the, relatively, 'protected' Iowa City environment, my usage of rude and coarse language became more common-place, and I came to feel that I wasn`t using language that would offend people`s sensibilities….much like the cheerleaders at the wrestling tournament, I suspect. My cursing started slowly at first as there really wasn`t much cussing in Basic Training. This may have been the result of two factors. First, we had several National Guardsmen in the company. Since foul language was likely NOT heard by them on an every day basis back in their home towns, perhaps they didn`t want to pick up any 'bad' habits. In fact, I actually can`t remember hearing any of them curse at all. But the second reason, which affected the majority of us who were new to the army, may be attributed to the fact that few of us ever expected to be going into the infantry. I wanted to be a Jewish chaplain`s assistant, after all, and I knew I certainly wouldn`t use offensive language in that m.o.s. Perhaps the other fellas may have ALSO figured on being assigned to jobs that required them to use a more genteel language. The bottom line was, however, Basic Training was not where I was inundated with profanity on a regular basis.

Advanced Infantry Training had a much different feel to it, however. Most of the soldiers in my company understood that they were headed to the Vietnam war zone, whether they wanted to or not. Let`s face it, bad things happen in war zones, up to and including death. I know I didn`t want to go there. Conversations between soldiers in A.I.T. were laced with profanity, even consisting of stringing one curse word after another, and nobody seemed to notice the language might be offensive to others in the area. I offended as much as the next guy. It was only after I got out of the army that I got back to the realization that only TWO groups of people should be allowed to speak in such uncivilized language....soldiers at war and prisoners. To me, those two classifications of humans have the right to show their disgust with their situations by speaking in an un-educated, low-class, disrespectful, and rude manner. After all, those folks ARE in the most crude environments imaginable, so speaking accordingly should be acceptable, right?

I do want to clarify my cursing a tad, though. I certainly used foul language WAY more than I ever thought possible. I was, however, in the position of platoon leader. In that capacity I actually felt the need to set SOME kind of parent-like standards. But I still cussed.... boy, did I cuss....just not as much as the majority of men around me.

Now that I am off THAT tangent, I will let you readers know that there will be very little profanity used in this book. Today, at sixty-seven, I don`t deem cursing as a necessary tool to express myself. Likely, the only 'hard core' language that will be used will come from conversations between soldiers, and even THEN the language will not be used to excess. I feel you can get the gist of the situations even if cursing is used sparingly. If you enjoy reading profanity-laced books, then you have the wrong book here. If you like good stories about the military, stay with me. You won`t be cheated because of the lack of f...king curse words.

The A.I.T. cadre was well aware of the sour attitudes in the company, and with the #1 do-nothing agitator out of the company, Lt. Aaron decided that Saturday night furloughs should be given out for our last five weekends. I mentioned that the 1st platoon got the first pass, and everybody knew they didn`t deserve it. The agitating soldier was gone just one day, but the announcement was made, so the worst platoon in the company was getting the first over-night furlough...given for most improved platoon. OF COURSE they were the most improved. They lost the worst soldier in the company, and didn`t have time to replace him with another major disruptor. The other three platoons complained bitterly to their individual tactical sergeants. Therefore, for the fifth weekend pass, our company commander decided to hold a tournament and let WINNING determine who gets away from base. The contest he chose was pugil-stick fighting. At the end of this event, one individual champion would be crowned and it would be HIS platoon getting TWO nights in Leesville. (Friday would be a bonus night) All platoons were allowed to earn this pass, even 1st Platoon, so they got particularly fired up. None of the other platoons wanted them to get a second pass before any of us got our first, so there was some animosity toward that group of soldiers even before we got started.

Pugil-stick fighting was kind of like jousting, only without the horses. Two combatants would stand on a six-inch wide plank, facing each other, and beginning ten feet apart. Each soldier wore a helmet but no other padding. On the command to begin, both warriors would move toward each other while holding a six-foot long stick. The sticks had some fairly heavy padding on both ends, and that made the weapon heavier than anyone expected. The object was to knock the opposing soldier off the narrow plank. However, even with padding on the ends of the sticks, and protective headgear, if a guy got hit by a forceful swing, pain was inevitable. The loser of each match would be out of the tournament, while the winner would still be alive to meet the next challenger.

All platoons were to select six representatives, and it wasn`t easy to find five other guys who were willing to compete for 4th Platoon. I knew I wanted to compete, and I chose Willie as our sixth entrant. He reluctantly agreed to represent us. Our company had recently had pugil-stick fighting classes, and people were just hauling off and hitting each other in the head. There didn`t seem to be many people who used strategy, like feigning, using jabs, or combinations of swings. During training, everyone just wanted to bust the guy across from him. Even though I had several gung-ho types in my platoon, only four volunteered to enter the contest. That seemed strange to me because EVERYBODY knew there was a pass waiting for the entire winning platoon. Willie was more or less forced to compete as our sixth entrant, but I didn`t have to work too hard to get him involved. He was a squad leader, so he knew he should lead by example. The fact was, Willie wanted to get out of the company area as much as anybody else, and he also knew there wasn`t a better competitor remaining in 4th Platoon. So he didn`t argue with me when I asked him to join the five of us, who were already involved. First Platoon was matched against 2nd Platoon in one contest, and we had to take on 3rd Platoon. The champion, in each of THOSE semi-finals, would face off for the furlough.

Second Platoon had to be the prohibitive favorites, based on brute strength. They had the two biggest soldiers in the company, and both were rowdy Southern Rebels. During the training class we had, those two brutes swung from the heels, and knocked their respective opponents off the plank in less than five seconds. Then they would each jump around and preen like peacocks while bellowing how great they were. They each only faced three opponents; all from their platoon, so I think intimidation had a lot to do with their quick wins. I have to admit, however, they were impressively large. The fact is, during the pugil-stick training, ALL soldiers had to compete against three other platoon mates. This brought familiarity into play, which resulted in some of the soldiers not taking the stick fighting seriously. Therefore, 100% effort was often questioned. Sadly, the three guys I faced from our platoon weren`t athletic at all, but they were the guys whom the instructors put me up against, so I didn`t complain. My first opponent was way off balance as he moved toward me, so I barely nudged him to finish the job. The second opponent came right after me all right, but when he took a mighty swing, he flew right off the plank. I never touched him at all. The last guy I faced wasn`t very coordinated. All I did was give him a jab to the solar plexus followed by a quick tap to the shoulder, and he, basically, jumped off the plank.

As I evaluated my chances in the tournament, I knew I had very little competition time during training, less than one minute of experience on the plank, as a matter of fact. Still, I also knew that I was pretty athletic, and very competitive. My four gung-ho soldiers, Willie, and I reported to the sergeant in charge of the event, and even though I wanted to be confident, I was VERY nervous.

The instructions seemed simple enough. The first two platoons would send their respective competitors against each other in the first round, followed by the second two platoons doing the same thing. Then survivors would have a second round in each semi-final contest. In the event that one platoon had more soldiers remaining after round one, the dominant platoon would match up two of its soldiers against one another. The platoon which had two of the FINAL three battlers, after that second round, had to decide which one of its teammates would stand by to watch the chosen member fight against the last surviving soldier of the opposing platoon. The last two undefeated combatants would then do battle. After EACH contest had a finalist, then those two would face off with the winner getting a weekend furlough for his platoon. On paper, this might look difficult to understand, but all the competitors had no problem comprehending. One of the 2nd platoon Southern Rebels bellowed, "All I know is that I would knock ALL these bastards off that board if it meant getting a night at a Leesville whorehouse." Yep, easy instructions…last man standing wins.

Third Platoon soldiers proved tougher than I first expected they would be. My Iowa buddy, Thomas Rockland, was a very strong person, physically, but chose NOT to compete. When I asked him later about it, he just said he was tired at the time. I guessed that his platoon had obviously stronger pugil-stickers, so I let it drop. In fact, all of Thomas` representatives were so strong, that only Willie and I remained for 4th Platoon after the first round. My first opponent actually slipped while coming at me, so a double right-hook, by me, knocked him off the plank very quickly. I was happy. My second opponent was a lot more athletic than I hoped he would be, so we sparred for a minute or so. I decided to give him a series of jabs to his stomach, but when I accidently nailed him good to his groin, (there was NO rule that said we couldn`t hit a guy in his genitals) he bent down and to his left. I took my strongest swing of the day and hit him behind his right knee. He buckled. Then a second hard swing smacked him on top of his bent head, and off he went.

Willie`s second opponent was pretty tough, too, but didn`t look as skilled as my opponent, for some reason. Still, Willie didn`t take advantage of some shots he had in front of him, and when his 3rd platoon foe hit him hard against the side of his head, Willie went flying off the plank. The third match, between two 3rd Platoon buddies was fun to watch, as neither really wanted to hurt the other one. They seemed to prance around forever until their tactical sergeant yelled at them to stop being sissies and start hitting. A minute later it appeared one of them just decided he had enough and fell gently from the plank. I watched the two remaining platoon mates battle, but it wasn`t a contest, really. The fella that beat Willie vanquished the weaker opponent almost as if given instructions by someone to do so. My bet was that Willie`s victor was the better hope of that platoon winning the pass, so every one of the other 3rd platoon members rooted for him. Therefore, he could challenge me and be a little fresher than he would have been in a longer contest with his buddy.

When I watched Willie`s match, I had noticed that his opponent went rather heavily in the direction of every feigned blow; thus, he would lose his balance temporarily. Willie never followed the feints with blows that might capitalize on his foe`s slight loss of balance. I jabbed and jabbed, and then he swung and miss. I had stepped backwards as he telegraphed the blow. Then I feigned left and right, and when that guy leaned a little too hard to HIS left, he was definitely off balance, but only a bit. However, it was noticeable to me. My quick smash from the left made him start swinging his arms to regain posture, but it was too late. I tapped him again, from the left, and off he went. I was the 3rd and 4th Platoon`s representative, which meant NOTHING to the other platoon, really. I was in the finals, and I wanted to win that furlough for my guys.

The 1st/2nd Platoon contest went as expected, and the two loud-mouthed Rebels ended up facing one another for a chance to battle me. Those two guys flew through their half of the tournament with little resistance, it seemed. Oh, the soldiers from the 1st platoon tried the same tactics as the 2nd platoon brutes, but THEIR hard swings were puny compared to Tweedle-dumber, and Tweedle-dumbass. The finals of their match was just a show of hard swings toward each other`s heads. There were a lot of 'ooohs' and 'aaahs' with each hit, and finally, one of them went flying off the plank. I had only one minute to recuperate after my match, but when the 2nd platoon bully was called to the plank, I was raring to go.

I can`t remember the guy`s name, as I have long put the antics of the Rebels out of my mind….including their names. What I DO remember is that he was the biggest person in our entire company, and since the removal of the #1jerk from 1st Platoon, this fellow inherited the reputation as the NEW major asshole amongst the trainees. As we positioned ourselves on the plank, ready to engage one another, chants of 'kill him' was started up by the Southern Rebels. I then started hearing chants of 'go, Stein, go' from, not only my platoon, but from 1st, and 3rd Platoons, too. I am pretty sure that a few of Goliath`s platoon members were secretly chanting for me to win, too, though they didn`t chant too boisterously as none of them wanted to be recognized by any of the Rebel supporters as traitors. Seems like those few fellas were willing to give up a chance at a weekend in Leesville in the hopes of seeing someone beat the big oaf. As the cheering got louder, I am ALSO pretty sure that I saw a couple of the cadre, standing in back of the crowd, cheering for me, too. Though I was quite nervous before we started to joust, I felt good that I had a lot of people in my corner.

Not to brag here, but beating that guy wasn`t too hard to do. When we were told to begin, he gave a mighty swing at my head. I backed up two steps, then countered with four quick jabs to his mid-section. They weren`t soft jabs, either, I gave some stiffness to them which seemed to upset him a great deal. His problem was his reliance, 100% of the time, on that heavy swing from his right to his left. They were easy blows to see coming, and the pattern continued for three straight encounters. He would swing, I would back up two steps, then return with four quick jabs to his gut. That would return him to the original starting position. He certainly had malice in his swings, but quickly became frustrated that he couldn`t hit me. Those swings, which were meant to hurt me while knocking me off the plank, caused him to lose his balance somewhat. So, on his fourth straight hard swing, I decided to NOT back-up as far as before, choosing to duck down instead. I squatted as low as I could, and felt the momentum of his mighty swing going right over my head. I heard this loud 'wooosh' above me, too. Since the big guy was moving rather quickly toward me with the force of the swing, and with him being slightly off balance I simply stood and hit him with three hard, rapid-fire blows to his right ribs. That big loudmouth couldn`t stop quickly enough to get his balance back, and ended up running right by me after he fell off the plank.

Pandemonium briefly followed. My platoon was ecstatic, the Southern Rebels seemed bent on teasing him for looking so inept, and his 2nd platoon screamed and moaned their disappointment at him for not winning a 'sure' furlough. And, while MY 2nd platoon supporters enjoyed yelling at him, they secretly nodded their approval in my direction. The bottom line was, at 1200 hours on the following day, 4th Platoon received a 48-hour pass to Leesville.

In some ways, Advanced Infantry Training was easier to get through then was Basic Training. Yelling, by company cadre, was much less than I experienced during my first nine weeks in the army. In fact, most of the shouting was directed toward individual soldiers with attitudes, and there were a LOT of them with poor attitudes. We certainly had the groups that could have caused havoc, and I am specifically referring to the Southern Rebels, the Black Brotherhood, and the Do-Nothing Agitators. But those groups seemed to have had the 'live and let live' mentality that kept tension, amongst themselves anyway, at a minimum. It was almost as if most of the soldiers in our company were resigned to the fact that they were soon going to be on the same side in the Vietnam War, and there was going to be plenty of time to vent anger against the REAL enemy. Harmony wasn`t exactly the order of the day, but it just seemed like a more plausible condition than constant bickering. I was certainly adapting better to being a soldier, too, so maybe I didn`t recognize as many stressful situations as I did in Basic Training.

The tactical sergeants were different in A.I.T., too. The three younger ones didn`t run rough shod over their respective platoons like the Basic sergeants did. In fact, the sergeant for 2nd Platoon seemed to have more trouble than he could handle, at times. The big rowdies in that platoon became the focus of Lt. Aaron, too. It seemed kind of strange, however, that the lieutenant was showing the young sergeant how to handle particularly aggressive soldiers. I couldn`t understand why Aaron wanted to constantly act like a big brother to that sergeant. After all, with the lieutenant taking charge of so many 2nd Platoon problems, how could that tactical sergeant EVER prove to himself that he would be in charge of tough situations in a war zone? Our tactical sergeant, Sgt. Huffington, showed us he was quite adept at leading in field exercises. When he ordered us to do something, we obeyed. However, he wasn`t as interested in leading when we were in camp….especially where work in the barracks was involved. In Basic Training, Sgt. Moreno would come into the barracks and start barking at us for poor bunk alignment, or un-polished brass, and he would take out a white glove to check for dust after we 'cleaned' the place. He was ALWAYS finding reasons to be unhappy with the barracks. Huffington, while good outside the barracks, left the inspections of our living quarters for me to handle. I can tell you now that we had nowhere close to the cleanliness we had in Basic. Sgt. Huffington wasn`t really thorough when he checked our work, either. Fortunately, I had some very good squad leaders. They ALL seem to have good report with their charges. So, while our barracks wasn`t EVER as 'finished' as our quarters in Basic, it was squared away just enough to pass inspection. The squad leaders were happy, I was happy, and Sgt. Huffington was happy. Thankfully, we never had an inspection by the c.o., which made EVERYBODY happy.

Training classes were taken more seriously, too. The Do-Nothing Agitators didn`t give 100% effort all the time, but when any instructor told us we 'could die' in Vietnam if we DIDN`T learn the material being given, even they became attentive. We had instruction on many more weapons than we had in Basic, too. The gung-ho types couldn`t get enough practice, nor could ANY of the problem groups in A.I.T. And that made life in camp much more relaxing to me, as opposed to the constant stress I endured during my first nine weeks in Basic Training....a stress which had been created by the conscientious objector Harry Johnson, and his broom rifle. In fact, EVERYBODY in A.I.T. liked handling the weaponry. One soldier even talked about wanting to take an M-72 bazooka-like weapon home to settle a score with the guy who stole his girlfriend. None of us, of course, could leave any training practice field with a weapon. After our nine weeks of advanced training was up, I actually felt like I was with a whole company of soldiers, instead of the eccentric, individual civilians I started with early in my army experience. And, whether these fellas WANTED to believe it or not, most of them finally realized that being infantrymen was their fate. They, also, understood that they would be headed overseas sooner or later, and that likely meant Vietnam.

Willie, Thomas and I decided that 'later' was better for us. We had chosen to go to the N.C.O. Academy in Ft. Benning, Georgia to become instant sergeants. I kept telling my two buddies that the longer we trained in the United States, the more likely it was that our government could work at getting America OUT of the war in Southeast Asia. We realized that not only would we get an extra twelve weeks training at 'shake-and-bake' school, we would ALSO get another nine weeks working as tactical sergeants in a second A.I.T. unit. Add to that a sizeable furlough before deploying overseas and I figured that the EXTRA time we would get to stay in the U.S.A. could be six months....or more. Surely, I figured, the President and Congress would see how futile it was to continue sending soldiers to Vietnam.

Thomas was concerned that when we DID go back to another A.I.T. company, we would likely get a WHOLE company of soldiers like those in OUR company`s 2nd platoon. Willie and I finally convinced him that wouldn`t happen, but the truth was, I worried about it, too. Since our N.C.O. class was scheduled to start two weeks after we graduated, the three of us headed back to Iowa for some much needed restful days.

I arrived at the Iowa City bus depot on a Sunday morning. The bus ride only took about 12-14 hours. It was like an eternity to me. I had been away from civilization for only five months at that point, but since Jill and I had only been married a short time before I reported to Des Moines to be sworn into the army, every minute on the bus seemed to drag by excruciatingly slowly. My wife HAD written me letters faithfully, while I was at Ft. Polk, and I was always so happy after receiving them. But I still thought of us as newlyweds, so I was MORE than excited about getting to BE with her again. As I got off the Greyhound I noticed my mom had come to greet me, too. I did love seeing my mom, but dropping her off at HER home was a priority for me. I just really needed some quality time with my bride. All right, I`ll admit it, I was horny.

Jill told me that she was on her last week of Spring Break from the University of Iowa, and that she had made arrangements with her school instructors to skip a class or two, AFTER school resumed, to spend more time with me. She really wanted to be with me, too, and I loved that. We owned a little trailer, located about three miles out of town, and with the exception of just a couple of short visits to see my mother, Jill and I stayed barricaded in our home for my entire leave. I never even told my friends I was back in town.

Unfortunately, my wife and I only got to spend eight days together. Willie had decided to drive his car for our trip to Ft. Benning, and since we had to report on a Saturday, we had to leave Iowa on the preceding Thursday. Willie had already picked Thomas up before they arrived at our trailer, and saying good-bye to Jill was every bit as hard as it was when I had to report to Basic Training.

VI

Earning Sergeant Stripes

As we left the trailer park, Willie decided he better tell the two of us passengers that his car had experienced a 'little problem' two days prior to his leaving and picking us up. But, he said in a reassuring voice, that his cousin knew cars 'kinda well,' and had checked it out. To quote Willie, quoting his cousin, "It seems fine to me." It WASN`T fine!

We had gotten to the outskirts of Ottumwa, Iowa, which is located about ninety miles from Iowa City, when all three of us started to hear a noise coming from the front of the car. Within seconds of us first hearing the sound, we saw a mechanic shop, so we whipped in there for a check by a REAL mechanic. I`m not sure what Willie`s cousin had looked at, but Willie told Thomas and me that he was going to have a 'serious' talk with his kin the very first chance he got. We were in that shop for nearly six hours. I certainly don`t remember exactly what the problem(s) turned out to be, but the repairs cost the three of us nearly two-thirds of our travel money. When we found out the expense, I can tell you that BOTH Thomas and I wanted to 'talk' to Willie`s cousin, too.

With all the waiting around, we three became quite exhausted both physically and mentally, and it got to be late afternoon before we took off for Georgia again. The car sounded great, so the expense was worth our peace-of-mind. However, we could travel no further than St. Louis, and all of us agreed to find a place to sleep for the night. We located a cheap place to stay, in a dark and dingy part of downtown St. Louis. Thomas suggested we stay there, as he had spotted a nightclub just down the street from the dumpy hotel. The neighborhood looked too seedy to me, so I made the suggestion we move on a bit. I was out-voted, so we checked in. This place had bars on the windows of every first-floor room that faced the street...bars on the front door, too. We rang a buzzer and there was a 'clicking sound' which released a lock allowing us to get inside and register. The clerk had a slovenly look about him, and when he gave us a key for our room, he said, "Your room is in the alley. There are four rooms there, and the key will fit them all. Just tell me which one you choose, so I don`t assign it to anyone else tonight."

We found the alley thirty-five feet from the entrance, but that area was so dark it was difficult to find the keyholes on the doors.

None of us had thought the desk clerk`s statement to be strange, at first, because we were all anxious to settle into a room. After entering our fourth room, however, I began thinking how creepy it was that our key could fit all FOUR doors. But when I mentioned my thoughts to the other two guys, neither of them seemed concerned at all. My fears would prove prophetic later that night, though. Anyway, we ended up choosing the furthest room from the street because it was the quietest, then we called the clerk to give him our room number. All rooms had a double bed and a roll-away bed, which is what we needed, but I also needed the quietest room we could get. I had started getting a headache, and took a couple of aspirin as soon as I could. After placing our belongings on the beds, we headed out to see about the night club Thomas had seen earlier.

I had been on two weekend passes with Willie, and we had gotten along like brothers. He was three years younger than I and had an opinion on EVERYTHING. He was also gullible about most topics, too, and since I had traveled a lot more than he had, he would eventually defer to my 'experienced' thoughts on most subjects. He was particularly agreeable if he had a beer or two in him.

Thomas Rockland was a different story. He was actually a couple of months older than I and had a degree from a small Iowa college. Generally, he was a quiet guy, and he had a real passion for weight lifting. From his long hours in the gym, over several years, he developed HUGE biceps, which he enjoyed showing off with muscle-baring t-shirts. With the last name of Rockland, Thomas told Willie and me that his friends back home just called him Rock. Since the three of us were traveling partners, we began calling him Rock as well. He had one main problem that was very noticeable...Rock was a 'quick' drunk. When he got a minimum of two beers in him, his personality changed from quiet to VERY loud and obnoxious. He was rather short, being only 5'8" tall, but when he got loud, people would just glance at him, see his bulging biceps, then turn away, allowing Rock to be as boisterous as he wanted to be. I knew Willie was a lightweight drinker, but this would be my first time in a bar with Rock. Since I was not much of a drinker of alcohol, it didn`t take but fifteen minutes in that club, for me to know that we were in for an interesting evening. I knew that I had to keep my wits about me, so I nursed one beer as long as I was there. After fifteen minutes, however, Rock had gotten his second beer.

The bar was packed with an eclectic group of people, too. There were several college kids there, which I found interesting until I noticed that no one was asking for age-proving identification cards. There were many well-dressed men and women, who likely had stopped there to get a drink after a long day at the office, and there were many office buildings in the area. There were locals scattered throughout the bar, as well, so like I said an eclectic group of people were drinking that night. The music began at 8:00 p.m., and that is when the noise level rose exponentially.

Women were everywhere, and many of them were staring at Rock and his huge arms. He was aware of their stares, and when he looked directly at any one of them, they would smile and give him a 'come hither' look. Though he had started getting loud BEFORE the music started, the women didn`t seem to mind much. He looked at Willie and me and said, "I`m off to dance, boys," and with that he left our table and headed toward the ladies.

Fifteen minutes passed, and Willie and I were surprised when Rock came back to our table with, not one, but three women. We were told that all were secretaries in one of the offices near the bar, enjoying a prolonged 'happy hour.'

But it was obvious that one of them had a serious interest in Rock. The other two were coaxed to join us as a 'favor' for Rock`s dancing partner. These were not girls, mind you, but women in their mid-forties. That was found out when Willie tactlessly asked them their ages, after he had finished his second beer. The woman sitting next to Willie was a non-stop talker and kept saying to him, "You remind me of my son."

All three women were married, and not particularly attractive. However, Rock and Willie were enjoying the attention they were getting. The third woman stayed about twenty minutes at the table, but then she abruptly got up and headed out the door. With no one to talk to I decided to leave. I also needed to get to my supply of aspirin as my headache had, once again, begun to throb. Neither Rock nor Willie was ready to leave with me, so before I headed back to our dive hotel, I said, "I`m going back to our place. I need to take care of this headache. Knock quietly when you are finished here, please. I would HATE loud banging on the door." With that I was gone.

It seemed like I had just crawled into the double bed that I was sharing with Willie, and apparently was sleeping like a baby, when I heard a loud KNOCK, KNOCK, KNOCK, being pounded on the door. I was so startled that I leapt out of bed and raced to the door so I could reprimand those two drunks. I swung open the door, but Rock pushed me back and said, "Get in quick and be quiet!"

He and Willie scampered into the room, and Rock closed the door just enough to barely be able to see through a sliver of an opening. "Oh, Jesus," he whispered quietly, "he`s got a gun!" Then he VERY quietly closed the door completely, and we all stood like statues for several seconds. Slowly we retreated into the darkness of the room.

"What is going on?" I whispered. Rock just put one finger to his lips and we listened for another minute, or so. I was thinking about what we would have to do if somebody came crashing into our room….with a GUN. Another minute or two passed, then Rock slinked back and re-slivered the door. When he appeared satisfied that there was nobody outside, he started to laugh quietly. I said, "What the hell?" Rock didn`t let me say anything else, as he began to speak a mile a minute, and Willie just nodded in agreement to everything that was said.

It sounded like gibberish to me, for the most part, but by the end of Rock`s rambling, I kind of got the gist of what had happened. Willie`s 'date' decided to leave the club, so he informed Rock that it was time to get back to the hotel. Rock`s 'date' was really into him, and asked our muscle-bound friend to go home with HER. She indicated that her husband was out of town on business, and she PROMISED to get him back to our hotel by five or six in the morning. However, it appeared, they would have had to take a cab to her home, since Willie`s date had car-pooled with Rock`s woman that day, and took the car when SHE left. Rock`s lady also complained to him that she was worried about taking a cab, by herself, at that time of night. Rock, seeing a night of passion ahead of him, but not wanting to be stranded at a woman`s house if she happened to NOT get him back at a decent hour, decided that he would go with her, but only if Willie could drive them. Willie wasn`t sure he wanted to do that, and that is when the horny woman told the young soldier that the refrigerator was stocked with food and beer, and he could have as much as he wanted while she and Rock were 'elsewhere' playing. With Rock talking a mile-a-minute, I was struggling with what he was saying. Like I mentioned, it sounded like gibberish to me, and I didn`t want to believe him, though supposedly, there HAD been somebody outside our hotel room with a gun. I uttered a muffled, "What?" when Rock told me about the Willie bribe, but I let him continue. He was on a roll.

"That house was at LEAST ten miles from here," Willie chimed in, while Rock continued with the story. After a half hour at the woman`s house, Rock was in the bedroom with his 'date,' while Willie was having a sandwich in the kitchen. Suddenly, all of them heard the distinct sound of a car motor outside the home, and it appeared that there was a vehicle coming up the driveway.

The woman of the house raced to the bedroom window and peeked outside. Then Rock tried to mimic what his sex partner said next, "Oh, no, it`s my husband getting home early from his trip," and Willie started to giggle at the high-voiced impression. Apparently, panic started setting in as both Rock and the woman hurried to get dressed. Willie, too, was freaking out, and he ran into the bedroom to see where Rock was. Both guys grabbed the rest of Rock`s clothing and his shoes, and stormed out the front door. They could hear shouting coming from inside the house while Willie fumbled to get the car keys, first into the door lock, then the ignition. Some guy then bolted through the front door just as Willie went screeching down the street. They DID see the man run toward the driveway, and soon they saw headlights, in the distance, following them.

With a sixth sense they didn`t know they had, according to Rock, both of the guys figured that the headlights in the rearview mirror HAD to belong to that angry husband, I shook my head when he told me that statement. They decided to park Willie`s car on a poorly-lit side street, two blocks from our hotel. As Willie said, "Well, I didn`t want that crazy bastard finding my car and vandalizing it." I told him that I could understand that reasoning, but I still had a hard time believing what I was hearing. The story continued.

My idiot soldier friends were racing toward the alley, when they spotted a set of headlights coming down the street. Since it wasn`t too late in the evening, they hoped that the lights DIDN`T belong to the husband`s vehicle, but when they saw the car picking up speed, and coming right at them, Rock and Willie scampered into the alley and directly to our room. "The rest," said Thomas finishing his narrative, "is history."

I had a hard time believing that story, and thought my 'friends' were pulling a prank on me. After all, I never actually got to see anyone in the alley with a gun. Yet, neither Willie nor Rock had laughed or teased me for looking so serious after I heard their tall tale. In fact, both of them seemed exhausted and went to sleep almost immediately upon their heads hitting the pillows. I, on the other hand, found it very difficult to get back to sleep.

It was approaching 3:00 a.m., and I was just on the verge of getting to sleep myself, when I heard the front door slam open and saw the lights go on. I bolted upright and looked at Rock and Willie. Neither of them moved one iota. I bounded from the bed and headed toward the door. I was tired of all the nonsense and didn`t care if there WAS a husband with a gun. I was angry enough to confront anyone at that moment.

There was a short wall obscuring the door from our bed, so I couldn`t actually see who was in the room. I scrambled around the wall, and saw nothing except the door, which was nearly closed again. I yanked it open and there was a man standing there. In his arms was a woman, who was wearing a short wedding veil on her head. Since I was just in my skivvies, I quickly closed the door until my body was hidden. Then I peered around it and said, "Why are you coming into my room?"

"We got married in Indiana earlier today," the man responded, "and we`re heading to Phoenix for a honeymoon. Coming through St. Louis, we decided to get a little rest, saw the vacancy sign on this hotel, and stopped to get some shut-eye before moving on."

"But, you`re in MY room," I said rather emphatically.

"The clerk gave us a key and told us that it would fit any room door in the alley, and that we should just pick one."

"What!" I said in disbelief. "He said the same thing to me....that moron!"

"Sorry," the groom said as he put his bride on her feet.

I hurriedly closed the door, woke my sleeping comrades, and with me having Willie`s car keys, we headed to the car. I was TIRED of that St. Louis area. After leaving the downtown proper, I asked my two traveling buddies where they thought we should go. They were sound asleep. Still, I was glad to be out of that dingy hotel, and I started to think about what might have happened if I went to the door in a snit, and there stood an angry husband with a gun. I found a quiet neighborhood at the edge of the city, and pulled into the darkest area I could find. Finally, I got some sleep.

We got to Birmingham, Alabama early Friday evening. We stopped to get something to eat, and Rock saw a dancehall just down the block from the eatery. Both he and Willie wanted to go there for a beer or two. I objected, slightly, because I knew two things. First, we were very low on monetary funds. And, secondly, Rock and alcohol just didn`t mix. Thomas swore to me that he wasn`t loud ALL the time, and that all he wanted to do was have one quiet drink and maybe have a dance or two. Willie said he was up for one beer, too, so we pulled into the dancehall parking lot, and in we went.

The place was a college hangout, apparently, and there were girls everywhere. We found a table away from the dance floor and ordered our ONLY beer for the night. Rock drank his right down while Willie sipped his and I just hung onto mine. The music had already started, so Rock took off on a search for dance partners right after he had finished guzzling his alcohol. He, naturally, had no trouble finding willing females, as once again, everybody was staring at his muscle t-shirt, or rather the guns he had hanging out of them. Then Willie got the itch to dance, and he was off to the floor, too. I was still missing Jill to the extent that just thinking of dancing with another girl seemed like cheating to me. So I sat there for hours and hours, first sipping my beer until it was gone, then sipping Willie`s beer until IT was gone. Both guys came around to make sure I was still there, and neither wanted to drink, so THAT made me happy. And, FINALLY, when it started to get late, I felt we should get to the car and get some sleep. I waved at the two guys to come to the table, and I got up to go. Willie returned to the table exhausted, which figured, since he had danced for nearly five hours straight. Rock had danced just as long, but when he began returning to our table, he wasn`t alone.

Thomas had been dancing with the same female for an hour straight. I thought he must have decided we should meet this girl before we departed, or so I prayed, as they approached. I had noticed this particular girl with Rock earlier, but since it had been a crowded dance floor, I really hadn`t gotten a GOOD look at her. When she got to the table, three things struck me immediately. She had HUGE boobs, but I had kind of seen that from afar. She was, at least, in her mid-forties, which I DIDN`T notice earlier because she had a lot of hair covering a good portion of her face. And she had a very noticeable limp, which made it seem like she was dragging her left leg when she walked, as opposed to stepping forward with it as in a normal gait. It`s hard to explain, but she definitely had something wrong with that wheel. I didn`t know what to stare at first....the boobs, the leg, or at how old she looked close up. Rock really DID seem to like his women older, that`s for sure.

"This here is," Rock started telling us, but the name was garbled due to the start of more music, so I never found out who she was, "and she wants us to go to her favorite club. It is an after-hours club, so we can stay there all night if we want to. Look, she bought me a beer," and he preceded to chug it down, which is something that I didn`t want to see, knowing how he was affected with too much booze.

Willie, using no tact what-so-ever, said, "What happened to your leg?"

She was extremely inebriated as she slurred her answer, "Car accident, but I don`t want to talk about it."

I quickly chimed in to Rock, "We can drop her off, or take her home, but you know we don`t have money to go to another club. Where`s her car, anyway?"

The older woman screwed up her face, and once again talked with a mumbled delivery, "My friends left me an hour ago when Rock told me he could take me home." I stared at Thomas in disbelief that he would tell her that. He just looked at me and smiled. She continued, "Rock says you`re soldiers. My ex-husband was a soldier. He was a bastard....but I still respect all OTHER soldiers. Don`t worry, whatever your name is, (and she kind of looked in my direction) I will buy everybody beer when we get to my club. It`s a GREAT club," and she became quiet.

I implored my traveling buddies to just let us drop her off at her house, then get some sleep. The thought of us reporting to Ft. Benning the next day was bad enough. To show up exhausted would not be the way to impress anyone. However, Willie said he would like to see the older woman`s 'speak-easy' club, so I was out-voted, and off we went.

I believed Birmingham had some kind of a 'no alcohol being served in public establishments after one in the morning' code. I wasn`t very sure about that, though, or I would have had more ammunition in my argument about NOT going to an after-hours bar. I also failed to mention how badly it would look for our futures, in the N.C.O. Academy, if we were to get arrested for drinking illegally. And Willie would have had EXTRA trouble, being that he wasn`t even of legal drinking age. However, I DIDN`T mention these things, so when we arrived at our destination, deposited the car in a full parking lot, and approached a non-descript building, I was more than a little apprehensive.

Around to an alley entrance we went. The door had a peephole on it, and when some guy opened it up and saw us, Rock`s 'date' said, "It`s me and I have three friends." I admit it was fun knowing that we were entering a Speak Easy-type bar, so I just decided to go with the flow. Rock and Willie had these huge smiles on their faces as we entered, which let me know that they weren`t thinking about anything but having fun. Normally, I didn`t consider myself to be very mature, even though I was a married man, but compared to my two soldier buddies, I turned out to be the poster child of responsibility during this journey.

The inside of this place was small, and it was packed with people. The music was not modern, more on the line of Glenn Miller, or the Dorsey Brothers. The people were quite a bit older than the crowd we saw at our first Birmingham club, too. I would say that the three of us were the youngest people there. Rock brought a couple of beers for Willie and me then said, "See ya later," as he took his lady`s hand and headed to the dance floor.

The two of us remaining travelers just shook our heads at the fact that Rock could have had just about any girl he wanted at our first bar, but he chose a woman old enough to be his mother, as a romantic interest. That was almost unbelievable to us, but we couldn`t leave town without him, so we wished him luck when he walked away. Then, Willie confessed to me that HE was finished dancing for the night, so the two of us just walked throughout the crowded club, nursing our beers. We finished drinking those brews in minutes, but we knew we couldn`t afford to purchase any more alcohol, not if we wanted to have enough gas-money to get us to Columbus, Georgia. After an hour, both Willie and I were ready to get somewhere, ANYWHERE, and sleep. We searched for Rock inside, then we decided to check around outside. As we strolled toward the parking lot, we spotted him sitting on the hood of Willie`s car. He had a sour look on his face, and we wondered if he had been ditched by his elderly date. "What`s going on, Romeo?" I teased as we neared his position.

"Look," he said as he gestured with his thumb toward the inside of the vehicle. Passed out in the back seat was Rock`s woman. Her blouse was un-buttoned and one boob was hanging out of its bra cup. Her tight-fitting Capri pants were halfway down her hips. "I couldn`t get her pants down," Rock said in a frustrated voice.

At that point, Willie got VERY nervous. He opened the door closest to her head, grabbed her under both arms, and pulled her from his car laying her next to the driver`s-side door. By that time her SECOND boob had fallen out of the bra. Willie looked quickly around the parking lot, and not seeing anyone in the area, he said, "Get in. We gotta get out of here now!" Rock and I scurried into the car, Willie gently backed out of his parking spot, and within seconds we were headed toward Ft. Benning. "I can`t believe you, Rock," Willie said as we sped down the highway. "You HAD to try something with an old lady, and now she is lying half-naked in a bar parking lot."

Thomas started to laugh and said, "Willie, she is not dead, just dead drunk. Think about how surprised someone is going to be finding a naked lady there." He continued to be amused, Willie continued to be upset, and I didn`t know what to do. I just hoped we wouldn`t hear on the news that something serious had happened to her….thankfully, we didn`t. I felt badly for many days following the dastardly, and cowardly act of running away and leaving her on the ground. I was sure she had to be mortified when she sobered up and realized what she went through. Even today, as I am writing this story, I can`t truly appreciate the humiliation she must have felt. However, to that lady, where EVER you might be, I want to apologize, from the bottom of my heart, for my participation in your embarrassment that night. I am very, VERY sorry!

Willie continued to drive until we reached Georgia. In the first small town we found, he pulled over into a darkened lot, and the three of us FINALLY got some sleep.

When we awoke, Willie drove us to the outskirts of Columbus, pulled into a gas station so we could clean our faces, then we headed to Ft. Benning. Once we checked into our company area, we were allowed to head to the barracks and catch a few more hours of sleep, which was desperately needed. Our first official formation was at 1500 hours, and all three of us Iowa boys were glad to be starting our N.C.O. Academy experience.

The company area at Ft. Benning was similar to all of my Ft. Polk sites. It was the cadre who were so very different. We had a captain as our commanding officer, with three E-6`s and an E-7 (sergeant first class) as platoon tactical sergeants. We were assigned barracks alphabetically, so Willie and I were in the 4th platoon once again. Our tac. was S.F.C. Fields, who had already served two tours in Vietnam and had earned his stripes over time. The other platoon sergeants were recent graduates from the Non-Commissioned Officer`s Academy, with all having finished as top graduates from their respective companies. Captain Helmuth had recently returned from Vietnam, too, so he and Sgt. Fields were given the utmost respect from everybody in the company….especially the other three platoon sergeants, who would be headed to the war after training our class of cadets. I respected every cadre member in our company, and paid close attention to anything any of them said.

There DID happen to be a lot of yelling, however, by the sergeants, so that hadn`t changed from my experiences at Ft. Polk. Still, the yelling at the Academy was directed at us in a more civil manner, and didn`t seem strictly punitive. For example, one day, during a training session on a trail where cadre were camouflaged and set into positions as snipers, I THOUGHT I saw some movement ahead of me. I decided to keep moving down the path anyway. Within ten more steps, I heard the discharge of a weapon, and was hit on my legs five times by a BB gun. The BB`s didn`t really hurt, only stung, but getting shot during training was never enjoyable. What DID hurt was what the sniper yelled at me right after the incident. "I saw you hesitate while I was moving from one bush to another," he bellowed. "You were unsure of what you saw, but you kept moving forward. Your lack of caution not only got you killed, but brought the rest of your squad closer to the ambush zone. It is your duty, when walking point, (lead man on the trail) to be sure of what you see before proceeding. Quit being in such a hurry, Cadet. That way you can stop getting yourself, and others with you, killed in combat. Is that understood?"

While this sergeant DID yell at me the entire time, he explained the situation and asked if I understood the consequences of my mistake. That was a lot different than sergeants who yelled in my Basic Training or Advanced Infantry Training units. Their reprimand would have been, 'You just got yourself killed, maggot. Your pretty little wife became an instant widow because of your stupidity. You won`t survive as a point man if you don`t use what little brains you were given. This is NOT a Sunday stroll through the park. The enemy is waiting to kill you, moron. You need to stop day-dreaming and get your head out of your ass when you are moving down a trail. You see something, you stop and check it out, or you could become a negative war statistic. Now you and ALL of this squad listen carefully to me. I`m not going to BE in Nam holding your hands. You better learn from this idiot`s mistakes right now, or y`all just might die over there.' The message may have been similar, but the delivery wasn`t. The N.C.O. cadre treated each of us as potential leaders. Earlier training sergeants treated us as a mob of recruits, expecting only the smart, attentive soldiers to learn and survive, while the non-learners....well, too bad for them.

Another major change at the Academy was that we were called cadets, and not referred to as slimeballs, maggots or any other derogatory label. This gave us more self-esteem, and since all 180 of us had signed up to try and become sergeants, attitudes in the barracks, and behaviors on the company grounds, were more positive. Orders were readily accepted. Every cadet had the opportunity to be a platoon leader, or a squad leader, at least one full week during our twelve weeks. Some of us were fortunate enough to serve in a leadership role more than once. I volunteered to be one of those soldiers.

Sergeant First Class Fields was an exceptional leader, in my eyes. Since he was a combat veteran, he had many 'small' tips to pass onto us about how to take care of our gear in rainy weather, or how to pack a rucksack efficiently. He KNEW what the conditions in Vietnam would be like, and he wanted his platoon to produce leaders who could lead efficiently from the get-go, as opposed to having to learn, on the fly, ALL the little tricks necessary for basic survival in a war zone. I will tell you now that his tidbits DID help me in several situations, but he barely scratched the surface of everything I needed to learn. That would come with on-the-job performance. Still, he was the best leader I ever knew.

One of the major changes, that I experienced in the N.C.O. Academy, was the lack of 'gangs.' It didn`t matter to the cadre what behavior we displayed before getting to Ft. Benning, but during our twelve weeks of training, each cadet was expected to treat EVERYONE with respect, and that included other cadets. It was all right to hang-out with several buddies during free time, but openly expressed taunting was not tolerated, and offenders were dealt with quickly and with precision. That usually meant expulsion from the program, and a one-way ticket to Vietnam.

Furloughs were handled differently at 'shake-and-bake' school, as well. After the second week, passes started to be issued. Most cadets could earn a pass, but it was not a 'given' privilege. Platoon sergeant had every right to withhold passes to individuals, or the whole platoon, if deemed necessary. Even when given the opportunity to spend the night away from the fort, many cadets found themselves needing to catch up on studies, as there was quite a bit of material given to us during each training session. Often, soldiers not given over-night or weekend passes, chose to go into Columbus for several hours on a Saturday, but they had to make sure they returned to the company area in time for bed check. In truth, there seemed to be a lot more instructional information given to us than SOME of the cadets could handle. This might cause some of them to ask to be excused from the company. In several cases, however, soldiers were simply dismissed from our ranks due to their lack of comprehending the material. Indeed, stress affected all of us. I studied a lot more than I thought I would have to do, but I DID enjoy the relaxed conditions that the weekends allowed us. However, with a high stress factor in play, I chose to only take two weekend passes.

Being accepted into the Academy was an honor, and it was rewarding, too. From the first day in the company, cadets were given a 'bump' in grade. We were considered E-4`s. It was hard for me to imagine that, after only six months in the army, I had blown through the three classes of private, to the respectable rank of corporal. AND, for cadets who could survive all twelve weeks of training, the rank of E-5, also known as buck sergeant, would be bestowed upon them at graduation. That is an important rank, even in today`s military. Becoming a sergeant indicates that accomplishments have been satisfactorily achieved. With any advancement in rank comes an advancement in pay, too. In 1969, making more money was meaningful to me. I felt the need to help Jill pay our bills, even though I was away. Her family had money, and would help us if we had trouble.

But it was important to me that Jill and I become a self-sufficient couple. I kept thinking how she must have been suffering with money problems, and I never wanted to ask anyone to help us financially. By becoming a sergeant, I knew I could DEFINITELY help my wife stop worrying about asking her parents for a loan.

There was also a pleasant surprise, announced by Captain Nemuth during our very first formation, which intrigued many cadets. He mentioned that the top SIX graduates would not only become sergeants, but they would skip the grade of E-5 to become E-6, staff sergeants. Those six, then, would be assigned to various companies at Ft. Benning to help develop a new cycle of cadets. I didn`t really care about the rank as much as I knew that, by staying in Benning as a tactical n.c.o., I could get an extra three weeks in the States. I had never wanted to give up hope that our government was working tirelessly to bring home our troops from Southeast Asia. I couldn`t help thinking that those twenty-one extra days might be JUST the right amount of time needed to ensure that I was not sent to a war zone. Also, by becoming a staff sergeant, I realized that I would be able to send even MORE money to Jill.

However, with Captain Nemuth`s announcement, I became instantly conflicted. While I really wanted to stay in the United States as long as possible, I also knew that if I WAS sent to Vietnam, as an E-6, I could find myself in a very important leadership role. The original plan, for my two years of surviving the military, was to stay quiet and do what I was told. I just wanted to slide through the army as invisibly as I could, known as a fellow who did his job admirably and without complaining. I never thought for a minute that I might attain a leadership role. Becoming a sergeant was scary enough. To become an E-6 staff sergeant meant that I would have to take on an even higher post of responsibility. My enrollment in the Academy had already closed the door of me getting through the army unnoticed. Still, I wasn`t sure about wanting to put out the work necessary to attain the rank of E-6, until I came to grips with the three truths I knew about myself. One, I wanted to stay as long as possible in the United States. Two, I would rather be helping make sergeants in another N.C.O. Academy company, than I would be fighting with disgruntled privates in another A.I.T. company. And, three, I was a very competitive person, therefore, finishing as one of the top six candidates was a challenge that I could relish. I didn`t let on, to Willie or Rock, my thought of becoming an honor graduate, as I knew they would tease me... especially Rock. But, I also realized that there were a lot of outstanding cadets in our company, so competition was going to be fierce. I didn`t even want to write Jill to tell her of my desire to be an E-6. I knew she wouldn`t approve of me as a LEADER in the army, when she wasn`t even happy that I was a soldier.

I listened intently when Capt. Helmuth spoke about the parameters of becoming an E-6. "Standing in front of me are future leaders, and it is my job, and that of the company cadre, to graduate those men who are ready to take on the responsibility of leadership. Six of you, however, will rise to a rank that normally takes an average soldier five years or more to achieve....the rank of staff sergeant. Every cadet here will be evaluated on two scales, academics and leadership. We are interested ONLY in graduating men who, not only know what to do in any situation, but can get himself, and the people in his charge, to a winning conclusion. Six of you will learn lessons better, and solve situational complexities more effectively, than the rest of your peers."

Hearing the captain use words like 'complexities' and 'peers' made it perfectly clear to me that I wasn`t with average people. Indeed, these were not the complaining, trouble-making Basic Training or A.I.T. soldiers with whom I lived at Ft. Polk. Everybody in THIS company was there for the same reason I was, to earn sergeant stripes. Knowing that most of my new training mates would also be trying to finish as an E-6 worried me somewhat, but I realized that we were all starting from square one. The bottom line was, I didn`t know most of the people around me, but they didn`t know me either.

Helmuth continued by saying, "Evaluations on every candidate will be updated weekly, but no one will learn who the 'honor graduates' are until our last day here in the company area. So, cadets, I wish you all good luck, and I hope that every one of you will accept the challenge of the N.C.O. Academy, and graduate as the outstanding sergeants that we expect you to be."

I glanced around to see how everyone else had received his challenge. Not that it mattered. I left that formation believing that I not only wanted to finish our twelve weeks of training as a sergeant, but I was also ready to fight for that extra staff sergeant stripe. I quietly whispered to myself, "Let the games begin."

While the living conditions around the company were much more civilized than any I experienced at Ft. Polk, the training was much, MUCH harder. Instructors were very quick and precise when doling out information. Perfect execution during field exercises was strived for, and the failure by cadets to achieve that perfection became the cause of MOST of the yelling which occurred throughout the twelve weeks. All cadets were given individual tasks as well as being assigned to group tasks. It was not unusual to have members of one platoon placed with members of OTHER platoons, when group tasks had to be resolved. It was known as the 'working with strangers' approach, and was used, somehow, to measure the adaptability that cadets would need to have while leading new and different personalities through difficult situations. Specifically, the cadre wanted to judge, for themselves, how effective each cadet might be when new replacements joined his unit in, say, a war zone. The fact was, however, that most cadets of our company wanted to do what they could to impress the sergeants. They did exactly what they were told to do when ANYBODY gave an order, including other cadets holding leadership positions. Not all platoon members, from companies in which I had served, would have been so cooperative, that`s for sure. You, the reader, could possibly think of several people, in both Basic Training and A.I.T., who would definitely have proven to be difficult co-workers. I know I can.

We had a variety of basic training classes, including weapons training, advanced hand-to-hand instruction, and more pugil-stick fighting. But, we also had many specialized sessions which were geared toward learning guerilla warfare tactics. It didn`t matter whether our training was individualized, or done in groups.... emphasis, in those classes, was centered on getting all cadets into 'surprising' or 'stressful' situations. The parameters were designed to emulate imagined, maybe even real, combat circumstances that might confront us in jungle settings. Those 'specialized' guerilla scenarios were highly valued by our platoon sergeants, too. It was a necessary way for the cadre to observe and measure all candidates` cognitive and reflexive reactions to difficult situations. Sadly, those exercises proved to be frustrating to many of us trainees.

Walking down sniper trails was one guerilla exercise that ALWAYS stressed me out. I can`t remember a single time when I WASN`T shot by BB guns. And it didn`t matter if I was hit by one or ten BB`s, I was declared dead each and every time. The scary part was that the cadre thought I was one of the more observant cadets, shot less than my fellow candidates most of the time.

We were instructed on, then got to fire, every hand-held weapon used by foot soldiers in war zones. These included the M-79 grenade launcher, the M-72 bazooka-like weapon, and the claymore anti-personnel mine. We were taught ways to rig C-4 explosives into a variety of booby-traps. It seemed like everything we handled could do heavy damage anywhere. It was necessary to learn all these 'destructive' weapons quickly and well, since we had limited, or NO chance to practice with them. It also became essential that every cadet learn both the logistics of when and where to use the weapons, AND how to clean the ones we did get to fire. We were constantly being told that everything we handled, during our training, had become mainstays of all platoons working the jungles of Vietnam. We could take notes, which I did, and we studied in our spare time. There were times when I thought I was back in college. We were given quizzes on material we had learned, which made it imperative that all cadets know the specific facets of each weapon. Sadly, the 'school work' was too difficult for several cadets, and they were removed from the company.

While academic proficiency was an important and necessary component to the well-rounded Academy student, many cadets, me included, preferred being involved in the field exercises. In fact, there were only two field experiences which I can say I really detested during my twelve weeks….the gas chamber, and the 4-man night compass trail.

The first time I came into contact with a military gas chamber was in Basic Training. The format at Ft. Polk was clear enough, and seemed simple and innocuous. I was, however, a bit concerned about being exposed to a 'noxious and irritating gas,' as it was described by our class instructor. As it happened, I may have started being just a little apprehensive before the exercise began, but I ended up having a moment in my life that bothers me to this day. Here`s how that unsettling Basic Training event unfolded. Inductees were ordered to put gas masks on.

One platoon at a time was told to walk single-file into a gas-filled room, and wait for an instructor to enter before continuing the experience. Once he was inside the gas chamber, the instructor walked in front of each man, and gave the command to begin. That was the signal for the trainee to take off his mask, state his name, rank and serial number, then walk calmly through the building`s exit. He was not to step toward the exit, however, until the instructor pointed at the door, and ordered him to 'move out.'

The gas made a man cough violently when it was inhaled. That information we were told before we entered the chamber. What none of us ever remember hearing was the fact that the gas also had detrimental affects when it came into contact with liquid…it burned when it interacted with ANY liquid. As soon as every single soldier took his mask off, he felt the urge to close his eyes immediately, due to that awful burning. But each soldier fought to keep his eyes open so that he could see the command signal to leave the area. However, that was given a full two seconds later. Certainly, the viscous liquid of the opened eyes burned badly enough to create enough discomfort, but if a soldier was sweating, he felt the perspiring areas burning, as well. In addition to having his eyes and sweaty areas feel like they were on fire, any soldier compelled to open his mouth due to the pain he was experiencing, discovered that the gas attacked the saliva in his mouth, AND started him to cough uncontrollably. It was down-right scary watching each platoon member recite his information, struggle while waiting to leave, then try to CALMLY depart, knowing that if he was deemed to have run he would be brought back into the chamber for another go. More than one soldier hit the wall next to the exit while trying to scramble blindly through the door. It was easy enough to hold one`s breath while reciting the required information, but when the gas started burning the eyes, panic would set in. Sadly, seeing us go through pain seemed to thoroughly entertain the chamber sergeant, as he appeared to be smiling behind his mask on more than one occasion.

Seeing men come through the exit door, sputtering and coughing, caused my fellow 4th platoon members and me to develop great apprehension, almost bordering on fear. I knew I was worried about what we had to face inside, and Sam Whitman, he kept telling anyone who would listen that he WASN`T going to participate…he did, though.

I believe that my gas chamber experience in Basic Training was more painful than most of the other troops in the company. I hadn`t really thought about the fact that I was a heavy sweater, but I DO remember standing in the middle of our single-file line, and suddenly feeling sweat beading on my forehead. Then my underarms began to perspire, as well as my crotch area. My recitation turn came too slowly for my liking, but when it DID arrive, I raced through the necessary information at a high rate of speed. To my chagrin I was also wiggling and squirming throughout the short speech. That was due to the agonizing burning I was experiencing in my private areas. My eyes began burning immediately, too, and I was forced to close them within two seconds of removing my mask. I must have made quite a hilarious sight. With me needing to keep my eyes closed tightly, I couldn`t SEE any signal indicating that I could leave, nor did I HEAR the sergeant give me the order to depart. In fact, I became more convinced, with each passing second, that the sadistic sergeant decided to delay sending me to the exit so he could get the full enjoyment of seeing an inductee writhe in pain. When I finally did get outside, I can`t tell you which was worse, the uncontrollable coughing, or the excruciating pain in my eyes or in the areas where I was sweating. I cringed in pain and hoped the feeling would be gone quickly….it wasn`t. Our less than sympathetic company cadre seemed overjoyed hearing us whimper, and appeared particularly happy to be able to label us 'big babies.' It shouldn`t be a surprise, then, that as soon as Academy cadre informed us that we were headed to a gas chamber, I became a little skittish. Going through another round of unbearable agony DID concern me, at first, as I knew that my eyes would burn and I would cough if I opened my mouth. So, I thought of a plan, which helped me be less apprehensive. I would simply position myself as the first cadet to enter the building. In that way, I would have less time to start sweating, and I would be closer to the door for a more rapid exit. To my surprise, I was actually looking forward to showing my fellow cadets how well I could accept the torture of a gas chamber.

Once we were finished with instruction, however, I realized that we all faced two potential problems, which made the exercise different than those I faced in Basic. First, we didn`t go through a chamber at all. Instead, four cadets were placed in a bunker, and there were several bunkers at the training site. Being in bunkers was supposed to emulate what the enemy might face if we would come across them in the jungles of Vietnam. Why we were to be ENEMY soldiers I couldn`t quite understand, but I was more worried about the gas then portraying an enemy combatant. The second difference scared me quite a bit. We were to sit in the bunkers with our masks OFF, and only allowed to place them over our faces when a gas grenade was hurled into the bunker and exploded. A sergeant would look into the bunker to make sure we had our masks off, then he would toss in our little 'surprise.' I began sweating almost immediately upon entering the hot bunker. To make matters even MORE interesting was the fact that the gas used in the exercise was CS gas, known to be the most powerful gas the army had in its arsenal. I became VERY concerned after hearing that news.

My three bunker-mates were from other platoons, and I discovered them already inside our cramped, stuffy cubbyhole when I got there. I, also, discovered that I couldn`t sit near the door as I had planned, either In fact, I was positioned the furthest away from the entrance/exit opening, and there was just the one tiny door-like aperture in the entire bunker. Apparently, the other cadets remembered THEIR Basic experience with gas, and crowded near the open doorway for a quick exit….smart bastards.

I still was not too worried as the instruction was much different than my first gas mask class. We were to be in a bunker, have a grenade thrown in, put on our masks as quickly as possible, and exit without panic. The instructor described it as a simple exercise. At least I knew we were going to get to wear the masks immediately, so breathing the toxic stuff wouldn`t be a problem to either my eyes or my breathing. The burning of my various sweaty areas still had me concerned, however. I tried to convince myself, that if my three bunker mates, flew out of there, I would be right on their tails, and therefore, out with minimal damage being done to any of my sensitive parts. And, like I mentioned, these guys HAD to be smart bastards. They would surely know to exit with expedience, or so I prayed. Meanwhile, I sat there trying NOT to sweat. As we waited for our turn to be gassed, each of us practiced putting our masks on as quickly as possible. Suddenly, a cadre member looked in at us, and after telling us to put our masks down, he hurled in the poisonous canister, which then exploded.

It was the guy sitting next to that teeny, tiny exit hole who caused the initial havoc. He began struggling to get his mask on. I had seen him practice, so I figured he must have panicked. Since he was a big boy, he suddenly became a formidable blockade to the only way out of that festering hellhole. I didn`t even see, or care, how the other two fellows were doing, as I quickly discovered that my mask was NOT functioning correctly. With my first breath I thought I was going to die. There was definitely something wrong with the filter. I tore the cursed thing off my head and hurled it to the ground. My eyes began burning like they were on fire, but I had to keep them open to see where to go. The two soldiers with masks on saw my dilemma, and moved aside, while 'roadblock' was apparently still trying to figure out which end of the mask goes on his face. He began to choke, too, but I didn`t care. I threw him aside, and clawed my way up and out of the trap, which I previously called a bunker. Through greatly labored choking and hacking I sought fresh air. I raced as fast as my feet could take me out into the countryside. Naturally, I started sweating profusely, which made my whole body feel like a suffocating ball of fire. SFC Fields had seen me bolt, and gave chase. I finally stopped and Fields caught up to me. He handed me a handkerchief, and told me to dab out the gas from my eyes. Thankfully, my eyes began to feel better within a minute. All my sweaty areas….not so much. In fact, it took over twenty minutes before I began to stop coughing, and even longer to get the burning pain to subside to a bearable level.

When the entire exercise was finished, and we convened for our evaluation, the instructor acknowledged that five cadets had trouble putting on the masks; thus, suffering the agony caused by gas. He told the company that one of the suffering cadets had a mask that was found to be malfunctioning. I just happened to be the proud owner of THAT lemon. He asked me to raise my hand, gave a quick 'sorry,' then continued to explain how rare it was to have faulty equipment, as filters were changed out frequently. But that was no consolation to me. I could still feel the ghost-like remnants of burning while he spoke. The big guy from my bunker, who had trouble getting his mask on, came over to me before we headed back to the company area. Surprisingly, he apologized to ME for blocking our hole. He must have been oblivious to the fact that I pushed him aside selfishly so that I could survive. He was one of the five 'sufferers,' so I just said, "That`s OK." I didn`t feel the need to cause any hard feelings between us.

The compass event occurred during either the 6th or 7th week of training, two days after instruction on how to use the instrument had been given. Each group of four men were given one compass, one map, and one set of 'azimuths'....a term the cadre preferred to use instead of the civilian term 'directions.' It was a two-mile course and the first foursome took off at dusk. It would turn out to be a very long night.

Since we got to pick our partners, Willie, Rock and I got together right away. But our fourth team member was a fellow named Vincenzo Petrocelli, who was in Rock`s platoon. He was from New Jersey, and while his strong Jersey accent was fun for an Iowan to hear, he was kind of a loud mouth. He was proud of his Italian heritage and the tough streets in his neighborhood. I found him both entertaining and obnoxious....almost cartoonish. He started most of his sentences with "Back in Jersey," then he would proceed to speak like he was a tough guy. His exploits of the trouble that he and 'his boys' got into, while he was growing up, contradicted his physical appearance. He was a skinny, pock-faced twenty-one-old with rail-thin arms. To be as tough as he said he was seemed only possible if he carried weapons on him at all times. He could barely do five push-ups, which made him the weakest cadet in the company, I do believe.

Anyway, he REALLY admired Rock, as Rock may have been the strongest cadet in the company. Thomas did push-ups constantly, during his spare time, and could do twice as many of them as any other soldier in our company. I just knew that Vinny, as he liked to be called, enjoyed spouting off feats of toughness knowing that he had Rock near him....kind of like having 'muscle' to back him up in case someone called him out for being the loudmouth that he was.

The MOST entertaining characteristic about Vinny was the choice of civilian clothes he wore when leaving base. He had shiny shirts and pants, patent leather shoes, and wore lots of rings, bracelets, and necklaces, all of which made him look like a pimp. His particular trademark was his hat. It was a Fedora, which seemed a couple of sizes too small, and he wore it down over his face to the point that it nearly covered his right eye. He had also driven his car to Ft. Benning, and it matched his personality. It was a huge, older Cadillac, which had been painted black. He had it fixed so that it rode very low to the ground. His tires had some gaudy wheel covers, and he had a ghastly hula girl hood ornament. The one time I rode in his car was uncomfortable, as he had a black interior, which caused me to sweat like a horse. He always wanted to be around Rock, however. So, by his constantly entertaining Thomas with his stories, AND polishing Rock`s ego by referring to the Iowa boy`s muscles at every conceivable occasion, it was a foregone conclusion that Vinny was to be our fourth compass companion. Willie and I didn`t really care if he joined us, but we also felt like we had no say in the matter, either.

When the exercise commenced, six different groups were sent on completely different azimuths. After a ten-minute wait, another six groups were sent out, and this continued until all groups had left camp. Cadre were positioned at checkpoints along each azimuth. However, there would be only THREE checkpoints on the respective trails, and to me, that wasn`t enough. Two miles in the dark, with little supervision, turned out to make all our journeys very long. It was comforting, though, to know that there would be SOME people checking our progress as we moved through the woods. As I remember it, that particular night was VERY dark….and I thought a little scary, too. Still, with each trail having ONLY the three checkpoints, there was plenty of room for groups to have interesting moments. For example, some groups were faster than others. If one team caught up with the group in front of them, the instructions became simple. They were NOT allowed to join forces. The 'caught' group was to wait ten minutes, then re-start the course from the point where they had been caught. No one wanted to wait in the dark, so apprehension started setting in for the foursome left behind. Sometimes there turned out to be a little cheating on 'wait' time, but the cadre was just anxious to get all troops back into camp safely by the end of the exercise, so no one was reprimanded for leaving a little early. At no time, however, did eight people show up together, at either the checkpoints or the finish area, so that never really became an issue.

The general instructions were simple enough. One cadet would check the azimuth required, by using his compass. A second cadet would move out in the direction noted, and would count his strides. The counting was done to approximate meters moved, as each step was assumed to be about one meter in length. The 'walker' would go in a straight line until he ran into an obstacle, then he would stop and call for his team to catch up. Sometimes the distance could be nearly one hundred meters, sometimes just twenty meters. We had been taught that sound was distorted by total darkness, therefore, even rendezvousing with the man out front became more difficult than many of us had hoped it would be. There were times when the 'point man' would NOT be calling us from the azimuth he was originally given. Maybe he had wandered a tad, due to bumping into small shrubs or rocks, or maybe he just plain got confused in the darkness. Whatever his reason for being out of line was inconsequential, but it often led to considerable conversation amongst the three remaining group members....to the point where arguing was inevitable. It then became necessary for the compass man, who was ultimately responsible to move the 'walker' a little to the left or right, to make the necessary azimuth corrections. Since it was also the responsibility of the compass man to get his compatriots TO the 'point man,' the troops were forced to move when the compass holder decided to go. That became the time for 'discussion' to cease. After gathering again as a group, the lead man would be sent further ahead on the appointed azimuth.

The azimuth debates continued to be a constant mess until the teams got to checkpoints. Fortunately, all checkpoints were located in large open areas, so groups could be off quite a distance on their azimuths, but got to correct their directional problems after spotting the fairly large lanterns, which the cadre had with them. From the 'spotter`s' position, each team would be sent on the new, correct azimuth, in hopes that the group walking could reach the next checkpoint safely. The instructions also mentioned that each team member was to take a turn at both walking out into the darkness, and reading the compass. That didn`t always work out to be equal work, however. Our group proved that point very well.

Vinny was given the compass by the instructor, and I was told to walk into the night at a certain azimuth. I was barely thirty-five meters into my journey when I ran into a large tree, so I called for the other guys to come to me. Not wanting to look like fools in front of the class instructor, the other three guys came walking toward me without any consultation. They just trusted that Vinny knew where I was. He didn`t. Soon I heard, "Damn it, Stein, where are you?" It took them five minutes to finally find my position. Willie was upset, so he took the compass from Petrocelli and asked Rock to walk for him. Thomas didn`t walk very far and called for us. He was a good twenty degrees off the course that Willie sent him, AND he hadn`t even gone twenty meters. At that rate, it might have taken us all night to finish our night course. We could even hear the instructor calling for the

NEXT group to 'mount up.' In embarrassment, I told Willie to walk point and I would read the compass. For some reason, Willie got so far that we could barely hear him when he asked us to join him. Both Vinny and Rock thought they knew from where Willie was calling, but they pointed in two completely DIFFERENT directions. I told them to trust me, and I kept saying, "Where are you, Willie," as I moved forward. With Willie answering my every call, we got to him rather quickly, and he seemed right on our azimuth. Everybody in the group seemed happy.

Willie didn`t have trouble reading the compass, and with me walking for him, he used my trick of constant calling to get to me. The other two guys didn`t fare too well. Rock could read the compass just fine, during daytime, but he lacked confidence at night. During the daylight, he liked to get the original direction, then look up to spot objects ON the azimuth. He would move to his object without consulting his compass again. That method worked fine in thin terrain, but in heavier forest land, he`d 'assume' landmarks in the distance, only to find out he was off the mark by several degrees. However, he wasn`t ever TOO far away from his assigned azimuth, so he passed his testing. During darkness, he couldn`t reconnoiter by the use of objects. This frustrated him a great deal, so after three or four turns on the compass, he asked to NOT be given any more turns....and we obliged.

Petrocelli was a different story. How he had made it through six weeks of training, including daytime compass testing, was beyond me. Rock served as his walker, but Vinny wanted to check with Willie or me to verify his azimuth every time he had the compass. Since Willie didn`t really care for Vinny, he kept saying, "Come on, Petrocelli, you`re going to have to EVENTUALLY be able to do this on your own." Me, wanting toget finished with the exercise sooner, rather than later, made sure he always had a proper direction toward Rock before we moved out. Petrocelli claimed having two main reasons why he wanted one of us to help him on every read. First he whined that he hadn`t ever even heard of a compass while growing up, boasting that because he knew every street in his Jersey hometown, he had no need to be around one. Willie tried to tell him that he WOULD have to be around compasses in Vietnam. But when Vinny just shrugged off the advice, Willie threw up his hands, walked away from the kid, and left me to deal with the situation. Like I questioned earlier, how did this guy pass his daytime compass testing? Never heard of them? Ridiculous! None of us had, unless we had been in the scouts.

Petrocelli`s second reason for asking Willie and my help was a pip. "Yuz guys is from Ioway, and deese tings come natchril for farmers." When that statement came out, Willie just shook his head and moved behind me, trying not to get into another argument with the idiot. I tried to explain to him that I was raised in Iowa City, which was a university town by nature, and I had only spent one night on a farm in my entire life. Vinny`s response, "Dat`s more den me, so help me or we ain`t going to do too good tonight." The fact that I was needed satisfied my ego, but Willie and I BOTH understood that Petrocelli hadn`t paid attention in class, and was looking for any excuse to NOT have to use the compass.

Even with the problems we seemed to have, we still were the second group to finish the assignment. The first six groups had sprinted out when they were told to leave camp. All of them wanted to get as much distance as possible before total darkness set in. That would be only ten minutes, though, as we were in the second wave of cadets to leave camp, and it was getting VERY dark when we were told to move forward. Add to that the fact that Vinny felt it necessary to ask the instructor, "Is dis ting showing the right direction?" Our dumb team member indicated that he just wanted to make sure he was reading the compass correctly on his 'first go-around.' The other five groups were leaving camp while the instructor was ONCE AGAIN explaining the term was azimuth, not direction. Then Petrocelli said he was sorry and blurted out, "Dis is the right AZMUTT, though, huh, Sarge?" The instructor got behind Vinny, moved the compass around Petrocelli`s hand a little, then pointed for me to get moving. I got to my first stopping point, called for Willie, Rock and Vinny, and they moved in the same general direction that I had gone. It was pitch-black by then.

Oddly, we didn`t catch up with any other group. The first team, using the same starting azimuth that we had, finished ahead of us. There were also two other cadets back in camp when we arrived. They never completed their trail. Those guys were members of one of the 'lead-off' groups. With the group trying to beat the dark, their second man with the compass had a misread, just as dusk was quickly turning to night. The group`s walker ended up going well off course. When the team got to the point man, one of the cadets thought he saw a 'rock' moving in the nearly complete darkness. Then, all cadets apparently saw objects moving. Seems they had run into a rock formation that housed abed of snakes. Terrified, the group raced back to their previous point of reference, corrected the azimuth, and moved until they got to their first checkpoint. Two of the cadets felt ill, due to their close encounter with the reptiles, and asked to be taken back to camp. When told they would receive no leadership OR academic points for the exercise if they quit, both of them gladly accepted, telling the sergeant, "We don`t want to run into any more snakes tonight, Sir." They were immediately reprimanded for calling the sergeant 'sir,' then a member of the cadre, using a flashlight, was dispatched from camp with orders to 'bring those cowards back.' The remaining pair had to wait until the next group of cadets arrived at the check-point, then all of THEM were allowed to continue in a group of six.

For the next two hours and more, groups arrived triumphantly into camp. After a short time, there was no in-coming activity, so it was assumed that all groups were accounted for. We cadets started to become restless. We knew it was already past our 'lights out' time, and thanks to the grueling task we had completed, sleep was the one thing most of us began craving. While we loitered around the deuce-and-a-half trucks, wishing we could get loaded and leave the cursed night course, it suddenly became apparent that something wasn`t quite right. Cadre began running around and seemed rather agitated.

No one wanted to ask any of the sergeants what the commotion was about, but information began to leak back to us that one group was still on the trail. Not only were they still 'out there,' but one of the cadets, while taking his turn at walking point, had taken a wrong azimuth which caused him to walk off a five-foot cliff. He supposedly had a broken leg. The rumor continued that one of his team members stayed with him while the other two cadets tried to correct the azimuth mistake and get to a checkpoint. THOSE two apparently got a little lost, too, and it took them quite a bit of time to find help. The scurrying around by sergeants turned out to be the organization of a recovery team. A jeep was dispatched, and twenty minutes after the rumor began, we were loading into our trucks. No one said anything on the ride home, as most of us were exhausted and disgusted by the whole ordeal. It was nearly 2300 hours when we got back to camp, and sleep was the only thing on my mind.

The next morning found everybody talking about the previous night`s events. We joked in the barracks about scratches and bruises received due to running into trees and various shrubberies. We laughed about how slow everybody`s movement was in the darkness, and the trouble following the sounds of the point men. However, when we got to our morning formation, the mood turned more serious. Captain Helmuth was NOT happy, and he let us know about it.

"The company lost three cadets due to last nights results," he began. "One man is in the infirmary for a fractured leg, and two men chose to quit when faced by adversity." The 'snake boys' were apparently removed from the company, as we later found out. "The overall effort by this company of cadets was dismal, at best, and I am VERY disappointed in your performance of our nighttime exercise. Your sergeants are so upset with you that they have asked me to re-schedule a second night of compass use." As it turned out our sergeants really DIDN`T want another night on the trails, but were used as scapegoats for the captain`s anger. "Unfortunately," the commandant continued, "our training program is too busy to accommodate a second night of compass practice. I am telling you now, however, that we are only half-way through our twelve weeks, and I had better see some drastic improvement from many of you, or we will have a very small graduating class. Is that understood?" We gave a robust 'YES, SIR,' not only to show that we understood, but just as equally for the news that we WOULDN`T have to go on another night compass trail.

The following week we actually had a second class of night training. It was a nighttime live-fire exercise, and some of the cadets seemed nearly as scared of being around live ammunition at night, as they had been frightened trying to negotiate a dark forest.

We were trucked to an interestingly laid-out field. There were two M-60 machine guns set up at one end. We were told that, throughout the exercise, those guns would be shooting short bursts of REAL bullets into a berm on the opposite side of the firing range. The course, itself, was forty meters long, and had barbed wire strung, in crisscross patterns, for thirty of those meters. With that wire only being strung three feet above ground, and the round dispersal barely a couple inches above the sharp barbs, we had been warned by our instructor to stay as flat as we could throughout the entire experience. In front of the berm was a starting trench. Six cadets at a time would leave that trench on bellies, roll over to their backs while placing their rifles on their stomachs, then crawl backwards under the entire thirty meters of barbed wire. Once they cleared the wire, they were told to roll back onto to their bellies, and CRAWL into the finish trench. Getting to the 'finish' trench turned out to be dangerous at times, as some cadets, having rolled to their stomachs, felt like rising up to get to safety. But, apparently, they had forgotten that the machine gun bursts were STILL only a little over three feet off the ground. Our cadre seemed to be constantly screaming, "Keep down!"

The course, itself, was at least twenty meters wide, so there was plenty of space between crawlers. However, there were also strategically-placed, simulated mine holes throughout that crawl area, so we had to avoid crawling near any of them, as well. Somehow, having helmets on seemed to make crawling on our backs a little more difficult, too. The mine areas were sandbagged, which was great. Those bags made sure that no cadet would be able to crawl into a simulated explosion hole, by accident. Even so, when those 'mines' exploded, they were VERY loud. No one even wanted to get near the sandbags, let alone crawl into the hole. Couple the explosions with the constant bursts of live ammunition going inches over our heads, and it became scary for those of us who had never had any reference point for that kind of activity. Add the nighttime atmosphere, and crawling for, what seemed like, an eternity, and the entire company of cadets was relieved when we were in our trucks headed back to camp. At the same time, though, I remember feeling that the 'realness' of the exercise was rather exhilarating, and also felt it to be my first close-to-being-a-soldier experience.

The remaining weeks of training WERE chock-full of field exercises and classes. One of our remaining assignments, however, nearly turned out to be a tragic event, and I can NEVER forget what happened that day.

Our company was trucked to a lake one afternoon, where there was an oddly-shaped course set out over the water near our instruction area. When we were seated for class, I observed a telephone pole situated four feet from the lake, to the right of the instruction site. Nailed to that pole were fifteen ascending wooden steps, situated about eighteen inches apart. From the top step, a two-foot-by-two-foot shelf was attached on the water side of the pole. A plank, which couldn`t have been more than fifteen or sixteen inches wide, stretched from the shelf to a set of stairs. The plank was a good twenty feet in length, and it was also twenty feet from the plank down to the water. These narrow stairs had three steps up to a landing, then three steps down to another plank. The second plank led to another telephone pole. Onto that SECOND pole was attached a thick rope. The rope was approximately thirty feet in length, and was strung completely across the water where it was secured to a final telephone pole. Though the last pole was sticking out of the water, it appeared to be a mere five meters from land. It was a weird and scary-looking set-up, but I was glad that it was suspended over water. A fall from that height to solid ground could have delivered some serious damage.

The instructions were as follows: climb the first pole, walk to the steps and go up and over them, walk to the second pole and sit, grab onto the rope and, with the use of both arms and legs, shinny to the center of the rope, hang there until told to drop into the water below, then swim to shore. In itself, that didn`t seem too difficult. However, when the first cadet was beginning his walk to the stairs, a second cadet was ordered to climb the first pole. That created a little swing of the pole, which made the plank seem narrower. To make matters worse, a third cadet was ordered to climb the pole as one cadet was moving across the rope and another cadet was negotiating 'the walk." With movement of three soldiers on the contraption at the same time, it was the WALKER who faced imminent danger. The rope shinny technique created a LOT of second pole sway. When added to the movement of pole #1 by a climber, that whole set-up moved sideways several inches. I know I was terrified when I walked, but I had a lunkhead who was in a hurry to get to the center of the rope, so he flew across the rope. Our cadre, and the class instructor, were kept busy by yelling for the 'rope' cadet to slow down, or the 'walking' cadet to keep moving. To make matters a bit worse, there was a gentle breeze that day, which added to the sway factor.

The sergeant in charge of our class tried to motivate us before the first cadet began climbing. "An Officer Candidate Class finished the course just before you arrived. They did an appalling job, and most of them looked terrified while executing this assignment. I am convinced that sergeants can do ANYTHING better than officers. Am I right?"

"Yes, Sergeant," was our enthusiastic response.

It should be noted again, that we were trained to NOT call sergeants, sir. As one of our first sergeant instructors noted, "I am a working stiff in this man`s army. Anything an officer THINKS he can do, I KNOW I can do." Interestingly, when I became a sergeant, those were words I used when called, sir.

A fearful situation can be paralyzing, and anyone, in our company, with a fear of heights, was asked to speak up before the exercise began. No one wanted to openly admit fear, but I know when I got to the top of the first pole and looked down, I was feeling a great deal of apprehension. The gentle breeze seemed like a raging hurricane when I started my plank walk, even though I knew it was the movement caused by the rope-moving cadet that was creating most of the swaying. I tried desperately to remember the words of the instructor as to how to handle fear of 'walking the plank,' as it became known. We were told to look about three feet ahead of us, as we walked, and NEVER to look at the water. Focusing on the board couldn`t be emphasized enough. Once I began, I never looked anywhere but at the board. When reaching the stairs, we were told to concentrate on one step at a time....first up, then down. I did that. By the time I had reached the second plank, the guy on the rope was already hanging, and ready to be told to drop into the water. So, the second walk was much simpler to negotiate. Since Willie followed me up the first pole, I inched my way across that rope, hoping to keep the swaying at a minimum. Still, I didn`t really relax until I was safely on shore after the short swim.

Company unity was in full evidence as each candidate received constant encouragement throughout the assignment, which seemed to please everybody, especially our company cadre. With this much support, not a single cadet complained about anything, but it was evident to see the relief on the faces of every candidate, too, when they exited the water. However, the festival of happiness came to a screeching halt as the LAST cadet reached the point of hanging from the rope. I can`t remember his name, but it became apparent as to why he placed himself as the last cadet to do the exercise. "OK, cadet, drop into the water," was the command by the sergeant who ran the drill.

"I can`t swim," was the unexpected response from the dangling soldier.

"This will be easy," ensured the instructor in an encouraging voice. "You`ll hit the water, bob to the surface, then slowly stroke your way to me on the shore. Even if you have to thrash your arms all the time, you`ll make the short distance to the bank, and I`ll pull you up. OK, soldier, drop."

This cadet was a big, heavily-muscled kid, but he did look terrified. Every cadet, including myself, moved to the shoreline to help encourage the guy, but he just kept hanging onto that rope.

"I REALLY can`t swim, Sergeant, and I don`t want to drown," the soldier said in a shaky voice.

"If you don`t rise to the top of the water within a couple of seconds, cadet, I will personally jump in and get you safely to land, where you`ve got all your buddies here to help you out of the lake. I have another sorry-assed O.C.S. company due here in a half hour, and you don`t want them to see you hanging there. Come on now, soldier, it`s time for you to let go of that rope."

Suddenly, the cadet released the rope and plummeted into the rather deep lake water. He DIDN`T rise as we all expected....not in five seconds, and not in ten seconds. The instructor had taken his shirt and boots off prior to the drop, and while all of us were looking at him, someone shouted, "Go get him!" The sergeant dived into the murky water, and all of us crowded together to see where either of them were. Our cadre began shouting at us to get back from the water`s edge, but it was easy to see how anxious they had all become, too. Finally, what seemed like an eternity, but in reality was probably closer to twenty-five seconds, we saw bubbles coming up, and suddenly the sergeant burst through the surface with the soldier in tow. With his hand cupping the chin of the cadet, and his elbow squarely in the middle of the victim`s back, the instructor side-stroked to the edge of the lake. Sgt. Fields, and another cadre member of our company, yanked the seemingly unconscious soldier from the water. Fields turned the man on his side, and gave a mighty whack to the cadet`s back. Water gushed from the big guy`s mouth, and our near-drown fellow started to sputter and gasp for air. He was going to be just fine.

That cadet had told everybody within hearing distance that he would have trouble once he hit the water, and that happened. I felt sorry for him. He had wanted SO badly to be part of our company, that he endangered his own life to prove himself....and that nearly cost him his life. The next day, however, we were one more troop short in the company, as the non-swimmer was dismissed from our class. Of the 180 cadets that started our company, sixty-seven would be removed for one reason or another. The training may have been somewhat rigorous, but I really only expected a half dozen soldiers, or so, to be released. Vinny Petrocelli would end up one of those let go, but not before he ended up nearly destroying one of my two-day, weekend passes.

I have mentioned that passes were readily gotten, but most were of the day variety. The Saturday passes helped many of us recuperate from a tough week of training by letting us go off grounds during day hours. But then we would be back in camp by nightfall, to study our notes, or practice hands-on lessons which had been given during the previous weeks. It was rare for soldiers to actually take a two-night furlough, but on the third weekend of our training cycle, Rock, Willie, and I felt that we needed a full weekend off. As Willie and I got ready to leave, Thomas brought Petrocelli into the barracks, and introduced him as a new friend. I know I hadn`t ever been around him before, but the way he dressed....well, I was skeptical when Rock asked us to allow Petrocelli to join us. Willie and I were so happy to be leaving camp, that we both just kind of shrugged our shoulders and indicated it would be all right with us. What a mistake.

Rock`s barracks buddy didn`t really seem to care what anybody thought. He simply made the assumption that if he was with Rock, he was going on the trip. "Hey," he started, "I`m Vincenzo Petrocelli from Newark. Everybody calls me Vinny. Rock, here, tells me yuz are good people, and dat`s good nuf for me." His introduction was delivered in a way that made it sound as if he was allowing US to join Rock and him for the weekend.

While Willie and I finished packing our duffle bags, Petrocelli would NOT stop talking. He absolutely wanted to make sure to point out how 'tight' he and Rock had become during the first three weeks of training. He spoke so quickly that it was often times difficult to understand his thick Jersey accent. In fact, I really wasn`t listening too closely, but I can tell you that he used profanity more than the three of us Iowa boys did as a group. When I hoisted my duffle onto a shoulder, Vinny took that as a sign that he could end his soliloquy. "I got dis smokin` ride dat I know yuz guys is gonna preciate ridin` in," he said. "Come on, let`s ditch dis place," and Petrocelli headed out the door.

Rock said, "He`s really not a bad guy, just full of shit sometimes, that`s all."

Willie chimed in, "Rock, I haven`t driven my car in three weeks, and we planned to take it to Calloway Gardens. Your friend better understand that, or he ain`t goin`." Rock nodded affirmatively, and we headed to the parking lot.

Once we got to Willie`s car, Rock whistled for Vinny to join us. As Petrocelli got to us he exclaimed, "Geez, my car flies, what kinda heap we go here?" Willie looked at me, shook his head, got behind the driver`s seat, and slammed the door. Rock told Petrocelli to 'just get in,'

Vinny wouldn`t stop talking after he got into the back seat with Thomas. "What kinda place we goin` to anyway?" he`d ask. "Could ya tell me yuz names again? Didn`t really catch `em." And with that, we were off for a two-night sabbatical from camp. As we left Ft. Benning, I wanted to have positive thoughts about Petrocelli joining us, so I kept telling myself, "We`ll all be friends by the end of the weekend…I just know it."

Just before we left the Columbus city limits, Petrocelli asked if we could stop and get some cold beer for the road. When I tried to explain that it was against the law to have open bottles of alcohol in a moving car, and that we should wait until we got to Calloway Gardens before drinking, Vinny looked at Rock and said, "Yuz told me deese guys was cool, Rock, baby." Then he tapped me on the shoulder and continued, "We can keep da beer lower`n da windows, Einstein. Ain`t nobody gonna see us drinkin` it."

Rock started to laugh and said, "His name is Stein, but you can call him Abe. Come on fellas, let`s have some fun. I could use a beer, too." Willie spotted a liquor store, pulled in, and we bought a case of cold beer, which Rock and Vinny had on the seat between them all the way to Calloway Gardens. I just hoped no one could see inside our car, but I didn`t say anything knowing I would just get a wise-crack retort from Petrocelli.

While I WAS worried about getting pulled over by the highway patrol, I worried more about my two buddies drinking while we were on the road. First, I knew Willie as a light-weight drinker having been with him when he had gotten drunk. He could be more than a little erratic, even incoherent, with beer in him. And Rock, good gracious, he almost ALWAYS got a little crazy after he drank a few beers. What didn`t help me stop worrying was when Vinny challenged, "I can out-drink all tree a yuz guys at da same time. If ya get tired, Willie, baby, I can drive whilst ya take a nap back here."

"I am only going to have the one beer until we get to Calloway Gardens," Willie replied. "Just save me a couple though. And nobody drives my car but me." With that being said, I stopped worrying so much about Willie.

After a half hour, we made our first stop along the roadside. The initial beer had apparently run right through all of us. Cars passed by and either honked or had someone lean out the window to holler something. I was also praying that no patrolman would see us squirting because if he stopped to check out what we were up to, well, that case of beer was easily seen on the back seat. THAT concern became secondary very quickly, for as we got back on the road, Vinny shocked us by asking a simple question, "Anybody want a stick of beef jerky?" He then proceeded to pull several sticks from his shiny coat pocket.

"Where`d you get those?" Rock said with a surprised tone in his voice. "I didn`t see you buy them at the store."

"Rocky, baby, come on, I`m from Jersey," Vinny said with pride. "I did tings like dis all da time in da `hood. Whilst yuz was payin` for beer, I was loadin` my pockets wit junk food. Nobody seen me, and dem stores rip us off all da time. Ain`t no biggie."

I instantly wanted to rip into Petrocelli, but Willie beat me to it. "Vinny, I don`t care how 'bad' you were back in your neighborhood. But we three don`t want to get kicked out of the Academy because of you doing stupid stuff. You try anything like that again, and you won`t be riding back to Benning in this car."

"OK, man, don`t have a cow. I taut yuz guys was up fer fun. Don`t worry, I won`t do nuttin to get yuz in trouble." And, for the first time since we met him, Petrocelli went silent for a nice period of time.

The rest of our trip moved along nicely, and eventually we started telling jokes. Vinny, having been scolded by Willie, stopped feeling sorry for himself, and tried to fit in again. He did have some crude jokes, but mostly he wanted to tell us about the 'fine goils' he knew back home. Once Petrocelli got talking about girls, the rest of us couldn`t get a word in edge-wise. "I got a special one for you, Willie," he would say. "An, Rock, you, man, could get dem ALL. Dem dumb broads like yuz strong guys. Abe, yur married, so none a dem would touch you wit a ten-foot pole." He just couldn`t help being obnoxious.

As we neared Calloway Gardens, Vinny asked us to stop a second time so he and Rock could pee on the side of the road again. I knew I had drunk one beer, and Willie only had the one beer. But, while Rock and Vinny were peeing, I checked our case of beer. Those two guys had finished three beers each, and had a fourth in hand as they were peeing. Drinking a beer, while peeing ouside, I just wanted to go back to Ft. Benning, but knew we had come too far to just turn around. Still, I had a terrible feeling that this was going to be a difficult weekend. I grabbed the remaining brews, and placed them under my jacket.

As those two knuckleheads entered the car, they were laughing very hard, and didn`t notice the missing beers. Finally, we read a sign that said 'Welcome to Calloway Gardens.'

The area was not what we expected. We saw a gas station, a flower shop, a liquor store, and three or four other small businesses. But, the area looked like several other rural towns that we had passed since leaving Ft. Benning. As we were leaving the commercial buildings in the rearview mirror, I remarked that I hadn`t even seen ONE motel. The others concurred with me. Suddenly, just ahead on the highway, we all spotted a huge sign that read 'Cabins,' and Willie turned onto the road leading to them. We saw a small shack, a few hundred meters off the main highway, and as we got close to it, an elderly gentleman departed the building and began waving both arms in a way that indicated that he wanted us to stop at the shack. As we did so, we began seeing several cabins behind a white picket fence, but they were somewhat camouflaged amongst the trees. A mere fifty meters inside the fence, and NOT camouflaged was one larger building, and what made this building interesting was the fact that there were six high school-aged girls walking away from it. They were not aware of our car, but Vinny certainly noticed THEM. "Goils!" he shouted out the window. They were giggling and talking so much that nary a one turned to see who was yelling.

"Be quiet, Vinny," I said to Petrocelli, "and roll up your window. Those girls are kids, and we don`t want this old guy checking us out and finding that we have been drinking. Come on, Willie, let`s see if he knows where there might be a motel."

Upon returning to the car, I reported back to Rock and Vinny. "There is a conference on leadership being held on this site, and all the girls are seniors from around the state who are deemed exceptional by their high schools."

"I saw a couple that looked exceptional to me," that pig Petrocelli blurted out.

"The guard says this place is off-limits to outsiders, but he mentioned where we could find a couple of motels. They are just down the highway and around the bend. They got restaurants there, too, so let`s go," I said and I suddenly felt very hungry. Willie turned the car around and we headed out to find a place to stay for the weekend.

"Hey, man," Vinny said excitedly, "Dey might be in high school, but some a dem GOT to be eighteen. And I know dey gotta have chaperones who`s older. Rock and me just wanna check `em out, right, Rock?"

Suddenly I felt like a chaperone. I knew Rock and I were twenty-three, Vinny was twenty-one, and Willie was still only nineteen, but these girls were high school girls, and definitely not people for ANY of us to mess with. "Vinny," I said, trying to sound like a father figure, "the guard was serious when he told Willie and me that this place was off limits. We are not looking to get arrested for trespassing, or harassing the girls in this camp. So, NO, we are NOT coming back here." And with that we arrived at a decent-looking motel, which happened to be less than a mile from the entrance to the cabins. We got two rooms....one for Willie and me and one for Rock and Petrocelli.

The original plan for Calloway Gardens was for Rock, Willie and me to play golf on Saturday, and relax the rest of the time. Rock was a serious golfer, and said he would call for a tee time. Around seven that night, we went to a restaurant next door to our motel. It looked like a dive, and probably was. But we didn`t care as none of us were carded when we ordered four beers to have with our meals. I casually asked Rock if he had gotten us a time to play golf on Saturday, and he mentioned that there was a fantastic course nearby that was really challenging. I was fairly new at the game, and Willie had never played before. As for Petrocelli, he said he didn`t want to play, but he would ride in Rock`s cart anyway. It WAS an exclusive course, and when Rock told us the price for a round of golf, I nearly choked on my beer. All three of the guys started to laugh uncontrollably when they saw beer spewing from my nose, then Rock said, "But, we`re not playing there. The resorts were ALL booked for tomorrow, but I found us a local municipal course with a decent price. We tee off at seven." With that being said, he chugged his beer.

Willie, Vinny and I all started, at the same time, to question Rock. I wanted to know why the early tee time. Willie wanted to know how much club rentals and golf balls would cost him. And Petrocelli wanted to know if we had to get to sleep early because of our early tee time; thus, leaving no time to party. It was chaos. Then Rock held up his hand to quiet us all down. "First," he said, "Seven was the only time we had available in the morning. We could have gotten the last tee time of the day, but there was no guarantee that we could get all eighteen holes in before darkness. Second, Willie, the cost of EVERYTHING is less than a quarter of what it would have cost us if we would have been able to get a round of golf at a fancy club. And, Vinny, yeah, we should get to bed early. BUT, we are here to have some fun, so it won`t be THAT early, right, boys?" And he looked at Willie and me for approval of what he said.

"Dats good, Rock, baby," Vinny responded. "I taut yuz guys wanted to sleep early so`s yuz can whack dat ball around, and be stars or sumpin. We came here to let off steam, not sleep da whole time? So we gotta go an` find us a few goils after we eat."

I actually found myself agreeing with Vinny about NOT going to bed too early. "Yeah, we get up at five every morning." I chimed in. "Since we can sleep in until six tomorrow, I think we should see what Calloway Gardens has in the way of fun tonight." With that being said, we ordered another round of beers, and there was no more complaining during dinner.

We were all a bit tipsy after we finished the meal, but decided to go find a place where adult women might be. Sadly, the FIRST couple of places we checked out were trashy-looking bars, where the local hooligans easily out-numbered the ladies by at least ten to one. Then, we checked out three fancy restaurant bars. In THOSE places, however, we stuck out like sore thumbs, thanks to our haircuts, casual civilian clothing, and the fact that everybody was dressed like they were going to proms. We even tried the local Elks Lodge, but were denied entry because we weren`t members. Finally, it was Rock who said, "Let`s go to that liquor store, pick up a couple of six-packs, and get back to the motel. The party life in this town stinks."

We got our beer and were heading down the road to our rooms, but when we got a quarter mile past the entrance of the cabins which housed all those high school girls, Vinny yelled out, "STOP!"

Willie, who was in a semi-stupor due to excess drinking on his part, pulled off onto the side of the road, and Vinny jumped out of the car. "I gotta see if any of dem goils in dare wanna party wit ol` Vinny tonight."

"Come on Vinny," I practically shouted. "Are you crazy? All you can find with high school girls is trouble. Get in the car….please."

"I ain`t tinkin` high school, Stein, I`m tinkin` female chaperones," and Petrocelli took off running toward the white fence that surrounded the cabin grounds.

Rock jumped out of the car, too, and yelled for Vinny to wait up, then he turned to me and said, "We`re just gonna convince some lady chaperones to come to our place with us. Ain`t no big thang." And with that being said HE took off running toward the fence.

I honestly didn`t know what to do, so I yelled after them, "Willie and I will wait right here for one half hour. If you`re not back by then, you can walk to the motel. Hear me?"

Rock just gave an acknowledging wave, and within seconds, he and Vinny were over the fence and headed to the cabins.

Willie grabbed two beers, got out of the car, and the two of us talked about the trouble those guys were going to encounter. Once we finished the brews, we went to the curb side of the vehicle and peed onto the grass.

I checked my watch and fifteen minutes had passed since the two guys went running off. "I`m going to get another beer," Willie said. "You want one?"

"One more, Willie, and I swear, if they aren`t back by the time we`re done drinking them, we will leave them here. They know where our place is."

"Oh SHIT!" I heard Willie yell out as he frantically began searching his pockets. "I don`t have my keys, and I locked the doors when I got out of the car."

"Why`d you lock the doors, Willie?"

"I don`t know. I don`t even remember doing it. I wasn`t thinking, I guess."

I looked into the car as Willie went through his pockets again. There, in the ignition, were the car keys. "Damn it, Willie, they`re still in the car."

"I can open the door with a coat hanger. I`ve done it before," Willie said while slurring his words. He turned toward the cabins, pointed in that direction, then said, "I gotta go in there and get a hanger."

I couldn`t think of anything else for us to do. I knew we weren`t going to break a window to get inside the car. Just as we had decided to head toward the restricted area, a vehicle exited the cabin-entrance road, and with its headlights turned on high beams, it came racing right at Willie and me.

We backed up as flat as we could against Willie`s car to ensure we wouldn`t get hit by that speeding moron, when suddenly, the crazy bastard slammed on the brakes, and the vehicle came to a stand-still right beside us. As the driver lowered the passenger-side window, I heard the familiar giggle of Rock, who said, "Get down and give me ten, soldier." I bent over a tad and saw both him and Vinny sitting in the backseat.

"Shut up," I heard the driver yell at Rock. Then he aimed his wrath at Willie and me. "Get into the car right now."

I bent lower to see who the speaker was and responded, "Are you kidding?"

The fellow behind the wheel was wearing a white dress shirt, and he had a holster strapped onto a belt at his waist. He pulled a pistol from that holster, pointed it right at my head, and said through gritted teeth, "Does this look like I`m kidding? Get in NOW!"

I got into the front seat, and Willie the back, and just as quickly as he had arrived at our car, the maniac driver whipped around and sped back to the cabin entrance, turned onto the road, finally stopping at the little shack where we four soldiers had encountered the old guard earlier in the day. While there were no flashing lights, I noticed three OTHER cars parked near the shack, and one of them was definitely marked as a sheriff`s vehicle.

Our nut-case of a driver told the four of us to get out of the car. We stood there silently for several seconds when finally he said, "I`m Detective Whatever. (I forgot his name as soon as I heard it) There was a call from this resort indicating some girls saw a pervert peeping into the window of their cabin. I just happened to be talking to those girls when I seen you two knuckleheads jumping the fence," and he looked right at Rock and Vinny. "When I confronted you, and then asked the girls if either of you guys looked familiar to them, I was told that the guy they saw in the window had long hair. By the looks of all your haircuts, I`m guessing you clowns are in the military."

Let me interject a Vinnyism here, to hammer home what kind of person Rock`s New Jersey buddy really was. Petrocelli later told the three of us, and I quote, "I wuz gonna say to that joik 'who yuz calling clowns, asshole,' and I had to bite my lip real hard to stop from doin` dat. I didn`t want to get yuz guys in trouble, dat`s all." I just shook my head and wondered how this idiot ever got into the Academy.

Anyway, the detective continued to talk to us. "When I asked this guy (and he pointed to Rock) why he climbed over the fence, he told me that you stopped the car because some of you had to piss. And when you tried to get back into the car, it seems like EVERYBODY had locked their door, but the keys were still inside. Are you ALL that stupid?" and he looked right at Vinny.

I couldn`t believe it. That was the truth, but Rock didn`t know that before he and numbnuts Petrocelli took off for the cabins. "That`s the truth," I chimed in.

"OK, wise guy," the detective said as he approached me, getting so close that we were nearly nose to nose. Then why did these guys jump the fence, and you two didn`t?"

"We needed something to pull up one of the locks, and my friends thought they saw a cabin. They just wanted to see if they could get a coat hanger from someone. Willie and I stayed back to guard the car," I said nervously.

"That`s what Dweedle-dummy said," and again the detective pointed at Rock. "You want me to believe that you didn`t know that there were over a hundred girls in here this weekend?"

"No, we didn`t," I continued. "We were headed back to our motel, and I told everybody that we needed to stop that very instant, or I was going to have an accident in the car. That`s when we pulled off the road."

Suddenly, before the detective could to say another word, there was a shout, 'We got him!"

A sheriff`s deputy was walking a shaggy-haired man to the big building. I could see that 'Shaggy,' as we later called him, was in handcuffs, and he wasn`t putting up any struggle.

"Stay here," our detective said as he moved toward the suspect`s position. When he was out of earshot, we four talked about how remarkably alike Rock and my stories were. We knew how lucky we had been, and all I could think about was being in our motel room sleeping.

A few minutes after our gun-toting, officer-of-the-law disappeared, he reappeared with good news. "Yeah, that creep fits the girls` description of the guy peeping on them. Seems like you fellas are in the clear. I`m going to drop the trespassing charges on you two idiots because I have a heart of gold. I`ve sent someone to get you a coat hanger, but when you are gone from here, don`t even THINK about coming back here. Understand?"

We nodded affirmatively, then he whirled around and headed back to the main building. About two-thirds of the way to his destination, he stopped to talk to a fellow who had a hanger in his hands. That 'fellow' turned out to be the guard with whom WE had met earlier in the day. As the old guard approached us, Willie suddenly blurted out, "Hey, remember us from earlier today?" The detective stiffened up a bit while turning his head slightly, then he continued on his way to the big building.

I grabbed Willie by the arm and said, "Keep your voice down. In fact, don`t say another word. Remember, we told the detective that we HADN`T ever been here before. We all just need to stay quiet and get out of here as quickly as we can." Willie just looked at me with glazed-over eyes as I took the hanger from the old man. As the four of us walked back to our car, I couldn`t believe how lucky we had been. After we got the car doors opened, and were heading to our motel, I convinced myself that I was traveling with a moron, a horny toad, and a guy who got loud and careless when he drank. I am not saying that I was a model human being in the whole mess, but compared to my three traveling companions, well, we were just lucky is all I can say. That night I thanked the good lord for allowing us to get through the 'cabin incident' with no punishment, and I asked him to keep us out of harm`s way until we could get back to Ft. Benning.

Our golf game the next day was horrible for everyone. None of us could shake off the alcohol effects from the night before, nor the stress of being detained by the law for doing stupid things. There certainly wasn`t any loud conversation, and I couldn`t take enough aspirin to get rid of my headache. The course, itself, was in great shape. However, the cost of renting clubs, buying golf balls and gloves, getting golf carts, AND the price of playing all eighteen holes, was WAY more expensive than the fun we derived from playing the game. To top off our poor outing, Vinny had no idea on how to play, NOR did he know anything about golf etiquette. Thank goodness for Rock. He showed great patience in educating Petrocelli in every facet of the game. Since the course was crowded that weekend, we had a self-imposed 10-shot limit for each hole, which meant that if we hadn`t gotten the ball in the hole after ten shots, we just picked the little dimpled-demon up. Vinny picked HIS ball up on all eighteen holes. But I give him credit for being a good sport about things. There was a foursome behind us, who was breathing down our necks the entire round, and Vinny was also embarrassed about how badly he was playing. Having been with Petrocelli just a couple of days, I knew things could have gone south in a hurry if he had gotten really frustrated.

Rock didn`t give up on trying to improve Vinny`s golfing knowledge, and for the first time I got a really positive vibe about his leadership ability. I was so impressed that I expressed my sentiments to him in a private moment after we finished the round. Rock, who is usually very quiet when he hasn`t been drinking, looked me in the eyes and said, "Thanks, I appreciate that."

We ALL decided to hit the sack early that night. When we awoke Sunday morning, we had a hearty breakfast and headed back to Benning. We arrived in the company area by 1300 hours, and I was SO glad that our two-night furlough was finished. I made two promises to myself….not to drink so much again when I am with Willie and Thomas, and never, EVER go anywhere with Vinny Petrocelli again. I was finished with Vinny, but Rock wasn`t.

Two weeks after the Calloway Gardens debacle, Willie and I got another two-night furlough. We didn`t know it at the time, but that would be our last two-night pass. Rock couldn`t join us, as his platoon had under-performed during the week, and his tactical sergeant decided to only allow day passes to Columbus, with a mandatory bed-check at nights. Willie and I decided to give Calloway Gardens a second chance, and try to play a round of golf with no stressful circumstances. We really just needed to get away and have some fun.

Rock came in after our Friday lunch formation, at which time the company was dismissed for the weekend. He had a frown on his face when he saw the two of us packing our duffle bags. It was pretty obvious that he had come to the barracks to ask if we wanted to join him and Vinny in Columbus that afternoon and evening, and likely Saturday, too, while knowing that we would have to make curfew both nights. Willie and my plan was deceitful, for sure. We had planned on NOT telling Rock about leaving for Calloway, as we knew he would be hurt by us going there without him. We expected to just sneak off base, and tell him we 'forgot' to tell him….but only after we returned on Sunday. It`s not what friends do, but we KNEW Rock wanted to spend time with Vinny, and that was definitely something that neither Willie nor I intended to do.

"Where you guys, goin`?" Rock asked with a surprised expression on his face.

It was Willie who answered, "Abe and I got two-day passes and thought we would like to try another round of golf in Calloway Gardens. We knew you COULDN`T go with us, so we were going to try to NOT hurt your feelings. We need to get away from army life for a couple of days, is all."

"Come on, fellas," Rock interjected. "You and me and Vinny will go into town tomorrow, maybe go to a strip club, have a few beers and a couple of laughs. You can relax by doing those things, and the four of us will have a great time."

"We would enjoy those things if it was just YOU, Rock," I said, sounding a little upset that Rock WASN`T going to be with us for the next two nights, "but Willie and I don`t enjoy being around Petrocelli as much as you do. And, we got a two-day pass, so we`re going to be leaving in a few minutes."

"He`s a blowhard, is all," Rock insisted. "He`s good people. He`s really harmless. Come on, Abe, just stay this weekend."

"Sorry, Thomas," I said while sticking to my guns. "We just gotta leave the area for two solid days. Don`t want to make bed-check each night, either."

"All right, you dickheads, if you gotta go, you gotta go. Where are you gonna spend the two nights?"

"I told you, we are going to Callaway Gardens again," Willie responded. "Gonna try playing golf again....this time sober. We really just need to relax, though."

"You guys really ARE dickheads, going to Callaway to play golf without me."

"Yeah, sorry about you not getting to be with us this weekend," I insisted. "The next time we THREE get a two-day furlough, Willie and I will go back to Callaway with you. Since your platoon can`t get out for two nights THIS weekend, well, we just have to pretend we AREN`T in the army for a while. Sorry, man."

"Damn," was all Rock said, and he pivoted and walked out of the barracks.

Willie and I had a very good trip, and DID enjoy our round of golf. When we got back on Sunday, Rock saw us heading to unpack, and he ran to be with us. "How was YOUR two days?" he asked, but with an impish lilt to his voice.

"We relaxed and had a better golf game this time around," Willie answered, but he didn`t get in another word about our trip.

"We had a LOT of excitement around here, that`s for sure," Rock said with enthusiasm.

It may have been a rude interruption to Willie`s description of our time in Callaway, but we hadn`t seen Rock this animated since we got to Benning. We sat on a bunk, and our muscle-bound friend continued with HIS story.

"Me and Vinny decided to go to Columbus for a couple of beers Friday. Sim Kerr was with us, too.

Willie and I didn`t know Simeon Kerr very well, but we DID know that he was a quiet, naïve, kid who came from a rural Georgia town. I had a hard time picturing him with Vinny, though we knew he was a Rock 'groupie, wishing he had ANY muscles on his scrawny body. Rock, Vinny, and Sim going out drinking together. I looked at Willie and said, "This can`t turn out well."

"Vinny drove us to Max`s, you know, the strip club that some of the other guys told us about a couple of weeks ago," Rock stated.

Willie and I looked at each other and just smiled.

Rock continued, "About ten o`clock this fat chick came out onto the stage. She had veils over a bikini, but she sure knew how to take everything off….really sexy for a big girl."

Willie began to laugh pretty hard, and I was wondering how big the bikini had to be to cover her.

"Her name is Tinkerbelle," Rock then said, and Willie laughed REALLY loudly. Now Rock knew he had us interested in his story. "Well, me and the boys had a lot to drink before she stripped, so I said to them, 'I`m going to get me some of that tonight.' Vinny looked at me and laughed. Sim thought I was crazy or something. When her music stopped, I said to the guys, 'Watch this.' I yelled up to her and said, 'Tinkerbelle, over here.' She saw me wave and without even puttin` her top on, she came over to our table."

"Are you kidding me?" Willie said in a surprised tone.

"No," Rock went on. "She came over and put both of her hands around my bicep (holding up his right arm to indicate which bicep) and then she said, 'Oooo, this feels great.' Then she sat on my lap. Felt like she was crushing my leg."

Willie was then laughing uncontrollably.

"And THEN," Rock said while starting to get a little more animated, "she leans over and whispers in my ear, 'I get off at one in the morning. Maybe you and me can go someplace for a while.' So I said I`d be back to get her. Then she went backstage somewhere. Then Vinny was going crazy….asking me if I`d really boink a fat lady, and wantin` me to see if she could get a friend for him. It was Sim who reminded us that we had to make midnight bed-check. Then Sim said to me, 'I don`t think you would have sex with her.' But, he was right about bed-check, so we had to leave."

"So nothing, then, huh, Rock?" Willie questioned.

"Hold on, young sergeant-to-be, the story is just beginning," Rock said with a gleam in his eyes. "While we were heading back to Benning, I said to Vinny, 'You know, we might just have to sneak off base AFTER bed-check, and with you driving this hot car, I`d be back in plenty of time to pick Tinkerbelle up before she gets off."

Willie let out another roar just at the mention of the name Tinkerbelle.

Rock just continued to talk away. “Sim, of course, thought that we would get caught if we skipped off the base. So, then, Vinny says to Kerr, ‘Who said yer goin, hayseed?’ But then Sim says to me, ‘If YOU don`t think we`d get caught, I`d like to join you, Rock.’ I laughed and said, ‘Sure.”

“You mean, Simeon Kerr, that gullible kid from Georgia, would take a risk of getting kicked out of the Academy, if YOU told him to join you?” I said in wonderment.

“That`s what the kid said,” continued Rock. “Then Vinny started complaining about having anyone but us two leaving the company, and how Kerr might just get us caught. But I said to Sim, “If you want to see how the big boys do it, and you can keep quiet, then sure, you can go. Vinny was pissed, but he didn`t say nothin’ else about Sim going.”

“So, you, Petrocelli, AND that innocent farm kid decided to leave camp after bed-check?” I asked incredulously.

“Yeah, why not? You know the sergeants just whip through the barracks most of the time, seeing that everything is quiet, then head back to bed themselves. They don`t really know who is on a weekend pass and who is restricted. So, yeah, we three were going to skip out of here. It wasn`t easy, though. Bed-check wasn`t finished until after twelve-thirty, so by the time we got dressed and out to the car, I was sure we were going to be too late to get Miss Tinkerbelle.” Then Rock looked at Willie, who immediately started to laugh again at the mention of the name Tinkerbelle.

“You didn`t make it on time, did you?” I questioned.

“Sure we did,” Rock said with some cockiness. “Vinny drove balls out, and I was more worried about cops getting us for speeding then if we could find Tinkerbelle. But, when we got to the strip club, she was leaving arm-in-arm with some guy. He took her to HER car, then he went and got in his car.”

“So you guys came back here, right?” I surmised.

"Hell, no," Rock said, sounding a bit agitated that I would even suggest that. "We followed `em. Vinny didn`t get too close, so`s we wouldn`t be recognized as tailin` `em, but he didn`t lose them either. And for a while, Vinny was telling Sim and me how he was going to beat the guy when we finally stopped somewhere. I`m sure he was just shootin` his mouth off, trying to convince Sim how tough people from Jersey are."

"Then what happened?" Willie asked, suddenly showing serious interest in the story.

"We follow them to a trailer park out in the country. Tinkerbelle stops in front of her trailer. The guy pulls up behind her, and they both get out of their cars. Vinny roars up behind THAT fella`s car, and all three of us get out, too."

"You guys didn`t really beat that man up, did you?" Willie queried.

"Naw, when we got out, Tinkerbelle said, 'Rock, what are you doin` here?' And the guy jumps back IN his car and flies outta there."

"OK, Rock, did you end up doing anything with the stripper or not?" I asked, knowing full well Rock would certainly keep pressing her for sex.

"I`m getting` there. Hold your horses, Abe," Rock continued. "So Tinkerbelle tells me that because I didn`t show up at one in the morning, like I said I would, that a girl has to take care of herself. She said that`s when she asked that weeny customer to make sure she got home safely. Safely, my ass, she was horny and just wanted a man. Since I wasn`t there, she settled for anyone who was available."

"Yeah, yeah," I said rather impatiently. "Tell us what happened, Rock, because we have formation in fifteen minutes."

"She grabbed my hand and led me to the trailer, that`s what happened," Rock said rather brusquely. "But, when we got to the steps, she pointed at Vinny and Sim and said, 'They have to stay outside.' I told the boys, 'Sorry,' and she and I went inside. Once we got inside she told me that she had two kids, but they were spending the night at her sister`s house, having a sleepover with their cousins, or something like that. Then she told me we had the whole place to ourselves, and started pulling my muscle-shirt over my head. I noticed a big, beautiful case by one of the walls, and it had medals, knives, and pistols inside. When I asked Tinkerbelle who those things belonged to, she told me those were her husband`s trophies and junk."

"Husband," I interrupted, remembering the incident in St. Louis. "Not again."

"Relax, Abe. It`s all good." Rock said, trying to sound mellow. "She told me he was a first sergeant, or master sergeant, I don`t remember, but she told me he was in Nam. She told me he`s making money over there, or he likes it, I wasn`t really listening. Anyway, what I DID hear was when she told me that she had the RIGHT to take care of her urges seein` that he was gone for so long. I was her 'Jody' for the night, I guess."

"Master sergeant," Willie repeated, with a serious look on his face.

"Hey, she said something like that. But, I gotta tell ya, I wasn`t listenin' real good because I was working hard at gettin` the rest of my clothes off. Then, we`re in her bedroom, and I`m trying to find the right wrinkle to probe, when we heard this loud crash coming from the living room."

"What the hell?" Willie blurted out, really getting into the story.

"No, it`s true, man, a LOUD crash," Rock exclaimed. "So I grabbed my clothes, knowing somehow that Vinny had to be involved with the noise, and I told Tinkerbelle that I was going to the living room to see what`s going on. I saw Petrocelli and Sims standing at attention, up against a wall, pretending like no one could see them if they were standing still. Those guys, apparently, decided to come into the trailer, and while Kerr was listening to the grunting going on in the bedroom, that dummy Vinny decided to steal Tinkerbelle`s tv. But, when he tried to get that television out the door, the dang thing slipped from his hands and crashed onto the floor, partially blocking the doorway. Just a huge mess.

Destroyed her set completely, and he was getting the thing out of the door entrance when I came in."

"You`ve got to be kidding me," I said while visualizing Petrocelli trying to carry a tv.

"Oh, it happened, Abe. I`m telling you guys the truth. Then it got worse. When Vinny understood that I saw him there playing statue, he just shrugged his shoulders and headed to the souvenir case. That`s when he noticed that the case wasn`t locked. Then Tinkerbelle yelled out and asked me what was going on. I kept telling her that I hadn`t found anything yet, but I was still looking. Meanwhile, I was desperately trying to get my shoes tied. Then she dragged her fat body into the living room, naked as a Jay bird. She saw Sim, who was pretending to be a statue again, up against the wall. She HAD to see the tv laying there, too. She hollered out, 'What the shit happened here?' then she ran back into the bedroom and screamed out she was going to call the cops."

"This is unbelievable," Willie said while shaking his head.

"Then, KERR said to me that he had never seen a naked lady before, and did I think she might let him cop a feel, or something. I told him I didn`t know, but if he went in there to find out, and she was on the phone, he better get his ass out to the car, pronto. So, Sim raced into the bedroom, and I heard this loud 'slap,' and Tinkerbelle was yelling, 'I ain`t no whore. I`m calling the cops, and I mean it.' We three scrambled to the car, and Vinny drove the car away like a bat out of hell. I notice Kerr rubbing his face where he got slapped, and then I saw that Petrocelli had a boatload of medals in his lap."

"He had WHAT?" Willie and I yelled at the same time.

"Medals, man, that maniac stole medals from the trophy case," Rock clamored. "I didn`t say nothin` to Vinny about those things when I saw them. I was more worried that we might get picked up by the cops for speeding. That Petrocelli is crazy. We FINALLY got back to camp, and sneaked into the barracks un-noticed. I couldn`t sleep, though. To top this whole thing off, Vinny dressed up in his pimp clothes yesterday, got to a Columbus pawn shop as soon as it opened, and SOLD his trailer booty for about $60. What a scumbag, stealing a guy`s medals, then selling them."

Rock had Willie and me promise not to tell anyone else about what happened, so we kept still. I knew that Rock finally realized what a jerk Petrocelli was, but I couldn`t help being really disappointed in him, AGAIN, for trying to take advantage of a lonely, married woman. This woman was the wife of a military man, too. I felt confident in the fact that Jill and I were still celebrating being newlyweds, so no Jody was going to hover around MY sweetie.

Ironically, both Kerr and Petrocelli washed out of the Academy early in the sixth week. Simeon just couldn`t show any kind of leadership. And Vinny, gosh, there were so many reasons I could give to get rid of him. He actually screwed up on too many field exercises to warrant keeping him in the program. I REALLY wanted to believe, however, that he was afraid of some kind of investigation, stemming from his night of thievery, and he wanted to make sure he wasn`t around if someone came sniffing around our company on the matter. Regardless of why he left, I was just glad Vincenzo Petrocelli was gone.

Nothing truly exciting happened for the duration of our training cycle, other than what I have already mentioned. Studying was intense, especially for me, as I had NO knowledge of anything military prior to being drafted. I hadn`t been the greatest student during my growth period in Iowa City, either. I was smart enough to do well, just never motivated enough to excel in the classroom. But, this was a different situation. I became practically fanatical about finishing at the top of my class; thus, becoming an E-6. I knew I was holding my own in most 'leadership' settings, as many times I was called on to 'solve' a situation after several failed attempts by other cadets. I just exuded confidence that I could get the job done when it was required. Oh, I had a bad day now and then, but leadership was my forte in that company. I wanted desperately to stay in the States as long as I could, and finishing as an Honor Graduate would secure me an extra three more weeks. Bottom line….I had to work my tail off during the final weeks, and didn`t have time to look for fun things to do.

During our last week as cadets, Willie, Rock and I started to talk about what we might be doing after graduation. We had trained together since our first day, but we three Iowa boys knew we`d be headed in different directions after earning our sergeant stripes. Rock was pretty certain his future included going back to another A.I.T, company, then, Vietnam. Willie told us he couldn`t handle another A.I.T., and he wasn`t even sure he knew enough about survival to be able to make it through Vietnam. So, he favored trying to get assigned to airborne/ranger training programs, at least that is what he told me, a week before we THREE began talking about our futures. Then Willie came right out and said it, "I applied for both airborne and ranger schools last week, and hope my orders will be waiting for me after graduation." The statement REALLY seemed to surprise Rock.

"I didn`t even know you thought about ranger training," Rock said rather disappointedly. "If I would have known about THAT, I might have given it a try, too." I was a little perplexed by Willie`s decision, too. I knew he liked the outdoors, but learning how to survive in the wilderness, using only what nature has to offer, that was too harsh for me to think about. It was right after Willie`s declaration that I realized how much I had under-estimated how tough that guy was.

Willie continued, "I know you aren`t crazy about roughing it, Rock, and, according to what I heard about the ranger program, we have to, first, survive six weeks in the cold mountains of North Carolina. Then, we have to survive six weeks in the swamps of Florida. It`s supposed to be a 'man surviving in nature' training format. I`m hoping I can hack it. I won`t even start ranger training until after I complete two weeks in jump school, which is held here at Benning, by the way. I`m sorry. I probably should have mentioned my plans to you."

"That`s all right, Willie," Rock said with a tired tone. "I`m getting real tired of training. It`s time for me to kick some butt at A.I.T., then go get my fighting in Nam over with." Then Rock looked at me, and asked, "What about you, Abe? We both think you will be an Honor Graduate, but what if you`re not? What are you gonna do?"

"I know there are at least 14 cadets here who probably qualify to get Honors," I answered. I am just going to keep fighting to be among the top six. I really want to stay at Benning for twelve more weeks, and train new sergeants. Ah, man, that sounds strange....me, training guys to be sergeants in the army. If I don`t get top six, I will probably have to go to an Advanced Infantry Training unit, too, Rock. If that`s the case, then I hope you and I will be assigned to the same one. I DON`T really want to think about going to Vietnam, though, that`s for sure. I`m praying that we get out of there within the next three months. Willie, I never considered ranger training because I found out, that in order to go TO survival training, I`d have to learn how to jump from planes. And if I sign up to learn how to jump, I`d have to extend my service time by two weeks. I don`t even want to stay one extra day in the army, let alone two weeks. But I know you will be a great ranger. And, Rock, no one is going to give you guff in A.I.T." We didn`t talk about our plans after that day, but I knew I had to work extra hard during that last week. I NEEDED to achieve my top-six goal. However, knowing that we Iowa buddies would be moving forward on our own, after graduation, I felt melancholy during those final Academy days, too. I knew I would miss them both.

Our training DID wind down quickly. However, with two days remaining until graduation, a rather strange occurrence took place, and it happened during our final physical training evaluations. S.F.C. Fields approached me just before our last test, the mile run. "Cadet Stein, you know Philly Beasley in the 1st platoon, right?"

"Yes, Sergeant, I do. In fact, he is a friend of mine," I answered with a quizzical look on my face.

"Well, today he`s not," Fields continued. "His sergeant tells me he`s going to whip you today in the mile run. I told him he was crazy. Bet a case of beer on it, in fact. You don`t want me to lose a case of beer do you, Cadet Stein?"

"No, Sergeant, I don`t," I said assertively. Then the un-smiling Fields nodded his head, wheeled around, and called for the platoon to get ready for the mile.

Philadelphia Beasley was not only a friend of mine, but I considered him to be one of the top three or four candidates in the company. I asked him once about his name being Philadelphia. "Conceived there," was his answer. "But only my mom calls me Philadelphia. My dad calls me Phil, but all my friends, and just about everybody else, call me Philly."

That guy had a charismatic personality and a dazzling ear-to-ear smile....very popular. As for the mile run, well, he had beaten me by two or three seconds on each of our first four p.t. evaluations. I wasn`t sure I could beat him. We both had run under six minutes, and that gave each of us 100 points for the event, which was the objective. Still, I felt that I had given it my all EVERY time I ran. I was a sprinter in high school, not a long-distance runner, and running a mile took all my energy. I didn`t want to let SFC Fields down, however, so I knew I was going to have to dig deeper than I ever did before. That way, if I was on the verge of collapsing across the finish line, Fields should be able to appreciate my effort. I couldn`t help wondering if Philly knew about the bet.

I really respected Sgt. Fields. He was the best military man I knew, a soldier`s soldier, if you will....at least in my eyes. He was tough, demanding, and kept talking about what it took to make a superior leader. He`d make comments like, 'Don`t EVER tell your troops to do something that you, yourself, wouldn`t do.' 'It is your responsibility to get your boys home safe and sound.' 'You lead your men even if it seems like you are on a suicide mission.'(that was a scary one) 'Be brave in the face of adversity, and you will get the respect that is earned from doing so.' Everyone in the company respected SFC Fields, and I felt lucky that he was our platoon`s tactical sergeant. As I headed to the starting line of the mile, I looked over at Fields. He saw me and nodded. I nodded back, and the race began.

There wasn`t loud cheering by any platoon sergeants, just the usual, 'Come on, cadet, pick up the pace.' Sgt. Fields stood at the fence, not far from the finish line. While he seemed to be encouraging every member of the 4th platoon, when I looked his way, he would clench his two fists, purse his lips, give me a slight nod, and say, 'You can do it.' In the past mile runs, I was sure that I had been doing the best that I could. However, there always seemed to be a pattern of running between Philly and me. He would pass me just before we would hit the curves, and I would overtake him down the stretches. That pattern held for all FOUR of our previous runs. The problem had been his kick. After passing me, coming into the last curve, he would just put his head down and sprint to the finish line. I just never felt the urge to try to match him, since getting six minutes was all we needed for maximum points. I did remember that I was ALWAYS tired after I finished, though. Philly beat me by about ten or fifteen meters every mile. I knew that this time out, I was going to have to go to a pain level that I hadn`t endured in any of my previous runs. In fact, I felt that the event had become a race to me, and not just a run. I also felt pumped to try and win it.

Philly and I played our 'I pass you, then you pass me' game for three and a half laps. Suddenly, with two hundred meters to go, I decided to run just as fast as my combat boots would let me. My lungs were on fire as I came off the last curve. Philly still hadn`t passed me. My legs started feeling like lead, but I knew that if I slowed down, Philly would blow right by me. I was grunting and groaning and DEFINITELY gasping for air, but I wouldn`t allow myself to ease up. With fifty meters to go I heard the crunching of Philly`s familiar gait. He was gaining rapidly, and I wondered where in the world that finish line moved. It wasn`t about the bet for a case of beer anymore, I was out to beat Philly in the mile run. I went heavily to my arms, and my mind went blank. With just a couple of meters until the finish line, I thought I heard Philly easing up on his pace. I just couldn`t allow myself to believe he was slowing, so I raced through the finish line like my City High track coaches taught me to do. I got him!

When the race was over, I leaned down to rest on my knees. I DIDN`T want to collapse onto the track. Philly came up to me and said, "Nice race, man. I thought I could catch ya. You were too good today."

I answered with barely audible gasps, "Thanks…..Philly." Then I stood upright and he and I gave each other a sincere, manly handshake. I was grateful for that, since I had no idea how to do the two-minute handshakes that I had witnessed in Basic Training, and that Philly and his buddies did all the time.

I saw S.F.C. Fields looking at me. He gave me a knowing wink and a little smile. (for crying out loud….a real smile) Then I heard Fields holler, "O.K., 4th Platoon, start forming up so we can get outta here!"

Philly and I were linked together, in a matter of speaking, one more time before graduation, and that occurred the day before the actual ceremonies were to take place. On that day Captain Helmuth called me to his office.

Once in his office I announced, "Cadet Stein reporting as ordered, Sir."

"Stand at ease, Cadet Stein," the Captain replied immediately. "I called you here to talk about tomorrow`s festivities."

That seemed like a strange comment for the captain to making to me. I knew that the Honor Graduates would be announced at graduation, so suddenly, I was feeling paranoid. I must have had a worried look on my face because Helmuth remarked, "Don`t look so worried, Stein. This is nothing bad, just unusual, but it is something that involves you. Let me start off by telling you that you are one of the six Honor Graduates in this company. So, well done, Cadet Stein."

I wanted to jump up and down while screaming 'Thank-you!' I wanted to verify that I was staying at Benning for twelve weeks, and not being sent to an A.I.T. company for nine weeks. I felt so proud of myself for making E-6 that I wanted to grab Helmuth and lift him high off the ground. I maintained my military bearing, however, and said with humble pride in my voice, "Thank-you, Captain Helmuth."

"That`s not all, Cadet Stein, the Captain continued. "You will be receiving the Leadership Award, as well, and will be recognized as finishing as the number one candidate in that category. In addition, you finished number seven in the academic category, giving you a combined number total of eight....best in the company. Congratulations on a job well done."

My heart was racing, but my chest was swelling up with pride as I said, "Thank-you, Captain Helmuth. I know my family will be very pleased." I was getting ready for a handshake from him, then being allowed to run to the phones to call Jill with my news. But the Captain just stood there.

"Cadet, Stein," the Captain continued, "While you had a total score of eight, you weren`t the only cadet to do so. Philadelphia Beasley ALSO scored a total of eight points. He was number two in leadership, while finishing number six in academics. There was a tie between the two of you. I have decided to reward Beasley as the Cadet of the Cycle, and he will receive a trophy indicating such."

I was confused, and with the Captain giving me time to speak, I took advantage of the opportunity. "Captain Helmuth," I started, "is it NOT true that if two candidates receive the same top scores, the candidate with the better leadership score is named cadet of the cycle?" I was happy that my studying was paying off.

"You are absolutely correct, Cadet Stein, for the most part," the Captain stated. "That is why I called you, and only you, here to my office. The cadre knows who the top six Honor Graduates are, but they don`t have access to the academic and leadership scores for any of you. TECHNICALLY, Cadet Stein, you should be named Cadet of the Cycle. However, in the case of a tie score at the top, the commandant of the company is allowed some leeway in making the decision for the company`s highest award. This is rare, but not without precedent. I think you are BOTH absolutely deserving to be named the number one cadet. However, we can receive political kudos from the military hierarchy if Beasley is named Cadet of the Cycle. He would be the first Black cadet, in this particular company`s history, to receive our most prestigious award. I aim to see that happens. It may seem unfair to you, Cadet Stein, but my choice of Beasley is for the good of all concerned."

The 'good of all' except for me, but I wasn`t personally offended that Philly would be named to receive our highest honor. I actually believed that our company WOULD get high praise if he was so named. I certainly wasn`t into politics, and didn`t care about medals or rewards from the military. What I DID cherish, however, was getting extra time in the United States, and I never wanted to lose hope that our president would end deployment to Vietnam. While THAT didn`t seem likely, I wondered if Beasley`s reward would keep him Stateside longer than I would be. "Captain Helmuth," I responded, "I would have NO problem with Cadet Beasley receiving the Cadet of the Cycle honor. He is smart, a good person and a strong leader. But, Sir, if his receiving this honor means that he will get a monetary reward, or be stationed Stateside longer than I will, then, Captain Helmuth, I would have to express an objection."

"Cadet Stein, there is no money attached to ANY honor from here. You and Cadet Beasley will be getting the same pay-grade as E-6`s, AND you will both be stationed right here at Ft. Benning, in the same company, mind you, during our next N.C.O. Academy training cycle. The orders to report to Vietnam will be given to both you and Beasley right after this next assignment. Neither of you will be exempt from serving in Southeast Asia. Just accept the situation. You are dismissed." Helmuth was done talking and appeared eager to get on with his work. I saluted and left the office.

As it turned out, I saw Philly in the Oakland airport the day we were both flying to Nam. He was actually on the plane leaving before mine. His getting named Cadet of the Cycle didn`t get him ANYTHING extra. In fact, my anxiety that he might get more time in the U.S. was quelled when I shook his hand and wished him well prior to HIS boarding the plane. So, in the battle to stay longer in America….I won. Ain`t being competitive grand?

The graduation ceremony went without a hitch. No company had a soldier carrying a broom, but then again, I didn`t REALLY expect to see any of that nonsense at Benning. There were only N.C.O. and O.C.S. graduates participating during that day`s exercise. I couldn`t help but to be in awe as I looked at all those future leaders on the graduation grounds. The ceremony was quite impressive, and I remember being very proud of myself for making staff sergeant in about nine-and-a-half months. I came to realize, that in a relatively short time frame, I went from knowing NOTHING about military life to becoming a fairly important member of the Armed Forces….well, in my mind I was important to the army. I couldn`t wait to see how happy my wife Jill would be of me.

I was proud of myself at our company`s last formation, too. There were 'ooooh`s' and 'aaaah`s' and cheers when the six 'Honor Graduates' were announced. There were loud cheers when the graduate who earned the Academic Award, (I have forgotten his name) Philly, and I were given our statuettes for the individual honors we garnished. I was proud to be a soldier that day. This graduation meant I was finished with my training, and I was expected to stand shoulder-to-shoulder with all the other defenders of our American way of life. That realization was terrifying to me, too. I was going to be sent off to war as a fighting man, and I was going to go as a leader. What did I really know about being a leader anyway? I DID know that before I actually got into combat in a lead capacity, I had better find out if I can really lead with responsibility. My first leadership opportunity was just around the corner. I was going to be responsible for training OTHER young men to become leaders. I wasn`t sure if I was confident enough to give orders to young men who knew less than I about being a leader, but I accepted the fact that I had better act like I knew what I was doing. The N.C.O. Academy graduation marked the end of my innocence, too. I knew that I still had a lot to learn, but would have to learn while on the job. The new cadets were going to expect me to know the right things to do ALL of the time. I wasn`t going to get any 'do overs' when I gave an instruction. I had a lot of doubt as I packed my duffle bag to leave camp.

My graduation was also a sad time for me. As Willie, Rock and I stood together in the middle of the camp, I thought about the 32 weeks we had known each other. Willie and I had been living in every barracks together, and Rock visited us every chance he got. We had survived a gaff-filled trip from Iowa to Georgia. We also survived a furlough with Vinny at Callaway Gardens. And how about all the drama of every training day in Basic Training, A.I.T., L.P.C., and the Academy? We had gone through a lot together. Suddenly, we had to come to grips with the fact that this was the end of the line for the three of us to be in each other`s lives. When the time finally came to say good-bye, it was Rock who finally said, "OK, you guys, it`s been fun. So, I guess I`ll see ya on the other side. I`ll miss ya." He hugged both Willie and me, whirled around, and Willie and I watched him head for the camp bus, which would take him to his transportation for Ft. Polk. Yep, he was assigned an A.I.T. unit at Polk, and he wasn`t too thrilled about it.

Willie and I had different busses to catch, too. He was headed to Jump School, which fortunately was located at Ft. Benning, and I was headed to my next Benning-based, N.C.O. Academy company, where I would be a tactical sergeant. We promised to see each other, but as it turned out, our schedules didn`t allow that to happen. We hugged then went to out separate busses. I felt a lump in my throat and tears welling up in my eyes. Those two guys were like brothers to me, and I felt like I was losing them. I was, and am, a very emotional person. Most of the soldiers, with whom I served in Vietnam, were like brothers to me, too. Losing my 'brothers' was something that I would have trouble accepting throughout the rest of my military days. My two Iowa buddies and I had been through a lot, but now our time together had come to an end. I felt very alone suddenly, and sadness turned again to fear as I knew that I was going to have to plunge forward, alone, for the first time since I was drafted.

VII

Rules & Responsibilities

Captain Helmuth had kept his word as both Philly and I were assigned to the same academy company. Our new commandant was a Vietnam vet by the name of Captain Carpinski. Both of the tactical sergeants assigned to our company were older E-6`s, though neither of them had served in Southeast Asia. One had been overseas in Germany, while the other had done a tour in Korea. They were good guys, but liked to tease Philly and me by constantly reminding us that they 'earned their stripes through many years of service.' Since all four of us were working as Academy sergeants for the first time, I felt Philly and I had an edge on the 'old-timers.' After all, we had been THROUGH the course already. The older sergeants, whose names I can`t remember, were married with families. Most of the time they were off work, they were in their off- base housing with their wives and kids. Philly and I were on friendly terms, but we never became close friends. He liked to go into Columbus, most nights, to meet some of his buddies, and I preferred to hang around camp, trying to look important. Most of the free time I had during the first ten days, however, I spent finding quiet places to write letters to Jill and my mom.

As it turned out, my solace would last only three weeks as Jill had finished her junior year at the University of Iowa, and we decided it would be great to be together in Georgia for seven weeks. That would be the amount of time she would have before returning to Iowa City to prepare for her last year at school. We both were looking forward to being together, and the days dragged by excruciatingly slowly as her arrival time neared.

I could have gotten military housing for us, but I knew Jill was anti-military, therefore living an army existence, with its rules and regulations would be like me poking a stick at a lion. I looked for off-base housing and Capt. Carpinski suggested we rent a trailer for two months. He came through in a big way as he knew a friend who owned a trailer in a park located 20 minutes from Ft. Benning. His buddy was looking to rent his place for six months, but Carpinski got us a two-month deal, which I really appreciated. Jill and I lived in a trailer in Iowa City, so trailer living would be just fine by us.

I made an appointment to see the trailer. I have to say I was quite disappointed. The place was larger than a camping trailer, but not by much. It didn`t have air-conditioning, rather one large fan that had to be moved from the living room to the bedroom at night, then back to the living room during the day. It was hot in Georgia during the summer months, and without having moving air, no one could survive living in the place. The furniture was minimal, but there was a stove, refrigerator, and a tv. The bed was a standard double bed, but I was informed that a larger bed was ordered and expected to arrive 'any day now.' In actuality, that bed didn`t arrive until Jill and I were finished with our fifth week of occupancy. The trailer WAS clean and bug-free which was important as there were some HUGE flying cockroaches in Georgia. However, most of the pipes were rusty, and the handle of the toilet had to be jiggled about every third flush in order to get the stopper to become snug. Rent was cheap, though, so I overlooked most of the faults. I just hoped Jill would.

I had called my wife the night before she was to get into our car and drive to Georgia. I mentioned that I had rented a trailer, at a very inexpensive price, but she just seemed thrilled by the prospect of being able to live with me for an extended period of time. This would be our first time living together, for more than two or three weeks, since we returned from our honeymoon. We talked about how we missed each other and about being safe on the road, and just as we exchanged 'I love you`s' for the umpteenth time, I ran out of quarters for the pay phone.

I expected it would likely take her three days to get to Ft. Benning, and found sleeping that first night to be very hard for me. I worried about her being alone on the road, but I couldn`t help but to be excited that she was actually coming to be with me. I was a nervous wreck. Time seemed to be moving at a snail`s pace. The second night`s sleep was equally difficult, as was the third night.

The day Jill arrived I had just returned from taking the company on a three-mile run. I was cleaning up in the cadre quarters when an announcement came over the loudspeaker, "Sergeant Stein, please report to the Captain Carpinski`s office." It was not unusual for cadre to be called to the commandant`s office, and since it wasn`t even noon yet, I wasn`t sure why I was being summoned. The two older sergeants were coming FROM the command building, and when they both gave me wolf whistles, my heart started beating rapidly, and I picked up my pace to a near run. Suddenly, Jill came racing through the front door of the building, and leaped into my arms, kissing me all over my face.

Captain Carpinski then came through the door, cleared his voice rather loudly, and called out, "Sergeant Stein."

The tone he used was meant to let me know that there would be no more public displays on company grounds. I peeled Jill off me, told her that I was very excited to see her, but had to gently tell her, "We can`t do this here. I`m working now and am expected to carry myself with a military bearing while on the job. I do love you very much."

Jill gave me a pouty look, grabbed hold of my hand, and turned toward the Captain with a big smile. The moment was a little awkward for me as now most of the men in camp were either huddled in doorways or peering though barracks windows. My awkwardness continued when I said, "Captain Carpinski, this is my wife Jill, whom I assume you`ve already met. Jill, this is my commanding officer, Captain Carpinski, whom I assume YOU`VE already met."

Jill kept hold of my hand as she reached out with her right hand, smiled, and said, "It`s nice meeting you, Mr. Carpinski."

"CAPTAIN Carpinski," I quickly corrected her.

"Captain Carpinski," my wife parroted.

Before I continue with my story, I must tell you a bit more about my wife. Jill was the only daughter in a family of five. Since she was ALSO the baby of her upper middle-class family, she was used to getting her way. She was definitely her daddy`s 'little girl' and could do know wrong as far as he was concerned. Jill was also very good-looking, and had a body that models dreamed of having…. only my wife was more voluptuous. She didn`t do physical exercise, ever, but her body was toned like an athlete. She flirted and used her sexuality to get what she wanted from men. She enjoyed dressing in clothes that accented her figure`s best feature, her boobs, to the point that when she would enter a room, not only did all the men look at her, so did all the women. She had a beautiful face, a great rear, and shapely legs. She may have been only 5'2" tall but she was the full female package. When Jill got her way, which really WAS most of the time, she was a delight to be around. However, if she DIDN`T get what she wanted, she was hell on wheels. Women generally didn`t like her as a person, for Jill demanded that SHE constantly be the focus of attention. My wife DID have the capacity of making a few good female friends, however, and every one of those friends was exceptionally loyal to her. When she worked her charms on men, it was almost embarrassing to witness. Guys would drop whatever it was that they were doing in order to do Jill`s bidding. There were times when a man would be in conversation with another woman, even his wife, when Jill would indicate she needed something done for her….and it was done immediately. It was easy to be ensnared by Jill`s wily ways, as I certainly was, but I was also very proud that I was the guy she chose to marry. We stayed married for nearly seven years. I know I wanted to grow old with her, but I was very naïve about what made Jill tick. In time, though, I came to understand that she wasn`t my soul-mate. For now, it is time to get back to the story, where YOU may soon begin to appreciate why we wouldn`t click as a life-long couple.

Captain Carpinski reached out his hand and said, "It`s my pleasure again, Mrs. Stein." While he was saying that, he was looking at Jill and my handholding, so I let go. I couldn`t tell if HE was charmed by her or not. "Sgt. Stein," he continued, "since your wife has just arrived, I`m going to allow you three hours to take her to the housing you`ve secured, and help her get settled a bit. I need you back here by 1300 hours. Mrs. Stein, welcome to Ft. Benning." Captain Carpinski gripped the bill of his hat with his thumb and two fingers, did an about-face, and returned to his office.

I was a bit surprised at how NOT taken by Jill the captain was, and I couldn`t help but ask myself, in an inner voice, 'Did he not notice her boobs, and how beautiful her face was?" I was convinced that the man had extreme will-power, or he was blind. Those were the only two rationales I could think of at the time.

My captain may not have noticed her, but every other pair of eyes in camp did. There was no movement, by anyone, as we left the area. I was proud to be leaving the company area with such a sexy woman, and Jill and I talked like honeymooners all the way to the trailer park.

The honeymoon talk stopped abruptly when I pulled up to the front of our trailer. Jill looked at me, with an unbelieving stare, shook her head, and said, "You`ve got to be kidding me, Abe. You`re not expecting us to live HERE for seven weeks, are you? This place is REALLY tiny."

"I know it is a bit smaller than our trailer in Iowa City, but, sweetheart, it is a place OFF base. No prying military eyes. You and I could live in a dumpy motel room for seven weeks. Think of this as an adventure. Even if we have nothing else we have each other. Come on, we`ll laugh about how much fun we`ll have here. You`ll see." Jill didn`t say another word as we got out of the car and walked to the front door. When she opened the door I expected a stream of profanity, knowing that Jill could curse with the best of them. She simply looked around, turned and hugged me, and said, "This will do just fine. You`re right, we`ll be sharing this together. Thanks for getting us a place." I`ve got to say that we were so happy to finally be alone with each other, I barely made it back to the company by 1300 hours. No more description of our reunion is necessary.

The rest of that afternoon in the company area dragged by for me. Everything I did was with a smile on my face, however, but that was not a good thing. Tactical

NCO`s are not known to smile more than a couple of times in a cycle, as everything has to be business to them while training cadets. People knew why I was smiling, however, so I was allowed to look happy, but only for that afternoon. It was business as usual throughout the rest of the twelve weeks.

The training we gave to the new cadets was remarkably similar to what I received when I was going through the class. There was no near-drowning, as my company experienced when I was a cadet. The night compass course was just as tough on this group of trainees, but no one ran into snakes this time around. I`m also pretty confident that there were fewer cadets leaving this class than the one I trained with. The major difference, to ME, was that I got to go home with my wife most nights, and that was VERY different. But going home wasn`t always a happy moment for me. Jill was a complainer, and she complained about EVERYTHING! She complained about Georgia being too hot, or too humid, and she really hated ALL bugs, especially the flying cockroaches. Her biggest complaint, however, was that she didn`t have anything to do when I was at work.

Jill demanded that she have the car while I was in Ft. Benning, but she complained about having to get up so early in the morning to get me there. I usually drove to my company, and Jill was quiet most of the time. But when she picked me up for our ride home, it was non-stop complaining. I tried to console her, but she never wanted to hear anything I had to say. And I NEVER remember her asking me how MY day went. She was constantly upset or angry. The 'honeymoon' feeling we had our first night in the trailer, disappeared by the second night. And it was pretty much absent for most of the seven weeks she was in Georgia.

The complaint that there was nothing for her to do when I was at Benning was a valid one, for the most part. She cleaned our home, but that was about all she did. She had no hobbies, nor did she try to find one. She thought Columbus to be a boring city, and didn`t venture there more than once or twice during her whole stay in Georgia. Even though we didn`t live in military housing, most of the trailers in the park were occupied by military personnel.

We actually tried to make friends with the couple in the trailer next to ours, but both of them were gung-ho about the military. If I haven`t already told you, let me make this perfectly clear….Jill hated EVERYTHING military. Our neighbors would come over to visit from time to time. It wouldn`t take long, however, before Jill would get a bored look on her face, leaving me to be the only one involved in the conversations with the neighbors. The only time my wife would perk up is if the other wife asked about make-up tips, or how to dress in a more sexy way. Jill could be charming, though, especially if either of our neighbors commented on how nice she looked. But, when the talk turned to sports, news of the world, or anything to do with the army, Jill would go outside for a smoke, pick up a magazine to peruse, or just plain close her eyes and pretend to be sleepy. She was so easy to read, but the neighbors never complained to me about her. When Jill looked like she didn`t want to be with us, someone would change the topic as quickly as possible. The ONE topic we all knew to avoid was politics. Jill wanted everyone to know how liberally-minded she was, and our neighbors caught on to that the first time they came over to introduce themselves. For seven weeks, all our conversations were designed to TRY to include Jill, which was difficult more times than not.

We never went to our neighbor`s trailer. Though it was quite a bit larger than ours, their place was loaded with weapons and pro-military slogans, so we always got together at our trailer. As nice as our neighbors were when they visited us, when they left, Jill would start in. "She is such a hayseed. Can you please tell him to stop scratching his crotch. Both of them need showers." She would vent a lot of frustration simply because she was unhappy, and she chose to rake them over the fires instead of me….thankfully.

During the entire seven weeks, there were few things that relieved her from feeling miserable. Three times I took her out to nice restaurants. She LOVED when we went out because it gave her a chance to dress up and look sexy. I knew Jill wasn`t happy staying at the trailer all the time. I wouldn`t have been, either, but I had very little time to show her fun things to do. Being a tactical n.c.o. was time-consuming, and when I was finished at the company, I was usually exhausted. Jill just didn`t make an effort to make lemonade out of lemons, as far as I was concerned.

We had ONE great weekend together, however. That`s when I took my wife to Callaway Gardens. We stayed in a beautiful resort for two nights. I rented golf clubs and, since Jill didn`t play the sport, she rode in the cart with me while I played. She was actually happy the entire weekend, and it made me feel great to finally see her that way. Those two days cost me nearly two months pay, but I didn`t care about the money. We had a marvelous time together, and I was hoping that feeling would extent to the following week, which was scheduled to be Jill`s last week in Georgia. I was VERY wrong!

It was Tuesday morning, and Jill dropped me off for work with her usual comment, "I can`t wait to get back to Iowa City, so I can sleep in." It only took two days for the Callaway Gardens high to return to reality.

When she picked me up later, she didn`t have her normal complaints about how she spent her day. She casually and defiantly said, "I`m supposed to go to a kangaroo military court in two days, but I`m not going,"

That got my attention more than her usual complaints, and I said rather sternly, "What?"

"This jackass military cop stopped me this morning when I was returning to the trailer. Said he got me speeding 10 miles over the limit, and that he was going to 'have' to give me a ticket." Jill then began to rant un-controllably. "I told him I WASN`T speeding, so I wasn`t going to pay any damn ticket. Then the bastard shoved that little piece of paper at me and told me I HAD to report to military court in two days. I wanted to call him a f..king Nazi, but I bit my tongue. Abe, I wasn`t speeding, and I`m NOT going to pay any ticket." Then she rested her mouth.

I was driving as I usually do after being picked up from work, but I was staring forward with my mouth agape. To my credit, I said calmly, "It doesn`t matter if you TOLD him you weren`t speeding. Hell, it doesn`t matter if you actually WEREN`T speeding at all. That m.p. has radar in his car, which indicated to HIM that you were speeding. So, you will go to the court in two days, and you WILL pay the fine."

Jill and I exchanged 'I won`t,' 'you will,' opinions a few times, but there comes a point when an opinionated discussion turns into an argument with neither party willing to accept the other`s opinion. Finally I said, "In the military I am responsible for every action my family does."

"That`s ridiculous!" Jill interrupted, "I`m the only one responsible for my actions. You have nothing to do with it!"

"I`m telling you, Jill, nothing will happen to YOU if you don`t pay the fine. But some kind of military action will be taken against me. I just don`t know what that action will be. It`s a little ticket. Pay it and we can move on."

"I wasn`t speeding! That clown m.p. knew I wasn`t speeding. He just wasn`t used to a woman disputing him. I`m NOT paying that ticket!"

Sleeping that night was tough. Going into the company area the next morning was tougher. I drove the car that morning, leaving Jill at the trailer. As soon as I checked into the command building, Captain Carpinski asked me to step into his office. I entered and saw him sitting at his desk, looking at some paper in his hand. "Sgt. Stein," he started, "I got a report here telling me your wife got a speeding ticket yesterday. The m.p., who wrote up the report, indicated that she not only told him she wasn`t going to pay the fine, she wasn`t even going to show up in court. The m.p. also stated that he was quite sure she called him a derogatory name, but he couldn`t be absolutely certain on that point. Did you talk to her about this incident last night?"

"I told her I was responsible for anything she says or does while she is here with me," I responded. "Sgt Stein, does that mean she IS going to be in court tomorrow paying the fine?" Carpinski said while giving me his sternest look. "Let me be more clear, Sergeant. If she DOESN`T show up, OR refuses to pay the fine, you will be docked one month`s pay, AND you will lose a stripe. Do you understand what I just told you, Sgt. Stein?"

"Perfectly," I answered in a firm voice. Then I was dismissed, and I felt terrible.

The day dragged by, and I practiced often what I would say to Jill when I got home. It was important that I make it absolutely clear, that nothing would happen to her, but MY world would come crashing down around me.

Jill seemed exhausted when I got home, but I asked her to sit down and listen without interrupting me. As I was giving her my presentation, she had a visible scowl on her face, but I finished strongly by saying, "I don`t think it`s fair that I lose a grade in rank because of your stubbornness."

She nodded her head, pursed her lips, and said, "All right, you take me tomorrow, I`ll pay the stupid ticket, and you`ll stay the rank you are right now. But I DO hate the army!" There was no 'honeymooning' that night.

The day in court went smoothly. The m.p., who gave the ticket wasn`t present, and I was glad about that. The presiding officer called Jill to his desk and said, "I have a sworn affidavit here from military police officer (I can`t remember his name) stating that he had you driving 45 m.p.h. in a 35 m.p.h. zone," and on he went. "How do you plead?"

Jill looked directly at me instead of the officer, gave a pregnant pause, and said, "Guilty." To say I was relieved is an understatement. I wanted to party when we returned to the trailer that night. Jill didn`t. Although we 'honeymooned' the night before Jill returned to Iowa City, as she was driving off, I could definitely feel tension between us.

The last two weeks at Benning were routine, and after graduation, I took a bus to Iowa City. I had a month-long furlough, but also had orders to report for a tour in Vietnam when that furlough was finished.

My wife picked me up at the bus depot, and while see seemed really happy to see me, I could sense that her feelings toward me had been affected by her visit to Ft. Benning. Our attitudes about life had gone in different directions. Though it was true that we spent a few good times together in Georgia, as the two-day trip to Callaway Gardens, and us celebrating our one-year anniversary at a nice restaurant come readily to mind, there had been a lot of tension during most of the seven weeks. Our happiest moments were those nights when we lay in bed and talked about our plans AFTER I got out of the service. Also, the fact that I had acclimated so well to being in the military bothered Jill immensely. I had become more of a hawk about life, whereas she had become a dove to the Nth degree. She never forgave me for NOT taking her side in the speeding ticket incident, and then there was her NEW life-style change, which became very evident to me as soon as I walked through our Iowa City trailer door.

Jill was a smoker, which really didn`t bother me that much since my mom was a smoker, and I had grown up in a house filled with secondary smoke. However, when I opened the door of my home, the smell of marijuana was nearly over-powering. The window curtains, the bedding, the furniture, even the walls themselves wreaked with the odor of the illegal drug. I felt like I was in a gas chamber, so I kept the door open in hopes of getting some fresh air to come into our home.

When I confronted Jill about the heavy smell she tried to explain that 'weed' helped her relax, and that she had recently increased her intake to deal with the trauma caused by her Georgia visit, and my impending Vietnam assignment. She was right in one respect. I was headed to a very dangerous situation. I had no idea how families coped with the possibility that a loved one might not come home from a war zone. I certainly didn`t want to add to her stress by arguing with her about her use of marijuana. I looked at her, then hugged her for a very long time. There was no more talk about drugs.

The time Jill and I spent before my deployment was pretty great. She agreed to NOT smoke dope while I was home, and I agreed to NOT talk about anything military. She was, however, smoking regular cigarettes at an alarming rate, and that did bother me. I had lost my dad to lung cancer when he was just 36 years of age. He had been a VERY heavy smoker and I believed Jill was close to his consumption level of daily cigarettes. We both worked hard at NOT finding reasons to disagree, and that resulted in me feeling the happiness I enjoyed before I was drafted. It was VERY difficult for both of us, and my mom, when the day arrived for my departure.

The scene at the Cedar Rapids airport was surreal to me. My mom kept reassuring me that it wouldn`t be THAT long before I would be back home, though I sensed the worry, and some doubt, emanating through her words. Jill, on the other hand, was explaining to me about the classes she was taking for her senior year at the University of Iowa. She appeared to be in denial as to my destination, and her mannerisms indicated that she might have thought she was just seeing me off to another training course. That was fine with me, as I hoped she would use her 'training in the States' mind-set as a coping mechanism. I definitely didn`t want her to worry. I also wanted her to stop smoking marijuana, though I didn`t say so at the airport. I have to admit that I was in a bit of shock, too. The time had come for me to actually go to Southeast Asia. My mind was playing mental leapfrog and there was so much that I wanted to say to the people that I loved. Finally, I just bit my lip, hugged both women, kissed Jill quickly, (her choice) and said, "I`ll be seeing you again real soon." I boarded the plane without looking back.

On the plane ride to Oakland, California, I tried to come to grips with my situation. I wasn`t the Jewish chaplain I tried desperately to become in Basic Training. All my training was geared toward me being a combat soldier. But I knew I was un-tested in the reality of war, and having attained a high rank so quickly, I doubted that I would be capable of leading REAL soldiers in times of crisis. I knew I would be expected to know what to do in every situation, but I still wasn`t even sure what I would face in Vietnam. Before being drafted I hadn`t thought much about Nam. I NEVER expected to be going there and fighting for my life. I thought of two things that I needed to do once I got to the war....get myself home alive, and apply for an early school drop. Yes, if I could start school in the fall of 1970, I wouldn`t have to be in Vietnam for one whole year. Throughout that flight, I was a mess mentally. I kept praying. I kept making promises to myself. I kept doubting myself. But mostly, I was scared.

My experience in Oakland was a bit strange, too. I was wearing battle fatigues, heading toward the gate where my flight would leave. In today`s society people have been known to shake soldier`s hands, and thank them for serving. In November of 1969, I saw people turning their faces away from me, as if I didn`t exist. I certainly wasn`t expecting any positive comments from other people in the airport, but it almost seemed like I was being shunned. In fact, I`m pretty sure that I heard two long-haired, hippie-type teens sneer in my direction before turning away. I knew that protesting the war had increased in intensity during the year that I was training in the United States. In fact, before I was drafted, I wasn`t in favor of our country being at war, either, especially since we hadn`t been attacked like we were at Pearl Harbor. The truth is, I never protested our military`s intervention, like many students were doing in early 1968. I not only loved America, I believed that our leaders knew what they were doing, though in retrospect, I was very immature and naïve about such matters. Yet, as a proud soldier walking through Oakland`s airport that November night, reporting for duty like all American soldiers were (and are) expected to do, I felt isolated from the other travelers. I was grateful and relieved when I saw many, many soldiers at my gate.

As I approached the large mass of uniformed men, I heard a very distinct, "Stein." I looked at the gate next to mine, and I got a brief glimpse of Philadelphia Beasley waving as he was moving quickly toward his gate. I waved back, but before I could acknowledge him verbally, he was gone. Philly was flying to Nam before me, and I kind of gloated about being in the States longer than he. Never heard from, nor saw him again.

Talk about a somber flight. We flew in a United Airlines plane, fully stocked with female flight attendants. They tried their best to be nice to us, but every person sitting on that plane was headed toward danger, so minds were not thinking about how friendly those women were. All the men had game-faces on, and there wasn`t a hint of any flirting with the attendants that I witnessed. Of course, I was nervously trying to be calm, so I really didn`t notice if there was laughing or even conversations going on around me.

For 19 straight hours we seemed to chase the darkness of night. We made two brief re-fueling stops on route to Nam....Hawaii and Guam. I had traveled to Canada, Mexico and down the Eastern seaboard during a crazy 20-month period of my early college years, but I never experienced anything like the one-hour lay-over we had in Hawaii.

We were allowed to leave the plane to stretch our legs, and I immediately felt an aura of relaxation. This was brought on by the many exotic Hawaiian flowers I saw and smelled when I first de-planed. I loved the unusual-sounding Polynesian music, too, that had been piped onto the open-air walkways of Honolulu`s airport. My senses were highly stimulated, and for a moment I nearly forgot where I was traveling. However, I was ALSO physically and emotionally drained, that was a certainty. Still, the gentle breezes I felt while walking, coupled with the smells, sights and sounds of Hawaii, relaxed me to the point where I felt like I could lie down and sleep instantly. I didn`t, but as I re-boarded the airplane, I said to myself that I HAD to return to Hawaii some day. I felt like I was leaving some sort of paradise.

Our stop in Guam was different. I didn`t leave the plane. In fact, the only thing I DO remember about that island was me becoming acutely aware that when the airplane took off, my next stop was going to be in Vietnam.

As the light of day was just appearing, I noticed from my window seat that there was water below us. It didn`t take long before whispers of 'land ahead' spread around the plane. I strained to look forward, and soon I did see a dark mass of land. Butterflies began filling my stomach. We started our decent and soon there was nothing but land beneath us. It was a beautiful dark green, but as we got lower I noticed puffs of smoke in the distance. As the plane descended further, and not far from the smoke, I began seeing red tracer bullets and green tracer bullets shooting at each other. I couldn`t believe it….I was witnessing people trying to kill each other. My mind instantly retreated to some of my training, specifically my sniper training. On each of those occasions I was theoretically killed when BB`s hit me while walking a 'salted' trail. With the sight of tracers, I understood training was over and the reality of people trying to kill each other was now my world. My head was throbbing with pain. To make matters worse, I was sure I saw the attendant, working my section of the plane, shed a tear, and I`m reasonably sure that I heard her whisper under her breath, "Why do we have to bring our brave, young men here to die?" I was thinking the same thing. I looked around the plane wondering how many of the 200 people aboard weren`t going to survive. Then the wheels touched down, and my butterflies turned to fruit bats. I was in the war!

VIII

On the Job Training

I sat in my seat realizing that I had better get my act together. Then the plane began to taxi, but unlike any taxi I remember in the States. In the U.S., planes taxied for many, many minutes, especially in the larger airports. Our plane was zipping along quickly, at a pace that would make any race car driver proud. Within seconds we were stopped, the front door was opened, and a member of the air force dashed into the cabin area. He announced," I want to welcome you to the Republic of South Vietnam. I had a longer speech prepared, but we were mortared fifteen minutes ago, and I`ve got to get you off quickly so that those going back to the Real World can get on. This bird needs to get airborne in short order." With that being said, he scampered back down the stairs with the rest of us scrambling right behind him in a single file.

While scooting down the stairs, it was NOT hard for me to notice a canopied shelter to my right side, which was set up within meters of the airplane`s nose. Under the canopy were the men who would be boarding once we de-planed. There were audible comments coming from them, 'Here come the replacements,' Give the gooks hell,' and my least favorite, 'Oh, man, I`m glad I`m not THEM.' There were men on litters, and many others bandaged up like zombies. All of them looked skinny, even scraggly. I had a sick feeling in my gut. I knew that even if I survived my tour, I would look like them when I was leaving.

With nothing but negative thoughts in my head, I followed the guys in front of me to waiting busses. Once loaded, the busses roared through the crowded streets, not stopping, or even slowing down for anything or anybody. We apparently had the right-of-way and civilians were scattering so as not to get hit by our hurtling carriers. I`m not sure if there was a posted speed limit anywhere, but our drivers never took their feet off the gas pedals, as we rocketed through the busy city center. Miraculously, no one seemed to have been hit, and it didn`t take long before we pulled into a U.S. military installation. We had arrived safely at a replacement center.

These 'centers' served several purposes. They gave in-coming personnel some time to acclimate to local weather and a different time zone. Some refresher courses were given on jungle survival. I got to witness a scary demonstration on how quickly the V.C. (Viet Cong) could infiltrate ANY compound`s perimeter, no matter how heavily barbed wired it was. I learned the term 'chu hoi' which referred to a former enemy soldier turned traitor against the Communist cause. I immediately told myself that I wasn`t going to trust ANY Vietnamese person, especially a chu hoi who could penetrate the thickest wiring and slit my throat. I was scared, and I was being overwhelmed with information that could end my life. I EVENTUALLY learned to lighten up on my feelings about being around the Vietnamese while in their country....well, maybe a little.

The main purpose of replacement centers was to refill soldier quotas for the various military units. When I arrived at my center, there were hundreds of new recruits ready to be snapped up by depleted companies. First-time soldiers usually got as long as a week to assimilate to being in Vietnam. Returning veterans, not as long. Staff sergeants seemed to be the highest ranking replacements at my center. I understood that we would likely not be around for more than a day or so before some unit claimed us.

After I viewed the 'sapper' wire demonstration, I moved to the tent used for housing the E-6`s. I was exhausted and wanted to lie down. When I entered the facility, I noticed two things. I was the youngest E-6 by at least ten years, and Philly Beasley WASN`T there. My rest didn`t last long, as the E-6 replacements were told to 'fall out' for a muster call. There were only about twenty of us, and we meandered out of the tent only to get into a rather sloppy formation of three lines. I noticed a specialist E-4 approaching with clipboard in hand.

"Oh, Christ," a sergeant behind me uttered, "the 199th needs an E-6. Please, Lord, don`t let it be me."

"Why not?" asked the sergeant next to him.

"All they do is hump in the jungle and get killed, that`s why not," the surly sergeant replied.

The young specialist stood before us, looked down at his board, and shouted, "Stein, Abraham D., come with me." I hoisted my duffle bag onto my shoulder, then he and I moved on our way without a word being spoken.

I hadn`t spent one night at the replacement center, and there I was, being placed into a company that had been bad-mouthed by a veteran E-6. My heart was in my throat, and I felt like I was moving in a zombie-like stupor. Scared and tired are NOT good qualities for a new guy, in Nam, to have. The E-4 and I finally arrived at our company`s truck.

The truck was a deuce-and-a half, which was the standard truck used for troop transport. I climbed into the back and noticed three privates already inside. I nodded toward them, sat down, and the truck moved out. We drove to Long Binh, where the rear echelon of the 199th Light Infantry Brigade was head-quartered. It was a relatively short trip from the replacement center. I was the first soldier off the truck, and not far from my exit was an older sergeant. He was 1st Sergeant Clarence Fish, the top sergeant in Delta Company. This guy was a very veteran soldier, and had more than three tours in Nam under his belt. Though Delta had captains and lieutenants, and those officers were the highest-ranking personnel in the company, nothing seemed to get done without the 1st sergeant`s say so….at least not in the rear area. Sgt. Fish called for me to come to his position.

"Sergeant Stein," he said as I approached, "welcome to Delta Company. Here is your M-16 rifle, which I have already zeroed in for you, and a full rucksack.

There is a chopper waiting for you at the heli pad, so you need to hurry and get there. You are now the platoon sergeant for 2nd Platoon."

I staggered toward him while in total shock, dropped off my duffle bag at his feet, threw on my rucksack, grabbed my weapon, and said, "Thank-you, First Sergeant. Could you do me a favor and start paperwork so I can go back to school next fall?"

"I can do that," he said in a rather gruff voice. "Now get moving," and he pointed toward the jeep that was to take me to the helicopter pad. I hadn`t been in Vietnam one full day, yet I was headed out to meet my platoon. Scared doesn`t cover how I felt. I was nearly petrified.

I was given a seat in the middle of the chopper, as the bird began ascending. At seven feet in the air we hesitated. I saw the pilot`s lips move. Then the right-side door gunner got out of his seat, moved to a chu hoi, who was sitting in the doorway, and with one swift move of his leg, the American shoved the little Vietnamese soldier out of the copter. My mouth gaped open in surprise. I had a hard time believing what I saw. I looked down and noticed that the chu hoi had landed on the rucksack he was wearing. Suddenly, he popped straight up, gave a thumbs up to the gunner, and yelled, "OK, G.I." I had to ask what happened. Apparently the pilot had decided that there was too much weight on board to be able to eventually reach the height needed for the journey, and the machine-gunner was asked to jettison some weight. The chu hoi was the most expedient way of losing the extra pounds. That move seemed strange and inhumane, but efficient, all at once. We moved up and away from Long Binh.

As it had become late afternoon, I was almost mesmerized by how beautifully dark and mysterious the jungle appeared to me. I also thought how ominous it was, and couldn`t help thinking that there were a lot of dangerous animals and people down there. The whirling blades of the helicopter were quite soothing, and the ride, itself, was very smooth. Had we not been in a war zone, I could have easily imagined this to be a wonderful ride in an American theme park. As we descended, I was finally gripped by reality. We had come to a pock-marked piece of land, where I saw a shirtless, American soldier, bent over a water-filled bomb crater, attempting to get a drink of water. He`d brush aside the scum, which was floating on top, then quickly cup his hands and raise the water to his mouth. The water had an ugly greenish tint to it, and I remember thinking that I would NEVER drink anything so disgusting-looking. Two days later, however, I was out of the water that 1st Sergeant Fish had packed on my rucksack, and I was trying to find ANY water source to quench my thirst. One of my first lessons in the jungle was how to conserve precious water. Fast-moving, fresh-water mountain streams would become more valuable to me than any gold mine.

When the chopper landed, everyone dismounted in haste. Within seconds that bird was gone. I didn`t stand there for more than a few seconds, when a soldier came up to me, grabbed my arm, and took me to meet members of the 2nd platoon. Then I was told to relax for the evening, and that I would be briefed in the morning. Darkness came quite suddenly, and I found a place to sleep, which ended up being very close to the soldier who had drunk the filthy water. As tired as I was, I had a hard time sleeping that first night, and there were several reasons for that. First, it was so dark that I couldn`t see my fingers moving no matter HOW closely I put them near my eyes. I kept wondering how I would be able to move around if, indeed, I had to. I had mosquitoes all over me, and the itching was driving me nuts. I was sleeping on the hardest ground imaginable. The drinker of the filthy water became ill, and vomited violently, which created a stench that was making ME feel queasy. I couldn`t remember a single face nor name of anybody I had met, including the soldier who was introducing me to the others. And I was scared of every sound I heard….including the retching of the sick soldier. That was just the first night of my jungle experience. How was I expected to survive a year?

As daylight broke, a 2nd lieutenant, named William Edwards, came over to me to introduce himself as the platoon leader. He was a serious-looking man who got right to the point. He explained his responsibilities and what he expected of me. I had such a headache that I couldn`t concentrate on what he was saying. I nodded knowingly, but I also knew I would have to get most of his information at least one more time before I understood my role in the platoon. After his quick welcoming speech he was gone. I must have looked as confused as I felt, and thankfully I heard, "Good morning,' Sarge." I`m sure I was introduced to him briefly the night before, but he hadn`t been the guy who fetched me from the helicopter. He continued, "I`m Sergeant Steven March, and I`m the squad leader for the 1st squad. I was the platoon sergeant for a couple of days until the company brought you in, and since you out-rank me, the job becomes yours," and he extended his hand.

"Good morning, Sergeant March," I said as I, too, extended my hand. "I`m afraid that I am very new at being in the jungle. Lt. Edwards tried to explain my duties out here, but I was just waking up, so things flew over my head. I`m going to need all the help from you that I can get."

"The lt. has only been with us a little more than than a week himself. Seems to know his stuff pretty good, though. I need to make sure you know everything I know a.s.a.p. `cause I`ll be gone soon, and I want to know that you are squared away before I go."

"Go?" I asked quizzically.

"Short, Sarge. Only three weeks left before I can head back to my family in Maine. I`m gettin` out of this man`s army when I leave Nam, too. Things are turning around pretty fast around here lately. Makes me nervous, getting so many f.n.g.`s (f…ing new guys) all at once. Guess I`d be jittery no matter who`s with me, though, kind of a short-timer's syndrome, if you know what I mean. I`m thinkin` the faster I can get you up to speed, the better for all of us. You come through shake-and bake?"

"Yeah, I did," I answered.

"No problem," March continued. "I washed outta there early. Too much spit and polish for me. But I know you`re gonna need help here….ALL new guys need help here. This shit here is o.j.t." (on the job training) Steve March continued to explain what I was responsible for, describing everything in very colorful language. Here, again, I am going to let you, the readers, know that the obscene language used amongst soldiers is generally used liberally. But the coarse language was amplified two or three-fold in Vietnam. I am somewhat sensitive to crude language in my today life, and will do the best I can to get the messages of my stories across without excessive offensive language. I can, however, tell you that soldiers in war zones get used to hearing and using foul language rather quickly. While I was in Nam, I fit right in with the others, and stringing three, four, sometimes five off-color words together in a sentence was very normal for me, too.

Steve continued, "Our lieutenant hasn`t seen any action yet, but he hasn`t got us lost yet, either. He gets us re-supplied out here without any problems, too, so I`m not un-happy with him, even though I`m not crazy about officers in general. Your main jobs include setting up night-time perimeters, leading the maneuver element when we make contact, and distributing job assignments when we get into forward firebases."

"I hope you don`t mind me asking, but how many guys are in the 2nd platoon," I interrupted.

"Right now, with you, we got 23," Steve answered. "That`s the most I remember us having in a long time. But, many of these guys are newbies. We got three privates who came in with the Edwards, got two the next day, and you yesterday. There`s gonna be a lot of cherries popped when we have our next run-in with the gooks." I found out later that 'cherries' meant the first time being fired at, and 'gooks' was the derogatory name used for the enemy.

I started opening an old W.W.II c-ration can of peaches that 1st Sergeant Fish had packed for me in my rucksack, while March continued with his introduction.

"That man over there?" Steve said while pointing to a black soldier. "That`s Smith. I`d say he`s the baddest ass in the platoon. Not the best soldier, mind you, just someone good to steer clear of, if you can. A while back him and two of his buddies went to the Enlisted Men`s Club in Long Binh, and started a free-for-all."

"What?" I questioned.

"Yep," March said matter-of factly. "Seems like he was getting a little impatient with one of the serving girls because she wasn`t stopping at his table to get his drink order. SHE claimed the club was very busy, and when she was finished delivering the drinks already on her tray, Smith`s table would have been next for her to serve. Apparently, Smith had grabbed her arm as she started walking by his table, nearly spilling the drink order she had with her. Then he says, 'Take our order, bitch.' Whereas SHE replied, 'Take your hands off me, ni…r.' (yep, that word) Then, all hell broke loose. He pushed her into a nearby table, spilling the drinks on the soldiers sitting there. Fists starting flying, and the military police were called. It was a mess. The bottom line was that Smith got busted back to p.f.c. This is his last mission, thank the Lord. He`s in my squad and doesn`t want to do anything I ask him to do. I don`t want to get shot, so I`m leaving him the hell alone. That bastard almost got into another scrape two weeks ago, too, when we still had Lt. McQueen as our lieutenant,"

"That guy sounds a bit crazy," I interjected while opening a small can of peanut butter which had also been packed for me. "What happened?"

"Well, there`s two parts to this story," March went on, "a good part and a Smith part. Second Platoon was settling into our nighttime, and our lieutenant took Stinson, his r.t.o. (radioman) with him to do a little re-con of the area. McQueen said he had a bad feelin`, or something like that, so that`s why he and Stinson went for a looky-see. Anyways, they found this trail, about four feet wide, and they could see a hundred feet and more, in both directions. The one direction was going up and over a little hill, but McQueen said he didn`t think about investigating what was on the other side. Just as him and Stinson got off the trail and were heading back to the platoon, one of them, I don`t remember which one, said he saw a helmet coming over the horizon of that hill. It was an N.V.A. soldier. They scrambled to get cover in some thick bushes right by the trail, so as not to be noticed themselves. McQueen tells Stinson that they are going to kill that gook when he gets close enough. THEN, they seen a second gook coming behind the first one, then another, then another. Our guys knew they couldn`t get `em all. In fact, they had to stay real quiet themselves hoping THEY don`t get caught. Hell, they were just next to the trail in some heavy brush, and Stinson said he was scared shitless. When all them gooks passed, McQueen rushed back and called our captain, claiming he counted 137 enemy soldiers walking down the trail."

March was getting quite animated, but he didn`t want anyone else to hear what he was saying, especially Smith, who was going to be the eventual guy getting ripped in this story.

"So," continued March more quietly, after he looked to see that others WEREN`T listening in, "the plan was for us to set up an ambush on that trail the next day. Third Platoon was called to join us. We stretched out along the trail, making sure that no one could see us while we were in those thick bushes. Guys had to careful, too, because that brush had some really big thorn-like stickers that felt like needles when you moved into them. We all put camou on our faces, and got our weapons ready to destroy whatever was in front of us. It was an awesome set-up, man. The guys at both ends of the ambush had a claymore pointed down their end of the trail, and when the last gook in line was in the kill zone, the guy in the rear was to blow his claymore. That was to be the signal for EVERYBODY to fire at what`s in front of him. The plan was to shoot for ten seconds, fall back about twenty meters, and McQueen would move us fifty MORE meters in one direction, then ANOTHER fifty meters in a second direction, while the other lieutenant was calling in a Cobra gunship to clean up the ambush area. We were THEN to go back and see what damage we did after the chopper was finished doing his thing."

A soldier, named Rodrigues, came over to see what was going on. March looked up at him, but continued with his story. "So eventually those gooks DID come over that hill, and we start watchin` `em go by us."

"Oh, the ambush," chimed in Rodrigues. "Yea, that was something all right."

"This is Rodrigues from my squad, Sarge. He was in the thick of it, too," March declared.

I gave a quick nod toward the fellow joining us, and he sat next to his sergeant. I had been having such a hard time believing March`s wild tale. But when Rodrigues joined us, and HE seemed to be confirming that the story was true, I began listening even more intently.

March continued. "McQueen was the main body counter, but when he got to 87 gooks, those bastards stopped and decided to take a break....right on the trail....right in front of all us guys setting up the ambush."

I looked at Rodrigues, he nodded and said, "It was really scary, man."

"Nobody knew what to do," March rambled on. "We were all lying there, quiet as we could be, waiting for some kind of signal so`s we could open up on `em. That signal came real quick, too. See that guy over there?" March pointed to a tall kid, who I found out was one of several guys from Texas. "His name is Moriarity. He was In Country (Vietnam) less than a month at the time. Anyway, he was humping an M-60 machine gun. This gook sits down right in front of Moriarity, and decides to lean back...you know, to stretch out or something'. But when he leans his head back, it goes a little into the brush, and the bastard bumps his head on Moriarity`s machine gun muzzle. So then the gook sits up and turns around to see what he hit his head on. He spreads the bush and is face-to-face with the end of the machine gun barrel. As Moriarity tells it, 'the gook`s eyes got REAL big,' and when Moriarity seen THAT, he just pulled the trigger."

"Oh, man," Rodrigues said while getting fidgety, "all hell broke loose then."

"Yeah, that`s right," March went on. "We all thought that was the signal, and EVERYBODY cut loose with their weapons. The shooting lasted just a couple of seconds, and we all ran back where McQueen got us going in one direction for awhile, then another direction for awhile. It was crazy for certain. Then we heard the Cobra come in and let loose with his weapons. THAT was a beautiful sound, man. Finally, we returned to the trail and counted 32 dead gooks layin` there, and some blood trails headed into the jungle. Not a single G.I. was even injured."

"The Brigade Commander said that our platoons had done a superior job on a 'highly-successful mission,' as he put it. He was particularly proud of us for NOT having any American casualties. So he declared that all members of 2nd or 3rd Platoon, who took part in the action, and any men who join our platoons for one solid year of the action, will get a Presidential Medal. That means you get a medal, too, Sarge, for just bein` part of our platoon. And you didn`t have to do nothin` to get it. Ain`t that a kick in the head?"

Rodrigues interrupted, "Don`t worry, Sarge, you`ll get plenty of chances to actually earn that medal," and he got up and returned to his rucksack.

It sent shivers down my back thinking I may, during my tour, have to be in confrontations like March described. I have to admit, however, that I was a little more at ease knowing I was among some real warriors, even though I couldn`t help wondering how I would react to circumstances like the ones faced on that trail. I was also curious as to how a hero, even one like the much-maligned Smith, could have problems, especially after coming through such a successful combat mission. "Sgt. March," I asked, "how could Smith be labeled a trouble-maker? Seems like he should have been treated like a heralded member of this platoon, just like the rest of you guys."

"Actually, being a hero is what got Smith OUT of some deep shit," March explained. "We were sent to The Rear, in Long Binh, for a 2-day stand-down. Higher Up musta thought we earned the rest after getting such a high body count, or somethin`, cuz we had just been back there a couple weeks earlier after a LONG time in the Bush. That earlier stand-down was the one when Smith had caused the riot in the bar I was telling` ya about. Anyways, when we got to Long Binh, we found out McQueen was leaving, and Edwards was coming aboard. During our first day, Smith tells us that he was just walking back from the px, or some place, minding his own business, when he began passing by a 1st lieutenant and a new 2nd louie. The new guy, I guess, decided to make points with the 1st louie and he shouts at Smith, 'Hey, soldier, you`re supposed to salute officers when you pass them. What unit are you with?'

I had to get a little closer to March as he was practically whispering so nobody else could hear what he was saying….especially Smith.

The sergeant continued. "According to our boy over there, (and March nods toward Smith`s position in camp) that 2nd lieutenant was sounding real uppity when he was shouting. So Smith says he turned around and shouted 'Delta 4/12!' and he was about to give the guy the finger, when the 1st louie asked, 'Wait, did you say you are with Delta Company in the 4/12?' Then Smith answered, real indignant-like, 'Yeah.' Then that same lieutenant asked, 'Are you in either their 2nd or 3rd platoon?' Smith then says he just nodded in the affirmative. Supposedly, the 1st lieutenant says to the 2nd lieutenant, 'This guy`s a hero. His company just killed a bunch of N.V.A. soldiers in a very successful ambush. Just let him pass on his way. Good job, soldier.' But then, according to Smith, that 2nd louie couldn`t leave it alone, and he says to our hero, 'We`re letting you go this time, Smith, (getting the name off the uniform) but next time you walk by an officer, you salute. Do you read me?' Smith got a real serious look on his face right about then, and told us that he said to the louie, 'Fuck off.' Then he says he turned away and walked back to camp. Like I said, that`s Smith`s story, but it does sound like things he`d say and do. This is his last mission with us, and I won`t miss him one bit."

Sgt. March took several more minutes pointing out various platoon members before he went back to his own business. I looked around, still over-whelmed by the moment. I asked myself, 'How could a Jewish boy from a small college town….a boy who, up until one year ago, had camped out just once in his life…. who had fired a small rifle just once in his life, be sitting in a jungle, eating W.W.II c-rations?' Suddenly, I had no time to feel sorry for myself. Lt. Edwards gave us the order to mount up. We were on the move.

There will be plenty of time to describe any 'action' that I encountered. But I couldn`t do the jungle of Vietnam any real justice without describing the flora and fauna that surrounded me during my tour. Beautiful, strange and dangerous are the three words that pop immediately to mind.

It`s true that the predominant colors in the jungle are green and brown. After all….trees….duh. In Vietnam I was struck, at least early-on, by the differences between American and Vietnamese vegetation. I had never seen bamboo in the States, but patches of bamboo were everywhere we walked in the jungle. I learned that bamboo was a grass, and I have to admit that I was in awe at how high it could grow. I called it the grass of dinosaurs because of its tremendous size, and couldn`t understand how it could be related to the tiny blades of grass that I cut regularly at home. Bamboo looked like small, skinny trees, not grass. For truly TALL grass, that looked like grass, Vietnam had something called elephant grass. The individual blades of grass were quite dense, and I swear that the grass could grow to be ten-feet tall or taller. In fact, the density of the many blades of elephant grass made it difficult to see what was up ahead. It was found in jungle clearings and was easy enough to hack through, which meant it didn`t delay our movement. But it was just a simple grass, and didn`t afford any REAL protection from bullets. So we generally skirted around it, and stayed in the treeline which surrounded the clearings.

The denseness, yet compatibility of the FORESTED jungle truly amazed me. In most of the areas where my unit operated, the trees formed a triple-canopy. There were the shorter trees, not quite apple tree short, but very thick with branches and leaves. Very near the smaller, bushy trees were taller trees that reminded me of elm trees back in Iowa. These trees had somewhat thick trunks, and the first real branches began to sprout, a good ten or fifteen feet off the ground. There were plenty of leaves on the branches, too. Again, think about the average elm tree in America, and you get the idea of what this second level of tree looked like. It was the third type of tree that really fascinated me, however. These trees were huge. Many of them had VERY thick trunks with gnarly bases. They shot straight up, well past the other two types of trees. Some of them had a plethora of vines hanging from them, like trees I used to see in Tarzan movies. The crowns were very thick, also, and the many branches had all kinds of birds and monkeys taking refuge in them. Their canopies were so large that it seemed impossible for sun to reach the earth, yet all the trees underneath, as well as all the underbrush, seemed to flourish in the darkness created by the giants of the jungle. The trees by themselves were majestic and beautiful, and soldiers had no difficulty navigating through them.

The underbrush, however, was a different story. Not only was there poisonous undergrowth which reminded me of poison ivy or poison oak back in Iowa, much of the bushier shrubbery had thorns on them....long thorns. It was not uncommon for our pointman to be hacking his way through a portion of heavy brush, then begin moving on rather quickly, when another soldier in the unit would say, 'wait a minute.' Thorns just seemed to reach out and grab uniforms. With the hacking of the thick underbrush, and the pleas by soldiers to be allowed to free themselves from sticking vines, is it no wonder that the enemy could hear American troops tromping through the jungle, and have time to set up ambushes? The jungle might even have been fun to walk through if it weren`t for those damn wait-a-minute vines....and maybe the poisonous plants, too.

The monotony of the brown and green colors was rarely interrupted. However, every now and then our platoon would come across a beautiful patch of flowers, or even one big red, or white or yellow flower, which seemed to have mutated in the sweltering, humid climate. While all the soldiers seemed to like the change of color, Lt. Edwards REALLY seemed to appreciate the change of color, and would often-times give the platoon a fifteen-minute break near the colorful flowers. The lieutenant was a squared-away soldier, there was no doubt about that, but he enjoyed the beauty of the occasional change of color in the jungle, at least that is what he said. I knew he liked the flowers, but so did we. Not only did we get to rest, but the short break allowed soldiers to break out their cameras to immortalize the rare beauties on film. The lieutenant, in the mean time, would use the time to check out his map. I appreciated the breaks, AND his not wanting to get us lost, but I never told him that. So, Lt Edwards, I tell you now, thanks for the flower breaks.

To me, the animals that I encountered in Vietnam were even more amazing. We trailed elephants, had a juvenile tiger blow itself up one night when it tripped a claymore mine that we had set out for our evening security, and we even slept under a family of giant apes one night. The apes were interesting. We hadn`t seen any evidence of them when we first settled in for the night. We DID hear some rustling in the branches above us, but we attributed that to breezes that had come up when we were developing our nighttime observation positions. Suddenly, one of the guys happened to look up into a tree above him, and pointed in a very dramatic fashion, while not saying anything. There, not twelve feet above the soldier, sitting on a huge branch, was a very large ape....not a monkey, as we were told later, but an ape. He wasn`t the size of a gorilla, but he was plenty big enough to cause a stir in our encampment. No one said a word, just looked around in the trees. Two other larger apes were spotted, and a couple of smaller ones. It was an awesome sight, and nobody showed any real fear that these beasts might come down to the ground where we were. We all moved about our business very slowly, while keeping an eye upward. The apes were watching, too, but never made a move toward us. Night ascended rather quickly and completely. It was VERY dark that night in the triple canopy. As we awoke the next morning it also looked like the apes were rising, too, but none of them moved from their respective branches. They just continued to stare at us in the same curious manner as they had the night before. Silently we had breakfast, loaded our gear, and moved out of the area. About twenty meters from the camp, we all stopped and looked back. From our observation position we saw the male giant ape come down from his perch, and scour our former site. Later, as a few of us talked about the event, we speculated that the big guy was likely rummaging through our garbage, just as a human would do when coming upon an abandoned campsite. That was a different, almost fun, experience for me.

Monkeys, by the way, were spotted all the time, but soldiers didn`t have time to watch them when we were on the move. I did hear one story, concerning monkeys and American G.I.s, that turned out to be a tragedy. It seems a platoon of soldiers had just settled into their nighttime positions, when a racket was heard in the jungle. As it was getting dark, the noise was getting louder, coming from one particular direction, and moving toward the American encampment. There was loud vocalization accompanied by a tremendous din coming from movement of vegetation. It was not uncommon for the enemy, thinking they had superior numbers of men, to loudly make a bulrush toward an American unit in hopes of over-running the G.I.s; thus, killing everyone and securing many weapons. The timing of this supposed 'charge' seemed odd to me, however, since it is VERY difficult to see anything at night in triple canopy, and total darkness was apparently minutes away. Even the enemy needed to see what they were doing, right?

The American platoon wasn`t taking any chances, however, and instead of trying to decide WHAT was making the deafening noise, they opened fire at the on-coming disturbance. Quickly, the loudness moved away from the soldiers, but vigilance was maintained all night by every member of the platoon, in case of another 'attack.' When day broke, and the previous night`s noise was investigated, dozens of monkey corpses were found. It was speculated that a LARGE group of monkeys was moving quickly toward their expected nighttime sleeping areas, in order to avoid total darkness themselves, and the American platoon was right on their path. I know it was a story, and couldn`t be verified, and I should have felt terrible for the monkeys if, indeed, this was a true story. But the fact is, under the same circumstances, our platoon would have reacted in the same manner toward unexpected and threatening noise at that time of the evening.

Darkness and fear go hand-in-hand, but in that case, innocent animals suffered from the experience. Sadly, I didn`t feel much sympathy for the animals then, but now, over forty years later, I feel terrible about the deaths of jungle inhabitants caught up in warfare.

Mutations in hot, steamy jungles are not just restricted to plants and flowers. We encountered several strange-looking animals in the jungles of Vietnam.

One day we were walking through the jungle in our single-file formation, when I noticed that up ahead was a large, rotted log on the path we were traveling. Usually men would step on a solid piece of the log and jump over, or simply hop over the impediment if there was advanced rotting. I noticed, however, that each soldier, as he approached the log, would hesitate, look intently down at the log, and stride very widely over the wood.

When it was my turn to go over the barrier, I looked down at the hollowed-out, center part of the log, and there sat a HUGE, blue scorpion. It faired comparably, in size, to what I considered a regular lobster one might see in the tanks at seafood restaurants. But it was definitely a scorpion! Its tail was quivering, waiting for someone to try and step on it, but nobody felt the urge to get stung. Once we all crossed over safely, we moved on our way.

There was also the day that the platoon took a break in an area which was thick with bamboo. I happened to sit down on a small, grassy trail between two thickets, when I suddenly heard a strange sound. The noise sounded a little like a motorboat engine, so I got to my belly to see if there was a vehicle coming down that long, narrow trail. Apparently, none of the other guys were on the trail, though a couple of men told me later that THEY heard the weird sound, too. Not seeing anything rolling my way, I quickly scampered to my feet and broke through the bamboo brush, and found a place safe enough where I could get a good look at what was making that unusual sound. I was hoping that I was covered enough, too, so as NOT to be seen by the on-coming intruder. It turned out that there was no vehicle coming my way. What I saw was a robin-sized wasp moving my way along the trail. It was zigzagging its way toward me, and quite slowly, I might add. The animal moved like it owned the whole trail, and I was sweating pretty profusely when it passed my spot on the side of the road. I saw the tell-tale body, of the black and gold physique on a normal wasp, only this thing was almost a hundred times larger than what I might see around Iowa City. I quietly turned my rifle so that the butt end was ready to swat the beast if it was anxious to investigate me. Thankfully it continued on its way, and I finally took a breath. To me, it was just another example of mutations that could be found in the jungle.

Another day that fascinated me was the day that our platoon came upon a savannah of grass and smallish trees. The grassy part of the field consisted of waist-length elephant grass, and the trees reminded me of apple trees in Iowa, only these trees were not growing any fruit that I could see. What these trees DID have, however, were spiders, HUGE spiders, and each tree had its own large web, which was inhabited by one large spider. I didn`t count how many trees were in that area, but there were dozens and dozens of them. The sinister-looking spiders were green and every one of them sat directly in the middle of its web. When I say they were big spiders, it appeared to me that each beast was larger than my hand with all my fingers extended. The bodies were not overly thick, but the legs were very long. As for the webs, all of them had to be four to five feet in diameter, the biggest webs I had ever seen. Add the somewhat foggy morning that existed when we came upon the savannah, and I felt like I was looking at a scene out of a horror film. I was a little surprised at what some of my soldiers did to the spiders 'for fun'. Each of us had been issued a large can of insect repellent, which was in a spray can. When Lt. Edwards decided the platoon needed to take a 'break' in the area, a few of the guys took their spray cans, walked carefully to the webs, and sprayed a heavy stream of repellent directly onto the individual spiders. Immediately those animals began to shrivel up, and eventually they ended up the size of a penny. Seeing how tiny those long-legged, intimidating spiders got, made me wonder what kind of corrosive chemicals were in the cans of repellent that we G.I.s sprayed on ourselves all the time. I know my guys were just trying to have some fun, but I chose not to get involved in the antics with them. I didn`t stop the carnage, either. In retrospect, I may have thought those acts to be cruel, but I also had become hardened to the fact that cruelty happened in the jungle all the time. My real reason for not joining the other fellows was a more practical one….I didn`t want to waste my repellent on animals that WEREN`T bothering me. It was the mosquito that was my true enemy.

The repellent became VERY necessary for me to use each night. I can`t even tell you how much I truly despised the onset of dusk. For each night, as the sun descended, droves of blood-sucking mosquitoes came to our vicinity. They were large, hungry and relentless pests. Once our platoon had established nighttime positions, I would begin to spray a heavy dose of repellent over EVERY inch of my skin and clothing. Spraying as heavily as possible STILL didn`t stop the hungriest of mosquitoes, however. Those nasty animals would 'bite' right through my uniform from time to time. I knew that some of the flying demons were carriers of malaria, and I loathed getting even ONE bite. Once I covered my entire uniform, I would spray heavily on my palms and rub every inch of exposed skin. I closed my eyelids tightly when I rubbed my face, so as not to get the irritating chemicals on my eyeballs. Even though I tried to get repellent as deeply inside my ear openings as possible, mosquitoes would seek to get where I COULDN`T reach. The on-again-off-again buzzing in my ears was most annoying. I remember lying there in the peace and quiet of the darkness, when all of a sudden, I would hear the buzzing of a hungry mosquito trying to get deep into my ear canal. That would cause me to slap myself on the ear, which in turn created a brief stoppage of the buzzing. Seconds later, though, the ritual continued; silence, buzzing, and slapping, until the bastards decided to move on. It seemed to me, however, as the night moved painfully forward, the numbers of bothersome mosquitoes lessened….thankfully. I once thought that the mosquitoes were playing their little buzzing game as a kind of insect entertainment, much like soldiers torturing giant, green spiders. I HATED those mosquitoes!

As bad as the mosquitoes were, fire ants were considered worse by many soldiers. Here`s an example of what happened when one of my men encountered ants. One day, as our platoon was headed through the jungle toward a specific destination, a fairly new fella was chosen to walk 'point' for us. His name was Mitchell Evans, a skinny kid from the U.P.of Michigan. Sadly, no one had told him about what to expect if he got attacked (and that is the right word where fire ants are concerned) by the irritating little insects. As Mitch moved slowly forward, he carelessly brushed a cluster of leaves situated on a tree. He could have, and should have, avoided knocking those leaves around, for they were teeming with fire ants. He smacked the leaves carelessly, and instantly the colony of ants dropped onto Evans and began racing all over his body and clothes. Fire ants are extremely aggressive, and within seconds, they were biting Evans` clothes, AND his bare skin. Mitch let out a loud, 'DAMN' and started to rip off his clothes as he began moving away from that tree. Moving may not be the best word to use….RUNNING away from the tree is a better description. His clothes were flying everywhere, and he was slapping at ants with every step. Within mere seconds, Evans was stark naked, and racing through the jungle. Since he was the whitest human I had ever seen, it was nearly comical, watching him scamper everywhere….like watching a ghost-like presence in full flight through a very dark jungle.

The rest of us in 2nd Platoon had a brief laugh, but then came the serious business of retrieving Evans` belongings. I was one of several soldiers who took turns snatching the gear with long sticks, running several meters from the attack, throwing the articles on the ground, then running to a different part of the jungle to knock off any ants that might be flying up the stick to bite us. Once we believed there were no ants on us, we`d return to get another load. Where the clothes and equipment were pitched, other soldiers would go and look for ants. All insects found were stomped with much passion. Finally, when the articles was deemed cleared of intruders, they were taken back to Evans, who, by the way, ended up having red welts all over his body. This action lasted an hour or more, and several soldiers got at least one bite while in retrieval action. I got just one bite, but I DO know why the beasts have the title 'fire ants.' When I got bitten, it felt like a person had stoked a cigarette in his mouth and immediately put it out on my arm. It`s true, that nobody had ever actually put a cigarette out on my arm, it just SEEMED like a reasonable comparison at the time. Mitchell was finished walking point for that day.

Far and away, however, the most feared animals in the jungle were the snakes. Not a day went by without someone in the platoon having an encounter with a snake. The best way I can characterize how I felt about snakes in Vietnam is the belief that if there were only ten types of snakes in the country, nine of them would be poisonous, and the tenth one could squeeze me to death. I never saw a friendly snake while in the jungle.

About six months into my tour, I had a member of the platoon come to me and say, "Hey, Sarge, you better go talk to the new squad leader," and he pointed to Sgt. Fimbres, who happened to be a recent graduate of the N.C.O. Academy. "He`s playing with a two-step, and I think he is going to get bit."

Fimbres was a rural kid from North Carolina, and fancied himself a Davy Crockett-type outdoorsman. When I got to him, he was poking a small stick into a hole, which was located in an abandoned ant hill. "Watcha doin', Fimbres?" I asked while getting down to get a better look at the pokee.

"Oh, just having some fun with the little snake inside the hole," was his answer.

I stood up, and backed away a tad. "What you have there is a viper, Sergeant, a mean one, too. It is poisonous, slithers through trees, and is well-camouflaged with its green color. We call it a two-step snake, and for a good reason. If it bites you, you take two steps and die. The anti-venom for this little beauty is the only snake medicine that Doc carries because so many G.I.s get bit out here. I have no idea why it got into the hollow of this hill, but, Fimbres, I am giving you this machete, and you need to take one swift stroke into the hole, and nail that snake. Believe me, you don`t want it to bite you, or ANYONE here. OK?"

Fimbres looked at me with the expression of a pissed-off kid, while some of the soldiers sitting nearby snickered a little. I may have sounded condescending, but this young Tar Heel did believe what I said to be true, and he took a mighty poke into the hole. I think his anger at me helped him with the intensity of the stabbing motion he delivered. When the sergeant slid the animal out with the machete, it was missing its head. "Nice job, Sergeant," I said, while grabbing the machete, and returning to my resting place so I could get back to cleaning my M-16. I do remember muttering under my breath, in a disgusted tone, 'newbies' as I was walking away, but I also figured that I had gotten the lesson taught BEFORE we had to disturb our medic because of a snake bite.

There was another guy who made a lasting impression on me due to HIS encounter with a snake. The soldier`s name was Marvin Royster, who was a 19-year-old kid from a tough part of Gary, Indiana. I had learned that he was one of two people in our platoon who had been given an ultimatum by his local court system. He could serve out a court-mandated five-year sentence in a prison, or he could serve a two-year hitch in the army, which included one year in Vietnam. Royster was a quiet kid, and a decent soldier. He didn`t like being in the jungle, but did his job, like most of the rest of us. One day, about two months after Marvin had joined our unit, the platoon was given a fifteen-minute break so that Lieutenant Edwards could get his bearings straight.

We had formed a fairly tight perimeter due to the thickness of the jungle, and Royster had decided to take refuge behind a tree. As he was just getting settled on the ground, the young soldier leapt to his feet, and after shouting a string of profanity-laced exhortations, went racing into the jungle.

One of our M-60 machine gunners, by the name of 'Bluto' Donovan, was setting up in HIS position, located just feet from where Royster had sat. Bluto, so nick-named because of his uncanny resemblance to the cartoon character in Popeye films, suddenly took the steel pot off his head, and smashed it twice onto the ground, crushing the snake`s head. "What`s the matter with you, you big baby," Donovan shouted in Marvin`s direction. "You afraid of an itty, bitty worm?"

Our platoon just happened to have a 2nd lieutenant assigned to us from the army artillery division. His job was to be a spotter and bring in howitzer rounds to aid our unit should we come under attack. He was called a forward observer, and we actually had him on several missions. He also happened to be an amateur herpetologist, an expert on snakes and other reptiles....at least that is what he told us. He did carry a book with descriptions and pictures of many, many snakes that were native to Southeast Asia. After looking into his book, the lieutenant identified the 'worm' as a krait, a snake with poison related to the cobra. It wasn`t a striking snake, like the cobra, but would bite something close by and hold on until its venom worked on the victim, a similar action taken by coral snakes, as our forward observer told any soldier interested in listening to him. Royster hadn`t sat long enough to allow the krait a good bite, but that snake sure did cause him, and me, trouble within the following week.

After a two-week mission in the deep jungle, our platoon was allowed to return to my favorite firebase, Firebase Ivy. Let me explain what a forward firebase was in 1969-1970. Those places were smallish encampments, set-up in a jungle clearing, or sometimes near a Vietnamese village in the jungle. They all had barbed wire surrounding the perimeter. Inside the barbed wire, itself, were trip flares, meant to expose movement, if set-off by enemy soldiers trying to get closer to the base. Also in the wire were claymore mines waiting to be tripped. Several meters inside the wire were located bunkers, set up strategically to cover the entire perimeter. Each of the bunkers was a single room, large enough to house three soldiers, and the exterior walls were fortified by several layers of sandbags. The roof had layers of sandbags as well, to prevent mortars from penetrating into the room. There were two or three firing portals in every bunker, from which G.I.s could fire rifles and machine guns. The placement of the portals established a cross fire with the other portals in that bunker, and other bunkers located nearby. This 'cross fire' gave the soldiers an ability to cover every inch of barbed wire if the base came under attacked. There were NO dead spots in the perimeter coverage.

Usually, rifle platoons, like those in Delta Company, housed their mortar platoons in forward firebases, and our 4th platoon loved having permanent residence in Ivy. The mortar men built individual hootches, and lived in relative comfort. There was also a command building in camp as well as a mess hall. The latter had the capability of serving hot food, and that was highly sought by those of us living on c-rations in the jungle. There was also a shower, which consisted of a structure having a VERY large bucket-like contraption on top. It was kept filled with water, and the water was warmed by the sun. This afforded warm showers for all people in camp. To soldiers who tromped around in jungles most of their tours, these firebases were very welcome sites.

Firebases were also places that got re-supplied by battalion and brigade trucks which arrived by convoy from Long Binh, or other rear echelon sites. Water for drinking and for the showers was brought by tanker trucks. Food for the mess hall came by truck, too. In fact, any supplies needed to maintain the firebases arrived almost daily to these forward havens.

The foot soldiers, arriving at the firebases to get a few days rest, got things from the Rear, too. Especially sought items included mail and care packages sent from home by the solders` families. G.I.s got new, dry clothing, picked up more c-rations for the jungle, and loaded up with fresh ammunition. Like I said, the two or three-day stand-downs, spent at places like Ivy, were cherished by grunts.

The only down side for any in-coming troops was that they had to man the bunkers, and take nighttime security. Sleep was NEVER a luxury afforded soldiers in the jungle or in firebase bunkers. Securing the base against attacks at night was necessary, so comfort was a trade-off for protecting places like Ivy.

My job, as platoon sergeant in these forward rest sites, not only included security watch, but I also had to dole out jobs that were base camp specific. The least desirable of which was the burning of honey pots. NOBODY wanted to burn those pots. Dragging the crap collectors from under the outhouses, pouring diesel fuel on them, then starting the fire was a nasty job. It wasn`t hard to get soldiers to volunteer for other camp jobs, but burning honey pots….I had to be very diplomatic if I wanted cooperation on THAT job. Perhaps the worst part of cleaning out the crappers was that the air was constantly fouled by the disgusting smell of burning human feces.

I remember giving Royster the job for one of the days we were in Ivy. He seemed all right with it, and seemed to forget about the snake incident. However, when it was time for us to head back out to the jungle, a problem arose with him.

My rucksack was loaded and I was getting ready to head to the helicopter pad, when Lt. Edwards approached me. He said, "Sgt. Stein, word has gotten to me that Royster is refusing to return to the jungle. Something about him being holed up in a bunker, threatening to shoot anyone who tries to make him go back out to the boonies. Go get him. The choppers are here right now." And with that, the lieutenant whirled away from me and he was gone.

The bunker was easy enough to spot, as several mortar guys were gathered around it. Royster was in the bunker opening, holding his M-16. When he saw me coming he moved to the back of the fortress. "Don`t come in, Sarge. I`ll shoot ANYONE who tries to make me go back out there with all those snakes."

I got to the side of the doorway and hollered in to him, "Marvin, you do NOT have to go out to the jungle again if you don`t want to. I promise. But, if you refuse to join us, you will have to face military justice. The army will have no choice but to discipline you….and that could mean a court-martial. On top of that you will also have to face civilian consequences, too. You know, from your problems back in Gary. The jungle isn`t all that bad, Marvin, compared to what you will probably face if you don`t go. What do you say, grab your stuff and let`s go."

"I ain`t goin` out there, Sarge. I can do time. I ain`t afraid of dealin` with people. But I sat on a snake, and I can still feel that thing moving out from under me right now. I HATE that feelin`. Just leave me alone."

"Can`t do that, Marvin. I need to get you out of there and into the c.p.., and I gotta hurry `cause the choppers are needed elsewhere after they take us out to our mission. I gotta come in, soldier. Just don`t shoot me." I stepped around the corner with my hands in the air. Royster was as far back in the bunker as he could get, but he did have his rifle pointed right at my mid-section. "I don`t have my weapon, Marvin, but you have to come out with me. There will be no more jungle for you. Let me just get you out of here so I can get going with the platoon."

I lowered my arms and extended them toward Royster. "I need your weapon, Marvin."

Royster was shaking horribly, but he stepped forward and handed me his M-16. "Thanks, Marvin," I said, realizing that I was shaking pretty badly, too. We walked outside, and a sergeant from the mortar platoon was waiting outside.

"Sarge," I said to the mortar man, "this is Marvin Royster. He`s a good guy, but is a little upset right now. Get him to the c.p. and call the military police. They will have to get him back to Long Binh where he will have to tell them about his refusing to go back out to the jungle. He knows he will have to face some kind of punishment. If anyone has any questions concerning his story, have them get in touch with me in the field."

The sergeant took Marvin by the arm, and another soldier carried the M-16, as they proceeded to the c.p. I grabbed my gear and raced to the helicopters. Everyone was just looking at me. They knew where I had been. The choppers took off right away and Specialist Forth Class Nelson asked me, "How`s Royster?"

"Don`t know," I answered. "He won`t be with us anymore." I never found out what happened to P.F.C. Royster. Nobody wanted to hear from me, so I minded my own business.

One of the more entertaining troops in our platoon was Specialist Fourth Class Rodney Nelson. He was a big, strong kid from a rough neighborhood in Flint, Michigan. He carried one of the M-60 machine guns for us, but also had an easy way about him. He was liked by just about everyone he met thanks to his natural sense of humor. He could make me laugh with just a look, but he also said some very funny things at unexpected times. He quickly developed the nickname Sweeper, which he seemed to enjoy. The name came to him rather naturally one day when he said in his usual comical way, "The girls back home KNOW that I`m sweet AND purdy." Someone commented, 'If you`re sweet and pretty, then we`ll call you Swee….per.' Nicknames were given freely in Nam, and some of them weren`t great, but Rodney liked his instantly. To solidify that moniker, I can tell you that Nelson was also a great machine gunner. Nobody could lay down 'cover' like Rodney, and as one of his squad members said one day, 'Ain`t nobody sweeps a contact area like OUR Sweeper.' The double entendre wasn`t intended, but it worked for Rodney Nelson.

What I particularly liked about Nelson was his readiness to encounter the enemy. He was NEVER afraid to get into the thick of any action. Most of the platoon`s machine gunners carried three 100-round belts of machine gun ammo, and that is quite a load to haul. One belt was heavy enough, but gunners needed a big supply of ammunition if the enemy was encountered. Rodney carried four belts. To be sure we had the M-60 ammo needed in firefights, most of the rest of us carried one belt of M-60 ammunition, too.

Weapons that Rodney carried weren`t restricted to just his machine gun and extra ammo. He also carried a machete, a Bowie knife, and a 45-caliber pistol, a weapon which was usually issued only to officers. I once asked Rodney why he carried extra ammo and three other weapons. His answer was simple, "Sarge," he said, "if I go down, I`m goin` down fightin`."

Sweeper was kind of a complainer about things in general, though, but when he complained he had this whiney delivery that was down-right humorous. It was hard to take Rodney seriously sometimes, as his complaints seemed more funny than serious.

What made Sweeper complain more than anything else were the animals he contacted in the jungle. "Look at all these skeeter bites," Rodney said one morning as he awoke. "Why don`t you guys help me out at night and take your share?" Since EVERYONE had his share of mosquito bites, Sweeper`s whiney comment brought out a couple of chuckles. He had many such entertaining complaints, and I considered him a main reason that many of us got our days started on a lighter note.

One dark night, just as everyone had settled into nighttime positions, there was a commotion in Nelson`s 3-man observation post. Suddenly, Rodney blurted out, "Someone get this deer off me! He`s doin` the James Brown on my head!" Apparently, a deer-like animal had wandered into camp, and nobody saw it approach due to the extreme darkness. As the animal began leaving the area, it walked right on to Rodney Nelson....his head to be exact. And when the beast stumbled around, trying to get away from its situation, it took a couple more clumsy steps, right ON Sweeper`s head. After the animal was gone, Rodney swore it was a deer, but no one else could identify what it was. We all heard the racket, and Sweeper DID have two separate nicks on his head....one on the left side of his head, up in the scalp, and one rather nasty one on the right side of his chin. It was Nelson`s constant, whiney complaining about the incident, the next morning, that kept the majority of us grunts giggling for hours. Memories of Sweeper make me laugh often, even forty years since I last saw him. Thanks for keeping things entertaining, Rodney.

If there was one animal that caused Sweeper the most drama and us the most comic relief, it was the snake. Usually, when Rodney heard that someone, ANYONE, was near a snake, he`d move as far away from the scene as he was allowed. Guys may have wanted to tease him about his snake phobia, but he was so well liked, that even the cruelest of his platoon mates left Nelson alone when he ran from the area of any reptile encounter. However, there were two incidents with snakes that solidified making Sweeper Nelson a memorable, COMICAL character for me.

One day, as the platoon was briskly walking on a trail next to a stream, our single-file column stopped suddenly. Everyone knelt down assuming that our point man had found evidence of enemy activity in the area.

Let me say here that following fresh water streams elevated our chances of contact with unfriendlies. That is common sense. Every living thing needs water, and jungles don`t have plumbing. North Vietnamese soldiers walked trails for expediency, as they headed southward to join in the fighting, so being near water was a necessity for them. Our missions were to find and engage enemy soldiers. Walking trails, which paralleled water, gave us a very high chance that we would eventually find trouble.

Our platoon members were spaced appropriately along the trail that day, but since I was near the end of the file, I hustled to the nearest radioman to see what action was occurring up front. Lt. Edwards had gone to the front, then passed the word back to the troops. "There is a large head in the brush just ahead of us," he said. "There is a long and thick body extending from the head. Tell Peppleman to take extra care when he passes by."

P.F.C. Walter Peppleman was the smallest guy in our unit. He would serve as our 'tunnel rat' whenever we would come upon a tunnel. Because of his physical size, however, he was the usual butt of jokes involving smallness. I was quite surprised that our lieutenant used him in an attempt at humor, as our platoon leader was very serious most of the time. Peppleman was two men ahead of me in line, and he was visibly shaken as he scooted by the snake. Sweeper Nelson actually walked into the jungle to avoid any sight of the animal, but that didn`t work, and he gave an audible 'damn' when he saw what was in the stream.

The point man was told to 'move out' as darkness would soon be approaching, and we`d have to find a nighttime position. As I passed the snake, I was astonished at its size. It was apparently enjoying the late afternoon sun, as its head was in the trail-side brush, but its body stretched across the three feet of sand on our side of the stream, covered the entire twelve feet of stream, passed over the three feet of sand on the OTHER side of the stream, and continued into the brush. Amazingly, the largest part of its girth was lying on the water/sand edge on the far shore. We just happened to have the same artilleryForward Observer with us, who had identified Marvin Royster`s nemesis as a krait. He whipped out his herpetology book, and proudly announced that we had walked past a reticulated python. He then told everyone that the guesstimated length of the beast was at least twenty-seven feet. In a move that I didn`t expect, the lieutenant decided that the platoon would bed down for the night IN the stream bed, AND only 100 meters from where that snake had been spotted. Peppleman was teased mercilessly as a 'midnight snake snack' by just about every member of the platoon. Sweeper Nelson didn`t say a word. He was actually conspicuous by his silence, and everyone was surprised when he volunteered to be in the observation position facing, and closest to, the huge python. I was in that position, as well, and it became humorous watching Sweeper prepare for his particular spot in the sand. First he stacked up some rather large boulders at his site.

Then he locked and loaded two hundred rounds of ammunition for instant use by his M-60 machine gun. I watched him gently place his machete, Bowie knife, and revolver, near him. Then he practiced again and again to see how quickly he could grab any, and all, of his weapons, like a gun fighter from the Old West might have done preparing for a duel. When I approached him to discuss the order of watch for the night, Rodney said, "Sarge, you are lucky to be with me tonight. I will NOT be sleeping at all. I know that snake will move sometime, and if it moves this way, I will blow it to Kingdom Come as soon as I see it. Don`t worry, the Sweeper is on guard….all night"

I kind of have-heartedly argued with him, as I did mention how tired he would be the next day, and how difficult it would be to stay up for the whole night. The truth was that I KNEW Rodney would stay up, and I really wanted to get a good night`s sleep. True to his word, Nelson watched for that snake the entire evening, and the other soldier in our position (forgot his name) and I slept through the entire evening. Sweeper was wasted the next day, though. As for Peppleman, it was reported that Walter was up the whole night, too. This was one time when Sweeper DIDN`T have a physical problem with a snake. A couple of weeks later, he wasn`t so lucky.

It is important to note that we left the python alone. Unless an animal is making threatening movements toward a G.I., the rule of 'live and let live' is usually adhered to pretty strictly. Soldiers didn`t want to have trouble with indigenous beasts, and we believed if an animal was given plenty of room to go about its business, it would do just that. In addition to being humane, soldiers needed to move around the jungle as quietly as possible. Shooting at animals, or making ANY unnecessary racket, most certainly alerted all within earshot that Americans were nearby.

Platoon leaders attempted to find clear land to traverse each day, and when that occurred, the platoons walked quite quickly in the standard single-file formation. Proper spacing between each man was encouraged for safety reasons. There were times when a fast-moving platoon actually walked right into a surprised enemy force, giving G.I.s an unexpected, but fairly fought, firefight. However, when reasonably open terrain was not in the area, and machetes were needed to hack through thick brush, movement was slowed considerably. Those times created lots of unwanted noise, AND it caused grunts to crowd too closely together. Worst of all, if there were Viet Cong or N.V.A. troops in the area, well-organized ambushes were set up against the bunched-up American soldiers. This kind of situation was NOT good for G.I.s. Sharp point men were crucial for all platoons on the move through the jungle, and spacing was important, too.

Sweeper Nelson never walked point mainly because he was big and slow-moving, AND he carried a lot of extra gear. He just slogged along and would often move a meter or two out of line in order to allow those behind to catch up with the soldiers ahead. Even with his squad leader encouraging Rodney to pick up the pace, inevitably Sweeper would find himself becoming the last man walking through the jungle. When this occurred for any length of time, it became necessary for the platoon to take five-minute breaks, allowing Rodney to reunite with his squad. One day, as he walked last in line and just off the beaten path, the big machine gunner ran into a scary situation.

Usually, a platoon experiences commotion from the front of the column, but, occasionally, action can come from the sides and even the back of the single-line movement. As we walked fairly brusquely through light brush, there was a sudden and loud ruckus coming from the end of the line. Reflexes caused all the soldiers in the platoon to spin around while kneeling to the ground. What we saw was Sweeper Nelson, his usual two meters to the side of our column, hacking the ground ferociously with his machete. While everyone maintained a vigil for enemy activity, I quickly scooted to the rear to investigate what Rodney had encountered. I got to Nelson just as he finished whacking the ground for the umpteenth time, and what I saw lying there was a nine-foot, mutilated snake. We didn`t need a herpetologist to tell us what kind of serpent it was, Sweeper told us in his usual humorous way. It was a large cobra. With Nelson walking off the beaten path, he happened to step right in front of the beast. Suddenly, the animal rose into the air, with its hood in glorious display, and struck at our man. Since it was a fairly slow-striking snake, Rodney just took a large step back, dropped his machine gun, pulled out his machete, and thrashed the serpent three or four dozen times. I cannot emulate the whining rendition given by Sweeper, but as we formed a perimeter around Rodney and his snake, I was surprised that the enemy, from as far as one hundred meters, couldn`t hear the laughter created by the 2nd platoon. Think of the funniest comedian lines you know, and perhaps you will understand the comical delivery, and the near uproarious laughter that was created at that scene. It was typical Sweeper schtick.

Sadly, we couldn`t move from that spot for a good hour or more. Sweeper just sat under a tree, and mumbled, "Snake, BIG snake."

I would answer, "Yes, Sweeper, and you slaughtered it. We have to move out now."

"BIG snake," Rodney would continue to say. "And he tried to bite the Sweeper, Sarge."

"I know, Sweeper, but that nasty thing can`t get you anymore. You got him good!"

"Big snake, Sarge, BIG snake," Sweeper continued, and so it went until the lieutenant finally told me to get everybody up, as we had a destination to make by nightfall.

Dogs played an interesting part in Vietnamese living, at least back in 1969-1970. I can best explain myself with two short stories where dogs took center stage with me, and the Vietnamese people that owned them.

Lt. Edwards and I were invited to a village chieftain`s home one day for lunch. Our platoon had been assigned operations in and around his small village. We got the assignment because our Intelligence people became suspicious that there was a strong Viet Cong influence in the area. We were sent to verify if the suspicions had merit or not. In order to show the Americans that his village was, indeed, a friendly village, un-touched by V.C., the top man in town invited the two of us infantrymen for a nice conversation over lunch. The chief`s wife had cooked an elaborate dinner consisting of appetizers, salad, soup, and a main dish of meat stew with rice. There was also a dessert that I couldn`t identify, but I thanked the chief and his wife for everything, while telling them that it was a great meal. Remember, though, that we had been eating canned food left over from WWII, so just eating REAL food was great. I had also remembered going to Long Binh for a short stand-down earlier in my tour. While there, I had gone to the N.C.O. Club and enjoyed a wonderful water buffalo steak. So, when the lieutenant and I finished our meal, I innocently asked if it had been water buffalo that was served in the meat stew. The chief gave a grin and then a curt response, "No, dog." Suddenly, I had memories of all the loveable dogs I had as a youth, and with those thoughts came an instant queasy feeling in my stomach, and probably a somewhat distressed look on my face. I had heard that dogs were sometimes raised as a protein source in Southeast Asia, but had no idea that I would be eating one….especially since I was expecting the chieftain to try to impress Edwards and me with buffalo meat. On the way back to our unit, I mentioned to the lieutenant that I was more than a little upset that we had eaten man`s best friend for lunch. All he did was tell me that we hadn`t eaten in a New York deli, but, rather, a home in the Third World, and I needed to suck it up. That guy was always serious, I tell you. Then he said he`d eat snake if it got us better relations with the village chief. I guessed he wasn`t a dog guy.

A month after the 'stew' incident, I got involved in another dog incident. If I remember correctly, it was President Nixon who informed the American public that the troops in Vietnam were no longer involved with search-and-destroy missions. Focus was on something called Pacification. This term indicated that American soldiers were involved in collaborative missions with South Vietnamese soldiers, and militiamen from various small villages. I can tell you that while my company WAS involved in some collaborative work, we also had our share of search-and-destroy throughout my tour.

Mac-V was the branch of the army whose primary goal was pacification, and combat units, like the ones in the 199th, were called upon to assist from time to time. It was on one of those cooperative assignments that a dog just about caused total chaos.

That would be the time when five members of my platoon and I were sent to assist Mac-V with a company of South Vietnamese soldiers. Our assignment was to instruct on, then demonstrate, the correct procedure for clover-leaf reconnaissance patrolling. The soldiers had a compound next to a small village, and in the days prior to our arrival there had been evidence of enemy activity just outside the village and compound. Nearby villages had been experiencing some of the same unwanted movement and the local townspeople were frightened by the prospects of having the enemy try to control them. They wished for the Vietnamese soldiers to do more to insure safeguards from V.C. or N.V.A. infiltration, and a couple of Mac-V soldiers were sent to assist. While the pacification guys did what they could, they sent for a working, combat-hardened unit to show how

Americans work the jungles around any threatened area. The six of us felt that it would be a simple matter of showing the Vietnamese troops how to perform a correct cloverleaf pattern around the town. We expected to work half a day and return to our company before dark.

As 2nd Platoon approached the compound, I spotted a large Mac-V sergeant. He had his back toward us as we moved to his position. He was also staring at a big circle of Vietnamese soldiers, who were laughing and yelling quite loudly. From inside the circle we heard some atrocious yelping and squealing. "What`s going on?" I asked when I got to the massive sergeant`s position.

"Just some soldiers having fun," he responded while turning and greeting my men and me to the compound.

This is a warning to any of you readers who may be squeamish, or have an intense love of dogs. You may want to skip the rest of this particular story. I love most all animals, and the re-telling of this story makes me angry, but it is part of my military experience, so must be included in the book.

The sergeant commenced to tell me that the Vietnamese were entertaining themselves. When I looked more closely at the mob of men to see what they did for fun, I became horrified. Inside the human circle was another circle created by razor-sharp concertina barbed wire. The wire circle wasn`t very large, and there was a dog inside its perimeter. The animal was definitely being tortured. The dog`s owner was planning on having the beast for lunch, but killing the dog quickly and mercifully wasn`t the way he chose to go. Instead the soldier broke both the dog`s front legs, yanked them around to the animal`s back, and bound them with concertina wire. If that wasn`t cruel enough, the dog`s mouth had been wired shut so if it tried to yelp too loudly it would lacerate the outside of its own nose. That was done to minimize the loudness of the dog`s noise, which obviously wasn`t working. I couldn`t believe what I was seeing, none of my men could.

The Mac-V man continued his explanation of Vietnamese 'fun' by telling us that what we were seeing wasn`t the normal way dogs were executed for meal preparation, but this dog`s owner wished to 'have some laughs' with his friends. He finished by telling us that there were no bowling alleys or movie theaters anywhere near the village, so soldiers did what they could to enjoy themselves, and killing the dog slowly before preparing a meal was meant to be an acceptable form of fun.

I was sick, and furious, at the sight of the dog in trouble. I was particularly unhappy with both the sergeant`s explanation and with him for allowing that kind of behavior. I saw that poor dog attempting to flee his predicament and pain by rising on its two hind legs and trying to hop over the too-high, wired fence. Most of the time the animal would lose its balance and fall into the coil of one-inch barbs. It was, in effect, stabbing itself to death, and would either die from loss of blood or shock due to continually impaling itself. I wasn`t going to let either of those things happen. "I`m going to stop the senseless torture of an innocent animal," I announced to the big sergeant.

"Not a good idea, Sergeant," Mac-V said. "There are two things that Vietnamese soldiers will not tolerate, messing with their women and stopping them from having fun. They`re liable to shoot you."

With that being said, I handed my M-16 to Peppleman, who had been standing next to me. I took my bayonet out of its sheath and put a smile on my face. Sweeper saw me prepare to engage the Vietnamese and he took his machine gun, placed it on a nearby berm, then locked and loaded the first round of a 100-round belt of ammunition into the chamber of his weapon. A second G.I. with my platoon, named Carmichael, also moved to the same wall, and trained his rifle on the mob, too. I looked back at the other grunts in my unit, and that`s when I saw that Nelson and Carmichael had my back in a very real way. I began to move slowly and nervously toward the circle of noise.

The South Vietnamese soldiers saw me coming and appeared happy that I had a smile on my face. They didn`t seem to mind that I had a bayonet in my hand, and I`m pretty sure none of them saw Sweeper and Carmichael ready to help me out in case of trouble. I wasn`t sure I was going to be able to converse effectively with people that didn`t speak English well, so I decided to attempt reaching them through Pigeon English, which was a common and accepted way of communicating between locals and G.I.s. "Numba one chop-chop," I stated as

I arrived at the perimeter of the human circle, and pointed toward the animal. It was my attempt at indicating that I understood that Vietnamese enjoyed having dog for meals.

"Numba one chop-chop," was the response from one of the soldiers, whom I assumed was the dog owner. He had a big grin on his face. He quickly said, "Numba one fun," and that got a lot of laughing in agreement from the other soldiers standing there.

"G.I. think numba one chop-chop, numba ten fun," and my smile disappeared as did those of the dog owner and many of the other soldiers. They then knew that I was NOT happy with what they were doing to the dog.

"No, numba one FUN now, G.I. Numba one chop-chop later," the owner repeated, and suddenly all eyes were on me, and there was NO laughing. There was no doubt that everyone there was unsure how to act toward my statement. In the meantime, the dog had attempted to get over the wire and again landed heavily on the barbs. No one laughed when that happened, so I said, "Numba ten fun," I said while pointing at the dog yelping in extreme pain. "G.I. think numba one chop-chop, numba ten fun. G.I. kill," I continued while using a slashing move across my own throat while still pointing. "You eat," I finished while moving my hand from the slashing motion to an eating motion.

"No, no," the soldiers all said in unison.

I looked as sternly as I could at the owner, and ONLY the owner, "G.I. kill…. you kill….kill now!" I demanded, and I took a step toward the barbed wire circle and the terrified dog.

I saw the owner quickly raise his hand to halt me, then he took out a knife that he carried on his side. He stepped slowly over the wire, pinned the dog to the ground, and killed it. The suffering was over. I nodded at him slightly, but with the stern look still on my face. I pivoted and headed back to my platoon members. No one said a word, especially the big Mac-V sergeant. I knew that I could never work in a Mac-V unit.

The combined clover-leaf mission worked well enough, but I couldn`t wait to leave those Vietnamese soldiers, and the Mac-V fellas. Since we never heard that the village had trouble from any enemy forces, I didn`t think about that dog again. I DID, however, thank Nelson and Carmichael for covering me in my time of need. I realize I should have left the Vietnam culture alone, as Mac-V suggested, and I wasn`t thinking, at the time, about any incidents that could have arisen from my interference. However, the torture of an innocent animal was something that I just couldn`t tolerate. I was thankful the incident ended the way it did. I was also thankful that Carmichael hadn`t opened fire on the Vietnamese soldiers. I considered that soldier a loose cannon.

I don`t ever remember Carmichael telling anyone his first name. When he came to us he just seemed a bit 'off' in the head, so nobody truly wanted to get to know him. Though he came to us a month after Royster was gone, he came via the same route. The court system in Baltimore, Maryland offered him five years in jail or two years of military service, including one year in Nam. So 2nd Platoon ended up with him. Carmichael wasn`t as calm as Royster, and he would do things to offend anyone and everyone as often as he could. Most of the time, when anyone referred to Carmichael, they would just call him the Baltimore nutcase. He was crude in his behavior as well as his language. The first time he was with the platoon at Firebase Ivy for a two-day stand-down, he immediately got drunk on warm Pabst beer, then wandered around the base mumbling obscenities to himself. I had to share a bunker with him at Ivy because nobody else wanted to be with him when he was drunk. In fact, when he confided in me that all he wanted to do in Nam was to kill V.C. and N.V.A. soldiers, I didn`t want to turn my back on him either….especially whenever he seemed like he was in a foul mood.

Fortunately, he took orders well, and did what his squad leader, or I, asked of him, though much of the time we had to ask him to stop some kind of inappropriate behavior. For example, he`d make kissing motions and sounds when he was around Vietnamese women whenever we were in villages. He also had a nasty habit of either farting or belching when people tried to talk to him. He just had a gross personality, but I still appreciated the fact that he respected me enough to watch my back during the 'dog and barbed wire' incident.

IX

It Can Get Scary

While most missions assigned to my company were meant to find the enemy and eliminate him, during the last four months of my tour, we grunt platoons were ordered to work with the local people, and the South Vietnamese army, more and more. I didn`t always enjoy the experiences. The tortured dog was just such an awful incident. Thankfully, that was just a one-day assignment. One particular three-day adventure with our allies tried my patience nearly as much as stopping the 'fun' encountered during our day with Mac-V and company.

Lt. Edwards was asked to have our platoon hike to a small village, to help the people there protect themselves from nightly incursions by enemy soldiers. The mission seemed easy enough. We would work with volunteers, both townspeople and nearby farmers, by showing them how to set up nighttime ambushes using claymore mines and trip flares. There had, apparently, been an incident a short time before we were given the assignment, where ransacking by some passing N.V.A. or V.C. soldiers had taken place at night. A few of the marauders entered houses, took things they wanted, then continued down the road until they were out of town. American troops didn`t usually travel at night, therefore the lieutenant and I knew that any nighttime ambushes, set up by locals, would be encountered only by the enemy.

The lieutenant and I expected to show locals how to booby-trap the main road, which ran through the town. Twenty volunteers showed up on the first night, so Lt. Edwards took half of them and moved to one side of town, while I had the second half and moved to the other end of town. My men and I showed the volunteers how to 'salt' the road with the appropriate number of trip wires attached to flares and mines. Since darkness had come upon us very quickly, I was anxious to move everyone off the road and set up observation positions. Before I got anyone moving, the leader of the volunteers pointed out to me that none of them had weapons that fired bullets, only knives, clubs, and other weapons meant to be used in close-in fighting. He said that while they had learned much about setting up the ambush, he thought it best if his people moved further up the road where they could be safe if actual fighting broke out. He mentioned, too, that if the enemy was observed moving on the road toward the town, he would race back, without being noticed, to alert us. I didn`t feel they could get the full impact of what an ambush was if they were forty feet up the road, but since they didn`t have any useful weapons in case of a firefight, I agreed to have him and his men work as spotters. I told him to make sure all his people knew that two people should be awake at all times, and looking for movement. He grinned, and nodded, and they moved quickly up the road.

As they left, my eight men and I moved to the side of the road to establish our own nighttime positions. It soon became very clear that the land that we had available for ambush cover was actually a former pig farm. Sadly, we had been so intent on setting out the hardware, we hadn`t really looked closely at the land which would be affording us cover from the enemy. While we were setting up the tripwires, we all noticed that there was a stench in the air. However, we justified the smell by believing that much of the Vietnam farmland we previously encountered had animal odors, so it must be a normal circumstance for farms. Also, we had chosen to leave the village later in the day, and get our position established quickly, just in case there were V.C. sympathizers watching us. The less time informants had to get our plans to the enemy, the safer we would be. Once we had left the village, and found an ideal place to set up the ambush, we disregarded any smells, focusing on the task at hand.

Our main cover terrain was located right in a pig sty, which, coincidently, had hog deposits still littering the area. One or two of my men ended up stepping in pig crap, which resulted in accentuating the air with an even stronger foul-smelling aroma. None of us was happy, but we didn`t have time to move our site. We all felt that the locals likely knew where we were laying out our ambush, they just didn`t tell us. Then they used a convenient excuse to move away from the smell. I couldn`t wait to talk to the leader the next day.

It wasn`t the stench that I ended up talking to the Vietnamese about, though. Around 4:00 a.m., we heard a lot of chattering, and it was loud, too. Since it was still dark, and we knew that the volunteers were a good forty feet from us, the nine of us scrambled into combat readiness. Suddenly we saw all our allies headed back toward us, RIGHT ON THE ROAD! I jumped to my feet, hollered for my guys NOT to shoot, and raced to stop the farmers from tripping any wires. "Where are you going?" I asked with an exasperated tone. I spread out my arms like a roadblock and all of our 'observers' stopped and stared at me. The leader, who was the only one who could reasonably converse in English, came running to the front of the column.

"So sorry, G.I. Farmers go to farms, we go back to town," he said somewhat sheepishly.

"No you don`t," I said in an elevated tone, bordering on screaming. "Gather all your people right here, right now." He smiled at me and did as I asked. While I was doing my best to explain how they would have killed themselves if they continued on the road to town, my soldiers were slowly and carefully trying to take down the tripwires. I asked the Vietnamese to sit down and wait until the danger was over. In the darkness, it took much longer than normal to disengage the wires, and after an hour the farmers began to grumble rather vociferously about how late it was getting and how they needed to get to their homes. When the trail was clean, we proceeded to town to wait for Lt. Edwards and the other grunts. He and his men walked into town less than fifteen minutes after we did. No pig sty, but his scenario was eerily similar to ours, right down to the Vietnamese with him not staying at the ambush site either.

Our lieutenant talked extensively with the village chief and volunteer leaders that second day. When he gathered with us to discuss the second night he said, "The Vietnamese expect to help set up the ambushes, but not stay at the ambush sites. They do not want to confront the enemy in battle, just have the claymores go off and let the N.V.A. deal with their own casualties. Farmers say they will set up the wires at night, then leave. That will allow them to work their fields early the next morning. The townspeople say they will take down the wires as the sun rises the next morning. After they work with us tonight on the set-up, they will volunteer to act as our spotters again....down the road like last night. That way they can join us when we call them. They want to be able to help us take the wires down. They promise not to leave the area until we tell them to, but they are also asking that they be allowed to finish early tomorrow.... right at dawn, actually. Some of them are refusing to be there with us at all, saying they have to be at work before the sun comes up, and that they will learn from the others in their own time."

Carefully, on the second night, the indigenous people were allowed to set up wires to the claymore mines and flares. There were half as many volunteers the second night, but all that showed up seemed competent enough to be able to lay out a good ambush by the time nighttime came. By necessity, and because we needed more time to allow the locals to work the equipment, and because there were no farm smells in the immediate area, we were forced to set the ambush up within sight of the village. Several village homes could actually be seen from the site we chose. The volunteers moved further away from town, serving as forward observers, so to speak, and we settled into a well-protected area to wait, and hope, that the enemy would choose that night to try to enter the village. No one came down the trail, however.

Around 2300 hours that evening, we heard the distinct crack of an AK-47 rifle, which is the weapon of choice used by the N.V.A. and the V.C. We all mobilized to protect ourselves. Then we heard another round fire off, and P.F.C. Peppleman whispered, "Hey, that shot whizzed right by me." When a third and fourth bullet flew near us, muzzle flashes were seen from one of the homes on the perimeter of the village. Bluto Donovan was the M-60 man with us, and he quickly trained his gun on that particular house. When he indicated that he was about to 'blow away the entire wall of that V.C. haven,' I had to tell him to NOT fire. Sure we saw flashes of light, but we couldn`t be sure that the sniping was coming from that home alone. I also indicated that if we all started to blow that house away, there could be innocent people being held hostage there, or there could be collateral damage to other homes in the area. Since we had substantial cover from any sniping, I told all my guys to just lie low, but on alert, to anything else coming from the town`s direction. None of us slept, watching both the trail and the town. There were no more pot shots that night, but the next morning, after we showed the locals how to dismantle the ambush site, I took the English-speaking townsman assigned to us, and we headed for that home.

An old woman answered the knock on the door, and the interpreter told her why we Americans were there, and that soldiers were going to go through her house looking fo evidence of sniping or V.C. activity. She complained with a hideous, cackling voice, something like witches I had heard in several movies, but HE invited us to check the house anyway. Three of us entered her place and she squawked non-stop. The rest of the platoon members searched the perimeter of the home. All we found were two small elementary-aged children in the one-room shack. There were no weapons or any indication that there had been trouble with intruders the night before.

Our Vietnamese volunteer tried to calm the lady down, but they continued to have a rather heated conversation the entire time we searched. We saw her shaking her head vigorously, and moving her hands from side to side like she was shooing flies. She was NOT happy with him or us. Still, we went about our business, and we were thorough.

When the inspection was finished and we had gathered outside, while still listening to the nasty rants of the old lady, the interpreter told us what he heard from her, "She say no one there last night. She say she no know any V.C. anywhere. I also tell you we have no V.C. in this village. We try STOP enemy from coming to our homes, yes?"

My guys were disgusted with everything they heard. We did take four rounds of sniper fire. And we DID see where they came from. Bluto seemed most agitated when we went back to meet up with the lieutenant. "I swear," he offered, "if we get fired upon tonight, even once, I will flatten the area of origin, and I hope it IS that little home. No, V.C., my ass."

The lieutenant and I decided that the third night would likely be our last night to assist the locals with ambush set-up. We didn`t care if the farmers were going to set out the equipment at night, and the townspeople were taking it down in the morning. Those decisions would be theirs. But, on the third night and subsequent morning, we weren`t going to touch anything connected with the ambush set-up or tear-down. Unless we saw them screwing up royally, we decided to just observe. The South Vietnamese people had already had two nights of training, and it was time for them to show they could do things without American help. And so they did. The mines, flares and wires were set up slowly but carefully, and the work looked quite satisfactory. The taking down of the equipment went about the same. Both farmers and townspeople did well enough. I was pleased.

The one difference we made, on the third night of ambush, was the insistence that we have locals IN our positions with us. I had no doubt that we would have been sniped at a second time, and we made sure that anyone looking at us setting up also saw that the townspeople were staying right next to us….kind of like shields. The way I got our volunteers to do that was to indicate that if there was ANY sniping at our positions, my men would level the house, or houses, where we suspected the shooting to be coming. The interpreter and his buddies weren`t delighted with the idea, but they knew we would do what we said we`d do. There was NO trouble that third night.

The lieutenant and I met with the village chief the next morning who indicated that his people felt like our services were no longer necessary. He was confident that the town could stop any unnecessary incursions with effective ambushes. Both the lieutenant and I wanted to tell him that it might be best if we watched the townspeople operate one more night. We would wait in town while the trap was set, sleep in the area in order to assist the town if necessary, and then we would leave when the wires were removed the next morning. We WANTED to say all that to the chief, but we didn`t. The truth was that my guys and I didn`t want any more pig crap near us. We were a bit worried that sniping might take place if someone watched where we were setting up. And, quite honestly, we didn`t want to deal with cackling old ladies again. That is why I didn`t chime up about staying one more night. My guess is the lieutenant had had his share of negative circumstances, as well, because he didn`t say anything, either. We both just agreed with the chief, and returned to Firebase Ivy.

Working with the indigenous people, in pacification-type missions, wasn`t what I nor my men had been trained to do. We were combat soldiers. Fortunately for me, I never had another assignment working directly with townspeople in any village. However, I DID work near villages and with South Vietnamese soldiers a couple more times during my time In Country.

One memorable time occurred after I returned from R&R in Hawaii. R&R gave us a week to get away from the stress of the war, and mine didn`t come until I had been in Nam nearly eight months. By that time I needed to rest and relax. Coming back, however, only added to any stress that I was under.

Prior to my R&R, the company had been assigned to work near a town called Vo Dat. Firebase Alice was built just above the village, but it was small, so missions operated out of there daily. There were several other American units working near that village as well. The reason for the heavy concentration was directly related to the Vo Dat Mountains. There was a LOT of enemy activity in, on, and around those mountains. Off-shoot trails coming from the Ho Chi Minh Trail honeycombed the area, making most operations very dangerous. For the month before my R&R 'vacation,' 2nd Platoon had lots of contact with either the N.V.A. or V.C. Some of the firefights were quickly ended, some took agonizingly long to resolve. The Vo Dat area wasn`t quiet, that`s for sure.

For the last mission before I went to Hawaii, our platoon got a brand new 2nd lieutenant. However, when I returned from Paradise, I was informed by the captain that the 'new' lieutenant would no longer be with us. He left for personal reasons. In fact, I was also informed that until further notice, I would be the 2nd platoon leader. I asked, and was told, that there would be no bump in pay for my up-grade in responsibility. Apparently, the 199th Light Infantry Brigade was in the process of down-sizing and preparing to leave the Vietnam theater, so finding competent officers was a problem, and senior non-coms were asked to take charge. Units who were still expected to stay in Nam must have been given precedence for any new officers arriving for their tours in the jungle. I was more than a little upset that we weren`t in line for officer replacement, especially when the captain gave my platoon an immediate assignment outside our firebase. Worse yet, I was told that there was no time schedule for the mission to be complete. The other two infantry platoons were working missions originating from the base, but got to return every couple of days or so. The captain told me that the mission was cushy, and would help me to work slowly into my new platoon leadership role. That was hog wash, but he was done talking to me about the subject.

One hour after I had reported back from R&R, my men and I were taken, by truck, seven kilometers south of Vo Dat where we noticed a mortar platoon and an artillery unit already setting up shop just outside a very small South Vietnamese base. Since there were only about a dozen soldiers in the Vietnamese camp, I assumed that it served as a listening outpost and nothing more, though I never got the opportunity to find out. Arty and the mortar people were placing their weapons strategically in order to be able to pivot and lay down fire in all directions if the situation called for it. The heavy mortar tubes and 105mm howitzers were as close as they could get without interfering with one another. I don`t remember how many of each there were, but they were spread out more than I liked to see. Our job was to give nighttime security to those heavy-weapon units throughout the night. We were to stop sappers from infiltrating the perimeter and wreaking havoc.

Our encampment was set right next to the only major road leading from the Rear to the many firebases in the Vo Dat area. It was called a highway, but most of it was dirt road. Since the enemy knew that American bases could re-supply its soldiers by truck, which was the preferable method to helicopters, the N.V.A. 33rd Heavy Artillery Battalion moved some of its forces into the area. Their mission was to find suitable sites, every other day or so, and ambush the American truck convoys. It may have only been 47 miles, approximately, from the Rear to Vo Dat, but the last 21 miles afforded great ambush sites. The area where the mortars, artillery and my platoon were located could look down a long stretch of straight road with heavy elephant grass on either side. The grass then extended approximately forty meters in both directions until reaching the jungle tree-line. The enemy had used that particular area on a couple of occasions to make hit-and-run ambushes, as the grass allowed foot troops to get close and open fire. While retreating, the 33rd`s artillery would give those troops support from the thick jungle. The American mission was to stop ambushes in the area, and since we had the high ground, we could see most of the road for nearly half a klick. (kilometer)

When my 16-man unit arrived at the site, it was after nine in the morning. I worried about our late start, but my men got right to laying all the barbed wire and installing wires for the appropriate amount of claymore mines and trip flares. I wondered briefly about the fact that no one came to greet us, but the thought was gone as soon as I realized how judiciously we`d have to work in order to be finished and prepared before darkness set in. Within three hours of our arrival, however, the precious time was interrupted. A small helicopter landed just on the other side of the road, and a good twenty-five meters from the wire we had in place. A one-star general hopped from the Loach, and looked around for a greeting party. Our camp`s command hootch, which had been hastily put together by troops from both mortars and artillery, suddenly had some very animated action around it. Two 1st lieutenants, whom I hadn`t seen since my unit got on location, came racing from the hootch door and headed straight toward the copter. They snapped to attention and saluted the general. After a short discussion, all of the officers moved toward the command post. It is interesting to note that the command post was put together with supplies sent specifically for hootch construction….not ONLY for a c.p., but for all the artillery and mortar soldier shelters, too. The infantry sent nothing for us to build anything. We were only prepared to lie in the open with no protection from the heavy monsoon rains which happened to be in full force during that time of year.

The officers hadn`t been inside the command center for more than two minutes when a member of mortars came to my work location. "Sergeant, I was sent to have your platoon leader report to the c.p. Where will I find him?"

"I`m the platoon leader," I said, though I still had trouble believing that was my new title.

Without showing his surprise at my answer he continued, "Anyway, the general wants to see your platoon leader right away," and with that he was gone.

Carmichael, who was working with me to set out perimeter wire, looked at me in disbelief "That prick wasn`t listenin`, was he?"

"Naw," I answered while grabbing a shirt to put on. I had to cover up the peace medallion I was wearing around my neck. Then I un-rolled my pant legs so I wouldn`t show the general the shorts I had formed. The monsoon season brought incredible heat and humidity, so many of us stripped down as much as possible to cope with uncomfortable daytime weather. I ran to the c.p., and when I entered I reported to the general with the military correctness that officers expected.

"Sergeant, are you the infantry platoon leader....in charge of perimeter security?" the general inquired.

"Yes, Sir," I stated with sincerity.

"OK," he said without showing any reaction to me being a non-commissioned officer, "Show me what you got."

It was pretty clear to me that the general was well aware of the brigade downsizing, so my being the platoon leader didn`t really phase him. I did, however, get quizzical looks from both lieutenants.

I walked the officers around the perimeter, showing them some of our finished wire. What they saw was an intricate overlay of strands of wire, with strategically placed trip wires attached to flares and claymore mines. I let them know that we would work until darkness, and would likely need a couple hours the next day to finish the entire perimeter. I received no response from any of them. When I showed the officers our proposed nightly observation positions, the general looked at me and gave me a nod and a wink of approval.

Once inside, the general got right down to business. "Your wire looks good, Sergeant, and your lines of fire look fine, too, but are you sure you have sufficient troops to cover the entire perimeter adequately?"

"I will have my M-79 guys ready with shotgun shells to cover our biggest areas of distance between o.p.s, and I`m placing our three M-60s in those same positions, along with one rifleman. That firepower will maximize the coverage of our largest distance between all the o.p.s," I said confidently. "We will have our medic in a four-man position with my best marksmen, and I will have two tremendous fighters with me, too. We can do the job, Sir," I said with pride. I also mentioned that I would be trying to get a few more troops with us in the coming days. I did know that we really needed six o.p.s to effectively cover the large perimeter, but I wanted to let everybody in the room know that we were a capable platoon.

The general turned to the 1st lieutenants and declared, "This will sound highly unusual to you two, but I have a necessary decision. Being an infantryman myself, I know this man (and he pointed at me) is here for one reason, to save your butts in case of military action directed at this camp. Your mission, lieutenants, is to stop ambushes from occurring on that stretch of road out there. Therefore, until further notice, Sergeant Stein will be base commander. You do nothing inside, or around this camp, without checking with him first. He has the last say. Is that understood?"

It was so quiet for the next few seconds, we could have heard a pin drop. I was surprised at the decision to put me in charge of the base....the lieutenants looked stunned. It must have really galled them, being experienced 1st lieutenants, to have to answer to a sergeant. To their credit, however, they both responded with a, "Yes, Sir."

The general looked at me and I quickly responded, "Yes, Sir. Without further ado, he whirled around and headed to his helicopter. The two lieutenants were right on his heels. I headed back to Carmichael`s position while taking my shirt off.

I had no real idea what it meant to be in charge of a base, but within the next two hours, I had my first encounter with the concept of 'who`s in charge.'

My men and I were working hard at getting the barbed wire in place when we noticed a South Vietnamese soldier, riding a scooter, come down the road from Vo Dat and turn into our encampment. He had a woman on the back of his vehicle, and he headed right toward the c.p. Since I was a good distance from him as he entered, I was a bit concerned that none of the guys from either mortars or artillery stopped him from going into the command hootch. In fact, those guys had just the opposite behaviors as they acted pleased that he was there. I was too busy to worry much about the lieutenants` safety, so I paid no heed to the stranger in our midst.

Within fifteen minutes, word got out to me that this 'scooter soldier' had brought his wife in with him, and that he was offering her services to all interested G.I.s for $20 per soldier. Not only that, but all the action was to take place in the c.p.

I looked at the lieutenants` hootch and noticed several mortar and artillery guys forming a line outside the entrance. I raced toward the mob as quickly as I could, and saw the Vietnamese soldier parking his scooter on the side of the building. "Hey," I yelled at him, "what are you doing here?"

He looked at me, rather indifferently, and said, (excuse the language here, folks) "Numba one fuckee, fuckee," and he pointed to the woman who was standing near him. "Twenty dolla….all the G.I….in here," he said while patting the side of the command post wall.

"No," I said as I was shaking my head. Suddenly some of the mortar and artillery fellas came to see what the commotion was about.

"Dah wee say so," he said rather indignantly. Dah wee was the term used to indicate 'leader' to the Vietnamese.

"I`m dah wee," I responded as I heard the murmers of the soldiers who had begun to surround us.

"You tee wee," (meaning underling) he declared and then he pointed to my hat with my E-6 stripes.

I looked at the increasingly restless group of soldiers and said, "Let`s settle this right now. Somebody get the lieutenants and have them come here right away." There was a call into the c.p. and both lieutenants emerged. "This guy thinks he can prostitute his wife for $20 per soldier, and he also thinks she can work out of the c.p.," I said in an irritated voice as they approached me. "I told him he couldn`t."

One lieutenant spoke up rather haughtily, "We do this all the time when we settle into some location for a while. The men have come to expect the service, Sergeant."

"Not gonna happen here," I said showing even more agitation in my voice than before.

The gathering soldiers were starting to get a bit boisterous upon hearing my statement, so the second lieutenant spoke up. "We don`t want to have a rebellion here, now do we, Sergeant?" And he TOO talked to me in a huffy tone.

The Vietnamese soldier looked at the two lieutenants and queried, "We do this, yes, dah wee?"

I then said rather emphatically, "You tell this guy that I`m the dah wee of the camp, and not either of you."

To say the lieutenants were upset is an understatement. Their faces grew red with anger, and both of them seem to be snarling. I can`t say I blamed them, for they did out-rank me. But if the general put me in charge, it was high time that everyone realized that. One of the lieutenants pointed at me and weakly said, "He`s dah wee."

If you can imagine cursing like one hears nowadays among junior high kids, then you know how the mortar and artillery personnel responded to the lieutenant`s statement. A huge look of surprise appeared on the Vietnamese soldier`s face, but he immediately began to try to convince me of his wife`s sexual prowess, suggesting that I would be first in line.

Both lieutenants were getting loud complaints, and Carmichael, who had come with me to the c.p., looked at me and shrugged his shoulders. Finally, I raised my voice above the din and said, "HEY! HEY! HEY!" and the noise subsided while everybody looked at me. "I understand that you have come to expect certain things while in a long-term setting. I am not looking for any trouble. But the general has put me in charge, even if temporarily, and I will try to make this happen. But it will be on my terms, or I send this guy packing." Suddenly, a large group of men had gathered around me, and everyone wanted to hear what I had to say, but there was still some low grumbling.

I turned toward the Vietnamese soldier and let him know what I had in mind. "I will NOT allow anyone but Americans inside my perimeter, but I saw a shady place over near that bush," and I pointed to the east about 30 ft. beyond the wire. You can have your wife work there, BUT no one will pay more than $5.

The husband raised his voice as he responded to my statement. "Five dolla no good! She numba one!" He continued in the same vein of ranting until I raised my hand.

"It`s $5 or she won`t be servicing ANYONE here. AND, today is the only day she will be allowed to work while I am in charge. If you want to make any money this afternoon, you will do as I say, or you can leave right now."

It got quiet as the soldier first looked at me, then the two lieutenants, then his wife. She nodded to him. "You rob me, but we go to bush."

"Five dollars, and we only see you here this day, no more, right?" I said, ending my conversation with him.

He nodded, they both got on the scooter and headed for the shady bush.

The mortar and artillery soldiers made a beeline to the bush and lined up. I asked the lieutenants to accompany me to the bush, I had one more demand, and their men may not like it. I sent Carmichael to round up the 2nd platoon to join us. When practically everyone in camp had come to my position, I stated loudly and clearly. "I did not ask to be in this position, but I am in charge of this camp right now, and that is the way it is. Everything done here under my command is my responsibility, and I want to make myself perfectly clear. My men and I have NEVER been in this kind of situation, involving a prostitute, since we`ve been in Nam. You guys have. Some of you may have a disease. I wouldn`t know about that. SO, I will have MY men get to the front of the line if they want to do this thing. None of them have anything nasty. That I DO know. Also, if any of you develop a problem while we are in this base, we have a great medic, and he has supplies to help you out."

Obscenities burst forth, and statements of 'you s.o.b.' and 'you can`t do that' came cascading my way. I raised my hand again, "LISTEN…. I don`t know you soldiers, and I can`t take a chance one of my people gets sick because of any of you." Again, curses and catcalls flew my way….kind of reminded me of when I stopped line-cutting in Basic Training. "MY guys go first, or she is sent packing…. your choice," and I waved to my platoon to move forward. "Any of you that want to do this, it`s your choice. Just get it done quick and get back to work. We still have a lot to do. I`m married, so I won`t be partaking. All right, line up and let`s get this over with." Carmichael was first in line, and while the rest of us endured some more vocal wrath, the Vietnamese husband told my man to go behind the bush. We only had a total of seven men get with the woman, but even that was more than I thought we`d have.

I then went to the lieutenants and said, "I don`t know if this IS something you normally do, Sirs, but I am pretty sure the general would not want to hear about it. You just make certain there is no trouble in this line. I was drafted, but you guys look like lifers to me. A bad report from here to Higher Up might not be so good for your careers." They gave me a 'if looks could kill' look and I walked away knowing that the 'draft' remark hit a sensitive spot with both of them. They stayed and controlled the line. I went with my men and we continued working on the perimeter.

The Vietnamese only had to work three hours, then they were gone. She must have been good, for she serviced over thirty guys in that time. I had no more trouble from anyone in mortars or artillery. Sadly, though, several days after the 'encounter' one of those guys approached my medic with a 'drip' and had to have our doc treat him. I never talked to the lieutenants again either, but plenty more went on during our twelve-day assignment at that location.

As infantrymen, my platoon and I were used to traveling someplace different every day before bedding down for the evening. During the monsoons we`d try to find large trees in the jungle`s triple canopy, not only for maximum protection, but to help minimize how much downpour we had to endure. Forward firebases afforded bunkers for shelter when we were to spend more than one night in a single place. This NEW base was going to be different for us. There was no overhead cover. We had no materials to make shelters of any kind, either. Both mortars and artillery were used to that kind of set-up and always built hootches immediately upon arrival to any new destination. They had arrived the day before my men and I had, and seemed very comfortable watching us on the perimeter when the rains started that first evening. And it poured! The nighttime was lighter than usual because of the lack of tree cover, but the dark clouds and heavy rain only allowed us to see things that were literally ten or fifteen feet from us.

As a matter of fact, where I operated in Vietnam, foot soldiers rarely had overhead cover like, say, pup tents. But that was for a good reason. The high profiles presented by tents, or any man-made overhead structures, had to be eliminated when we slept in the deep jungle. Grunts wanted to stay as low to the ground as possible in case the enemy suddenly appeared in their area. It`s also true that since infantrymen carried everything on their backs, about the only items they humped, which helped them be more comfortable in nighttime positions, were rubber mats to keep them from lying in the dirt, and poncho liners, which they used to keep themselves warm and to keep the rain from directly pelting their clothing and faces during monsoon seasons.

When night descended that first rainy night, I had a devil of a time getting to sleep. After all, I had just returned from R&R, been sent on a long-term mission where a general put me in charge of a base that had two 1st lieutenants already in camp, AND my men and I had tried to construct a safe perimeter, during which time I had to fight with just about everybody over a prostitute wanting to use our base as a brothel. I did indeed have one or two things on my mind when I lay down to catch forty winks. Compounding my sleeplessness was the torrential rain pounding me while I curled up in a fetus position under my poncho liner. I felt like I was just about to slumber off when I heard Bobby Jim Spiker, a young kid from somewhere in the boonies of Texas, talking into my ear through the liner, "Hey, Sarge, it`s your watch," he said. An hour had passed in what seemed like a minute, but I arose from the liner, and saw Bobby Jim looking up at the sky. "You know, Sarge," he continued, "if it don`t rain tonight, it`s gonna miss a good chance."

His slow, down-home delivery of that country phrase, took me away from my stress instantly. At that moment, I believed those words from Spiker to be the funniest comment I could ever imagine hearing, and they came at a time when I needed something to help me forget the awful day I had just endured. I started to laugh and laugh. Bobby Jim looked at me with his usual dead-pan expression, then grabbed his poncho liner, flopped onto his rubber mat, and disappeared. I giggled for my entire hour of watch, and still had a huge grin on my face when I woke Carmichael up for his watch. I would like to thank Bobby Jim Spiker right now, for helping to relax a man who was about to lose his mind.

When the sun arose the next morning, my platoon took about an hour to finish the wire and its 'gifts,' then we focused on our secondary responsibility at the base....setting up a roadblock. Since we knew there was a lot of V.C. activity in the village of Vo Dat, we also knew that the enemy had to get re-supplied any way they could. The main highway was the most logical point of entry. We searched every vehicle and all people heading toward Vo Dat on that road. P.F.C. Carmichael turned out to be an enigma at the check point, however. And I ended up removing him from that particular duty before the morning became noon. While his commitment to the job wasn`t the issue, his actions became questionable. Here`s what happened.

A bus was the first vehicle that rolled up for inspection. Peppleman wanted to just board the vehicle and walk through it for a quick eyeball search. Bluto Donovan, the third man on the three-man unit at the time, was all right with Peppleman`s suggestion of strolling through the bus. Not Carmichael. He stopped our tunnel rat from boarding, walked up the steps, and ordered EVERYONE off the bus. As his two partners searched the bus itself, Carmichael started to pat down each and every South Vietnamese citizen before they could re-board. A ten-year-old kid was spotted hesitating when it became his turn to be frisked, so Carmichael grabbed him roughly and gave him a thorough check. Voila, twenty vials of penicillin were discovered strapped to the boy`s back. I called our headquarters in Vo Dat and the captain sent a jeep to get the boy and have him returned to the village for interrogation. Carmichael was praised by all of us for his actions.

That praise didn`t last very long. Ten minutes after the jeep took the kid away, a dilapidated car rolled up. Carmichael ordered the occupants to get of the automobile, and out stepped six people, four elderly males, one elderly female, and one teenage girl. The older five folks were given the quick, once-over pat-down and they seemed fine with that. But when Carmichael decided that the girl might be a sympathizer for the V.C., like the boy he had discovered, he went overboard. First, he patted the teenager on her back, giving the butt area a few extra pats. Then he decided she must have been carrying something important on her front, so he proceeded to literally 'feel her up.' She let out a scream, which caused me and several other soldiers to race to his position, weapons at the ready. It was a disgusting use of power, and after some prolonged apologies, the car was sent on its way. Carmichael thought it to be somewhat funny, for some reason, but I told him that if there was another complaint from any female, I would have to relieve him of check point duty. I continued by telling him that I really didn`t want to embarrass him, especially since he had done something positive, but that I`d have no choice. I finished by letting him also know that I had heard some positive comments from some of the fellas in the platoon, and that was a good thing. But, since I was upset with him I may also have said some things too bluntly. I eventually told him that he needed to change the image many of the soldiers had of him as a loud, gross, trouble-making, crazy kid from Baltimore. I suggested that he just develop into a regular grunt, doing his duty WITHOUT drawing attention to himself. I actually felt good after my lecture, rant, counseling, I don`t know what to call it. And I felt like I had reached Carmichael when he nodded in the affirmative and went back to be with Peppleman and Donovan.

A second vehicle, then a third passed through our check with no problems. Suddenly, there was some very loud caterwauling coming from a van that had arrived. Once again I raced to the roadblock, this time to a woman pointing at Carmichael and claiming that he had put his hands all over her....everywhere! She was livid. Peppleman and Donovan told me that they didn`t see Carmichael when he was with the girl, but I knew what I had to do. Again, there were sincere apologies from me, and the van took off toward Vo Dat. I pulled Carmichael aside and let him know that I didn`t have time to address every screaming woman he decided to molest. I had finally come to realize that he was a total misfit in social settings, and that I had to keep him away from women. Certainly, he was angry when I informed him his checkpoint days were over, but the move worked out fine for the platoon. We had no more real complaints about searches over the next eleven days. AND the grunts who did work the checks were very thorough, doing so without over-familiarizing themselves with anyone. We found no more contraband either.

Carmichael, as good as he was in the jungle, was a disaster in our little base, too, no matter where he was. He became prominent in two other events during the days after his demotion, that`s for sure, but those stories come up a little later.

Once the original checkpoint had been set up, I gathered up the rest of the platoon and decided to send three patrols out to do basic cloverleaf reconnaissance, with each extending at least fifty meters from the perimeter. None of the patrols returned until after the first checkpoint fiasco, but they all came back with some distressing news. Human activity had been discovered as close as twenty meters to our base. Matted grassy areas, accompanied by empty sardine cans meant only one thing to us....either the V.C. or even an N.V.A. unit had been out there in the rain, spying on us and trying to detect exactly where we had placed our positions within the wire.

I radioed our captain in Vo Dat with the news. Captain Mertz was the third captain to command our company. I got to know him best of the three, but I really didn`t like officers in general, therefore I never got too close to any of them. He had come to Delta Company just prior to my taking R&R. Since he ordered my platoon to form our own little base protecting mortars and artillery, I only remember having one mission with him, and I wasn`t happy with his leadership then. I knew we needed help with such a big perimeter, and I was relying on Mertz to get me that help. But when I reported my patrols` findings, he was very curt in his reply, "Monitor the situation for the next few days. You can handle it, Sgt. Stein." That was it. He had no other words to say, but I had a terrible feeling in my gut which made me believe that the test for us to 'handle it' was going to come sooner rather than later.

The second night brought the heavy monsoon rains once again. To make matters worse, arty and mortars had started accumulating garbage, which ended up not far from my o.p. And it had begun smelling up the area. I had never been in a situation where we had days of collected garbage, but common sense told me that the rotten smell of so much food would eventually bring critters in to investigate the horrible aroma. I was right.

After my first 'watch' I quickly got to my mat, scrambled under my poncho liner, and because the rain was so heavy at that moment I pulled the liner over my head. Suddenly, I thought I felt a movement against my leg….under the poncho. I bolted upright instantly and lowered the liner. Immediately, an animal crawled up the front of my shirt and sat on my shoulders. It may have been dark, but I could still make out the form of the largest rat I had ever seen. To make matters worse, the beast bent down and started licking my moustache. That`s right, I said the thing bent DOWN before starting to lick! That rodent was huge. I yelled out loudly, "RAT!" and swatted the monster off my shoulder. An aside here….to this day, when I think of the horrible moment when that licking was done, I can still feel the sensation of that animal`s tongue on my upper lip!

After my shout, the rest of the guys in my o.p. quickly sat up and looked at me. I explained what happened and all of us searched the area….no rat was found. We actually stayed awake for hours, with bayonets in our hands, but that beast didn`t return. The next morning everyone in the platoon looked for big clubs. All o.p.s found suitable ones, and everybody was prepared to look for rats INSIDE our perimeter as well as watching for enemy activity outside the wire.

In the early afternoon of the third day, I ordered ALL garbage to be taken seventy-five meters from our base and placed in a heap. We also placed a large sign stating that nobody was allowed to rummage around in the pile. Mortars and artillery agreed to take their garbage out, too, but neither of those groups was too worried about rats. One of the groups had a dog that they had trained to be a 'ratter.' The canine walked their area all night long looking for varmints. The second group had a mongoose trained to do the same thing. Both of those animals slept most of the day. We, the infantry, only had our clubs, but we were ready to engage any wild animal that came into our area during the nights.

I hadn`t thought about moving the garbage until I witnessed an event that happened while we were eating our c-rations for lunch. The garbage pile near my o.p. was the main drop-off for most of the guys when they had finished eating. While we grunts were eating, a couple of fellas from mortars (or artillery, I don`t remember which) brought the mongoose over to our position so we could see what one looked like. While all of us were talking, the mongoose decided to take a nap. Suddenly, a huge rat came scurrying into the camp and raced directly to the garbage pile. The mongoose caught a quick glimpse of the beast and immediately rose to its feet. In a split second the weasel-like guard animal bounded into the pile, and all hell broke loose. Garbage was flying everywhere! The two animals rolled round and round trying to get the better of the other. All of us were cheering the mongoose on, and I had a club in hand just in case the giant rodent bested the smaller mongoose. Several minutes passed before there was a stoppage of action, and the mongoose had the rodent in its mouth. The dead rat was heavy, but the determined mongoose was dragging it away from the garbage. It ripped and tore into its prey to the cheers of all of us who were still finishing our meals. We actually took THAT as entertainment. When lunch was over, the garbage was removed from camp.

The new trash site hadn`t been in place, nor the sign put up, for even fifteen minutes when children moved onto the trash pile. They were kids who walked the seven kilometers, from Vo Dat, every day in order to sell junk to us Americans. Their curiosity apparently got to them, and they chose to scour the garbage for hidden treasures. The sign we placed was large and the warning was written in both Vietnamese and English, but the kids didn`t seem to care. Several members of 2nd Platoon were yelling at the children to get away from the trash, but to no avail. Suddenly, Carmichael joined the other grunts, and he had his M-16 locked and loaded. Without a warning to anyone, that Maryland bastard was firing shots in the kids` direction.

I had been headed toward my guys when I heard the screaming, but when I hear the rifle shots, I raced to that location. "Damn it, Carmichael," I hollered as I approached and saw what he was doing. "Quit shooting at friendlies and conserve your ammunition! What`s the matter with you?"

"I was just havin` fun, Sarge," he answered casually. "I`m not trying to hit `em, just gettin` in some marksmanship practice. Hell, I`m shooting well behind their feet, forcing them to leave that pile of trash."

I didn`t approve of his method, but the kids WERE racing back up the road to our location, AND none of them ever went back to inspect the garbage. I told you, he was crude and gross, but many times what he did worked very well.

I had more on my mind than Carmichael playing with children. Our third morning re-cons found more evidence that our base was being observed....lots more matted grass and empty food cans were discovered. I had been wanting to call Captain Mertz to tell him of my increased concern, but given my worried tone the previous day, and his response, I didn`t want to sound like the boy who cried wolf with only grass and empty tins as my proof.

Around 1400 hours of that third day, however, the American convoy began to approach us from the south. When I saw the children moving off the road I thought they were preparing to cheer the tanks, tracks, trucks, jeeps, etc. while the vehicles moved north on their re-supply mission. This was to be the first convoy passing us since we had set up our outpost, and we were getting ready to cheer, too. However, when I looked at the kids a minute or two later, I saw they WEREN`T preparation for cheering. All the children were headed into the brush, and I have to admit it now.... I was too naïve to recognize why they were doing that. Suddenly, with the convoy within half mile of our position, an ambush was sprung by the N.V.A. Heads began popping up from the tallish elephant grass, and the people belonging to those heads fired singular shots or short bursts of ammo toward the line of vehicles. Half dozen rocket-propelled grenades were launched, as well. There was, however, NO support for the ambush coming from the jungle tree-line. Just as quickly as they rose up, the enemy would duck down, trying not be seen. But we in the camp saw them going up and down, and THAT was also when I realized that the children must have known about the ambush and were seeking cover from stray bullets. But kids were the last thing I was worried about once the shooting started.

Immediately I radioed the captain and advised him of the situation. Meanwhile our mortars and artillery were peppering the grassy area. The convoy`s lead truck had been damaged, and none of the other vehicles could pass it on that road. Tanks and tracks, assigned to chaperone the convoy, opened fire onto the fields as well, but none of them moved toward the enemy, which kind of surprised me.

Within fifteen minutes, a lone deuce-and-a-half truck, filled with all the remaining G.I.s from Delta Company, came roaring past our location. The soldiers looked like a rag-tag bunch for sure. Some were wearing soft hats, others hard hats, and some had no hats on at all. Some weren`t wearing shirts, either, and most of those who HAD shirts on didn`t bother to button them. While everyone did have pants on, thank goodness, most of the pants had been rolled up to make shorts. It also seemed like every one of the 'not-looking-ready-to-fight' grunts had cigarettes dangling from their mouths. To make an even worse appearance, the way they were hanging all over the truck reminded me of the movies starring the Keystone Cops....too many people for just one truck. But their behavior was more bizarre than their appearance. They sounded like drunken fraternity boys after they had had too many beers, hooting and hollering and cursing at the top of their lungs. I was wondering who was in charge of that motley group. I couldn`t tell if they were cheering or complaining about the fact that they were headed into combat. Thankfully, they didn`t have room for us to join them on the truck. In fact, they never even slowed down to see if we might want to join them. They just sped on toward the action. The South Vietnamese started up THEIR truck, though, and the sixteen of us hitched a ride with the few soldiers they had on their base. We headed into the danger zone, too.

Mortars, artillery and the American armor vehicles started concentrating on the jungle tree-line once the infantry arrived, and the enemy was making a hasty retreat even before Delta Company hit the ground. We all charged through the grass, which wasn`t a good tactic, but every one of us was full of adrenaline, or something. Suddenly, an AK-47 cracking sound rang out from one of the closer trees. My platoon`s Bluto Donovan was looking right at that specific tree when the shot was fired. Since our gunner had already loaded a belt of M-60 ammo, he immediately raised his weapon and fired a long blast in the direction of the branches where the shot originated. Bluto and some of the other guys saw a body drop to the ground, and they all ran to finish the job, if need be. Yes, Donovan had, indeed, killed the sniper, but the lone shot by the enemy soldier HAD wounded one of the South Vietnamese soldiers who had ridden into battle with us. Thankfully, our ally wasn`t seriously wounded, nor was anyone in the convoy. A few vehicles had damage, but since nothing bigger than rifles, automatic weapons and a couple of r.p.g.s had been used by the enemy, the destruction wasn`t considered too bad. Within an hour of the sniper shooting, the convoy continued on its course northward.

That incident was described as a nuisance ambush by leaders of the convoy.

When we returned to our compound, I couldn`t help thinking about what had just happened. If the rumors were true about the N.V.A. forces being from the 33rd Heavy Artillery Battalion, where were the big guns? I began wondering how many enemy soldiers were involved in the ambush. I recalled seeing many, many heads popping up and down before reinforcements came rolling in from Vo Dat. Suddenly, I got back to reality for us. I couldn`t afford to conjecture about what might be in the area. What I DID know was that we had enemy soldiers VERY near our base, and I had no doubt that our little camp would have trouble from them sooner rather than later.

Just before nightfall, I radioed the captain and finally told him of the increased evidence we had found outside our perimeter. I didn`t care if it sounded like begging or not, but I made it perfectly clear that we would need some help in securing the camp, and we would need that help in short order. The captain didn`t sound impressed by my pleas.

The next morning my platoon worked as one sole unit while executing a cloverleaf around the perimeter. I knew if we were to encounter trouble outside the wire, we`d be better able to take on the enemy with a force of fifteen, as opposed to getting caught with three, five-man re-cons working separately. Luckily, there was no one out there setting up an ambush. There was, however, evidence that we had been observed by a very large group of humans. We were surprised at how well-worn some of the trails, leading to the matted, grassy, observation sites, had become over night. There was an inordinate supply of empty sardine cans and discarded cigarette butts, too, and I felt quite paranoid when we returned to camp. I knew that an attack was imminent. I just wasn`t sure when that time was coming....one more day....two. I just had an eerie feeling of doom.

When the children arrived on the fourth day, it was around mid-morning. One of the boys, approximately twelve years of age, approached me and said, "This is the night, G.I. You be overrun tonight." He was gone in an instant, like he didn`t want to be noticed talking to me one-on-one. But I certainly understood his message, even becoming a little panicky.

I got right on the horn and called Capt. Mertz, explaining what we discovered on our morning cloverleaf and what I heard from the kid. It was evident to me that an attack was going to happen within the next twenty-four hours, and I felt like we were in real trouble.

The captain explained to me that he had sent out his other two infantry platoons on a two-day, joint mission with a South Vietnamese company, so we wouldn`t be getting any help from Delta. I tried to sound VERY distressed and told him that my 12-year-old informant indicated that a HUGE element was going to be involved in swarming our encampment. (the kid never told me how large the invading force would actually be, but I had to sound dramatic) Then to top off my plea of desperation, I actually told the captain that I didn`t really need more troops, I needed track vehicles, and as many tanks as he could find. I definitely let him know that I felt we were going to be in real trouble after the sun went down. He assured me that he heard the distress in my voice, and he would do what he could. At 1030 hours, my call to Mertz was terminated.

Though I hadn`t worked with Captain Mertz long, I was well aware of his extensive military service, and the connections he had with many other combat units. He wasn`t a warm and fuzzy person, but he was savvy, and I WANTED to trust him when he said he`d try to find us some solid help....I really did want to trust him.

When 1300 hours came and went, I called Mertz again. "I AM on it, Sergeant!" he said rather impatiently, "But every unit I`ve called is currently involved in its own mission. Now let me get back to work getting you some help," and with those few words, he was off the radio.

I took a moment and thought about the situation. I had returned from my Hawaiian R&R four days earlier, then put in charge of the 2nd platoon. My platoon was sent on a 'cushy' assignment, where I was told to take charge of an entire camp....by a general. I had over-whelming evidence of a wave-attack likely going to hit our encampment that very night. I also had two lieutenants who didn`t want to listen to anything I had to say, so I was wasting my breath trying to tell them to prepare for a fight. Finally, I thought about the fact that my platoon and I might have been experiencing the last hours of our lives. I was nervous, angry, sad, and scared. I prayed for help to arrive.

By 1700 hours, when all the civilians had returned to the village, I called my captain once again. It didn`t matter to me how annoyed he would be with a third call, I HAD to successfully convey the urgency of our little base`s situation. "Captain Mertz," I began, "We are within two hours of darkness, and I guarantee that something catastrophic is going to happen here tonight."

"I hear you loud and clear, Sgt. Stein, and believe me when I tell you I am working with a couple of channels to get you relief. If I can`t get you help tonight, I will, for sure, get you help tomorrow."

"Captain," I said with finality, "if we don`t get help in a big way this very evening, this will be the last time you hear my voice, or the voices of anyone else in this encampment." I hung up without giving Mertz a chance to respond. I may have been using Jewish guilt on him, but I really believed what I was saying to be true.

About a half hour before sunset, my men and I heard machinery rolling toward us from the south. Suddenly, we saw a whole company of tanks and other tracked vehicles rolling our way. When the lead tank arrived at our perimeter, a captain peered down at me and asked, "Who`s in charge here? We`ve been ordered to assist this site until further notice."

"There are two lieutenants here, and I am in charge of the infantrymen. But, Sir, if you are here indefinitely, that means YOU are base commander. And, Sir, we are ALL grateful that you have arrived. Tonight is to be the night we have real trouble coming our way, and…."

I was interrupted by both lieutenants arriving at the tank, and saluting the captain. The two babbling ninnies had nothing of importance to say during the next minute or so, therefore the captain stopped them, looked at me, and asked, "What IS the situation, Sergeant? We need to get set in before darkness comes completely." The lieutenants just glared at me again, and I explained what I knew. The captain got his vehicles inside the perimeter and they were positioned in short order. It was beautiful! While the area was too large for my small platoon, it barely held a platoon of tanks and tracks. Finally, the captain approached and asked me to tell him where, specifically, we found evidence of enemy in the area. I explained that we had evidence in every direction he could look, and with that information he just smiled and said, "Tell your people to cover their ears if they don`t like noises." Then he ordered his men to 'prepare for a nighttime show of intimidation to let the gooks know we are here.'

What we heard was loud, all right, but also music to our ears. Big gun muzzles flashed from tanks and tracked vehicles alike. Mounted M-50 machine guns, too, contributed light and noise inside the compound. I watched the show like it was a Fourth of July fireworks display. And we all cheered….infantry, mortars, and artillery. It was a beautiful sight to see, if not hear. Needless to say, there was NO enemy activity that night. When we re-conned the area the next morning, it appeared as if the tree line had receded at least fifteen meters due to downed and shredded trees and shrubbery.

Maybe just as delightful to me and my men, that first night, was the fact that we got to share guard duty with the armor people, which meant more sleep for everyone. We even got to attach our poncho liners to various vehicles, making some overhead cover for our positions. Suddenly, the rain wasn`t so depressing to us grunts. I thanked the Lord all night long that Captain Mertz had come through for us. Even greater news came when the armor company was ordered to stay with us for the next eight nights. In fact, after those eight days, my platoon was ordered elsewhere while the tracks remained. The presence of the armor, in that outpost, also meant quicker response time to ambushes within ten miles of Vo Dat. The decision was made, by a higher command, to leave them in the area quite a bit longer than originally planned, and that was all right with me. I have to tell you, the last eight nights of that particular mission were the best duty nights I had during my entire tour in Nam. I got some extra sleep, and I felt safe.

With the armor company controlling the perimeter, the most important duty left to my platoon was the checkpoint on the road to Vo Dat. With Carmichael being restricted from working that duty, things went smoothly.

Still, Carmichael wasn`t quite finished with his antics. As I`ve mentioned, children would walk from the village to our checkpoint every day. They not only sold us soda pop and other trinkets, they were looking to see if the G.I.s would give them things like tins of peanut butter from the c-ration packs. There was give and take, and bargaining on both sides. Anywhere from twenty to twenty-five kids would show up on any given day. My platoon ended up staying in that camp for twelve days, and on the sixth day a kid came to visit with an unusual item that he DIDN`T want to barter for or sell. He brought a baby baboon. Carmichael took a shine to the little monkey, and casually said to the young boy, "How much for the monkey?"

The kid didn`t look concerned and answered, "Mine….not sell,"

Carmichael was undeterred, and he reached into his pocket, pulling out military script, which was what we used instead of real American money. All he had was fifty cents worth of script, so he said, "I give you fifty cents for the little ape."

The ten-year-old child got irritated and vigorously shook his head. "Not sell, G.I., not sell."

Carmichael got a little irritated himself and bent down to get nose to nose with the youngster. He said in a really serious voice, "I SAID I`ll give you fifty cents."

The kid, apparently seeing he was in trouble, tried to use his instinct as best he could. In the spirit used by all the children who were there to make money the child stated, "OK, G.I., I sell....five dolla."

Carmichael then calmly stood up, locked and loaded his M-16, and put the barrel of the rifle to that kid`s forehead. "Fifty cents," he snarled.

With no one coming to his aid, the kid was petrified. "OK, G.I., fifty cent," and with that being said, Carmichael had himself a baby baboon. That particular child never returned to our camp.

Everybody in the outfit liked to play with Carmichael`s baboon. Most of the guys would let the monkey ride on their shoulders, with the ape holding onto ears or hair in order to keep balance. Every now and then, however, one of the fellas would shout, "Get him OFF!" No, the monkey wasn`t rough with the ears, or pulling hair, but he WAS still a baby....and babies have 'accidents.' Carmichael didn`t let anyone from armor, artillery or mortars play with his pet, however.... said he didn`t like any of them. That was Carmichael, pure and simple.

I didn`t want to get peed on, or worse, but I enjoyed my turn with our hairy pet, too. I carried the platoon rope, which was used to ford some of the swifter-moving mountain streams. In fact, I used the rope as my pillow and usually awoke with rope burns on my neck. When I played with the monkey, I would make a little noose on one end of therope, and place it around the skinny little beast`s neck. I would proceed to walk up and down the road while the children would laugh at how funny he looked in a noose. Suddenly, a youngster would leap in front of the baboon, make a face, and run away as fast as he could. The monkey hated being laughed at, so he would chase the kid with the intent of doing some harm to the little tease. I would let out enough rope to allow the animal to just about reach the little brat, then I would pull back in a way that caused the animal to give a slight gagging sound, but not hard enough to hurt it. The monkey would return to my position while I reeled in the rope, then we would continue the walk. Suddenly, another child would make a face in front of the beast, and the chase was renewed. This happened quite a bit when I walked up and down the road with our pet.

However, on the third day of having the pet, I began walking the baboon as usual. Suddenly, a kid, maybe six-years-old, did something he shouldn`t have done. He stepped in front of the little ape, but instead of making a face and run, he tossed a pebble, which hit the animal right between the eyes….THEN he ran. I thought hitting an animal with a stone was uncalled for, so instead of holding the rope until it was time to yank the monkey back, I jogged along WITH the beast. The kid`s eyes grew saucer-size when he saw me running, too, and he started to scream while still running. Our baboon caught that child in a flash, wrapped both arms AND legs around one of the kid`s legs, and the rock-thrower began screaming even louder, like he was being eaten by a shark..

Remember, though, this animal was just a baby, and he would often bite us grunts, but he could never break the skin. We`d just slap him along side his head, and the monkey would stop teething, as it were.

This time, however, the ferocity of the attack DID cause a couple of little puncture wounds, which drew a drop or two of blood; therefore, I began to appreciate why the kid was screaming like he was being eaten alive. I worked fast to get the baboon off the kid. First, I peeled one arm, then two from the youngster, but the animal held on with both legs and continued his biting. I FINALLY got all four limbs off the victim, and the monkey scampered up my arm, wrapped his legs around my neck, and grabbed my hair. Then I could feel his face right next to mine and his head began bobbing back and forth as he looked at the kid. I interpreted this action to be his way of saying to the kid, 'I got you good, and if you do that again, I`ll get you again.' Everyone was laughing except for the pebble thrower. I got Doc to put a couple of Band Aids on the kid, and all of a sudden the other children crowded around the six-year-old like he was a hero. Still, no one ever hit that monkey with anything again.

When we had to leave the comfort of our little base, I heard that Carmichael got $5 in script for his monkey. I approached him and asked how he got so much when he paid so little. In typical Carmichael fashion he bragged, "Yeah, the guy wanted to pay me fifty cents. I told him I wanted five dollars or I was taking the ape into the jungle and slit its throat. I got my money." It was just hard trying to be friends with a guy like that.

X

Bring on the Enemy

The American foot soldier operating in Vietnam had a fairly nomadic life-style, at least my unit did when I was there in 1969 and 1970. The jungle was our home, and I have to admit that there were many times when I enjoyed being in nature. I had grown up in a college town, seldom ever getting to investigate what a farm had to offer, let alone going to the wooded areas outside Iowa City to explore area wilderness. In Nam, my platoon seldom stayed in one location for more than two days, and every day we moved about I discovered beautiful, as well as unusual and even bizarre, sights and sounds in the tropical jungles. Most of the time Delta Company worked in the mountainous areas of central Vietnam. The South Vietnamese war arena was divided into four major areas, called cores. Saigon was in the Delta area of the country, and was designated as IV (Four) Core. I (eye) Core was in the northern part of the arena, on the North Vietnam border. II (Two) and III (Three) Cores were central South Vietnam, and were heavily mountainous from the Cam Ranh Bay to the Cambodian border. My company, Delta Company, operated in both II and III Cores, and the majority of our operating areas were nearer the Cambodian border than the bay side.

Though not officially called a 'search and destroy' brigade, the 199th Light Infantry was designed to be very mobile, and able to move to any enemy activity with a very little time of notice. Both the II and III Cores were honey-combed with many, many trails used as off-shoots of the Ho Chi Minh Trail, which was the major jungle highway used by N.V.A. moving into South Vietnam for combat.

When American Intelligence got word of enemy movement on those trails, units of the 199th were quickly dispatched to the 'hot' areas, and expected to intercept and engage any hostiles found.

Those of us who humped in the jungle for a living affectionately called ourselves 'grunts'. That was because when we headed to engage the enemy, we carried everything we needed, as well as items we wanted, on our bodies. The loads we carried could get very heavy, which caused grunting on occasion. Our rucksacks were jammed full of clothing, food, and anything else a soldier might deem necessary to survive missions oftwo or three weeks. While in the field, we were re-supplied as often as possible, but it always seemed that water and food ran out in short order. Soldiers wanted to make sure, especially at the start of a mission, that they had all the necessary items they could carry just in case re-supply couldn`t get to us as scheduled. 'Wanted` items, while coveted, would only be added to an individual`s rucksack if there was room. While poncho liners and rubber mats were not essential to have, most grunts carried them for comfort. Those two items took up a lot of space in rucksacks, however, so other 'comfort' items were left behind. Clothing was good to take, but THEY took up a lot of room, too. Many of us chose to carry just one extra clothing item....socks. Keeping dry feet during the rainy, monsoon seasons was essential, so I carried three extra pairs of socks, and no other articles of clothing.

We filled our pants pockets, and strapped as many 'extras as we could to our bodies and rucksacks. Every soldier carried as much ammunition as possible for his weapon. No one wanted to be caught short of ammo if a firefight broke out. Most of us carried a bandolier of extra machine gun ammunition for our gunners, too, slung over our shoulders, bandito style. Most soldiers carried claymore mines, grenades, (high explosive and smoke) bayonets or other knives, with at least one machete assigned to each platoon. One soldier per platoon was given a one-shell, bazooka-type weapon called an M-72 to carry. Medics and radiomen needed extra, specialized equipment, and I carried the rope necessary for crossing some raging rivers. On and on it went. We were loaded down with 'stuff' when we 'moved out' from our rear areas to the jungle. We looked like pack animals, but whatever we carried, we had to be able to operate sufficiently while climbing up and down tough mountainous terrain, through heavy brush, in ninety degree daytime heat accompanied with stifling humidity, all while we were hunting down the enemy. Each man knew the limit he could carry, and I can tell you this, there were no wimps amongst the grunts that I served with.

I carried around ninety pounds, when fully loaded. I was a picky eater and the cases of W.W.II c-ration cans we had as our food source, offered a limited variety of options. The only food choices I could stand were beans and franks, or beans and meatballs. Every other 'entrée' option was repulsive to me….powdered egg meals, ham packed heavily in some sort of gelatinous goo….ich! I liked the small cans of cheese or peanut butter, and EVERYBODY tried to get their hands on pound cake, which went well with the cans of peaches, but there were just a few cans of cakes in each case of C-rations, so that treat was hard to get hold of. My saving grace came in 'care packages' that I got from home. My mom knew what I liked, and she was diligent in sending me food. My wife….not so much. We carried sterno packs to prepare hot food, and packets of fairly coarse tissue paper to use as either napkins or butt wipes. I carried a large spray can of insect repellent and a diary. Other people carried cameras, but I didn`t. I wrote in my diary every night, and that was going to serve as my reference to memories from my Vietnam days. Every grunt carried something special to make his life more comfortable, or at least more bearable.

Easily, the second heaviest item I carried (ammunition was first) was water. We toted water bags, and each bag could be filled with three quarts of water, or maybe a full gallon, I can`t remember right now. No matter what the actual size, they were HEAVY! I sweated so much that I carried TWO water bags, and even THAT much water wasn`t enough. Fresh water could be found in mountain streams, but we knew we would also find enemy soldiers near those streams, too. Getting our water first, before encountering the enemy, seemed prudent to me, though there were times when just the opposite occurred.

If we weren`t near any streams, we would get our water re-supplied by helicopter.

Sometimes we found a field for the helos to land, and that was the easiest way to get water. If there was no place for the helicopter to land, the water would be dropped to us, loaded into various containers. The most popular way to drop water was by the use of weenie bags. They were nothing more than huge, hotdog-shaped, balloon-like containers. The trouble with the bags was the fact that they were thin-skinned, and could be punctured way too easily. Dropping a bag in the jungle, and trying to get it through the triple-canopy tree configuration without bursting, was nearly impossible. A second option, and the one more likely to survive a tough journey through heavy forestation, was the use of artillery casings….not used artillery shells, but the metal casings in which the artillery rounds were housed before being used. First, not very much water could be stored in those casings, and worse than that, as far as I was concerned, the water had a distinct metallic taste. I hated the taste of water stored in artillery cases! Most G.I.s, humping the jungles, were thirsty most of the time. To this day I cherish good, clean, drinking water, and I NEVER take water for granted. When I see waste of clean water, I get very upset.

My favorite personal item to carry was an eight by ten and a half, notebook that served as a diary for me. I`d wrap it in plastic so the rain couldn`t get to it, and I found as much time as I could to jot down daily events. I loved that diary! While I did write about strange animal events or about some of the beautiful flowers and terrain I got to see, most of my writing was centered on the combats my platoon had. I counted more than thirty firefights, (quick-ending, or longer in endurance) where bullets, or other weaponry ordinance, came very close to me. As I searched for a suitable release for the stress of each combat encounter, writing in my diary, followed by reading from the book Hawaii, which I also carried, worked best for me. It was imperative that each soldier find a way to release the effects of a terrible day in the field. By writing about the gruesome events that had occurred during any particular day, then reading something far removed from war, I found a mostly satisfactory escape from my horrific reality. It was important that we forgot disastrous incidents as quickly as possible in order to keep our wits about us. However, the ending of one event NEVER meant the end of the danger around us. We had to constantly try to mentally self-medicate…either that or have a breakdown.

In Vietnam, a grunt never knew when he might become a direct target of enemy fire. He was trained to fight when in combat, that`s a given fact, but when real bullets came his way, actually trying to kill him, a soldier learned rapidly what he is made of. Tradition in many infantry units of the Vietnam conflict, and probably every war in U.S. history, held that a G.I., being shot at for the first time, was said to have lost his cherry….he was no longer a combat virgin. And when that same soldier found himself directly involved in his first firefight, he could feel his initial panic and fear turning into the act of retaliation and the use of common sense….but not always. Though there seemed to be negative emotions (fear or panic were the most common for ME) involved with the start of each subsequent firefight, that same new guy in the jungle was expected to gain more and more confidence in his ability to react quickly to any situation. Eventually, he went from being a rookie to becoming a battle-hardened, veteran, American fighting machine. Also, the combat metamorphosis had to develop pretty quickly, if any new soldier expected to survive a tour in Vietnam. It should be noted that while all soldiers recognize any other soldier as a brother, soldiers who have actually seen combat have a special bond of brotherhood, which stems from a deep understanding of having 'been there.'

I trained in the States for one year, but the first time I heard gunfire in the war zone, and it was in the vicinity of my platoon, the adrenalin rush I experienced nearly had me in pure panic mode. That first 'contact' occurred when our point man walked right up to two enemy soldiers guarding a cache of rice. One of the guards was killed immediately, while the other ran quickly into dense jungle. When I saw one of my platoon members indicate in which direction the second guard ran, I took off after him….by myself. I got so excited that an enemy soldier was on the loose, I disregarded everything I had been taught in my training about proper protocol in such a scenario. I actually pursued that guy by myself. Apparently, nobody else had the same idea, nor did they question why I was wandering into no-man`s land, but after a twenty to thirty meter chase, and having NO idea what I was doing in the jungle, I returned to my troops. Sadly, I had gotten a little turned around in my quest, and it took intuitional re-conning to find my way back. By that time, observation posts had been established, and I headed right into one. Suddenly, I heard, "Hey, is that you, Sarge?" It was Carl Allison, a radio transmission operator in our company, and he was with one other grunt on o.p. duty.

"Yeah," I replied, surprised to see them, but glad to have found my platoon again.

"We saw someone coming," Allison continued. "Couldn`t tell who it was at first, and we were both about to shoot, when I recognized your American uniform. Since you`re new, and all, I got to tell you, Sarge, you just can`t wander around after contact. If the enemy don`t get you, we might. We never want to see any movement OUTSIDE our perimeter."

"Thanks for NOT shooting. Lesson learned," I said, knowing that I would have to learn a great deal more about actual jungle procedure. And I was sure my learning would come through on-the-job training. I also learned that I hadn`t gotten my cherry popped because no one had shot at me….thankfully, that included Allison.

There were a few more skirmishes over the next few weeks, but I was never directly involved in any of those firefights. However, on December 21st, 1969, all that changed, and I got caught up in a real catastrophe.

For that particular mission our company commander, Captain Smithers, had decided to attach his little entourage to our 2nd platoon. We didn`t see any evidence of enemy activity during the first six days of the assignment. So, early on the morning of December 21st, the captain decided to move us to a mountain stream, which had a hard-packed dirt trail paralleling it on our side of the bank. We moved slowly along that trail, knowing that eventually we would find the enemy somewhere. As I have said, the N.V.A. stayed close to water sources, while utilizing trails to get southward in a hurry.

Finding enemy activity, somewhere along THAT trail, was a no-brainer. Eventually, we came upon an area that was an obvious rest site for the enemy. Thankfully, the camp site was empty, so we investigated.

Inside the area we found three house-like structures or hootches, but more importantly, we found a fire pit with some still warm embers. Just outside the camp area an apparent restroom dump site was discovered, and it supposedly had warm feces in it. I can`t tell you how any of the soldiers determined that the feces were still warm, but the captain was impressed. A three-man re-con patrol also found a well-worn grassy trail coming into the camp from the rear, indicating that enemy could enter while coming from the jungle, too. We didn`t have just the one dirt trail to worry about anymore.

Captain Smithers was convinced that if we ambushed the trail on the bank of the stream, we would eventually catch the enemy coming in for a rest stop. He decided to keep the lieutenant and most of two squads with him. But he asked Lt. Edwards to send his 'new platoon sergeant' to watch the grass trail in the back of the camp. I wasn`t upset that the captain didn`t want to know my name. In fact, I was impressed that he decided that I was ready to be in charge of my own ambush force. Up to that moment I hadn`t done ANYTHING without working with Lt. Edwards in the same area with me.

I had eight men with me, which included one medic, one r.t.o., and one machine gunner. But, as we went out the back-end of the camp, we immediately saw two OTHER grassy trails connecting with the main grassy trail right at the rear entrance. That hadn`t been reported to the captain. They tied into the main grassy trail from two different directions, and both closely paralleled the edge of the camp. While they didn`t look too heavily used, they certainly had had some traffic on them. We moved out on the main grassy trail, and got only twenty meters, when we discovered that the one main trail forked into two heavily-used trails, and those trails led away from the camp in two different directions. NONE of the four 'new' trails had been reported, but I knew we had to defend them, and I only had the nine of us to use. Since the captain had nearly twenty men ambushing one trail, the thought of asking for more men crossed my mind. But, I was thinking the same way he was, that the most likely entrance into that rest area was by way of the dirt trail on the stream. So I commenced to distribute my men.

I had Sgt. Thompson`s six-man squad with me, and they were the most veteran squad in the platoon. However, Thompson was on R&R, so it was solely up to me to configure an effective four-trail ambush. There were no useable standing trees available to us for the ambush. What we did have, for some solid protection, were a few fallen trees, some of which were rotting, and several tree trunks of varying diameters. We also had very thick underbrush, but unfortunately, none of it was thick enough to stop a bullet. The men were going to have to find a nearby tree stump or maybe a fallen tree for any real hope of protection. The brush could effectively hide us, and I felt confident that the veteran men in the squad would be able to find something to use for protection from live ammunition.

I chose to send Tex Foracker and the newest member of the 2nd platoon (sorry, forgot his name) to cover one of the parallel trails near the camp. From their vantage point both men could look down THEIR trail, while still being able to look a few feet down one of the forked trails, right where it merged onto the main grassy trail. Tex was a big, slow-speaking Texan, with a known reputation as a warrior in combat. I felt comfortable having him being able to see activity happening on two of the four trails. The second parallel trail was much more difficult to defend, but it didn`t go far into the jungle. I`m pretty sure it was the trail that led to the crapper pit, but there had been no mention of there being a trail when the 'hot shit' was reported. Still, I would never send one man to an o.p. by himself, no matter how innocent the assignment might look. Spec.4 Andrade, and another fellow, whose name I have forgotten, (now I understand why the captain didn`t know my name) were sent past the end of the trail, with instructions that if they saw ANY movement coming their way, they were to scramble back to the rest of us so we could readjust our positions and get ready to engage.

The medic, r.t.o. and I focused on one of the forked trails, while the second forked trail, and the one that looked like it might get the most action, was covered by our machine gunner, Spec.4 Pfleuger, and another tough Texan, Spec.4 Middleton. Even knowing that Foracker could also spy down the Pflueger and Middleton trail put me somewhat at ease, the whole ambush site seemed quite cramped to me. We were as spread out as we could get while watching all four trails, but the configuration just seemed like a tight fit, and I felt uncomfortable about it. But I also felt confident that we all had found sufficient cover in case any surprise visitors came walking into our area.

The nine of us lay there, on our bellies, as silently and motionless as we could, for two excruciating hours. Suddenly, Allison got a call on his radio. The lieutenant needed me to get a re-supply list together, as we were scheduled to get supplies the following day. I carried a pen and small pad of paper, too, and estimated what we would need. While Carl and I had the same trail as our primary target of observation, we had two different stumps for protection, though they were a mere two feet apart. Between us was a thick 'wait-a-minute' bush, which made passing the re-supply list through it, impossible. I stood up, took a step toward Allison, and asked him if he could read my handwriting. He also arose and we stood there, shoulder to shoulder, as he read the list. I then noticed that both Pflueger and Middleton decided to take the moment to move to their sides and look back at us while Allison was reading. It turned out to be a bad moment for BOTH of them to be staring at Carl. I looked at the two guys on the ground, then gave a brief peek down their trail, where I noticed a man moving quickly on the trail, and he was coming right at us.

Two prominent things stuck out to me when I saw that on-coming person....he wore a bright, blue hat on his head, and he had a rifle on his hip, which was pointed down the trail in front of him. He may have appeared to be coming from nowhere, but he was coming right at us at a high rate of speed. When I saw him, my eyes opened really widely, and I pointed in his direction. Immediately behind him was a second man, then a third. As soon as I pointed at the intruders, I mumbled rather weakly, "Gooks." I looked at Pflueger and Middleton, who looked back at me with puzzled looks on their faces. "GOOKS," I said with more force, as I instinctively reached back to retrieve my rifle, which was lying against my stump of protection. The fella in the blue hat had closed to within ten meters of us when he noticed us, too, and his eyes got as big as saucers. He stopped and stared right into my eyes. I took another short step backward for my rifle, trying not to take my eyes off him. But as I did so, my left heal butted up against a small tree, tripping me, and I found myself falling straight backwards onto my back.

As I hit the ground I heard the unmistakable crack of an AK-47, and I also heard the firing of an M-60 machinegun and an M-16 rifle, too. Instantly, there were loud popping noises on either side of my head, and large clods of dirt flew skyward, which was the result of the AK bullets hitting the ground near me. The dislodged soil came raining down on my face. I grabbed my rifle and rose to fire at the enemy, but there was nobody to shoot. The soldier with the blue hat lay dead on the trail. I pointed toward the jungle, leading away from our o.p., and yelled, "Pflueger, they ran into the jungle over there. Shoot `em, shoot `em!"

"Can`t….he`s been hit," I heard Middleton say, and he had quickly gotten to the radio to make contact with the lieutenant.

Since Middleton had hustled back and had gotten on the horn, I saw Allison lying within a few meters of Pflueger`s M-60. (yes, the o.p.s were that close) "Carl," I bellowed, "get to the gun and fire at their escape route!"

Middleton looked at Allison then said to me, "Can`t….he`s been hit, too."

All of a sudden, the flight of the enemy became unimportant. I looked at Carl, lying just one meter from me, and he was facing my way while rolled up in a fetal position. I could hear him moaning softly. I could also hear shouts of, 'medic' coming from both the Andrade and Foracker positions, but I moved to Allison as fast as I could. I gently rolled him toward me, and saw that three bullets had ripped into his back. I then rolled him gently away from me, and was greeted with three ghastly exit wounds. Pooling blood and part of Carl`s intestines lay on the ground.

Allison`s first aid kit was visible on his rucksack, so I scrambled to find bandages or tape of any kind. I couldn`t tell how seriously Allison`s wounds really were, but they looked bad to me. From my stateside training I was sure that I remembered needing to get his organs back inside him, asap, and wrap him tightly so as not to expose his open wounds to the open air for very long. His body needed to maintain a certain heat, and I truly believed he could die from shock if I didn`t get him wrapped immediately. Before I could even start to wrap Carl, Doc Buckland was right there. He had seen Carl when I turned him, and Allison became his first priority. With madman speed, and superior skill, Doc had Carl wrapped tightly, with large pads and a lot of tape, within mere seconds, it seemed. I stayed with Allison while Doc moved toward Foracker`s position. I`ve got to say right now that the medics I worked with in the field, were truly heroes. Carl was awake, and even alert after Buckland moved away.

Captain Smithers, Lieutenant Edwards, and the rest of 2nd Platoon came swarming into our area. "What happened, Sgt. Stein?" I heard Edwards ask. I was still sitting with Carl Allison, and I have to admit I was in shock myself. Though I had seen dead enemy soldiers since I had landed In Country, (A reference referring to Vietnam) this was the first time I had seen an American soldier in distress.

The captain was right behind Edwards, and he was demanding to hear the details of the botched ambush. I related the incident to the best of my ability and was relieved to see that neither officer was angry. In fact, Lt. Edwards just walked away when I finished my account, and the captain suddenly began talking to the med-evac helicopter, which had just arrived at our location. I was left alone to contemplate what occurred, and I watched people placing Carl on the chopper. He was awake and seemed to give someone a smile as he was loaded. The doctor on board the helicopter told Doc Buckland that he had done 'a hellava good job on that gut wound.' I just remember wanting to throw up, and I was wracked with guilt.

Spec. 4 Allison wasn`t the only casualty of the fast-moving firefight. Machine gunner Pflueger had much of his right hand missing. Andrade had caught a stray bullet in the foot. And Foracker, who was the G.I. firing at the enemy, and was the guy given credit for killing the man with the blue hat, had his head wrapped very heavily. He lost an eye as a result of the conflict, and was going to a hospital outside of Vietnam before being sent home. The war was over for him and for Pflueger, too, though Andrade was rotated to somewhere in the Rear.

When we moved to our nighttime position that evening, there was a pall of gloom over the entire platoon. For me, it was an endless night of sorrow and NO sleep. I had been put in charge of an ambush that resulted in one dead enemy soldier, and four wounded Americans. I prayed often during the night that all four of my injured platoon members would heal quickly, and end up leading great lives. For most of the night, however, I decided to chastise myself about everything that happened. I was upset that I hadn`t reported having to cover four trails instead of just the one mentioned by our re-con. I lamented the lack of satisfactory defensive positions, leaving some of my guys grossly exposed to enemy fire from various trail directions. I was angry at the thought at how cramped Pflueger`s and my positions were, therefore putting five men in direct fire from the fellow in the blue hat. I was also very angry at myself for having to stand, which forced Allison to rise in order for me to get him my re-supply list. That couldn`t have happened at a more inopportune time, especially since our standing apparently signaled Pflueger and Middleton to watch what Carl and I were doing, thus relaxing their eyes from the trail they had been watching. But, most of all, I was nearly overwhelmed with guilt wondering how I was not even scratched in the firefight, while Carl, who was standing within inches of me, was shot three times. I had lost my cherry, that`s for sure, but the price was overwhelming to me.

The next day we got our re-supply. In with the supplies was an official-looking letter, which came from Brigade Command. It simply read, "Specialist 4th Class Carl Allison died on the operating table at the medical facility in Long Binh. Cause of death was massive internal bleeding resulting from his grievous wounds."

When Captain Smithers read that message to us, numbness came over the entire platoon. The captain said he`d look further into how Carl could be gone, considering Allison`s condition when he was put onto the copter, and the remarks made to Doc Buckland by the doctor who took charge of our soldier. I wandered behind a tree to be by myself….and I wept. The first American I had seen shot was a person I considered a friend of mine, and he died. I felt like my heart was broken, and I mentally beat myself up for the next two days. We were sent to a firebase to be able to give Carl a decent good-bye.

It was tradition, in most combat units serving in Nam, to hold a short memorial service for fallen comrades, when the mission was ended. While the usual speaker, at most memorial ceremonies, was the platoon leader, Lt. Edwards asked me to organize the service, AND to be the main speaker. I told him I would be honored, and called the platoon to the service site. We placed Allison`s rifle, with bayonet attached, into the ground. His helmet was then placed on the butt end of the rifle. All the men got seated onto the ground, and I moved to the rifle to say a few words about our lost comrade.

I had heard from several 'experts' that getting too close to another soldier, in a war zone, was not a wise thing to do. It makes LOSING that friend really, really hard to accept. I had not seen an impromptu service for any soldier before, but was told that the eulogy should list the very basic information, and stay away from any words that might solicit emotion….just a very professional eulogy.

But the fact is, I HAD made friends with Carl, and we HAD talked about his life and family back in Ohio. I felt it was important that the whole platoon hear about the Carl Allison that I had come to know in such a short time. While the thought of doing that was courageous, the reality of it never materialized. In fact, I never got one word out. I stood in front of my platoon members, and a huge lump came into my throat. I looked out at the sad faces, and tears came immediately to my eyes. I tried to swallow hard and try speaking, but water began streaming down my cheeks instead. Then I saw tears welling up in the eyes of all the tough soldiers in front of me. I just stood there, shaking my head, and allowing the tears to flow non-stop down my cheeks. Specialist 4th Class, Richard Hart, whom I considered the best soldier in the platoon, rose to his feet, came to my position, and with his hand on my arm he said, "We know, Sarge." And with those few words, he walked me away from the gathering. The memorial service was over.

I had gotten word that Captain Smithers actually did seek to get more information surrounding Allison`s demise, but no news came forth placing blame on anyone. I think of Carl all the time, and the wound that his death created in me, will never heal.

About two weeks into 1970, our company was rotated to the Rear for a two-day stand-down. Long Binh headquartered the 199th Light Infantry Brigade, and having a two-day stand-down there was considered the safest place any of us could enjoy while in Vietnam. Of course, the Tet Offensive of 1968 let every American know that there was truly NO safe area in the war-torn country.

A stand-down in Long Binh afforded us grunts some comforts that no forward firebase could match. There was a huge quantity of military personnel assigned and working in the Rear. There were many civilians working there, too. I knew Long Binh had a superior medical facility, and I also knew there was a place where we could buy most any civilian goods imaginable. I think it was called a px, but all military branches seemed to have similar stores, identified in various ways. I`m pretty sure that in Nam, we in the army referred to our store as the px, which stood for post exchange. That being said, I can tell you that the most popular places in the Rear were the service clubs, though bars that played loud music, while serving liquor and food may be the best description of the clubs we had.

When we were excused from our initial formation in Long Binh, I headed right to the N.C.O. Club. Popular music was blaring, beautiful waitresses were serving drinks, and I could hardly wait to sink my teeth into a water buffalo steak. Soldiers, with various patches I had never seen before, and some I recognized from other fighting units, were congregating in small groups at various tables. I wanted to be by myself, so I sat at the end of the bar and watched everything that was going on. After a good meal, some cold beers, and singing with some of the music that was being played by the d.j., I actually felt like I was healing from spending a couple of months in the jungle, and maybe even some from the tragedy of losing Allison.

As I left the club and headed back to the Redcatcher (our brigade nickname) area, I remember looking forward to having a second day of relaxation, hot food and cold beer. But as I entered my company area, I was greeted by Lt. Edwards. "Just got word," he began, "we have to head out and help a platoon of the 1st Cav., as they fear they are about to be overrun by gooks. Didn`t catch all the details, but the captain is mounting up the entire company for this mission. You have to get everybody you can, right now. We are leaving on trucks in twenty minutes, headed to the helipad. We fly out at 2030 hours, so get the men packed and ready to move out, Stein." Edwards looked at his watch, walked to the command post, while I started to feel the pressure of getting everybody in my platoon ready to leave in a very short time.

Word had already been sent to the Enlisted Men`s Club by runners, and men were staggering back into camp. I knew I hadn`t heard anything about this emergency while at the N.C.O. Club, so I prayed I had all our squad leaders in the area.

I ran to the barracks, got my partially-loaded rucksack, and was issued an M-16 rifle from the armory. I was hollering at everyone to hurry, but that wasn`t really necessary. We all knew what being in Long Binh entailed. This was my first stand-down in the Rear since I arrived in Vietnam, as it was for most for the platoon members. Stand-downs in Long Binh were rare to get, but being the support company for most emergencies was inherent with the privilege. It didn`t make any of us happy, however, that we didn`t get to spend even ONE night in the Rear, let alone the two days we were told we`d be getting.

In the area where we hold company formations, I saw a man lying on his back. I knew him as Stretch, and he was the lieutenant`s radio man. He had apparently passed out due to inebriation, and Doc Buckland was with him, even putting a mirror under the fallen man`s nose to make sure he was alive. Doc kind of chuckled and said, "He ain`t goin` on any mission tonight. I just want to get him inside."

I helped Buckland pick up the six-foot seven, 160 pound r.t.o., and we dumped him on a cot in the nearest barracks. Doc went to look for other R&R casualties, while I scampered about seeing who I needed to help get ready.

I saw a guy, who looked like a 14-yr.-old kid, standing around near the c.p. building. "Are you new to Delta Company?" I asked.

"Yes, Sir," he answered, "but I`m not sure what to do."

"First, you don`t call me sir. I`m Sgt Stein, and you are now in this platoon. You stay with me," and he and I headed toward the trucks. "What`s your name, new guy?"

"P.F.C. Martin Hoyt," was his answer. "I`m from Nashville, Tennessee, and I just finished A.I.T. at Polk, got a short stay at home, and here I am."

"Stay close, Hoyt," I said with a voice that sounded like I had gone out on night missions before, and I hadn`t. "I`ll help you get through this mission." I was sounding like a veteran, though I hadn`t been in Vietnam even three full months yet. I must have sounded like I knew what I was doing because that kid was on my heels all the way to the trucks.

At 2030 hours, exactly, Delta`s three infantry platoons, all about three-quarters full, took off in the black night sky, headed to….well, none of us in my chopper knew.

The First Cavalry Division supplied the helicopters, which only seemed fair since it was a platoon from the 1st Cav. who was having trouble. Hoyt and I were in the second helicopter of the formation, and that journey sobered up everybody on my bird. Not only was it pitch black outside due to heavy cloud cover, all the helicopters flew with their lights out. The next twenty minutes were terrifying. We could barely see each other in the helicopter, let alone ANYTHING outside, and there wasn`t a single word spoken the entire trip. All of a sudden, we all saw where we were headed, and it was a scary sight. I was seated in the doorway, with my feet dangling outside. I leaned toward Hoyt, who was sitting in the seat right next to the door, and said, "You stay with me, Hoyt. You`ll be fine." I wasn`t sure if I was trying to reassure him that he was going to be fine, or I said that to reassure myself that I would be fine. I was about to soil myself when I saw where we were going to land.

There was a thirty-foot wide, black space in the middle of where red tracer bullets were shooting at green tracer bullets, and we were going to land right in between the opposing forces. Suddenly, every chopper machine gunner in our single-file formation, on the side facing the enemy`s green tracers, (my side, by the way) opened up with non-stop firing. It was an awesome sight, but I knew that when we landed, I was on the enemy side of the conflict, and we would literally be given just five seconds for everyone on the chopper to dismount and move to cover. The helos would not stay down more than five seconds, and it didn`t matter where a soldier was sitting, or which direction he was dismounting, getting off any of the helicopters would last a mere five seconds....maximum.

Luckily, all shooting stopped just as we neared the road separating the fighting units. I jumped off before the chopper hit the ground and ran to the side of the road looking for shelter, ANY shelter. Hoyt was right with me. With no trees anywhere near me, I just hit the ground, trying not to be a target for any nearby enemy soldier. Hoyt was running right next to me, but instead of diving to the ground, he tripped and fell. "Sergeant," he yelled, "There`s a guy here. I fell over him. What do I do?"

"Is he American?" I yelled, though the baby-faced new guy was less than three feet from me.

"NO!" was Hoyt`s reply. "He`s missing an arm, but he`s alive `cause he`s trying to get his gun with his other arm."

"Shoot him, right now!" I screamed. Hoyt sat up, shot two rounds into the enemy soldier, then rolled toward me. On his first mission In Country, Martin Hoyt had killed a man, and I couldn`t believe how callously I gave the order to do so. It was true. I had changed dramatically in the two, or so, months I had been in the jungle. I was no longer the innocent Jewish boy from Iowa City, who wished to become a Jewish chaplain`s assistant. I had become a hardened veteran, to whom enemy lives meant nothing, and I was able to adapt to my surroundings in order to survive. I looked at Hoyt, and I could see the dazed look on his face. He had popped his cherry, all right, and he appeared confused and in shock at what he had just done. I had to try to help him recover from the incident, so I said, "You did what you had to, Hoyt. He was going to try to kill you, but you didn`t give him the chance. You are here to be a fighting soldier, death comes with the territory. You eliminated one soldier who can no longer hurt Americans, AND you proved to me that you can be trusted to have my back. You`ll be fine, Hoyt. Now let`s get back across the road where the good guys are."

As we moved to the American side of the road, and helped secure the area for the First Cav., I suddenly began thinking about Carl Allison. Guilt started to wrack my mind once again. I had hoped that the R&R in Long Binh would help me heal from the mental pain I hadn`t been able to shake since Carl passed. The night assault re-kindled, in me, the reality of my being in a life and death situation once again. The survival quandary was triggered when that new kid from Tennessee sought advice from me, as to what he should do about an enemy soldier reaching for a rifle. The entire time he had been by my side that evening, I had told him not to worry, I would take care of him. When I heard the indecision in his question, I instinctively yelled at Hoyt to shoot the one-armed combatant. I knew that if that soldier could have gotten his weapon, he would have killed both Martin Hoyt AND me. All that night I couldn`t stop thinking about who should live and who should die. I had a LOT of trouble sleeping. I couldn`t stop wondering how I had put Carl in his fatal situation, while I, who was standing right next to him, didn`t suffer a scratch. I thought about the order I gave Hoyt to shoot a man, and how that may have saved us both. I was in bad mental shape all night long. Then, when morning broke, and Stretch arrived with the other lucky drunks, Delta Company took off on another assignment in the jungle. I finally, FINALLY convinced myself that I HAD to stop thinking about death, and that included losing Carl. I needed to get hold of my mind if I was going to be able to function as a leader in my platoon. The reality of being in a war zone automatically meant that anybody could perish at any time. For me to get fixated on events that I couldn`t change would only hinder me from what I decided was my true job in Vietnam.... to keep my men and me as safe as I possibly could until we went home.

March 13th, 1970, started out normally enough. Delta Company hadn`t seen a lot of action since our night assault. We had been in a few contacts, but they all ended rather quickly. In no skirmish did we have anyone even wounded, let alone killed. We did have a firefight where one of my 2nd platoon soldiers accidently put his head in a hornet`s nest while seeking protection from gunfire. His head swelled up like a basketball, our new medic gave him some pain reliever, and he was dusted off for medical attention in Long Binh. But that grunt was back with our unit the very next day, AND he didn`t show any affects from the severe stinging he had received. Delta Company was filled with very capable G.I.s. However, with the lack of sustained combat, many of us were actually becoming complacent. I remember even finding jungle life to be rather enjoyable. March 13th changed my way of thinking that we were invincible, however, and in a big way. Second Platoon had a very bad day.

On the morning of the 13th, my platoon was just finishing a breakfast of c-rations, when Lt. Edwards got a call from our new company commander, Captain Rivers. Rivers had joined our company in mid-February, when he volunteered to lead a field company for a short time. He was on his third tour, and needed some jungle combat experience to expedite his grade bump to becoming a major. Apparently, his first two assignments in Nam were some cushy jobs in The Rear. According to rumors, he was seriously lacking in ANY combat exposure, and that he was going to lead Delta for a couple of months, get his share of field action, then move on with his career somewhere much more safe than the jungles of Vietnam. He talked like he couldn`t wait to 'tear up some gook ass,' and many of us wondered if his bite was as tough as his bark. Some of the guys laughingly wondered if he had even had his cherry popped. The truth was that while our company did have several small contacts, during his first five or six weeks with us, Capt. Rivers was never anywhere near any of the actual action.. Still, he was counting all of Delta Company`s skirmishes as HIS getting combat experience.

Our company had been working in the southern end of III Core, in the Central Highlands, and 2nd Platoon was working an area about nine hundred meters higher on the mountain then the area where Capt. Rivers, his entourage, and the 1st platoon had been working. The call to Lt Edwards was to let our lieutenant know that a two-platoon mission was being planned for the next several days, and 2nd Platoon needed to come down the mountain to join forces with 1st Platoon.

Within half an hour, we were packed up and ready to move and rendezvous with the captain. Randy Williamson was to be our point man, but he had asked our lieutenant to allow him to train a new fella, named Jaime Vega, to be point as we moved down the mountain.

I considered Williamson and 'Little Dickie' Hart to be the two best point men in our platoon. Both were uncanny at finding signs of enemy activity, and both men were relatively quiet as they walked point. Noisy point men were dangerous, often times triggering ambushes while crashing through brush, so I felt comfortable with either guy out front. Sadly, Hart had already been in Nam for nearly nine months, and wished NOT to walk point. He earned that right. Williamson had been In Country for a little over seven months, and was trying to be able to walk further back in our single-file formations….sooner rather than later. Training capable replacements to walk point was a necessary and important skill, and Randy Williamson was good at it. He had already trained one or two men before Vega, and this was to be his last trainee.

Jaime Vega, on the other hand, had only been in Delta for two weeks, which was a very short time to be thought of as point man material. But he seemed quite bright and was very eager to prove himself a good soldier. Sgt. Taggert, squad leader of both Williamson and Vega, was consulted on the training session. "It`s fine with me, as long as Randy is right behind Jaime, and BOTH are vigilant.

The part of the jungle we had been working wasn`t particularly loaded with really thick underbrush, so movement toward 1st Platoon progressed quickly. When point men move at a brisk pace, the single-file begins to spread out, and sometimes as much as fifty meters can be measured between point and drag. (last man in line) My position was the fifth man from the back of the formation, with only newly promoted Sgt. Dickie Hart and the three remaining men of his squad behind me. Squads were typically small, so Hart`s squad of four was not unusual. He actually had a squad of six, but two of his men had recently been on R&R, and were scheduled to be flown out to rejoin the platoon on the very next re-supply mission. The men in Hart`s squad, on that March day, included Sweeper Nelson, with his M-60 machine gun, Mickey Samuels, one of the best r.t.o. operators I saw in Nam. What I liked about Samuels was the fact that he carried an M-16 rifle, and was considered one of the best marksmen in the platoon. The fourth member in the squad was a brand new guy on his first mission. His name was Paul Randle, and he was a gung-ho type grunt from somewhere in the New England part of the U.S. These four fellows and I would share some very harrowing moments, so I could never forget them.

Our platoon made good time down the mountain, and by my reckoning, was closing in on the captain and the 1st platoon`s location. Suddenly, though, the column stopped moving. As is custom, when stopped during a move through the jungle, everyone knelt down and looked for any unusual activity nearby. I moved two men behind me to Samuel`s location so I could monitor the conversation that Lt. Edwards was having with Captain Rivers. "Captain," my lieutenant started, "we have found stumps indicating we could have enemy activity in our area."

A brief explanation is needed here. 'Stumps' referred to the remains of trees, having been cut down, which were all 8-10 inches in diameter. What made the stumps that Vega and Williamson discovered, different from ordinary tree stumps that loggers may have cut, was the fact that sand had been placed on top of our tree find. The sand would dry the exposed sap very quickly; thus creating the illusion of aged trees The N.V.A. used this tactic to fool people into thinking the logs had been taken several months, if not years, before the actual cutting.

The newly cut logs were used to build bunkers. The enemy bunkers consisted of digging a good-sized hole in the ground, covering the top of the hole with sturdy logs which could withstand mortar shells, artillery shells, and even large bomb fragments, if any of that kind of ordinance happened to get through the triple-canopy above them. The structure was then camouflaged with a thick layer of dirt and leaves. Most bunkers usually had a rear entrance, which was protected by the slope of a mountain. The business end of the bunker had a front firing portal pointing toward an area of openness. The enemy could see the Americans coming WELL before any bunkers were detected. There was a shelf of protection OVER each portal, too, which allowed firing from the bunker to be wide open, while anyone trying to get bullets into the opening would have to be prone on the ground. With the 'shelf' being two-feet in length, anything shot from a standing position, would merely ricochet upward creating, at best, only dirt hitting the soldier inside.

Randy Williamson and Lt. Edwards had seen sanded stumps before, and were very certain that bunkers were in the area. But Capt. Rivers didn`t concur. "Lieutenant Edwards," Rivers said after the lieutenant voiced concern, "we`ve re-conned the area and found NO evidence of bunker activity. Bang your helmet against a tree so I can give you and azimuth and approximate distance to our location."

"Whoa," I heard Dickie Hart whisper. That order of 'bang a tree' surprised me, too. G.I.s are taught to move silently through the bush. Only if using machetes, when absolutely necessary, is it ok to make noise. Sound travels a long distance. Enemy in OUR area would most certainly hear a helmet hitting against a tree.

But, the crack of the steel pot was made, and I heard the captain say, "I have you at (such and such) azimuth, approximately 100 meters from our location. Keep moving."

Everyone got to his feet and commenced to descend. Within a minute or two, the file of men knelt down again. Not much further down the mountain, Vega and Williamson came upon a fast-moving stream. It was about fifteen feet wide, and there were large rocks in the middle of the water. First Platoon had begun to step onto the boulders, get across the water, and go up a small rise on the other side of the bank. That is where the point men stopped, causing the rest of us to stop, as well. On top of the rise was a three-foot wide dirt trail. Lt. Edwards called Capt. Rivers to report the findings, and I listened on Samuel`s radio. "Captain, we`ve found this stream and on the top of the bank is a trail that has plenty of tire-sole shoe marks on it. They look pretty fresh to us. We believe the enemy has been here recently."

"Look, Lieutenant," the captain said with some impatience, "we`ve re-conned that very trail and found nothing suspicious. "You can`t be far from us. Bang your helmet." Again loud clanking could be heard. "You`re only about fifty meters on the same azimuth. Come on in."

Just as I was standing back up, there was a sickening sound of large explosions and the cracking of AK-47`s at the front of our single-file formation. After hitting the ground, I turned to Hart and we yelled in unison, "Ambush!"

Immediately I shouted to Sgt. Fimbres to get his 3rd squad to the river and secure the position, also telling him that Sgt. Hart and I were going to execute a maneuver. A maneuver occurs after a platoon comes under attack, and defensive positions have been established. A small group of grunts then attempts a flanking movement on the enemy. A successful maneuver will create a pincer action, thereby having the defensive positions in front of the enemy, and the maneuver element on the side of the enemy. This allows a cross-fire effect to be established which should expose some, if not all, of the enemy positions to aggressive American retaliation fire.

Hart and I identified a large tree along the nearside bank but about twenty meters away from us. We would need to get to that tree in order to cross the fast-moving stream and get a good angle on the ambushers. Getting there was going to be a problem, however. While the tree was very near the stream, AND there was a slight slant in our favor, which would give us a low profile for anybody shooting at us, we would have to low-crawl slowly, face in the dirt, until we reached the tree. Moving slowly helped reduce the movement of shrubbery around us, and that would hide how low we were and how fast we were inching along. Several bullets did soar over our heads and bodies throughout the entire low crawl, and they were just a matter on inches, too, but we could NOT be seen clearly, so it was a guessing game by the N.V.A. as to where we were at any one time. I figured they probably believed we were going to try to get to the giant tree in order to have maximum cover, but they couldn`t zero in on any of us at any time.

We had a near-tragedy, though, as Rodney Nelson got one of his 100-round belts of M-60 ammo caught in some brush. He rose to his knees to untangle the bullets, and a couple of AK rounds tore into the bush right in front of Sweeper`s face. He slammed himself to the ground and untangled his equipment, with some difficulty, while in a prone position. It took more time than we wanted, but all five of us got to the tree safely.

The sound of Bluto Donovan cursing loudly as he continually lay down bursts of machinegun fire, was easily identifiable. There was a constant staccato of rifle fire, both M-16 and AK-47, and an occasional grenade explosion, too. I knew that we HAD to get across that stream and get an angle on the enemy. We needed to help our brothers. What I couldn`t hear was help coming from anyone else. Where were the captain and the 1st platoon?

I spotted a similar tree to our giant protector, and it was almost exactly across from our position. I talked to Sgt. Hart and we identified four large rocks that everyone would need to run across safely, then we made sure that the other three men saw those boulders, too. I didn`t have to order Hart to take off across the stream, as he suddenly bolted over all four rocks and dived behind the large tree on the other side. It startled the enemy that anyone tried to cross, and only one shot was fired at Dickie. But he WAS the only one on the other side….with the enemy, so we had to move quickly. "Crawl up the mountain a bit, and make room for us," I shouted, and Hart did so, giving us a thumbs up when he got to another tree.

"Randle," I said, "new guy next." Paul dashed across all four identified boulders and dived behind the large tree. Three or four shots were fired at him, but again, nothing seemed to come close to him. Both Hart and Randle moved up the mountain so the three of us could have the large tree to jump behind.

“Come on, Samuels, we`re up,” I said to our radioman. I`m not exactly sure why I had two of us crossing the stream at the same time. Perhaps it was because I wanted to make sure I had a radio near me so I could listen to all the chatter on the phone….naw. Maybe I didn`t think the enemy could hit either of us since they did such a poor job of shooting at Randle. No, that couldn`t be it. Sitting here today, though, I likely WAS thinking that having a radioman with me gave the enemy two targets. I`m ashamed to admit that I probably figured that the N.V.A. would benefit from shooting a man with a radio, thus stopping our communication line. However, shooting the person WITH the radioman was just as probable, for THAT man was likely in charge of the unit involved in the contact. Oy, I`m getting a headache thinking about it, AND I am digressing.

I took off around the tree and as my foot hit the first rock, there was a loud pinging sound as an AK-47 smashed into the stone just inches from where I landed, and apparently disintegrated a good-sized chunk of the boulder into dust. My eyes widened, my speed across the stream increased, and I dived behind the large tree. Samuels dived on top of me and I asked, “Are you OK, Mickey?”

“Yeah, fine, Sarge,” was his answer and the four of us moved cautiously up the mountain to make room for Nelson and his machinegun, which we would need desperately if we contacted the enemy.

“Come on, Sweeper, get over here. We need you and your gun,” I yelled.

What I didn`t previously know about Rodney Nelson was that he couldn`t swim, so I just stared in amazement when I saw Sweeper stand, adjust the belts of ammo, place his M-60 on his shoulder, and WALK across the four large rocks. He didn`t even dive behind the protective tree, he ambled behind it. The enemy did shoot at him for a good 15-20 seconds, and that was twice as long as they shot at any of the four of us who preceded him. He was apparently more terrified about slipping off a rock and drowning in the raging water then he was about getting shot. None-the-less he looked at my position, one tree above him, and queried, “What now, Sarge?”

"Stay alert, everybody, so I can see what the situation is with our guys," I answered as Samuels and I listened in on the horn.

The fact is, only one person at a time can speak on a field radio. By holding down the 'talk' button, everyone else is prevented from speaking. As we listened, the chatter on the phone was non-stop. Sadly, the amount of gunfire and explosions was non-stop, as well.

I heard Lt. Edwards frantically declaring, "We`re getting wiped out here. We need help NOW!"

The captain, who had established his position as being just fifty meters from the lieutenant BEFORE the ambush began, was not involving the platoon he was with at all. Instead, when he came onto the radio, Rivers seemed to be calling the company`s 3rd platoon to rush to our location. Turned out they were a good 1000 meters from the rest of us when the fighting started, and were moving through some thick jungle. The 3rd platoon leader, for his part, was desperately trying to get the exact location of the ambush whenever HE could get through on the radio.

We also had observers in the air above us, too. Our battalion commander (forgot his name) was in a Loach helicopter, and the brigade commander, General Dobler, was in a second Loach. Both of THEM wanted to know the situation as often as they could get into the conversation. Five people, all wanting to have a say on the radio, consequently, the air waves were never silent.

Suddenly, a new voice broke through on the radio. "This is Diamondback Niner. I am on location. Pop smoke," It was the pilot of a Cobra gunship declaring he was in the area and was there to help.

The gunship was basically a flying arsenal of weapons. It had two gattling guns on board, which were machinegun-like, only they fired larger caliber bullets than a basic M-60 fired, and it fired those rounds four times (or so) faster than the regular machinegun, too. I saw a Cobra work out at a nighttime support mission, and with every fourth round of ammo being tipped with a red tracer, it looked like one continuous, glowing, red line from the ship to the ground. The helicopter could also be outfitted with two seven-pod (maybe it was eight, I don`t remember) rocket attachments, one on either side of the bird. There were a variety of rockets available to be loaded into the pods, too. White phosphorus, or willie pete, as we called them, was used to burn up whatever it fired upon. High explosive rounds were the standard rockets used when things had to be blown up. Finally, there were rockets loaded with razor-sharp metal scraps, which tore through heavy foilage, and were the rocket of choice when the Cobra needed penetration for 'close-in' jungle combat. We knew those beasts to be called flachette rockets, and they were thought to be quite effective by those who had been helped in predicaments like we faced at that moment.

The order to 'pop smoke' was simple to understand. Every combat unit had several men assigned to carry smoke grenades. Those were used to give G.I. locations for re-supply helos, med-evac helos, and in our case, to show where the good guys were hunkering down. Samuels hurled a smoke in front of us, and toward the enemy positions.

"I identify a triangle of yellow, and a purple 500 meters away. I`m going to make a pass inside the triangle. Cover yourselves." With that statement, Diamondback Niner prepared to rip the enemy apart. I couldn`t help thinking, as I grabbed my tree as closely as I could, that the pilot had identified my lieutenant, the captain, and us, as forming a triangle. Meanwhile, Captain Rivers was demanding that a third platoon come to our aide instead of using the one he was with, which was sitting right behind the enemy.

The pilot`s words would normally have been comforting to hear. However, there was a rather stiff breeze blowing that morning, and the smoke grenade, that Mickey Samuels had thrown, was drifting back into our faces, and ended up being right behind us as Diamondback Niner opened up with gattling guns and a couple of flachettes. Indeed, the N.V.A. soldiers weren`t in the center of the triangle, the five of us on the maneuver element were.

It was literally raining metal on us. The ground around Samuels and me was 'trenched.' The tree that Mickey and I used for protection from above, had a large branch situated right above us....probably saved our lives. Unfortunately, one piece of shrapnel, apparently from a flachette, DID rip through my boot and made a painful, jagged gash in my left ankle. "Everyone all right?" I asked and was glad to get affirmatives from all my men.

The chatter on the radio picked up even more than before, and that amazed me. Both the general and colonel were getting more anxious about the situation on the ground. The captain and 3rd Platoon were still trying to figure out where each of them was and how long it would take for help to get to us. My lieutenant sounded more frantic as he pleaded for someone, ANYONE, to 'stop the gooks from ripping us apart.' Somehow, Diamondback Niner got onto the channel and announced, "I`m in position to make a second run at the triangle."

R.T.O. Samuels handed me the horn and said with a bit of excitement in his voice, "Here, Sarge, you better talk to them. That guy is going to kill someone next time."

I started jamming the radio by pressing, then letting up, the talk button very rapidly, therefore creating the tough scenario where no one was able to get out a continuous message. Then there was a brief moment of silence, and I spoke immediately, "This is the niner-niner element (maneuver unit) and we are in position. This is what the situation is as I see it. Our one-niner (the lieutenant`s men) is in real trouble. Three-niner (3rd Platoon) is a long way off. And Diamondback Niner about wiped us out with his first pass. All Americans stop firing. I say again, we are in position and all Americans need to stop firing because the next people you`ll hit will be us."

Immediately, shouts of 'cease fire,' and 'Sarge is in position,' were coming from down in the stream.

"What are we going to do, Sarge?" Hart questioned.

When I was on the radio, I had NO idea what we would do. I just didn`t want the gunship to kill us. A few seconds passed then I said, "Has anybody seen the movie where John Wayne charged the enemy?" I had no idea if there WAS a movie like that, but I had to sound like I had a workable plan, and by presenting an American hero, like John Wayne, using the tactic successfully, I thought that I might have a shot at convincing the other four that my plan would work.

"We`re gonna do WHAT!" screamed Little Dicky Hart.

"When I count to three, the five of us are going to charge right AT the enemy. We`ll have our weapons at the ready (waist high, safety off) and we WON`T stop running until we are in the creek with the rest of our platoon. (I used creek instead of river or stream to help Sweeper visualize a gentler body of moving water) If you see anyone in a different uniform than ours, shoot him. We`ll find out what army he`s in later. But, here`s the trick, guys, and this is serious. We run as fast as we can AND we scream at the top of our lungs. We need to make five soldiers sound like fifty. We can do this! Get ready! One, two three," and the maneuver element was racing straight at the enemy, and we were ALL yelling like mad men.

Suddenly, there was a single shot, and Hart, still screaming, stated, "Got one!" And he did, too. Seems that the guy was trying to protect a retreat by his men by firing a couple of shots our way, but Hart saw him first and nailed him right in the chest.

"AAAAH," we continued to yell as we ran, and within seconds we found ourselves standing next to our fellow 2nd platoon members, who were crouched behind large rocks in the water.

I saw Sgt. Taggert right away. His shirt was soaked with blood. "Where are they, Taggert?" I said, realizing I was highly amped with excitement.

"Over the rise, Sarge. But be careful, some of them might still be there. Do me a favor, though. When you can….find my glasses. I can`t see anything without my glasses."

I nodded then charged over the rise. The enemy was no longer there, but Vega and Williamson were.

For those of you who get a bit squeamish, you might want to skip the next paragraph or two, as I feel compelled to describe what I saw, and it might be too graphic for some. Sorry.

What I saw were three bunkers, all in their near-finished state. They HAD to be easy to see by our point soldiers. The only explanation I can give, even today, as to why my men didn`t react to bunkers, may be the fact that Captain Rivers had told our platoon his unit was close, and he had re-conned the area thoroughly. Williamson MUST have thought that 1st Platoon had found the bunkers and cleared them.

As Vega moved in the lead, he stepped right in front of a 40-pound, Chi-Com command- detonated mine, which was filled with scraps of metal similar to a flachette rocket. The blast from that huge mine left Vega`s body almost unrecognizable. When someone fired that mine, all hell broke loose from the N.V.A. Williamson was the recipient of a rare shot made by an r.p.g. (rocket-propelled grenade) It barely struck the young soldier on the top of his head as it whizzed by, but that was enough to rip the top half of the skull away from the rest of the head. Taggert was third in line, and had just started down the incline from the trail toward the bunkers when the attack began. Shrapnel from both the mine and the r.p.g. ripped into the him, and he was knocked to the ground from the explosions. As Sgt. Taggert rolled over onto his stomach, he reached out to find his glasses, which were dislodged due to the concussion of the blasts. His radioman Cecil Turner, a great kid from Kansas City, had fallen flat onto the trail as the firing began, but seeing his sergeant in trouble, he hollered, "Up here, Sarge!" Turner hadn`t received even one piece of shrapnel from the explosions, and stood up on his knees as he yelled to Taggert. While not being able to see his comrade, the sergeant DID hear Turner`s voice and scrambled to his feet, heading toward the sound of his r.t.o. Within one meter of Cecil`s location, Sgt. Taggert was shot four times in the back and started to fall backwards. Instinctively, Cecil Turner reached toward his sergeant, grabbed onto the front of the wounded man`s shirt, and flung him over his head, into the stream. Sadly, a bullet ripped through Turner`s bicep, tearing the muscle from the body.

After I satisfied Taggert`s request to find his glasses, I stood in front of the remains of our two fallen comrades. When Hart and Samuels joined me, we stood silently. Dickie pointed to the three bunkers and said, "How come Randy didn`t see these?" I was in shock at that moment, but when Paul Randle came over the rise to join us, I told both him and Dickie to 'gas' the enemy fortresses.

That being done within a minute or two, I asked Mickey Samuels to 'give me the horn.' Once again I had to jam the airwaves from all chatter, but once that was finished I simply said, "The maneuver element has secured the area. It`s safe to come in," and I gave the phone back to Mickey. Within seconds I heard voices coming from the tree line behind the bunkers, and then I saw American soldiers coming from behind trees and stumps, and other protective positions. It was 1st Platoon, and Capt. Rivers had exaggerated the distance they were from the bunkers. It wasn`t fifty meters, but more like thirty. I saw Rivers. As he approached me he had a quizzical look on his face, and was scratching the side of his head.

"I didn`t know they were this close," he said, but I didn`t let him say another word.

"You`re a liar and a coward, and if you EVER put my platoon in a dangerous situation again, I will take you to the I.G." (Inspecting General) I whirled around and ran to see how the rest of 2nd Platoon`s troops were doing. I felt Lt. Edwards must have been seriously wounded, judging by the wailing I heard from him when I monitored the radio.

I saw Specialist 4th Class Johnny Middleton, the lieutenant`s r.t.o. He had been wounded slightly by two enemy rounds, but he wasn`t complaining at all. I asked where Edwards was and Middleton pointed over his shoulder to the man sharing the same tree with him. "Never even looked around the tree," Johnny said while giving a little grimace caused by his wounds. "Just cried into the horn the whole time." The lieutenant had obviously been severely traumatized by the ambush, and that was to be his last mission in the field. He may not have been a dynamic leader, perhaps, but the guy took care of his platoon, and the men and I missed him.

Upon checking with the rest of the men, word got to me that seven N.V.A. soldiers had run down the trail as the maneuver element began its charge. They actually ran by a couple of the guys in 3rd Squad. "Why didn`t you shoot them?" I asked with wonder in my voice.

"Sarge," one of the fellows answered, "you guys were right behind them. We didn`t want to miss them and shoot you."

"Thank-you," was all I could say.

Med-evacs dusted off our dead and wounded, but Lt. Edwards stayed with us. Second Platoon DID end up with the captain and 1st Platoon for the night. Third Platoon, after joining us at the ambush site, was given a separate assignment, then they disappeared.

Early the next morning, my platoon was picked up by helicopters and flown to Firebase Ivy for a two-day stand-down. We held a memorial service for our fallen comrades, and once again I had to be led back to my seat when I tried to give the eulogy. As I had looked at the two rifles with helmets on them, I knew the ceremony was to honor Randy Williamson and Jaime Vega, but I couldn`t even get finished talking about what fine people they were. I was just a basket case, so Dickie took me away when I started to break down. Once back in my bunker, though, I finished my tribute to those two guys, AND I began talking to myself about the other four soldiers who wouldn`t be back in the jungle with us….Lt. Edwards, Cecil Turner, Sgt. Taggert, and Spec. 4 Johnny Middleton. I had known all six men, not just as fine combat soldiers, but as loved sons and brothers in their respective families. The firebase ceremonies ALWAYS destroyed me, but I knew I would never forget any of those fallen heroes. In fact, with the re-telling of this story, I am re-living my sorrow right now….forty-three years later.

I never saw Captain Rivers again….thankfully. When we headed out for our next mission, we had a new captain, a new 2nd lieutenant, and three p.f.c soldiers fresh from the States. I wasn`t sure how well I wanted to get to know any of them. I was sick of having to say an eternal good-bye to men I called friends.

There were some follow-ups to that ambush that I feel you need to know. Sgt. Taggert had extensive surgery where doctors took out NINETY- TWO pieces of shrapnel from the initial explosions, and spent a long time repairing the damage done to his body by the four AK rounds that ripped him. He lived in Arkansas the last I heard.

Sgt. Fimbres was the 3rd squad leader, and it was he that I sent to defend the stream while the maneuver element moved toward the big tree. Fimbres got the best nickname in the platoon, AND he had a souvenir to prove he deserved it. As the sergeant reached a huge rock in the stream, he went up to see where the enemy was. A bullet ripped through his helmet AND helmet liner....completely through, without touching a hair on his head. He very carefully hid behind that rock during the rest of the conflict, and that was understandable. While he expected people to call him Sgt. Fimbres, he was called Sgt. Lucky by EVERYONE for a good month and a half after the battle, AND whenever one of us looked at the hole that went through his steel pot. The large hole was a special representation of his jungle action, but I don`t think he got to take his helmet home as a trophy, though.

Finally, what the maneuver unit did to end the hostilities, didn`t go unnoticed. Amongst our platoon, the debate as to whether the 'charge' was only something crazy people did, or if the action HAD to be done before other Americans were killed, occupied time in nighttime positions. Heroic action was fairly commonplace in the Vietnam theater, but taking a chance of losing five men on an empty charge made several soldiers wonder what they would have done in the same situation.

General Dobler wanted to make the questionable act one of heroism, though. As I was told by the company clerk several weeks later, the general thought the five of us were very brave, and put us in for bravery medals. I was in line to get a Silver Star, the third highest award an army soldier could get back then. Hart, Nelson, Samuels, and Randle were to receive Bronze Stars with a 'V' device, (for valor) and those were rare for grunts to get, too.

The company did present us with medals, all right, but NOT the ones anyone expected us to receive. It seems that a few weeks after our ambush, General

Dobler had landed his chopper to direct troop movement in another skirmish. An American Cobra gunship 'accidently' shot, and killed him during the exercise. My platoon`s paperwork was still in the 'in-box' of the general replacing Dobler at the time of the general`s death. When awards for our action were finally being considered, it was thought our 'charge' to be VERY dramatic. However, since I hadn`t declared that I was wounded during the action, the new general faced a perplexing decision. According to the clerk, the replacement general rationalized giving medals based on facts that he understood. Men were given Silver Stars for heroic action, AND for dying, or at least being wounded in the process. It was with that reasoning that there was no way that I, Abraham Dicker Stein, should have been given such a prestigious medal. Excuse me for sounding a bit bitter. I WAS wounded by shrapnel from the Cobra, but the men who died, or were seriously wounded in the fight, got Purple Hearts, and deservedly so. But I didn`t feel, when that combat write-up was sent in, that I deserved getting a Purple Heart like my comrades, since I never left the jungle because of a slightly bleeding sliced ankle. Politics....phooey!

Bottom line....I did receive a Bronze Star with a 'V' device, and the other four heroes of the 'charge' received regular Bronze Stars. The kicker to this medal story was that Captain Rivers, in honor of it being his last field assignment, and because he was AT the action site during the whole ordeal, well, he ALSO received a Bronze Star with a 'V' device. Medals really didn`t mean anything to me while I was serving in Nam, but for an officer to get a medal for doing nothing more than showing complete cowardice....I was furious when I got that news.

Though morale in Delta Company was quite low for the four or five weeks following the stream ambush, no one had time to sulk for very long. Intelligence had picked up a significant amount of evidence that N.V.A. troops were infiltrating into the South, in large numbers, using the Ho Chi Minh Trail with its tributaries, and a relatively safe set of trails from a supposed neutral country. Cambodian was just a little west and north of my battalion`s usual area of operation, but it was through that neighboring country that the enemy was sending a teeming number of troops and resources into Vietnam. American big wigs had decided to pull-off a surprise raid into Cambodia, and because of the 4/12 battalion`s proximity to the border, we were the first combat unit selected to be the raiders.

However, while the plan was still being formalized, the entire 4/12 had a very bad month. My platoon led Delta`s losses, that was a given, but 1st Platoon had lost a man, and 3rd Platoon had two seriously wounded soldiers who were sent out of Nam. Charlie Company had a major set-back one night, and suffered significant casualties, while the other two companies in the 4/12 had sustained more than their share of casualties, as well. Our entire battalion was depleted and was, consequently, ordered to just move NEAR the border as a support force. Our sister battalion, the 5/12, was given the order to move across the border, in a surprise raid, and wreak havoc on unsuspecting N.V.A. campsites.

While in support, however, the 4/12 saw INCREASED contact with the enemy, with a couple more casualties to show for it. Meanwhile, the 5/12 raid went rather smoothly and had little resistance during the entire mission. They took the enemy so completely by surprise, that many of the raiding forces found large caches of weaponry and food sources. The move was deemed a success, and the victors were allowed to bring back, into Vietnam, many, many personal souvenirs. Their casualties were very few, if any, but the spoils were great. The whole operation was thought to be a major accomplishment at that time of the war.

Meanwhile, we, who were low in esteem and morale before the raid, were having nearly daily firefights while our colleagues were raking in the Cambodian loot. The fighting wasn`t anything we couldn`t handle, but there just didn`t seem to be any significant stretch of days where we could get ourselves stronger physically and mentally. My platoon`s veteran soldiers, like Hart and Nelson, seemed really upset at the fact that we were fighting our butts off with nothing to show for it, while our sister battalion had a highly successful mission, and had reaped a ton of rewards for their efforts. It is important to mention that most soldiers wanted to take a souvenir, earned in combat, home. We struggled to find anything from our firefights that was worth taking, while 5/12 literally walked into more than they needed, and got them with very little resistance. Even though I had a diary as MY main souvenir, I felt badly for Hart, Nelson, and the others who wanted to take home a captured weapon. (which would be rendered unusable, by the way) I admit to having been a little bitter toward the 5/12 at the time, too.

The only positive thing that 2nd Platoon received, during the several weeks following the stream ambush, was the fact that throughout the many skirmishes we contested, we suffered no more loss of life….and THAT was a blessing. The same can`t be said for the other platoons in Delta, or the other companies in the 4/12 battalion. Like I said, it was easy to tell that morale throughout the entire battalion was poor, though I did feel that my platoon was actually becoming an effective fighting unit.

To increase morale amongst his troops, the battalion commander decided to give the entire 4/12 battalion a one-day stand-down….a respite from the war, so to speak. The entire force was to be bussed to Cam Ranh Bay where we could enjoy the beach for a good part of one day. I`m not sure where our company was taken by truck, but it was a long ride for Delta Company. The battalion was supposedly to meet at a fairly safe gathering place where more than fifty busses would rendezvous then caravan to the water. Several hundred men were loaded onto cushy busses, and suddenly we were headed for a 'vacation.' I appreciated the gesture, to be sure, but felt VERY naked without having my rifle near me. We were still in Vietnam, but none of us were allowed to have any weapons with us, and I was pretty sure that neither the N.V.A. nor Viet Cong would look away if a chance to wipe out hundreds of defenseless American soldiers presented itself. I got over my paranoia once we got to the South China Sea, however.

The sun was shining as we pulled into a large parking area, not far from the water. We couldn`t readily see the beach, but we did see a sight for sore eyes….a couple of thousand prostitutes….and they were waiting for us. The men were drooling as we neared the women, and morale seemed to REALLY shoot upward when the busses stopped. Before we were allowed to leave the transportation, however, we were given a short speech by some battalion officer. No one really paid attention, as the girls were begging us to get off the busses and join them for some fun. The gist of the speech, however, explained that there had been shark sightings the day before, there was a report of poisonous sea snakes in the local water that very morning, and there were a lot of jellyfish floating nearby, too. Therefore, if any of us got bitten or stung, there would be medics available. Mainly, though, we heard that the girls outside our busses WERE working girls.

They had all been medically checked for diseases, so we had nothing to worry about in that respect. We were also given the time we needed to be ready to disembark the area, and just as our speaker began telling us to have a good time, the bus door opened, and that poor guy was nearly run over by a stampede of men anxious to get some 'satisfaction.'

The men were swarmed by hundreds of women, and G.I.s were taking the closest girl then running toward the beach. We had been told of an 'accommodation' building, with six rooms to be used for 'relief,' and within minutes there was a lengthy line waiting for rooms to open up. Interestingly enough, the walls on this building were only four feet high, and there was no roof at all, so intimacy was never going to happen. There was an older woman monitoring the line and telling each couple which room to use. Those using the house didn`t seem to mind having voyeurs staring at them. I, however, had some serious doubts as to the sanitary conditions of the rooms as dozens and dozens of excited grunts used them. The shyer soldiers headed into the sea, and there was coupling EVERYWHERE in the chest-high water just off shore. Sounds of ecstasy were heard far and wide, especially during the first ten minutes of us departing the busses.

You might have thought that married men, engaged men, and men with steady girlfriends would have some doubt as to whether or not to partake in the sexual circus. You would be wrong. I saw less than thirty fellows without girls wrapped around them. Even though Jill and I hadn`t hit it off so well, since I got drafted. I still FELT like a newlywed, and didn`t want to do anything that might jeopardize my marriage. I always heard my mom`s voice in my head telling me to do everything I could to hang onto my marriage.

That day in Cam Ranh WAS a challenge to me, however, as a beautiful and quite buxom young lady approached me as I exited the bus. I was flattered because she had to fend off several grunts, AND other ladies to get to me. It seems that I had a rather high rank, being an E-6, and the girls thought it prestigious to be with soldiers of higher rank. This girl was feisty and physical with every girl trying to entice me, and I can tell you she was the most beautiful girl I saw during the entire stand-down. I was impressed with her on many levels, but when she told me that for $20 she would be with me for the entire time we were at the beach, I told her I was married. She shrugged her shoulders and said, "No matter. EVERYBODY married. I take care of you BIG time."

I was tempted, for sure, and it was easy to understand why many men took advantage of the moment believing they would never tell their wives of their improprieties. I, on the other hand, had a serious conscience, and knew I could NEVER hurt my wife by being unfaithful. Besides, I was supposed to meet Jill in Hawaii, for R&R, in less than a month. I couldn`t wait to see my spouse, so I tried again to beg off the advance of the sexy woman in front of me. "I`m really sorry," I said trying to be as gentle as possible with my put-down, "but I just can`t....sorry."

She looked at me seductively then pulled me toward her, making sure her boobs hit my arm. She whispered in my ear, "But you look so nice to me. I save myself for you. I promise you like. I`m best girl here."

At that moment I spotted Paul Randle nearby. He was just a kid, and had only been in country about six weeks. But he was a proven combat veteran to me, so I called him over. "Randle, where is your girl?"

"I don`t have any money, Sarge. I was trying to find somebody to loan me $20, but all my friends are busy."

"This is numba one G.I.," I said as I looked at the girl on my arm and pointed to Randle. He is VERY nice. You be with him and I give you $25." (in script, of course) I handed her the folded script, and she took it while giving me a bit of a pouty lip. She unraveled the paper and looked to make sure it was worth $25. Then she gave a quick look around, took hold of Paul`s hand and said, "OK," and she started to drag him toward the entertainment building. So much for her intense desire to be with me, I thought as the two of them moved on.

Randle looked back at me and said, "Thanks, Sarge. I`ll pay you back when we next get paid." The look on his smiling face thanked me plenty, and I just headed toward the water.

Getting the men back on the busses was a chore, even though everyone knew that we all had to return to our individual bases of operation by nightfall. A few men had suffered from jellyfish stings, but not serious enough to be told that they were exempt from returning to the jungle. Nobody got bitten, which didn`t stop a couple guys from telling anyone who would listen that their 'dates' bit them, and the 'whores may have been carrying rabies.' Being sunburn was the biggest complaint, but most of the grunts cherished that condition, knowing they may not get to see the sun much for several weeks while operating in triple-canopy tree cover.

The busses flew back to our unit originations, and the happy faces I saw everywhere on the beach were once again stern-looking. The battalion had done its job and given a few hours of joy to some very 'down' men, but the fun was over, and everyone knew they had to get their game faces on as we entered the tough mountains once again.

The following weeks dragged by for me as I was counting every minute until I could be reunited with my wife in Hawaii. After passing on beach passion, I knew Jill would more than make me believe that SHE was the only female I would ever need to satisfy my....well, needs.

The first several contacts we had with the enemy were like blips on a movie screen. They came, and almost instantly, they finished. Here is an example. While moving through the jungle one day, Little Dickie Hart had a 'feeling' that the enemy was nearby. Since I believed him to be uncanny in his ability to sense things like that, I mentioned to our new lieutenant, Lt. Stoker, that we might have some V.C. following us, (that is what Hart thought was happening) and we might consider a surprise move to test the theory. The plan included finding an appropriate setting to spring an ambush. The lieutenant looked on his map and discovered an open field, which was situated less than fifty meters from our current location. We mounted up and reached the open area quite quickly. The entire platoon fanned out and moved cautiously across the grass. While the majority of us continued moving forward, maybe an additional fifty meters, Sgt. Hart stopped his squad just inside the tree line, set up a hasty ambush position facing back across the open field, then waited to see if anything would develop. Sure enough, within minutes of the speedy ambush set-up, three V.C. soldiers were spotted moving into the opening. One of them carried a portable mortar, and the other two carried three mortar rounds each. There was no one else with them, but they must have had people nearby, as those were the only weapons any of them carried. Our guess was that the smallish V.C. force heard us breaking through the jungle, and the three mortar men decided to follow us. When there was a proper attack moment, those three guys would shell us six times, then scamper back to their unit. It would be a simple nuisance assignment for them, but if they should hit us directly, they would have scored big with their bosses.

Hart had Paul Randle with him, and Randle had just taken over on the M-60 machine gun. As the three V.C. began to move into the opening, Paul opened up with a burst of ammo. Sgt. Hart had NOT given the signal to fire, and Randles` premature discharge was not accurate enough. The three enemy soldiers had only been five feet in the kill zone, so it was easy for them to flee back into the heavy foliage, and the protection of the trees. Hart had wanted the three antagonists to be at least twenty feet into the trap, then all five of the soldiers in the squad could lay down some withering fire. Randle jumped the gun, and not even a blood trail could be found. We had no more trouble from that band of V.C., but once again, Dickie Hart proved to me how valuable he and his sixth sense were.

Two weeks prior to my R&R date, I felt very comfortable with the members of 2nd Platoon. We had Randle as the new gunner, and he joined our two experienced M-60 men, Sweeper Nelson and Bluto Donovan. Those guys all knew how to fight, and all were fearless. Dickie Hart was the best soldier in the company, let alone our platoon, and I depended on him whenever I needed help in any situation. The problem with Dickie, though, revolved around him being 'short.' He had been In Country longer than any of us, and it was just a short matter of time before he was going to be shipping out of Nam.

I still could rely on Walter Peppleman, too, even though he, too, was getting shorter, (in field time, not stature) and he didn`t volunteer for duties like he did as a rookie. We would use him as our only tunnel rat, that is for sure, but I enjoyed the fact that he didn`t mind doing the menial tasks asked of him whenever we were in forward firebases. He actually volunteered for honey pot burning, a duty that guys like Nelson and Hart hated more than combat. Whenever Fritz asked to do the burning of crap, he would find TWO warm P.B.R`s (Pabst Blue Ribbon beers) waiting for him at the end of his mission....compliments of Nelson and Hart. Peppleman may have asked out of walking point, as his time dwindled, but if action commenced, he could be counted on to be right in the thick of the action. He was a great little warrior.

Lt. Lance Stoker was our new lieutenant, straight out of the R.O.T.C. program at one of the Big 12 schools....Kansas, I believe. He actually came to me and admitted that he could use all the help he could get, as he really wasn`t fond of being in the infantry. He was an artillery lieutenant, by m.o.s., who couldn`t get a slot in that arena yet. He relied on me for strategy, so I liked him. To help him out even more, R.T.O. Mickey Samuels was assigned as his radioman.

Captain Mertz was the new c.o. of the company, and came to us following the Capt. Rivers debacle at the stream ambush. He was a veteran leader who was known to be gung-ho, but not reckless. He even talked like he was a hard-core lifer, so I wasn`t really interested in becoming a confidant of his. Mertz seemed to relish combat situations, and he always wanted to know every detail of every skirmish. A rumor that preceded him, that DID endear me to him was the fact that he would not commit any of his troops to track down, then engage, the enemy without having support already in place....and more available with an instant phone call. He seemed to be very connected to outside sources, whom he could rely on instantly. I liked the idea of having support being at our beckoned call.

There are a couple of other platoon members that I would like to mention before moving on to another story. James Remington is one of them. In May of 1970, he was considered a veteran combat soldier that got along with everybody. He was left-handed, so was asked to walk either point, or second man when his squad had the lead for the day. The reason for that was that he carried his rifle facing to the right when we moved. Most right-handers felt more comfortable carrying a rifle pointed to the left. With one rifle pointed right, and the second rifle pointed left, the reaction time to return fire, which was needed in times of sudden ambushes, was lessened. That may not make too much sense to most of you readers, so let me just say that Remington was considered a great marksman, and his squad leader wanted accurate return fire INSTANTLY if things turned badly on a walking mission. Both Hart and Samuels took issue with James being declared the best shot in the platoon, and those three guys would hold contests while zeroing in their weapons at forward firebases. I didn`t care who was the best shot, as long as all of them were great when we needed them.

One of the privates who came to us with Lt. Stoker was another sharpshooter by the name of Sven Laaken. He was proud of his Scandinavian heritage, and carried an M-79 grenade launcher. He enjoyed walking point while having a shotgun shell in his weapon. Shotgun shells were devastating at close range, and Laaken was deadly accurate with his 'baby,' as he called it. Most of the grunts called him Steve, however, since they couldn`t remember to call him Sven.

Carmichael had joined us after the stream incident, too, but you know plenty about him already.

One important soldier to join our platoon, came two weeks after Taggert was shot. We had Walter Peppleman filling in as squad leader, and he did a good job. But when we got Calvin Janowitz, who was a full-blown E-6, Walter returned to becoming a veteran soldier in the 1st platoon. Janowitz had already been in Vietnam for quite awhile, but he had been attached to the Big Red One, an army unit where he had become the leader of a track platoon. Apparently, he commanded his own tank, too, though I was never clear about that. However, his unit was being rotated back to the States, and Calvin hadn`t quite earned enough time in the war zone to warrant a trip home with his armor buddies.

Instead, he was sent to an infantry platoon…mine, to serve out the second half of his required duty. Calvin Janowitz was NOT a happy camper when he got his assignment to the 199th, and not because he hadn`t had to hump his way around the jungle before he got to us, either.

The fact is that he and I trained together in shake-and-bake school in Ft. Benning. We weren`t in the same platoon, while becoming sergeants, but he graduated an E-5, while I graduated an E-6, and he kind of held a grudge. He actually WAS a finalist to make Honor Graduate, but only six staff sergeants were allowed in any one class, and he was one of the odd men out. He had made E-6 while serving with the tanks, and was very upset to find out that he was going to be a staff sergeant squad leader, as opposed to a platoon sergeant. And when he found out I was his superior in rank, well, that was upsetting to him.

To be fair, though, he really DIDN`T take suggestions well from anyone, even though he was a new guy to infantry tactics. For instance, Bluto Donovan tried to help Calvin by advising him on the necessary items packed in a rucksack before a two-week mission to the jungle. He pointed out things that most grunts considered frivolous, even wasteful, and shouldn`t be taken. Bluto emphasized survival was the key for a grunt, not comfort. The sergeant was trying to fit such items as a small stove that he brought from his tank. Donovan told his squad leader that stoves were cumbersome and unnecessary, as all field soldiers could build very useful cooking pits. Sgt. Janowitz was packing a heavy-duty rain poncho even though Bluto told him that everyone got wet no matter what, AND rain pinging loudly off the hard poncho, could make enough noise to alert any nearby enemy. The sergeant wanted to take some text books he had, which he could brush-up on, and be ready for a job interview when finished with his service time. Bluto explained that a lot of soldiers took reading material, but three thick books took up space needed for important items, like insect repellent, AND they were heavy to carry, as well. Janowitz simply said, "Thank-you....I got this." Donovan just walked away as Calvin packed most of the items that wouldn`t be useful to hump around.

I had two important talks with Sgt. Janowitz. When he first arrived with the platoon, I knew it was important to explain certain guerrilla warfare tactics that we employed in the boonies. When I finished, Calvin simply shrugged his shoulders and said, "If we had my tank we`d....," and I had to break in to remind him that we DIDN`T have tanks.

With ten days to go before I was to head for Hawaii, I went to Janowitz to explain the platoon sergeant`s duties at forward firebases, as well as in the jungle. And I mentioned that being the platoon sergeant in my absence didn`t mean that he would have to experience everything cold turkey. He could get a lot of help from the veterans, if he needed it. All he had to do was ask, and no one would think lesser of him if he did so. Again, Calvin nodded then wondered if I was finished with the lecture.

He was a hardhead much of the time but, fortunately, he DID listen to both the lieutenant`s and my orders. He became a fairly competent infantry soldier after three weeks in the jungle. But Calvin Janowitz also had a stubborn streak. He refused to call me Sarge, like everyone else in the platoon did. He insisted on calling me Abe. There wasn`t a sergeant in our outfit who wasn`t called 'Sarge' by Janowitz. I was the lone exception. If I had to render a guess, it would be that when I gave him an assignment to do, or even an order, he wanted to let those around us know that he was my equal, and that he was doing me a favor, therefore, his answer was always the same, "O.K., Abe." It didn`t really bother me that he wouldn`t show me the respect generally accorded a platoon sergeant, he just seemed to feel better when calling me by my first name. We both just kind of avoided each other unless working together became necessary. Calvin Janowitz WASN`T a warm and fuzzy bear, but he was a member of 2nd Platoon, and that was good enough for me.

Six days before my R&R was scheduled, which would allow me to get my mind away from war for a full week, Delta Company was flown to a forward artillery base. The perimeter was very small and contained both 105mm howitzers and the much bigger 155mm howitzers. Finding room for an entire infantry company to bed down was challenging to be sure, but we would need rest before heading out to find the enemy. Our mission site had been shifted to an area in the Central Highlands where Intelligence indicated heavy enemy activity, MUCH heavier than the area where we had recently been working. An artillery base was, therefore, quickly developed near the enemy-infested section of the Highlands, so the guns could prep the mountains for several days before ground troops were sent in to engage the N.V.A. The mountains looked particularly dark as I stared up at them, maybe even a little scary. I prayed to make it to my R&R.

Two things about being in that small camp bothered me, too. First, the ONLY place I could find to lie down at night was located directly under one of the 155 barrels. I packed my ears with 'stuff' trying to cushion them from the concussion created by the blasts of the big gun, but the roars were still deafening. Sleep was impossible. I have had some hearing loss since that night.

Secondly, I had a new captain, who seemed to seek out combat, and a new lieutenant whose training was mostly with artillery. It is true that Lt. Stoker was with the platoon when we had the four or five most recent little encounters with the enemy, but he was never close to the action. The example of THAT was easily provable by the incident when we were followed by the mortar threesome. Yes, we made contact, but the lieutenant was no where NEAR Randle when he opened fire on the V.C. And, we never did get mortared. We had some enemy action, yes, but was the new lieutenant ever directly involved, no. He still had his cherry, and I was a bit nervous knowing that.

My gut told me that we would face more than our share of N.V.A., and I knew the lieutenant would have to be prepared for close-in combat. I didn`t know how he would react the first time he was in the enemy`s line of fire, and I don`t think he knew, either. The fact is NO ONE knows how he is going to react the first time being shot at. All I didknow was that I really, really, REALLY wanted to get to Hawaii, and I needed to depend on Stoker to be prepared to lead in battle.

I had a good pep talk with him as we were waiting to board the helicopters for jungle insertion. I tried to keep things as light-hearted as I could, telling him he had come a long way from his first day with us, and other words meant to encourage him. That was the first time I had ever given a rah-rah speech to anyone in Nam. He may have been my platoon leader, but I knew I had experience on him when it came to guerrilla warfare, and I was going to need him if I was going to get to Hawaii and Jill. I felt better about things after I spoke to my lieutenant, which was just before we got on the choppers. Lt. Stoker looked scared to death, though.

The platoon was set down in a quiet clearing, and we immediately moved into the tree line. After humping for approximately two clicks we settled in for the night. There was nothing out of the ordinary where we were, and we didn`t hear about anything extraordinary where the other two platoons were placed, either. When the second day was a repeat of the first, I was actually feeling a bit more secure about the mission, AND I only had four more days remaining until I would be plucked from the jungle, taken to the Rear, and sent on my way to Paradise to be with my wife.

The third day would prove to be different, however, MUCH different! Second Platoon had just finished breakfast when we heard a lot of gunfire. We weren`t exactly sure at first who was seeing action, but it had to be a tough situation since we heard AK-47s, and their distinctive cracking sounds, WAY more than we heard regular M-16 or M-60 sounds.

Suddenly, we heard Lt. Stoker holler, "Mount up. First Platoon needs our help. They just walked into an ambush," and within minutes we were moving quickly to support our brother platoon.

As we got closer to the ambush location, there was a sickening smell of death in the air, a smell that many of us had experienced before. The veterans in our platoon just knew we were going into a bad situation.

While the ambush had lasted just a short time in duration, we witnessed plenty of American carnage when we arrived at 1st Platoon`s position. One soldier had been killed, and three were wounded seriously enough that a med-evac helicopter was sent to take the wounded back to the Rear for immediate medical attention. Shortly after 2nd Platoon arrived, 3rd Platoon, with Captain Mertz in tow, joined us.

I recognized one of the wounded soldiers. He had been on the truck with me as we left the replacement center and headed to our brigade location in Long Binh. Though we hadn`t talked much, during that ride, I did know he was from Joliet, Illinois. He was with a platoon mate of his when I approached. We talked briefly, and I gave him my address in Iowa City. I told him to call me in exactly one year, and we could make plans for a rendezvous. The talk was cut short as he was suddenly being loaded onto, what was called, a jungle penetrator. Then he was hoisted up through the triple-canopy trees to the chopper, which was hovering just above the trees.

When helicopters couldn`t land because of the thickness of the jungle, they would sit above the foliage and lower a sturdy wire to the ground. Casualties were placed on either a seat or platform, depending on the severity of the injury, strapped on, then lifted up to the waiting medical helicopter. The journey back through the trees had harrowing moments, at times, as branches could hinder or delay upward movement.

My Joliet buddy had a mangled leg, and was the least seriously wounded of the three soldiers being airlifted out of there. A litter was finally sent down so that the deceased soldier could be taken away, too. As the body was just about through the last of the difficult branches, there was a short burst of AK-47 rifle fire.

The shooting meant that the helicopter had to rise straight up, which was done to insure that the wire, with litter and body bag attached, could get freed more quickly from the trees than would have been the case if the slow retraction process by motor had continued. The helicopter pilot had no alternative but to rise upward. He knew that if he had just taken off at the first rifle shot, the body bag and litter would have been hauled sideways through the tops of several trees, causing entanglement and possible loss of the litter. He also didn`t want to take the risk of getting the body bag, or even worse, the soldier inside the bag, ripped and mutilated.. Either way, any side movement meant that the precious cargo could have suffered further disaster. The pilot was well aware that he would be able to reel in the body when his chopper had cleared the trees and the immediate danger area. Unfortunately, by rising, the med-evac had to move itself away from its low hovering position and the camouflage it was afforded by the trees. Strangely, the helo became more exposed to the enemy as it rose upward. With it becoming more clearly visible with the naked eye, the ambush soldiers were able to send some heavy fire toward the defenseless medical helicopter.

Everybody at the ambush site took cover with the increased firing, but couldn`t figure out where the shooting was originating. We watched the helo start to move away, but then were shocked to see it take a direct hit from a rocket-propelled grenade. Smoke began billowing from the chopper as it desperately tried to move toward ANY safe area to land. It disappeared from our site, but then we heard an awful explosion. We didn`t have to see what happened, everybody knew the medical helicopter was gone. I thought about who was on board....a pilot, co-pilot, two machine gunners, a doctor or other medical personnel, and the three wounded soldiers from 1st Platoon. I was sick to my stomach knowing that it wasn't even eight in the morning, and we had lost nine Americans....

nine men who were never going to get to see their families ever again. It was obvious that Delta Company was having a bad, bad day. Losing one soldier is bad, this ambush was a catastrophe. I also couldn`t shake the feeling that the 'bad' wasn`t going to stop for me, in particular, and I became very nervous about just living, let alone going to Hawaii.

Captain Mertz was immediately on the radio calling for help, from any outside sources, to move toward the helicopter`s possible crash site, and secure the area. He was going to move in that direction, too, with the rest of the 1st platoon, but he felt that he might need help even finding the downed med-evac copter, let alone securing the wide area of a horrific crash.

Mertz had the look in his eye of a man wanting to kill someone, and he decided that 2nd and 3rd Platoons were the two instruments who were going to exact the revenge he sought.

Lt. Stoker and I were called to his side, and through gritted teeth, the captain said, "The murdering rat bastards shot at the helo from over in that direction," and he pointed northward. "Take your platoon and find them. Then call and let me know what your coordinates are, and we will rain fire on their asses." While we stayed with him, he called 3rd Platoon`s leader to him, too. "Second Platoon is going after them. You move your platoon 100 meters west of their position, and move parallel with them, ready to render aide if they need it."

I wanted to tell the captain that I was just days away from R&R, and I would feel better if WE were the platoon prepared to aide the 3rd platoon, or maybe be the platoon to search for and secure the helicopter. But the captain cut me off before I could speak. "Second Platoon has the more veteran and battle-tested troops, and in case of unexpected engagement by gooks, they will be better prepared to defend themselves."

I moved silently back to the men and Lt. Stoker had asked me to get the men ready to move out. He wanted to ask the captain to identify nearby artillery units, who could be raised if the need arises, AND if we would have access to any air force support, also if needed.

I immediately walked over to Dickie Hart and said, "I know you are a squad leader and you haven`t walked point in over a month. I also know how 'short' you are....what, maybe five or six weeks left In Country?"

"Five weeks, Sarge....early June," Hart shot back.

"I understand, Dickie, but we have a mission that you are the only person in this whole company who I would trust to walk point and know what to do if you find something. Most of these guys would walk us right into danger, and I know you won`t. You`ve got to do me a favor and walk point on this assignment."

Richard Hart really liked it when someone massaged his ego. By the simple statement that I thought he was the best soldier in the entire company, his reply to my favor request was short and simple, "Roger that." At least I had my best soldier ready to go, and when the men saw him walking point, they were more willing to move toward the enemy, too.

We moved north and west from the ambush site, and almost immediately found a small mountain stream, small enough to likely be classified as a creek, but it had moving water in it, and there was a trail moving along its banks. We had been given a coordinate that the captain expected us to reach by nightfall, if possible. I prayed that we would be able to reach that objective without further problems arising, but we WERE moving on an azimuth that the captain expected that we might run into N.V.A. resistance. Hart decided that the heavy foliage in the area required that we walk on the trail, at least for a while. We could walk more quickly and quietly, and the silent move would lessen the likelihood of the enemy hearing us before we found them. Besides, the trail was almost exactly on our given azimuth, so off the platoon bloodhound went, following the trail.

As I have mentioned before, walking trails that follow water sources is dangerous, but Dickie was the one guy who seemed to be able to sense unusual oddities around him. He not only could see what others couldn`t, he could hear and even 'feel' differences in his surroundings. He claimed the trait was passed down to him by his father, and grandfather, who were great soldiers during their times in the service. I didn`t care where he got the 'sense' trait, I just believed in him.

I had asked the lieutenant to walk in my usual place in line, just in front of the last squad, and he thought that a great idea. I then asked our platoon sharp shooter, James Remington, to walk second in line, and I would be right behind him. I just wanted to be as prepared as I felt the platoon could be, and I wanted to get to our objective as soon as possible. The trail was moving us right along, but nobody was relaxing.

Suddenly, Sgt. Hart came to a dead stop, and knelt down. Everyone else followed suit. I moved to his position and asked, "What is it, Dickie?"

Hart pointed to the trail and then asked ME, "What do you see, Sarge?" I stared for a moment, seeing nothing out of the ordinary, and then Dickie continued. "Get close to the ground." I crouched down trying with all my might to see something unusual. I didn`t see a thing, at first. But all of a sudden I thought I saw a thread, stretched across the two-foot wide trail.

"There`s a thread there, Dickie," I said almost triumphantly. It was no thicker than a sewing thread. It was very taut and stretched from a bush on one side of the trail, and when it reached the other side, it went slightly into the brush where we found it attached to a well-camouflaged, 250 lb., American high explosive bomb. The thread wasn`t more than six inches off the ground and seemed to blend into the trail. I shook my head at the fact that Hart saw it and had the know-with-all to stop before someone tripped it and blew all of us up. R.T.O. Samuels called in our find, we marked the wire with tissue paper that someone had in his rucksack, and then we continued down the trail.

Fifty meters further along the trail, Dickie Hart stopped again. "What you got now, Sergeant?" I asked when I reached the kneeling Hart.

"Notice anything different about the trail in THIS area?" he responded while giving a sweeping motion with his finger, and ALMOST sounding like he may have been trying to taunt me because of my inability to NOT be able to see what he could.

"The trail looks like a trail to me," I answered, wanting Hart to get on with it.

"Well, Sarge, there are LOTS of leaves on this area of the trail, but they seem particularly heavy in that one spot," and he pointed toward the ground a couple of feet from where we were standing.

Although all the leaves appeared messy and scattered to me at first, I got down and took a closer look. The spot that Dickie was concerned most about, not only had a slight pattern look to it, there was little doubt I was staring at an undeniable, over-lapping weave between several of the leaves. I nodded to Hart and he gently placed the patterned leaves aside, which soon exposed a nearly transparent film covering a gaping hole in the ground. Carefully, the film was taken away and there was a two-foot diameter pit. Though only about four feet deep, there were seven sharpened bamboo stakes stuck into the bottom of the hole. Both ends of the bamboo had been sharpened, with one end stabbed deeply into the ground, and the other end facing upward. The tops of each stick had human waste spread all over them, and the crap extended downward for about a foot. Sergeant Hart had discovered a one-man punji pit, and if a man tried to walk across the slight film, he would have dropped straight onto the poisoned bamboo, and impaled himself. A human might not die immediately upon being punctured, but the impending infections, caused by the feces, could most certainly lead to fatal infections. I was glad that Dickie found that pit!

We called in our second find, marked the area for further walkers to see, then Hart and I decided we needed to get OFF the obviously 'salted' trail. We did need, however, to continually follow that creek, which lay on the ordered direction of our dangerous mission.

Our movement was slowed considerably at first by shrubbery, but after twenty minutes, the wait-a-minute vines and other bushes started to get less thick, and we started finding patches of clearer land on which to walk. Ten minutes more passed, and 2nd Platoon was moving at a brisk pace through the trees and underbrush, when all of a sudden, we heard a couple of bursts of AK fire. It was behind us and a bit west of our location, so the lieutenant got on the radio to see if we were needed to help out.

Third Platoon, on its mission to parallel, then support us if WE had trouble, walked into an ambush. It was a hit-and-run type situation, but the platoon DID incur a fatality. We were ordered to stay put as a med-evac was on its way to help remove the k.i.a. soldier.

We also heard that the chopper would then fly to the location of the first downed helicopter. It seemed that the captain had found the crash site, and there were bodies to be recovered from that disaster. An order was also given to 3rd Platoon that they were to report to the captain`s position once their dust-off was completed. As we found out later, there were remains of G.I.s scattered over a wide area, and the captain wanted to get every American collected and sent to the Rear before nightfall. At the time of the second ambush, it was only 1100 hours.

While our two brother platoons would be together, that left only 2nd Platoon to seek out the enemy, and we weren`t sure what kind of support we could get from the company if we DID make contact. Lt. Stoker decided to call the captain to ask if our orders had changed, too. The captain adamantly declared 'NO,' but he said help was on its way. It was 'help' that terrified me! We were to dig in as best we could because our supportive captain had decided to ask for navy jet fighters, stationed on a carrier in the South China Sea, to run a mission for us. The assignment was to fly to our coordinates, then drop eight high explosive bombs, of indeterminate size, as near to us as possible, in hopes that the show of force would scare the N.V.A. into abandoning the area. Near us….I was positive they would end up dropping the bombs right on us. The captain, and the two platoons who would be with him, would be a good 500 meters from the bombing run. The captain told Lt. Stoker that the men he had with him were intending to set out after the salvage job was done, THEN ascertain how best to support us. Oy Vay!

I remembered that a Cobra gunship about wiped my men and me out once before, with ammunition that could tear up the surrounding jungle. Bombs could make much bigger holes in the ground. However, there WERE some good-sized trees at our site, and with us being in triple-canopy, I could only pray that most of the explosions would occur in the tree tops, not even making it to the ground. However, I rationalized, that if a bomb DID hit the ground before exploding, it wouldn`t have mattered HOW deeply we had dug in, it wouldn`t have been deep enough. I couldn`t stop arguing with myself. I also knew that gooks had prepared bunkers for just such occasions. Other than a direct hit on top of the little fortresses, shrapnel would likely NOT penetrate the interior of any bunker. I had learned to respect the survival skills of the N.V.A. and V.C. in the jungle. Our platoon worked areas that had been napalmed, burned out with Agent Orange, even carpet bombed. We never found evidence of many, if any, dead enemy soldiers. Kind of reminded me of a story I heard in my 8th grade science class where cockroaches were able to survive a nuclear attack. The enemy was that tough in my mind. As far as I was concerned, in the jungle, weapons that were intended to inflict great numbers of dead Communists, did minimal damage at best. The only tried and true method of clearing out enemy soldiers was to send in the ground troops. Grunts could get the job done.

By the time I was finished using my entrenching tool to dig a hole under a huge tree root, the jets were upon us. I knew the hole wasn`t big enough, and I suspected that IF a bomb made it to the ground in our area, the only casualties would be from 2nd Platoon.

In an instant, there were eight very loud explosions, and the ground shook non-stop, but nothing landed anywhere near our platoon….thank goodness. Just as quickly as they arrived, the jets were gone, and since it was just past noon, everybody decided to open c-rations for lunch. What else would soldiers want to do after surviving a bombing attack? During our 'break' I went to Lt. Stoker, who was still a bit shaken from the navy mission, and he hadn`t had anything to eat, either. I said, "Lieutenant, it has been an hour since you last talked to the captain. Maybe you can call him and find out if anything has changed. I feel very naked out here with no friendlies in the area." Understand, it isn`t usual for sergeants to make such suggestions to lieutenants. But Stoker was clearly out of his element.

All his previous missions in the jungle, while not entirely safe, didn`t have the danger attached to it like this one seemed to have. AND, on the lieutenant`s other missions, there were other platoons always around if we needed them to come help us out. Our last transmission to Mertz made it sound like our platoon might be going it alone for quite some time. Even though the captain TRIED to convince us that support would be nearby at all times, I didn`t buy it. Bombing our position wasn`t the kind of support any of us felt comfortable with. I hoped that with time having gone by since the second ambush, Captain Mertz would have calmed down enough to want to gather ALL his troops together and work as a single entity. The lieutenant made the call.

By the look on his face, I knew the lieutenant didn`t get good news. Stoker came to my position and said, "The captain rejected my idea that we come to his location. Just the opposite. He said 'you and your platoon are to continue to pursue the bastards, and we will join you when we can.' Sgt. Stein, let`s get the men ready to roll."

The look of despair was on Stoker`s face, and I am sure he felt much like I did....that our platoon may very well be on a suicide mission. I thought about Jill again, and I knew we would have to alter the captain`s azimuth somewhat if I ever hoped to see my wife again. I mentioned to my lieutenant that following the creek would most certainly lead to more trouble. We needed to get AWAY from the water, and get to the coordinates that were assigned to us by a different route. Lt. Stoker agreed, and Sgt. Hart led our single-file formation as he started to ascend the thirty to forty-foot rise leading away from the creek.

As Dickie reached the top of the rise, he suddenly let loose with two short bursts from his M-16. Everyone hit the ground and I quickly yelled up to his position. What`s going on, Hart?" I shouted.

"Two gooks, Sarge....smoking pot....probably relaxing after watching the jets work out." Dickie`s attempt at humor escaped me as I crawled to where he and I were lying side by side, staring at an open field before us. "I was surprised to see anyone, Sarge, and when I fired on `em, one ran to the left and the other to the right. Both are in the jungle now, but I don`t think they went far."

The lieutenant had then made his way to our position and wanted a status report. I explained what Hart had told me, minus the pot and jet comments, then I made a suggestion. "Lieutenant," I started, "I need for you to bring up the rear squad and protect the clearing with Sgt. Hart`s squad. I will take Sgt. Janowitz`s squad and make a move to flush out the guy who went to the right. The lieutenant seemed relieved that we were going to do something, and he seemed VERY relieved to be in charge of the troops protecting my men`s backs.

As the rest of the platoon moved into defensive fire lines, I huddled up with Janowitz. "Calvin," I began, "Sgt. Hart saw a gook run over there. (I pointed to the right) Your squad and I are going to get him. We need to spread out on a line, no more than five to ten feet apart. Once we are on line, facing the gook`s last known position, we use fire-and-maneuver tactics to move forward until we spot him and kill the bastard. You understand?"

"If we had my tank, we`d just run over that gook," was his answer.

"Sgt. Janowitz," I continued, trying to get my point across, "it is important that nobody advances forward without having protective fire. We have NO tank, and we`re not exactly sure where that gook is. He might have others with him, too. We fire then move quickly to cover….got it?"

"Got it, Sgt Stein," Janowitz said in his omnipresent negative tone toward me. I didn`t want to sound 'bossy.' But it was important that I convey to my newest squad leader how the infantry is used to working in the jungle WITHOUT tracks at hand.

Once the seven of us were on a decent firing line, facing the site where the enemy was last seen running, I fired a burst of ammunition. When I finished, several other grunts started to shoot while I moved forward quickly to my next source of protection. The fire-and-maneuver tactic seemed to be working, as we had no return fire from anywhere. Sgt. Janowitz was five feet away from me, and he was following procedure beautifully for forty to fifty feet. Then, for no apparent reason, Calvin fired off a few rounds of ammo, moved from his tree, then slowly moved forward in a crouching position. That was not only NOT protocol, it was something that he hadn`t done once since we began advancing. His timing couldn`t have come at a worse time, either. EVERYBODY else in the squad was re-loading, so there were no Americans shooting during Calvin`s time in the open. Janowitz had spotted a giant anthill for his next protective site, that was easy to see, and he probably COULD have made it to the hill, if he would have run like he did every other time he moved forward. But, there he was, creeping along slowly, and without support. Calvin`s exposure time, without supportive fire, spanned only two to three seconds, but it seemed like forever when I recalled the event later.

A three-shot volley from an AK-47 rang out and Calvin Janowitz went down. He was a mere five feet to my right, but eight feet ahead of me. "Janowitz," I yelled, but he was just lying there, on his stomach, with his open eyes staring back at me. There was a bullet lodged in his head, and the point was just barely visible, as it didn`t escape the skull.

His squad had commenced firing again, but everybody ceased when I shouted his name. At that moment I instinctively moved from my position to get to the fallen soldier. Two more AK rounds exploded, and I heard them whiz by me, as I scrambled back to my cover.

"Bluto," I shouted, "Sergeant Janowitz is down, and I need help getting him back to my position. Put short bursts in that direction," and I saw Donovan nodding that he understood where to fire. Peppleman had hustled to my position, and with ALL the rest of the squad firing at once, Walter and I raced out to Calvin, grabbed him by the shirt, and dragged him to safety. Janowitz`s squad continued to use fire-and-maneuver, but we were moving back to the ridge with Calvin. Once back with the rest of the platoon, Janowitz`s entire squad looked with shocked faces as they stared at their leader`s listless body.

It was Lt. Stoker who seemed to have his wits about him more than any of the rest of us. He got onto the horn and called Capt. Mertz with the report of what happened. The lieutenant also suggested, rather vehemently I might add, that we be allowed to rendezvous with the rest of our decimated company. The captain agreed.

When the lieutenant came to my position to explain what the captain`s coordinates were, I knew I had to snap out of my funk, and in a hurry. We were in a very dangerous area, and everybody knew it. With Stoker next to me, we plotted the azimuth necessary to get us back to the rest of Delta Company. It appeared to be a distance of just over 500 meters. However, the direction would take us BACK toward the creek, but we needed to dust Janowitz off first before we could move to the captain. Sven Laaken and Dickie Hart were called to join the lieutenant and me. We were going to have to secure the open grassy field in order to get a med-evac to help us.

When moving across open areas, toward heavy jungle, it seemed prudent to me to have a weapon available which could disperse a large spread of ammunition toward the enemy if we were suddenly fired upon. Sven carried an M-79 grenade launcher, in which he always had a shotgun shell loaded, ready to produce mayhem. Also, when the shotgun round was fired, it made a startlingly loud noise. The pellets, packed inside the large shell, may or may not always take out a target over fifty feet away, but it DOES cover a vast area. The noise and the wide spread of BB`s was what I felt we needed to make the enemy seek shelter, even if for a short time. While grass was no real cover for humans, we all knew to hit the ground immediately if the shooting started, then low-crawl to the nearest protection. I prayed that we could traverse the open area unnoticed. Laaken just needed to lead me and the rest of his squad to the tree line, where we would be able to establish some defensive positions. While the 'field' squad was on the move, Sgt. Hart would be moving HIS squad back into the tree line where Janowitz had been shot, and stop anyone from advancing toward the open, grassy area from that direction. The lieutenant would stay in our current position, with the 3rd squad, and set up a defensive line to protect from any enemy forces coming up from the creek. The plan was for ALL of us to secure the field, and then call in a med-evac to dust off Janowitz quickly.

The grassy area wasn`t all that large, but our movement toward that left-side tree line was slightly uphill. In a mere 25-30 seconds, Laaken had traversed the majority of the field, and was within steps of getting to the trees, when the sickening crack of another AK-47 was heard. Sven Laaken crashed to the ground and screamed, "I`m hit. I`m hit!"

Steve (Sven) was a couple of meters in front of me, and to my right. I could clearly see him writhing in pain. I looked in front of him and there was the unmistakable firing portal of an N.V.A. bunker situated just inside the tree line. Anyone shooting from inside that perfectly placed portal had to be able to cover the entire open field. I yelled, "Bunker at twelve o'clock," and the six of us who had gotten onto the grassy plain started to shoot right at the portal`s opening. For Steve to not see such an obvious bunker was bewildering to me, and I never got to ask him how he missed it.

Sweeper Nelson was just to my left, and was laying a semi-steady stream of short bursts at the opening, but most of his rounds were just tearing into the roof over the portal. Laaken was crawling back toward us. Then I saw that James Remington had crawled to the right of Steve`s position. He was firing single rounds at the portal, too, but nothing was getting inside. Meanwhile the sniper was laying his rifle onto the floor of the opening and shooting blindly. Luckily, the tilt of the land was just enough to force his shots to go over our heads. Two members of Laaken`s platoon crawled forward to Steve, then dragged him back to the tree line, and away from the danger.

I knew what we were doing was not working, and if the gook decided to lower his muzzle he might just get lucky and shoot one of us. I yelled over to Remington, "James, you and I have to get closer to the opening. We`ll use fire and move tactics here, and Sweeper will be continuously firing bursts at the portal. When we get close enough one of us is going to have to toss a grenade INTO the opening. If we get too close, though, that bastard might hit one of us. We can`t crawl so high up toward him where his shooting would be level with us." The plan was in place, and Nelson kept the enemy soldier`s head down, while I fired then moved, then Remington fired then moved.

We were, sadly, getting close enough that Sweeper`s firing became dangerous for me, too. He had to stop support, and that left just James and me to shoot, and we were both using a lot of ammo and clips. Finally, James said, "I think I can get one in, Sarge," and with that statement he pulled the pin and let a grenade go toward the portal. Both he and I were in the kill zone, so getting the weapon inside was a must. I saw it fly, then saw it bounce up and off the portal opening ceiling, stopping right there. It hadn`t gone in! All I heard, after I lay as flat as I could, and covered my head with my arms was the sounds of a single AK round being fired, followed by one loud explosion, and a definite'whoooshing' sound accompanying the forceful grenade concussion wave going over my head. I also FELT a burning sensation on the back of my right hand. The tilted land had saved us.

"Remington, are you all right?" I hollered.

With his assurance that he was fine, we both rushed the bunker, coming around the backside and firing several shots into the entrance. We crept in slowly and found a headless body inside. We both surmised that the gook must have come up to fire when he couldn`t hear the constant rattle of our weapons, and then the grenade detonated. The guy must have seen the grenade lying in his opening, but didn`t have time to do anything but fire one round instinctively. He didn`t feel a thing, but I did. I had a small piece of shrapnel still sticking in the back of my right hand, and it was giving me a burning sensation. I carefully pulled it from my skin and hurled it to the ground. James and I were lucky, for sure, but we knew we couldn`t believe that THAT gook was the only enemy soldier we might face in the area. We hustled back to our unit.

Lt. Stoker had called for a dust-off helicopter, and soon the bird was hovering over our basketball court-sized open field. The chopper couldn`t land, however, as the canopy of the very large trees in the area were draped over much of the grassy plain. A jungle penetrator with seat was lowered for Laaken. Unfortunately, Stoker had failed to tell the med-evac copter, BEFORE it left its base, we had Janowitz with us, too. Apparently, no body bag or litter was brought to our action. Lt. Stoker told me later that he had just panicked when he saw Laaken, and wanted to get Sven help right away. We would have to keep Janowitz with us until morning when another medical helicopter could be sent. Darkness was rapidly on the way, as the helo took Steve back to Ling Binh.

I didn`t get to actually see what happened to Sven Laaken, but rumor had it that when the enemy soldier opened up on the point man, one round ricocheted off one of the high explosive grenade rounds, that Steve carried in his grenade vest, and tore upward. It took a small piece of Laaken`s cheek and his right eye, too, but the injury, as a whole, wasn`t thought to be too serious by the medical staff on board. Steve was one tough kid. A couple of months after the ambush, Laaken sent the platoon a picture of himself, as he was preparing to become a drill sergeant in a Basic Training company. The army not only let him stay in the service, but thought he would make an imposing-looking D.I. in his Smokey the Bear hat and a patch over one eye.

With nightfall less than an hour away, Lt. Stoker decided that we would settle in on the creek side of the grassy opening. We did know there was at least one gook in the area, but he would be to the right side of the perimeter with an M-60 pointing his way. The creek, itself, seemed to be enemy free, but there WAS a trail there, so setting out the o.p.s became very important that night. It was my job to not only place the observation posts correctly, but make sure they had coordinated cross-firing patterns which supported one another. Since I had only seventeen able bodies available, I decided to place a five-man o.p. whose job would be to cover the entire field AND be able to help if trouble came from either the left or right tree lines. Since I knew we had earlier encountered a gook to the right side of our perimeter, a four-man o.p. was placed, with Paul Randle and his M-60, focused directly on the area where Janowitz had been shot. The rest of Sgt. Hart`s squad would cover the remaining right side of the tree line to the creek, and half of the creek, too. 'Lucky' Fimbres` squad was set up to cover the entire left side of the perimeter, from the tree line to the creek, and the second half of the creek, too. There was no area unaccounted for with both small arms and machine guns having over-lapping firing lanes. Claymore mines were placed out front of each position as well. The order was given that nobody was to sleep that night. WE knew we were in a bad area, and we had to be prepared to react instantly if trouble came our way.

The lieutenant, the r.t.o. Samuels, and the medic were placed as close to the center of the perimeter as possible, though that perimeter was VERY small. They could render aid anywhere needed if trouble arose. For his part, Lt. Stoker had started calling in supporting mortar support as soon as he had his position for the night. The support plan was to have mortar rounds pulled in as close as fifty meters of our nighttime positions. There were five drop points around the perimeter, and Stoker had asked that one shell be sent in, in any of the five points, every fifteen minutes. The mortar platoon should also be prepared to drop rounds on all five points simultaneously if we came under attack. And the rounds DID land close by, as one of grunts in the 'field' o.p. caught a piece of shrapnel, from a mortar round, sometime during the night.

I decided to give more support to the creek side of the perimeter. Since we had two four-person o.p.s expected to be able to cover both the tree line and creek trail, I felt that I needed to give my full attention to the creek. After all, if the N.V.A. moved at night, they would take the path of least resistance. The creek offered a trail that could move people in a hurry, though this particular creek had booby traps set on it. I still had a bad feeling about movement coming from below us. Perhaps I was getting a little of that Dickie Hart 'sixth sense' intuition, but I found a log exactly halfway between the two 'creek' o.p.s, and that is where I set up for the night.

Two things bothered me almost immediately. The log was seven feet in length, and eight inches in diameter, but it wouldn`t stop a bullet from ripping through it since it was rotted out to the extent of nearly being hollow. Secondly, the body of Sgt. Janowitz had been laid four feet from the log, due to the small size of the entire perimeter, which meant he would be two feet from me after I was settled in next to the log. There was no time to move the body, as everybody was incredibly busy preparing for their nighttimes, and darkness came with lightening speed. What bothered me nearly as much as my first two dilemmas was the fact that it had been a cloudy day and there was absolutely NO moon or star light that evening. I knew there would be no light under triple canopy, but with the field nearby, I had hoped for some illumination from above….but it was not to be.

The only positive that I knew I could count on was the dropping of a mortar round, every fifteen minutes, all night long. That alone gave me a sense of security. I also prayed a lot. I just wanted the sun to rise so we could get out of that tragic area.

There was a sweet music that I listened for every night in the dark jungle…. the sound of crickets. While it was always so dark in the jungle that no perceptible movement could ever be seen, even with one`s own hand waving in front of the face, it was the chirping of crickets that became MY way of knowing that the jungle was at peace. On nights where there was a lack of cricket sound, I believed there must be something moving outside our perimeter, and that always worried me. Sadly, on that moonless night, there were NO cricket sounds, so I lay behind my log trying to be extra quiet, and extra alert.

I wore a watch whose hands and numbers glowed in the darkness. I wore it with the face on my inner wrist, so no one else could see the glow, and I always carefully tilted my wrist upward so I could get a glimpse of the time. Around 2200 hours, on that scary night, I heard the distinct 'wooosh' of an in-coming mortar round, then the explosion of its shell on one of the pre-determined five drop zones. That sound was immediately followed by the customary whizzing of shrapnel through the trees, which was then followed by dead silence.

About two or three minutes after the noises created by that mortar round ceased, I thought I heard a crunching sound. While sound is distorted in total darkness, I felt pretty confident that the crunch came from the creek. The first crunch was then followed by a second crunch, and a third. They were slow deliberate sounds, and even though it was impossible to tell exactly where the crunches originated, I felt nearly positive that there was a human walking close by. With the crunches seemingly getting louder, I determined that this man was moving from the creek toward our perimeter. I just couldn`t determine how close he was.

My M-16 rifle was lying on the ground between Janowitz`s body and me, but I didn`t dare pick it up. By doing that I could have made a noise that might have alerted the 'walker' to the fact that he wasn`t alone in the area. I HAD to maintain quiet. I did, however, sleep with my bayonet next to me as well as my rifle. With one more crunching sound I quietly picked up my bayonet, and since I had been lying on my back, I slowly moved to a half sit-up position. Unfortunately, I had grabbed the bayonet with my left hand, which wasn`t good since I was terrible doing anything with a knife in my left hand. I NEVER used a knife when I held it in my left hand. Still, there I was, in a half sit-up position, resting on my elbows, knife in my left hand, trying to figure out where this guy was and what I needed to do about the situation.

I heard a fourth crunch, then a fifth, suddenly there was a tremendous explosion. This was not a mortar round landing, it was someone in Hart`s position setting off a claymore mine. The blast was very loud, and burning leaves were falling from the trees along the creek. “Oh, good,” I said with my inner voice, “We got the bastard!” But I was wrong. We didn`t get ANYONE! Seconds after the mine was discharged, I heard two more crunches, only this time they sounded like they were coming FROM Hart`s o.p. heading in MY direction. Apparently, the gook had already penetrated inside Hart`s area of the perimeter. My heart began racing like I couldn`t ever remember it racing before. I had little time to think, when suddenly I heard the sound of a foot striking the end of my protective log. Through a quick, panicked analysis, I realized that the log was only seven feet long, and I was six feet tall. I couldn`t see him, but he couldn`t see me, either. To make matters worse, when he hit the end of the log, I heard him slap some kind of rifle-like weapon against his side. My eyes were wide as saucers when I realized that this enemy soldier was about to make a decision himself. He could choose to walk on the creek side of the log, and head away from me, OR he could choose to walk on my side of the log, and walk right on me! I knew I had to be quick if I felt him stepping on me, and I would have to stab at him again and again, and again, until either I got him, or he shot at me when he heard me moving.

Fortunately, he chose to move toward the creek. But with two more crunches, and believing him to be right next to me, my stomach growled. It wasn`t a little squeaky growl, but a longish, hungry growl. Immediately, this guy hit the ground, and in doing so he hit his head on the log….right next to where my head was. I could feel his heat, and I heard the faint sound of ‘ooof’ coming from him. Instantly, I heard him shuffling away from the log. I was frozen with fear.

Within seconds of his shuffling away, I heard the familiar sound of a mortar round descending. With the explosion, I lay my bayonet down, grabbed my M-16, placed it on my chest while trying to lay there as flat as a pancake, and set my weapon to the ‘panic’ mode. I was ready to fire all twenty rounds in my clip at once, if I had to.

I just lay there, wondering how close he was to me. I never heard another crunching noise, or shuffling sound, so I felt he had to be within feet of me. The only time I dared make any movement myself was when I heard the in-coming sound of another mortar round. THEN, I only moved from one butt cheek to the other. I wanted to roll away from that log desperately, but doing so would mean to try and roll OVER Janowitz. That would have created a great amount of noise. I didn`t want to make ANY noise since I knew how fragile that log was. That piece of wood was a mere security blanket for me when I chose to use it for cover, and at the time of my choosing it I was just thinking that I`d be adding firepower from between two o.p.s. I never really did take into consideration that if I was fired at from the creek, that hollow log would make me a dead duck. Noise was my enemy, so the longer I lay there in complete silence, the better I thought my chances were of the enemy forgetting exactly where my position was.

For most of the next six hours I started arguing with myself, "Abe what the hell. Just sit up, spray twenty rounds from left to right, and leap to the other side of Janowitz." "No," I would counter, "if I fire and miss the gook, he would surely see my muzzle flashing in the darkness, and shoot me dead BEFORE I could roll away." I did NOT know what I was going to do.

After lying there for those many horrifying hours, I began to think about daylight. When I looked at my watch and saw the time was approaching 0500 hours, I had an over-whelmingly terrible thought. Lately, 0500 had been about that time when the first light of day began appearing in the eastern part of the sky. This enemy soldier lay west of me, therefore I would be silhouetted against the sky WELL before I could get my first glimpse of HIM. I also realized that the eight-inch diameter log, I was hiding behind, would not hide my profile no matter HOW thinly I tried to make myself. I began thinking about Jill and my mother, and how I was going to miss them, when all of a sudden, a man stood up, not six feet from me. I could see HIS outline very clearly. He began racing toward the creek. I sat up, placed the rifle against my cheek, and tried like hell to fire my weapon. I wanted to kill that bastard....I really did. But I couldn`t move my finger. It was nearly paralyzed on the trigger. In fact, it took me several minutes to massage that digit before I could even remove it from its position. Being in that stressful situation for such a long time had frozen my hand in place. I was so perplexed at my unusual situation, that I never even saw where that enemy soldier headed once he got to the creek.

When light was just beginning to make things on the ground clear enough to see, I hustled to the lieutenant`s position. He asked immediately what had happened with the claymore. I told him my story briefly, and we agreed that we had to vacate the premises as quickly and quietly as possible. We knew of at least one, and maybe two, enemy soldiers to the right side of our perimeter, so we decided to move to the left and around the bunker with the dead gook inside. That direction happened to be on the azimuth where we would find the captain, so with Sgt. Hart walking point, we moved out.

Movement was incredibly slow, however. Calvin Janowitz`s body had swollen during the night, and gotten to a very heavy weight. It took six soldiers at one time to carry the body, and we had to switch off often. Not only did we have to carry Calvin, but he was just being carried in a poncho liner, so his body was visible the whole time we moved him. With the tension from the day before, and the sight of a fallen comrade being carried, the morale of the entire platoon was diminishing, and in a short amount of time, too. Within an hour`s walk we FINALLY found a field big enough to accommodate a med-evac, and Lt Stoker made the call.

During all three ambushes of our company the prior day, med-evac choppers were never later than fifteen minutes before arriving at any of our locations. We were STILL in an area that we believed was swarming with N.V.A., and we knew that the enemy probably knew where we were, too. An agonizing hour went by and no helicopter. During that whole time, I was once again stationed in an area where Calvin lay right beside me. I started to think about him and me at the N.C.O. Academy. I thought of how he came grudgingly to our infantry platoon from his tank company, and then developed into a first-rate, grunt squad leader. I also couldn`t help thinking about his family, and the anguish they would suffer at the news of his demise. I didn`t have to wait for a memorial at any firebase. I shed many tears while waiting for that medical helicopter to arrive. Finally, an hour and ten minutes after the lieutenant called, a med-evac came for Calvin Janowitz.

I raced to the chopper and yelled, "Where have you been?" I knew I was spewing irrational venom at the wrong people. They hadn`t done anything wrong, but I just needed to unload my pent-up anger, guilt, and sadness on somebody. The medical staff member on board must have known I wasn`t really yelling at him specifically, just whoever got to me first, and he said, "Sorry we`re late, Sarge, but we got him now. We`re gonna take real good care of your buddy."

Tears welled up in my eyes again as I backed away from the rising med-evac, and I uttered, "Good-bye, Calvin. You can rest in peace now," and I felt tears once again falling down my cheeks. I wiped my face and turned around. Hart and Nelson were looking at me. They both just nodded in my direction, which told me that they understood my tearful good-bye to Janowitz, then Hart said, "Come on Sarge, the lieutenant is in a hurry to get to the captain. We moved out in short order, and arrived with Capt. Mertz and the other two platoons less than an hour later.

XI

Life Can Hurt, Too

The day after I saw Calvin being taken away, I was removed from the jungle by helicopter, and flown to the Rear. One day later, I was headed to Hawaii on a 'freedom bird,' where I was finally going to get to be with my wife for one great week.

Paradise is the way I would describe Hawaii. I have been to those islands many times since my R&R of 1970. The gentle breezes created by the Trade Winds, the smell of Plumeria, the beautiful colors of the Bird of Paradise and other island flowers, the taste of exotic drinks like Mai Tais or Pina Coladas or just watching lovely girls dancing the hula to the unique sounds of island musical instruments and vocals….Hawaii is a place where people can forget the grind of everyday problems back home, and truly relax in the serene surroundings which make up these magical islands.

Military people had choices for their R&R weeks, Sydney, Australia was one, so was Bangkok, Thailand. Those were places where single guys and gals went to blow off steam before returning to Vietnam. Married men and women, however, were really looking for a place to cuddle with their significant others, and do nothing else but lay back and re-charge the emotional bonds which were inevitably strained by the assignment of one or the other spouse to a war zone. As for me, I had endured seven months in a kill-or-be-killed environment, and I NEEDED to be in the loving arms of my sexy wife. I kept wondering why that plane was taking so long to get me to Hawaii.

As we began descending into the Honolulu airport, I started to worry about whether I was going to be accepted, or rejected, by Jill`s arms. First, I thought about my time with her at Ft. Benning….it was horrible. That was when she couldn`t tell me ENOUGH how much she hated everything about the army, and the fact that I had adapted so well to the lifestyle. There were certainly no loving arms enveloping me just before I saw her get into the car and head back to school. However, I also thought about my returning to Iowa City, before my deployment to Vietnam. Jill and I seemed to re-develop a very healthy relationship before I flew to California. She finally accepted the fact that I was going to be away for nearly a year. But she also believed that upon my return from the war, and my discharge from the army, she would be able to think of the military as just a bad chapter in her life. I desperately wanted to be with the woman I left at the airport in Cedar Rapids, not the person who nearly got me reduced in rank in Columbus, Georgia. I also wanted to stop making mountains out of mole hills. I looked around the plane, and when I saw how many military people had huge smiles on their faces, I calmed myself down. I frantically wanted to believe that our week in the Hawaiian Islands was going to transport Jill and me back to the feelings we had for one another during our honeymoon.

The plane landed and busses loaded us on board. Soon we were headed to Ft. DeRussy on Waikiki. That is where our loved ones would be waiting for us. As we entered the road leading to the reception center at DeRussy, I spotted Jill immediately. Disembarkment wasn`t as hectic as the day we spent at Cam Ranh Bay, but people were definitely scrambling to get off the busses as soon as possible. I rushed to Jill, grabbed her in my arms, then said loud enough for everyone around me could hear, "I love you so much," then I gave her a near-death bear hug.

"I want you to do me a favor," she said.

I wasn`t sure I heard her correctly. I thought she said 'do me a favor,' NOT 'I love you,' or 'I`ve missed you,' not even a 'hi.' The first words out of my wife`s mouth, after seven months of separation, were, "I want you to do me a favor."

Easing up on the bear hug, but still with a huge smile on my face, I looked into her eyes and said incredulously, "You want me to do you a favor? What kind of favor?" She broke free from my arms, and with much excitement in her voice she said, "I want you to try these with me." She opened her purse exposing four perfectly wrapped marijuana joints.

As we started to walk away from DeRussy, I tried to explain a few things to Jill. I told her Vietnam was FILLED with drugs. Barbers would offer G.I.s nickel bags of heroine after a haircut. I then told her about a evening that our platoon had a nighttime position IN a field of wildly-growing marijuana. And since we were headed to a forward firebase the next day, the men crammed every inch of their depleted rucksacks with the weed. Once at the base the captain ordered grunts to un-load every single plant they took to the base, and pile it in one huge stack in the center of the grounds. I told her smoking dope wasn`t uncommon in The Rear, but getting caught would mean getting an Article 15 disciplinary action taken against the smoker. Drugs were illegal for soldiers to have EVEN in a war zone, and smoking in the jungle was an invitation for the enemy to smell it from a good distance away then surprise us with an ambush. I did lighten the story up a bit by telling her that the captain had the pile of marijuana lit on fire, and soldiers spent a LOT of time, during the early part of the stand-down, hanging out near the fire.

I knew Jill was a smoker when I married her, but she also knew that I had never even taken a drag from a single cigarette in my entire life. It really bothered me that within minutes of my long-awaited reunion with her, my wife not only wanted me to smoke, but to smoke an illegal substance. When I rejected her offer, she remained quiet for a very long time, and the first day was mostly spent in silence.

It was during that silent period that I really had a chance to think about Jill`s support for me during the time I had already spent in Nam. Since I kept a journal, I also carried paper and envelopes so I could write loved ones, and friends, letters whenever possible. In the jungle I didn`t find enough time to write to anyone very often. However, in forward firebases, I was a prolific writer, and would write at least two letters a day, one to Jill and one to my mom. Then I would write to as many other people as time permitted.

The correspondence I received was quite interesting. I DID get several letters from the people I wrote to. My mother wrote me more than anyone, which kind of surprised me because I knew she was holding down three jobs to make ends meet. I couldn`t figure out how she had the time to write so many letters to me, but they made me happy. Jill sent me letters, too, one to every three of my mom`s, though. She claimed to be busy, but how much busier than my mother could she possibly be. My mom sent me at least one 'care package' a week, filled with lots of goodies that she knew I liked and couldn`t get in Nam, like pie fillings, and I LOVED eating the apricot pie filling she would send me. Jill sent me a 'care package' about once a month. Hers were small, however, and contained things that didn`t go well in the jungle, like peanuts….salted peanuts. With water being so scarce in the jungle, the last thing I wanted to do was eat a bag of peanuts and get insatiably thirsty.

The letters Jill sent me were unusual, too. They were short and usually informational…how her classes were going, who she met for this lunch or that breakfast. I didn`t know most of the people she wrote to me about, so I had very little interest in Jill`s meals with them.

There weren`t any, let`s say, mushy words or phrases in my wife`s letters, either. While I saw letters from other soldier`s wives saying such things as, 'I am counting down the days until I am with you again,' or 'there is no woman who can love a man more than I love you.' Jill`s letters NEVER had the phrase, 'I love you.' The best I got from her was, 'hope you`re doing fine,' and her usual letter sign off , 'with love, Jill.' I hated to share my letters with guys in the platoon…except for the last one I received, which I got the day before the mission of the three ambushes. Jill actually said in her letter, 'I`m really excited about going to Hawaii and seeing you again.' She still signed off with, 'with love, Jill.' Still, I became very happy when I read that she was 'excited to see me.' Man, was I reaching for warmth from her.

Even though the first day didn`t start well, we remedied the long, quiet period by having sex later that afternoon. We just touched each other, almost by accident, then we found ourselves in an embrace. Having that moment to have sex was important to both Jill and me, as we had always enjoyed having sex. It was our go-to activity. During the week in Hawaii we had MANY moments of sex. We enjoyed eating at restaurants, too. For me, eating all the great food almost made me forget c-rations….almost. We walked hand-in-hand along the Ala Wai Canal, but the conversations we had, for the rest of the week, NEVER centered on Vietnam or anything else having to do with the military.

Whenever I wrote a letter to Jill, or my mom for that matter, I made sure that I NEVER talked about any of the dangerous missions I had been on. I wanted both women to visualize me having duties in a safe part of Nam, where missions into the jungle weren`t all that exciting. My letters were filled with descriptions of flowers, plants, and even animals that I might have seen. I also talked a lot about the guys in my unit and some of the crazy things they said and did in the jungle or at our forward firebases. Jill couldn`t believe I had people burning feces in 'honey pots.' She thought America ought to do something about getting sanitary bathrooms for soldiers in ALL our firebases. While my information was innocuous, I would ask many questions about how work was going, school, the weather, or about what my family and friends were up to. Anything that was necessary to say, that would not make Jill or my mom worry about me, I would include in my letters.

Even while avoiding talking about ANYTHING military that week, Jill and I could both feel the tension between us. For instance, we had a terrible argument one day involving money.

I kept very little money from the monthly paycheck the army paid me. I didn`t need money in the jungle, so I sent all but $20 to Jill every month. I was making more money than I ever thought I would make as a soldier, too. I received E-6 pay, overseas pay, AND combat pay just because I was sent to Vietnam. I was sending a LOT of money home. Jill had told me, in one of her letters, she decided to rent out OUR trailer because her father had gotten her an apartment in downtown Iowa City. That was done so she wouldn`t have to drive from the mobile home park to the university every day. Her dad worried about her living alone out in the country. With the rent we received from our trailer, and having Jill`s dad pay for an apartment, I believed we were saving some really good money. Jill sweetened the pot by telling me that her apartment was so big that she could take in one of her former sorority sisters as a roommate. She claimed having a friend living with her made her feel less lonely for me. Jill collected a little rent from her 'sister,' too. While Rosie, the roommate, didn`t pay a lot of rent, she did pay SOMETHING. Finally, Jill told me she had taken a part-time job in the book store, which was located directly under her apartment. I was thrilled at the idea of Jill being so responsible and saving a lot of money. I couldn`t wait to hear about the size of the nest egg we`d have when I got discharged from the service. Then one day in Hawaii, we discussed all that money. That`s when the other shoe dropped.

"There isn`t as much money as you might think," She answered when I asked her to give me an 'in the area' amount of funds in our savings. "I`ve had lots of clothes to buy for school, groceries to buy, there are utilities to pay." I stopped her right there.

"Jill, what utilities?" I asked. "I thought the renters in the trailer paid for their utilities, and your dad paid for the utilities in your apartment. What utilities?" If there was one thing my wife could not do, and never WANTED to do, it was to tell a lie. "All right," she said with conviction, "I`ll tell you about where the money went." She started to tell me about parties that she threw in her apartment. About how expensive it was to buy marijuana, and all the paraphernalia what went with the drug. She told me about trips she and Rosie took, where Jill picked up most all of the bills because 'Rosie couldn`t afford to go with me, and I didn`t want to go alone.' I couldn`t believe my ears, she was partying and having a great time being with her friends, AND buying lots and lots of clothes, while I was in Vietnam doing my duty to my country. I know it sounds a bit maudlin, but that is how I expressed myself to her when she told me the 'truth.' I wanted her to feel guilty about spending so much of our money. She didn`t. She had been used to getting things her way all her life, AND she wasn`t going to change her search for a good time just because I was not around. That was NOT one of the fun days we had.

We had a huge argument about cats, too. Jill wanted to get a cat as a pet. I told her I was allergic to cats, but I would love it if she got a puppy. That 'discussion' arose a few times during our week, and each time, we finished arguing by going silent on one another.

Our loudest argument happened as I was about finished packing my bags, and preparing to head for Ft. DeRussy and the bus taking me to the airport. "You remember when you asked me how I was spending so much money with not much to show for it?" she asked. I nodded, and then she continued talking while pulling an envelope out of her purse. "I got us two tickets to Canada," she said proudly. "I am willing to leave everything here in America and start a new life with you in Canada. Our plane is scheduled to leave one hour before that plane headed back to Vietnam. I have ALL our money with me now. Come on, Abe, let`s do this, please?" I took the envelope, opened it up, and looked at the contents. I saw the two tickets to Vancouver, all right, and I just glared at Jill. Then, I just lost it. For the first and only time, during the entire week on Oahu, I actually yelled at my wife. "Are you crazy? I have about three months left to serve in the army because I am getting an early out to go back to school. I have done EVERYTHING I can to make you, my mom, our friends, EVERYONE proud of my service to America. I have EARNED respect, and now you want me to go with you to Canada, be labeled a deserter, and never be allowed to return to the country I love again? I CAN`T believe you did this, you bitch!"

That is when Jill let loose with seven days of pent-up anger toward me. She cussed me up one side, then down the other. She told me she hated the military, and if I wasn`t willing to leave for Canada with her, she hated me, too. I just listened to her as she ranted on, but when I was all packed and headed for the door, I turned to her and said, "I still love you, Jill, and if you still want to be married to me, you`ll have to think about what you tried to make me do, understanding that I love this country, and would NEVER desert it. I`ll be back before you know it, and we can work at making a beautiful life together." I opened the door, realizing that I would be walking to DeRussy by myself, then I turned toward Jill and tried to say, with a little humor in my voice, "And DON`T get a CAT." She just turned away, and I was gone.

The plane ride back to Vietnam was a lot different than the ride to Hawaii, as you might have guessed. The looks on everybody`s faces were pensive to serious, not a smile from anyone on the entire journey. Personally, I felt tortured, but I remember my mom telling me, after I had just gotten married to Jill, that I would need to constantly work at my marriage, trying to never let it die without fighting to save it. She had mentioned there would be some tough times, especially since I was about to serve two years for Uncle Sam, but if I truly loved my wife, I would need to be strong to endure. Since I respected my mom more than anyone I ever knew, I convinced myself that I was going to do everything in my power to keep Jill.

I wrote Jill more than a dozen letters after my return to the war zone. She wrote only two to me. Both of her letters had that 'Dear John' sound to them. She said, "I`m not sure I can stay with you anymore. You were SO changed in Hawaii. I`m not even sure I know what love is anymore."

I didn`t feel I had anyone in Nam to talk to about my failing marriage. And, knowing that, I convinced myself to NEVER show any weaknesses in the field while constantly reassuring my platoon that I was a leader they could count on at ALL times. However, whenever I would slink off to be alone, and I re-read both of Jill`s letters, I just felt helpless and a little sick to my stomach. It was in Jill`s second and last letter to me that she told me that she was going to get a cat. That made me angry, as she knew it would.

For my part, I told my wife that I still loved her very much, and I felt confident that if we worked hard together that we could not only save our marriage, we could make it stronger than anyone could have ever imagined it would be. I implored her to 'hang in there with me,' as my time in the military was rapidly coming to a close. She would need to 'give us a chance to work things out.' I also mentioned, on more than one occasion, that I really, REALLY didn`t want her to get a cat until I got home. I tried very hard at selling her on the fact that we could get us a cute puppy, and she would love that puppy. Finally, I ALWAYS finished each letter with the phrase, "I love you, Jill!" I felt I did everything I could to try and save our marriage from long distance. I just needed her to wait for me to return to Iowa. I really wanted to believe that we could become lovers and friends again while being a married couple.

Upon my return to Long Binh, I was given two bits of interesting information. First, Lt. Stoker had been reassigned to a non-infantry platoon somewhere. Apparently, his first true combat mission in the jungle caused him so much stress that he deemed himself inadequate as an infantry leader in the jungle. At least that is what First Sergeant Fish told me. That news was a little hard for me to figure out. That 'triple ambush' mission made ALL of us edgy. It`s what close-up combat does to most every human being. The lieutenant seemed fine when I left for my R&R. He MUST have gotten the ear of someone with pull because he sure wasn`t with our platoon anymore.

The second bit of news shocked me even more. As the 199th Light Infantry Brigade was down-sizing, in preparation to be rotated back to the United States, new second lieutenants were becoming scarce. So, 1st Sergeant Fish informed me that I, Abraham Dicker Stein, was to be the acting 2nd platoon leader until a replacement could be found.

I wanted to ask Fish about several procedures associated with being platoon leader, like....was I going to get platoon leader pay, etc., but he didn`t seem interested in talking to me anymore about my temporary promotion. I did know that I should not upset the man. He was the person in charge of getting me the early school drop. That 'drop' would take two and a half months off my two-year hitch in the army. First Sergeant Fish was the most powerful man in Delta Company, and for me to upset him in any way could prove to be detrimental to my getting out of the service early, so I just said, "Thank-you for the good news, 1st Sergeant."

He did have some interesting and welcome news for me, however. He said that there was a chopper waiting for me, so I had to move it, BUT he also mentioned that our company was working out of the village of Vo Dat in a pacification capacity. Knowing that we would have shorter missions, and we wouldn`t have to work the dangerous area where we had just lost so many men, was pleasant news to my ears.

When I arrived in our encampment next to the village, I reported to Capt. Mertz. He welcomed me as the new platoon leader then immediately sent me and my men on that security mission. You remember, the location was seven klicks from Vo Dat, right next to that little South Vietnamese outpost, where we ended up protecting the American mortar and howitzer platoons for twelve days.(with LOTS of help from a track unit) When I was first given that assignment I DO remember wanting to tell the captain that I was a little exhausted from my trip from Hawaii, and that I had a terrible time with my wife, so perhaps he could send either of the other platoons instead of 2nd Platoon. However, within fifteen hours of leaving an upset Jill, I was laying barbed wire in an enemy-controlled area of Vietnam.

As it turned out, THAT mission, while causing me great stress for the first four days, turned out to be more relaxing and gave me a more 'needed' feeling than my R&R. Go figure.

After a short jungle mission with my company, the rest of my nine weeks in Vietnam proved quite interesting. On one of my missions, my platoon worked a joint mission with a South Vietnamese platoon. The lack of work ethic they exhibited convinced me they would be no match for the extraordinary fighters from the North. On that mission, I witnessed some of the laziest, noisiest, most careless, and down-right non-committal behavior I could imagine seeing in professional soldiers.

Here`s an example of what occurred. Our combined platoons were asked to make a sweep of a certain part of jungle near Vo Dat, then report to a larger unit of South Vietnamese troops, in a second part of that area, for a mission set for the following day. As we were moving along nicely, we came across a pepper field, or maybe it was a peanut field. Anyway, you`d have thought we came across a gold mine. Those guys just plopped themselves down and started to pick, whatever it was, and pop them in their mouths. They were having a grand old time. It didn`t seem to matter to them that the field had no protected cover from an enemy attack. The eating frenzy led to a smoke and joke session for them, too, as most every one of those soldiers lit up cigarettes, and started having VERY loud conversations with one another. My platoon moved to one end of the tree line and set up some o.p.s, you know, just in case the enemy WAS in the area. When we arrived at our final destination, I got the South Vietnamese platoon leader alone and asked this question, "What are you going to do when the Americans leave you, and you have to fight the Communists by yourselves?" I then pointed out some of the lax and seemingly undisciplined behavior in the pepper (peanut) field that could have gotten them killed.

He really only seemed concerned with my question, and not all that bothered by the short-comings I saw amongst of troops. He answered with a statement that both surprised me AND angered me. "America NEVER leave here. They make too much money for their war business back home." Then he addressed his troop issue. "We had you with us. If you fight, then we would fight. We ALWAYS have you help us fight. No problem, Sergeant." He then left to talk to his troops about what I reported. No one looked too concerned by his words. The next day the large force we had joined swept a lot of jungle. When we found nothing by midday, we all went back to our compounds.

We were assigned the same Vietnamese platoon on a couple more two-day missions, one week after the joint mission. Apparently, the leader HAD been upset with the lack of discipline his soldiers showed us on our first go-around. He wanted my platoon to show his people PROPER technique to use when operating in jungles and fields. The captain okayed the request, so we spent two full days showing that sloppy platoon how to work in the jungle. Less than a week later, and after practice on their own, the Vietnamese leader wanted to show my platoon what his troops had LEARNED. If pacification meant teaching what we knew to others, then I felt like we made some progress in that area. However, if what we saw during the second two-day mission was meant to show us VAST learning had taken place, then the assignment fell short. Honestly, we would have had to work strictly with that one small unit for many more days to eliminate most of the poor field behavior exhibited by them. We weren`t Mac-V. We were not trained to teach, we were trained to fight. The assignment was more failure than success, and nobody in my platoon had the desire or patience to work with that South Vietnamese platoon for more than those two short missions. Luckily, the captain had other assignments for us to perform, so that was the end of our 'teaching' sessions.

By comparison, though, my platoon got to work a two-day mission with a crack South Korean platoon. Those troops were eager to learn anything we could teach them during our first day together, and on the second day they were anxious to show us what they learned. It was beautiful! I was so impressed with the extreme discipline the Korean troops had. Here is what I am talking about. The leader of the Vietnamese platoon, with whom we had worked, talked to his troops with very little emotion, kind of suggesting that they should pay attention and TRY to learn from us. He seemed like he didn`t want to upset anyone. From what I could tell, his troops hadn`t apparently had any real hard discipline put on them in previous training, so being animated in speech might have turned his men off, and made motivation next to impossible to achieve.

The ROK troops were elite. They were professional soldiers, who took their craft seriously, and they were MUCH more disciplined than the American troops I was around, I do know that. On the second morning of our mission with the South Koreans, the ROK platoon leader called his troops to morning formation. They stood silently at attention as he inspected them. He would admonish his men for even the slightest infractions, which resulted in push-ups being done by the offending soldier. I knew none of that would fly with American troops in the jungle. We were 'officially' professional troops, but many of us were drafted, a couple guys were court-ordered to be there….it was just different with U.S soldiers. In fact, there were incidences where some American leaders had been 'fragged' or 'accidently' shot during firefights after a leader was particularly harsh to certain soldiers. There were several ways to get respect, and while I respected the discipline that was exhibited by the ROK leader and his men, I knew I could never get away with that program. But I DID know that the South Vietnamese leader could have used a stricter approach to get things done with his troops. Balance was the key for me.

Working with the South Koreans was eye-opening, and working with the South Vietnamese ended up being somewhat satisfying, after I was told they were actually trying to learn from my platoon. But I STILL preferred working my missions with American troops. I didn`t like conversing in pigeon English much, so during my last two and a half months in Nam, I was happiest being around men who could just speak plain English. Also, I was MUCH happier when we only had to work the two and three-day missions as opposed to the two and three-week missions we had been given during the first seven months of my tour. I was getting pretty picky, huh?

One of my favorite missions had us working with army dogs and their handlers in a place known for tunnels. We still had Peppleman, but HE was happy that he wouldn`t have to crawl inside tunnels as long as we had dogs. And the dog teams were extremely professional....no extra noise....all business when we were on the move....I had hoped we could work with that team a few more times, but we only had them for three days. We did find tunnels, but there was never any contact with the enemy. We didn`t even find caches of ANYTHING which surprised the dog handler. Still, we knew that those tunnels had been used, and likely will be used, so we gassed them and moved on. That was a memorable mission for me because I learned to have a lot of respect for specialized troops and their canine companions.

The final five weeks of my tour weren`t too memorable, as far as having contact with the enemy went. Thanks to the Cambodian incursion a month earlier, fewer N.V.A. forces seemed to be coming into South Vietnam through areas where our brigade was working. It seemed the raid sapped a lot of the enemy resources, which apparently, took some time to replace. The Vo Dat Mountains had less activity, too. Even though there was evidence of many hard-core enemy cadre remaining in the mountains, we just didn`t get into many firefights. I can`t really tell you why that was, either. There was still plenty of fighting in other parts of the country, just not much involving Delta Company. I was very thankful for that, too, because my time In Country was getting short. I felt more anxious every time we were sent into the jungle on any mission. I knew I couldn`t avoid combat all together, I just didn`t want to take unnecessary chances if I didn`t have to, and previous ambushes started to haunt me, too. Yes, I was becoming nervous as my days dwindled.

The only mission I remember where I was VERY uncomfortable happened in IV Core, which was South Vietnam`s Delta region. My platoon was attached to a larger operation and we had to hump through open rice paddies. I hadn`t ever been so exposed before, and I worried that there might be V.C. popping up from every rice paddy. It was a very uneasy feeling. I wasn`t even sure what our mission was, to be honest. We were ordered to be part of the assignment for one day, so my platoon went. The only things we DID encounter were leeches. I had one get on my hand, and an experienced paddy soldier used lighter fluid to get the thing off me....at least I think it was lighter fluid. That was the most miserable mission I had during my waning weeks in Nam.

The day before I was to leave Vietnam, which was three days before I was to actually get my discharge from the army, I was called to the captain`s hootch. My platoon had been reduced to fifteen men at the time. Dickie Hart had not been with us since I returned from R&R. Both Bluto Donovan and Sweeper Nelson had been rotated to the States several weeks before it was my turn to go. It`s not that we didn`t still had some mighty fine veteran soldiers left in the platoon: Paul Randle, Sgt. Fimbres, Walter Peppleman, and Carmichael, who was a good troop, just not a fun person to be around. The rest of the 2nd platoon members, however, were relatively new guys, and none of them had really been tested in combat yet. In fact, the whole brigade seemed to be marching in place, waiting to leave the Southeast Asian theater. I felt like I was one of the last real Redcatchers, just a remnant of a once proud, fighting brigade.

The meeting with Captain Mertz was un-emotional and to the point. "A chopper is on route to get you back to Long Binh. I understand you are scheduled to leave Nam tomorrow and will be getting out of the army in three days. Good luck to you, Sergeant. In the meantime, Sgt. Fimbres will assume the platoon leader position, at least one or two days or until we get someone of E-6 rank or higher to take over as the new 2nd platoon leader. That`s all, Sgt. Stein….you are dismissed."

All right, I wasn`t expecting a hug, maybe not even a handshake, since I did know Capt. Mertz to be a no-nonsense commander. And, even though I wasn`t crazy about officers in general, (pun intended) Captain Mertz likely saved my life. I knew I could NEVER forget him. It was Mertz who got me tanks when I desperately needed them. It`s true, however, that I never really thanked him for doing that. At the time I felt it was his duty to do everything he could to get help to the 2nd platoon in time of crisis, which he did. After all, we were his men, and it wouldn`t have looked good if he let a whole platoon perish. In retrospect, I should have thanked him.

When I left the captain, Sgt. Fimbres was just arriving. "Captain Mertz wants to see me, Sarge. I wonder what that`s all about." I smiled and walked away.

As the chopper was arriving, Walter Peppleman sought me out. "I`m gonna miss you, Sarge, and I just want to thank you for being my friend. And as a friend,

I am going to tell you the nickname that the fellas made up for you WAY back when Hart and Nelson were with us. Only ones who know that name now are Randle and me."

"What are you talking about, Walter? What nickname....I never had a nickname."

"Actually, you DID, Sarge, but some of the guys thought it might offend you, so no one ever used it on you. We just used it behind your back `cause Hart and Nelson thought it fit you, and they made it up."

"Tell me, Walter, before I have to get on the helo."

"Jewish Jungle Boy, Sarge, that`s what a few of us liked to call you. Hart and Nelson were calling everyone by their nicknames one day in Ivy, and Dickie said we needed to give you a fitting nickname. Said all sergeants are called sarge, but we wanted you to be a special sarge. When Hart blurted out Jewish Jungle Boy, and Nelson laughed, then it was done. Some of us thought you might get upset with the name, you being Jewish and all. But it was because you WERE Jewish and operated well in the jungle that we all thought it a fair name. Guys would come up and say, 'Jewish Jungle Boy is going to be in our nighttime tonight,' or 'Jewish Jungle Boy wants us to mount up now.' It may not have been a great name, Sarge, but by giving you a nickname, well, it made everybody feel that you were more like us, just a fellow grunt fighting the gooks. Hope you don`t mind. I just thought you might want to know we gave you a nickname, that`s all."

Walter was smiling from ear to ear as I turned to move out toward the chopper. "Love it, Walter. Thanks," I shouted back at him as I moved toward the helicopter.

Normally, anti-Semitic name-calling would result in hard feelings, maybe even physical confrontations. Walter just wanted to let me know that the guys I respected also accepted me as an equal, and there was NO prejudice associated with the nickname. I was just one of them....and I felt very good when my ride got airborne.

Getting 'short' can elicit every emotion a G.I. has in him. I knew I was getting very skittish, maybe even a bit worried, nervous….all right, scared for several days prior to my evacuation from Vo Dat. I had gone through a lot of tough times during my ten plus months in Nam, and I didn`t want anything to happen to me, especially when I got under ten days left before I was to get my honorable discharge from the service.

Once on company grounds in Long Binh, I reported to 1st Sergeant Fish, where I received my orders for the freedom bird, scheduled to leave late the next night. As soon as I walked out of Fish`s office, I began feeling quite relieved, almost happy just knowing I would soon be a civilian. My plans would be simple. I`d catch my transportation to the airport at 2200 hours, board the plane, then take off while re-assuring myself that I was leaving the war for good. Once airborne, I would will myself to forget everything I went through during my time in Vietnam. I also planned to pray so hard that things between my wife and me would return back to the way they were before I got my draft notice. Yep, it was a great plan. My immediate problem, however, was that I couldn`t figure out how to turn my brain off. I just couldn`t stop thinking about EVERYTHING!

I was still upset, maybe even angry at the way Jill and I left things in Hawaii, and how I felt after reading the two upsetting letters I got from her once I reported back to my unit. I tried to practice what I would say to her that could make our relationship get back to the honeymoon feelings I desperately sought for both of us. I struggled all afternoon with those thoughts.

That first night in the Rear got worse as the night progressed, too. Oh, I went to the N.C.O. Club all right, had a water buffalo steak and a few beers, listened to the music blaring, but I wasn`t enjoying any of them. I decided to return to the barracks early, trying to rid myself of the melancholy I had been suffering the entire time I was at the club. As I lay on my cot, I needed to fight back tears when I began thinking about the men I couldn`t get safely home to their families. I remembered everything I knew about Allison, Williamson, Vega, and Janowitz. The guilt and sadness I felt with those memories caused me to toss and turn so badly that I did not sleep one minute all night.

I got up early the next morning, had breakfast, then returned to my bunk. I was lamenting about how bored I would be just hanging around the company area all day. I was also sulking because I just couldn`t release some of my horrible memories, either. Suddenly, Sgt. Jesse Minister, the company supply sergeant, walked into the barracks. His story was interesting. He was a member of the 1st platoon, and was rotated to The Rear a scant week before the medical helicopter was shot down during the horrible three- ambush day. He was so upset by the loss of so many platoon brothers, he told First Sergeant Fish that he wanted to re-up for another year in Nam. He also told the 1st sergeant he would do most any job needed, but he couldn`t go back out to the field. Since 1st Sgt. Fish had gone through several supply sergeants in recent months, and was getting tired of training new ones all the time, he got orders for Jesse to stay in Delta Company for an additional year. Once the orders came through, Minister was assigned, by 1st Sergeant Fish himself, permanent company supply sergeant. He did, indeed, become known as the Fish`s right hand man, and was constantly running errands for his boss. Jesse Minister told me he was on the fast track to make E-6, too.

The Minister (as everyone called him) had come to the barracks to find someone to ride shotgun for him, as he was getting ready to deliver re-supply to Delta Company in Vo Dat. There were a couple of guys around the barracks, but neither of them wanted to 'spend all morning waiting for a convoy to get established at the checkpoint, ride through ambush country to deliver a few supplies, then wait most of the afternoon for the convoy to RETURN to get them, finishing up by driving through ambush country a second time,' as one of them stated. Each of them had done that journey before, and each of them got back between 1800-1900 hours, essentially wasting an entire day. They pleaded with The Minister to find someone else.

I remembered working that 'ambush' road for twelve days. I wasn`t against going back and seeing where my platoon had set up a civilian checkpoint, and perhaps remembering some of the GOOD times we had there. In fact, I hadn`t heard of any ambushes taking place on that road over the past ten or twelve days. Without thinking twice I said," I`ll go with you, Jesse."

"Sarge," Minister whined, which was his usual speaking tone, "you`re going home tonight. Why in the world would you want to go back to the boonies. You do know that we could end up in an ambush, right?"

"We`ll be just fine, Sgt. Minister," I said knowing I was happier having something to do during my final day, more than I was worried we would be in an ambush. "When do we go?"

"In five, Sarge, if you`re sure you want to do this."

At 0830 hours, on my last day in Vietnam I found myself heading out toward Vo Dat with re-supply for my company. It was going to prove to be an interesting 94-mile round trip.

Jesse Minister was a nervous character. Besides being a chain smoker, he spoke a mile-a-minute in a voice that reminded me of nails going down a chalkboard….very annoying. But the guy was very efficient in his job. If a soldier needed a pair of boots immediately, along with a new poncho liner, an extra high explosive grenade, AND half dozen clips for his M-16, The Minister would make sure the order was filled for the next re-supply. I imagine most supply people were just as efficient, but Jesse never messed any order up, and 1st Sergeant Fish liked that. He kind of reminded me of the tv character Barney Fife with his herky-jerky movements. I couldn`t help but smile when I saw the guy. What can I say, he entertained me.

The first thirty miles of the journey to Vo Dat was on a relatively easy highway-type road through open lands and farms. It was at the end of the thirty miles where convoys were formed to insure safety for military vehicles moving north through dangerous territory. The road from the check-point onward was a narrow, curvy, severely-rutted dirt road, with open fields bordered by thick jungle tree lines containing plenty of sites for the N.V.A. forces to set up ambushes. While the seventeen, or so, 'dangerous' miles were seeing less and less ambushes, it was mandatory that no American vehicle be allowed to leave the checkpoint without at least a track and tank escort. The roads were considered dangerous enough that Cobras were always on call for immediate support, too.

Ambushes took days to set up. Patience was a virtue of the N.V.A. The enemy always prepared for a quick strike, using foot soldiers and mortars, followed by a well-planned retreat at the first sign of retaliation by tanks or gunships. In recent months, however, the N.V.A. seemed to have a lot of difficulty finding ambush sites that fit their needs. Truly, there hadn`t been an ambush on that road for the last several days, but according to Sgt. Minister, he felt certain that one would occur in the next day or two. Though The Minister was generally a nervous worrier, that information made me re-visit my paranoia. I DID have the desire to see my former checkpoint, and my platoon mates one last time, so I didn`t react negatively to Jesse or my fears. Besides, it was well-known that the local Vietnamese people were using that road much more, in recent weeks, than they had when the ambushes were frequent. I felt quite certain we`d be fine on my last day In Country. Let`s face it, when I was in the jeep, my mind was playing tricks on me.

Once The Minister got to the military checkpoint, we were directed to a spot where other vehicles were waiting to be inspected. It was required that military police first find out where each vehicle was headed, and what cargo was being hauled, before anyone was allowed to move to the holding area. When the m.p. was finished looking our jeep over, I asked him what time we could expect to get rolling. He said the usual track company was finishing up an early morning assignment, but the convoy would likely pull out in about three hours. My jaw dropped as we headed to the holding area. The Minister had warned me it would be a long wait before any convoy was ready to proceed, but three hours was unacceptable to me.

We had been placed far away from the checkpoint area, in order to accommodate more vehicles needing to join the convoy. Vehicles started pouring in, and soon there were almost two dozen trucks and jeeps between us and the guys checking everybody. When I saw that there were no visible soldiers standing at the checkpoint, and all of them had their heads looking into trucks, I said to Jesse, "Sergeant, get on the road right now, and let`s get to Vo Dat."

"Sgt. Stein," the supply sergeant objected, "ALL American vehicles are required to be escorted north in a convoy. We could get into big trouble, AND we could be ambushed….with no support."

"Just move NOW, Sgt. Minister. I`ll explain my actions later. You won`t get into trouble because I am taking full responsibility for this action. And I PROMISE you we won`t get ambushed. Put the petal to the metal, Sergeant, and let`s move before the checkpoint guys see us." The Minister just shook his head, but he flew down the road. I looked back continuously, but saw nobody even slightly concerned with our departure. Within two minutes we had gone around our first curve, and we were out of the sight of any convoy personnel.

Sgt. Minister`s eyes were glued to the road. He didn`t seem capable of speaking, but his gas petal foot remained flat on the floor most of the time. He didn`t miss many pot holes, I`ve got say, and my kidneys were feeling it. However, there were no problems with the supplies as The Minister had strapped them down tightly.

"Jesse," I said as I began to explain why we were alone. "if you were the leader of an N.V.A. ambush, the first one you were springing in over a week, and you found the perfect ambush site, would you choose to blow the surprise on one lone jeep, or wait until the big prize came along? You MIGHT even think that one single jeep, going down the road, could be acting as a decoy, with Cobra gunships ready to swoop in at the first sign of an ambush? If the jeep WAS just a decoy, then you`d let it go, right? I know I would. No leader would want to blow a chance to get a very important convoy, by losing it on one little jeep. What do you think, Jesse?"

"I don`t get paid to think, Sarge. I`m just going as fast as this thing can move, like you told me to."

"That`s great, Jesse, but is there any way you can miss even ONE of the ruts in the road?" I just prayed that I was right about my reasoning, but I had my rifle ready to let loose with twenty rounds at the first sight of any trouble.

Our total time from the check point toVo Dat was a little over thirty-five minutes, which was actually longer than I expected. Normally, The Minister could have covered seventeen miles in less than half an hour, but the country was in the middle of its monsoon season, which caused Jesse to slow down on the slippery dirt curves. Once we passed the little South Vietnamese outpost, where 2nd Platoon had set up its own outpost for twelve days, the road was a pretty straight drive right into town. I was sad as we passed our former checkpoint, however. The barbed wire was gone. The grass had grown high enough to cover any of the track marks made by tanks. There was just that crummy, little Vietnamese encampment, so I didn`t even think long about what went on while we were in the area.

We pulled into the Delta Company compound but the place looked nearly deserted. I found out, as I was un-loading the cargo with a new guy from 1st Platoon, that both the 2nd and 3rd platoons were involved in another joint venture with a whole company of South Vietnamese soldiers. Sgt. Minister had gone to report in to Capt. Mertz, but within minutes he was back at the jeep. "The captain wants to talk to you, Sarge." By the intonation in his voice, Jesse`s message almost sounded foreboding.

As I got to the entrance of the command hootch, the captain saw me and immediately bellowed, "Sgt. Stein, why are you here, and WHERE is the convoy?"

"Sir," I began, "Sgt. Minister needed a shotgun companion, and with nobody else wishing to go, I told him I was available. As for the convoy, we were told that the tanks would be late arrivals to the checkpoint, so we were unsure what time we could even leave for Vo Dat. I got worried that I might miss my flight back to the States tonight if we had a long wait, so I told the sergeant to drive hard and we could get here in no time at all. Plus, Sir, I had gotten intel that there would be no ambushes today. The intel must have been right because here we are."

The captain tapped his fingers on the table for a few seconds, arose from his chair, moved to where I was standing, and looked me right in the eye. "Sgt. Stein, you know as well as I that there is NEVER any intel on when an ambush will take place. You were lucky. Now, you may have a death wish, but you are NOT to include Minister. Is that understood?"

"Yes, Sir."

"You have a late flight tonight, so you won`t be missing anything. I am ordering you to stay on the company grounds until the convoy comes BACK through here on its return trip to the Rear. Do you understand that?"

"Yes, Sir."

"If Minister so much as gets a splinter on the return trip, I am holding you personally responsible. Now you better understand that, too."

"Yes, Sir,"

"Go find something to do for the rest of the day, but report to me when the convoy is returning and you are headed back to Long Binh. Get out of here, Staff Sergeant Stein.... and have a safe trip back to your family."

"Thank-you, Sir," and I snapped to attention, gave Capt. Mertz a salute, pivoted, and headed to see where The Minister was. The captain`s last words almost sounded like he cared for me, and I left his office with a smile on my face.

When Jesse saw me entering the supply tent, he rushed up to me and asked nervously, "What did the captain say? Are we in trouble?"

"No, nothing like that, Jesse," I answered. "He was just surprised to see us so early, is all. Wished me a safe trip back home tonight. Which reminds me, are we done un-loading? I have a big steak waiting for me at the N.C.O. Club, and I want to leave as soon as possible so I can go enjoy it sooner rather than later."

"We`re done, Sgt. Stein. Let me go tell the captain we`re ready to head back," Minister said in his usual whining tone, as he started to leave the tent. "Then we can....."

I gently grabbed The Minister`s arm and stopped him from exiting, then I said quickly, "Already told him we would be headed out just as soon as the supplies were out of the jeep. Told him I thought we would be done in the next five minutes....which we are. Come on, Jesse, I`m kind of in a hurry here."

Minister stared at me for a second or two, with a comical look on his face, then he shook his head and said in a very shaky voice, "You`re going to get us in so much trouble." We hopped into the jeep and sped back the way we came.

To this day I can`t really explain to anyone why I acted so stupidly and recklessly by driving that dangerous road alone....and forcing Jesse Minister to be with me was VERY wrong. My first thought is that I must have just wanted to see Peppleman, Fimbres, and Randle one last time, but then I got upset when I thought that the lateness of the tanks would put a crimp in the plan. I likely would have reasoned that a long wait time would not only DELAY me from seeing my buddies, it would have vastly shortened the reunion time, too. Sadly, I didn`t get to see them anyway, but I didn`t know that at the checkpoint. Perhaps I was just plain sick and tired of the military`s 'hurry up and wait' routine. Ever since Basic Training, it had bothered me that the army would get us some place in a hurry, then we`d sit and practically go stir crazy waiting for something to happen.. So, when the m.p.s indicated we`d have a long wait, and then Mertz DEMANDED that I wait, perhaps frustration got the better of me, maybe I decided to 'thumb my nose' at the military policy. Then again, perhaps the captain was right....maybe I DID have a death wish. I had beaten myself up pretty well my first night in Long Binh. Guilt from losing combat brothers, the uncertainty of what life would be like trying to make things work out with a wife who told me she wasn`t sure she wanted to be married to me. I was just plain tired of chastising myself. Maybe I`d hoped that I would be in an ambush, fight like a madman, then everyone would have their final thoughts of me going out like a man.

On the return trip down that slippery, dirt road, I was WAY more frightened than when we went to Vo Dat. I was one mixed-up human being....that was for certain. For his part, The Minister pressed the gas pedal even harder on the way back, and we passed right through the m.p. checkpoint in less than a half hour. I smiled at the m.p.s, and they just stared at us as we continued to our rear company area. "By the way, Jesse, I DON`T think you should report back to the 1st sergeant until much later today." I said to my driver as we pulled onto the company grounds. "He may not be as accommodating as the captain. No reason for you to get into trouble with him, and I don`t want to have any trouble getting out of the company area, and to the airport. I just realized, I have GOT to get out of this stinking country, and I need to do it soon."

"Sarge, I`m not going to see Fish at ALL for the rest of the day. I can hide out, count on that. What we did today was nuts, and I NEVER want to have to go through something like that again," The Minister said.

"See ya, Jesse," I said. Then the two of us went our separate ways. I wanted to thank him for doing what I had asked of him during our ordeal, but I chose NOT to say another word because it was easy to see how upset he was. Once the two of us departed, I immediately headed to the N.C.O. Club. I had lost 47 pounds during my tour in Nam, so I was really looking forward to having a huge water buffalo steak with all the trimmings. And I needed a cold beer, too.

I was actually expecting someone from Delta Company to come get me at the club and take me to face 1st Sgt. Fish. I was sure that he`d either want to ream me out for taking his supply sergeant into unnecessary danger, or have me sign a disciplinary action taken out on me by Captain Mertz. I was surprised and delighted when no one showed up. I intended to enjoy the club until fifteen or twenty minutes before I had to catch my ride for the airport.

At 2000 hours, two sergeants entered the bar and one of them announced loudly, "Oooh shit, did we have a rough go today. The re-supply convoy we were in, which was headed north, got hit about seven or eight kilometers short of the village of Vo Dat. There were some injuries but no one died. Got to see a Cobra come in and give those gooks hell, and that was fun to see. Then a couple of the tracks chased those bastards into the jungle, but nothing came of it. Lots of excitement, though. Damn, we`re just gettin` back now!" Two thoughts raced through my mind at that news. First, I knew almost EXACTLY where that ambush took place. Secondly, I felt pretty good about my rationale as to why our jeep WOULDN`T be ambushed. Then I shuttered thinking about the fact that The Minister and I would have actually BEEN in that ambush if we had waited for the track outfit to join us. I had another beer, and gave a prayer of thanks. The Good Lord had to be watching over my stupidity that day.

At 2130 hours I headed back to my barracks, finished packing my duffle bag, and only had to wait twenty minutes until my ride to the airport picked me up. No one was around to say good-bye, but that was fine with me. At 2230 hours, I boarded an air force plane with about sixty other vets. The guy sitting across the aisle from me said in a very quiet voice, but loud enough for me to hear him, "Let`s get outta here!"

That`s apparently how everybody on board felt, as not another word could be heard as we taxied before take-off. I just stared out the window, wondering why it was taking so long to get off the ground. When we finally got airborne nobody moved for several minutes. I just prayed that the enemy would let us get up and away without firing anything at us. Suddenly, a voice came over the loudspeaker, "Gentlemen, we have officially moved out of Vietnam`s airspace.... let`s go home."

The cheering was indescribable, but only lasted a minute or two. Everyone, me included, was exhausted, and sleep became the rule of the flight. I don`t remember stopping anywhere. What I do remember was being physically, mentally and emotionally drained, and I just needed to collect myself. The long flight helped me do that.

It became daylight several hours before we landed, but I didn`t open my eyes until the captain came on the loudspeaker for one last time. We are starting our descent into the Seattle area airport. You`ll be on America soil in half an hour.

This was truly my freedom bird. I looked out my window and smiled at ships, and buildings, and cars....and there were lots of cars. I was so happy because I knew I would be getting my discharge from the military within two days. I would be DONE fighting any wars. There would be no more shooting from me, or at me. I was willing to tell people, if asked, how I survived the jungle, the elements, the food, and the danger that was around me every day....but not the combat. I wasn`t sure I could handle talking about the death of my platoon`s real heroes without breaking down. I may not have been a happy camper when I was drafted, but I served my country admirably and with honor.

I knew deep down inside me that I was ALWAYS going to be a proud veteran, but I also knew that I was going to have to win back my wife, too. To do THAT, I believed I would never be able to talk about the military in her presence again. I believed it to be a simple formula....if I ever wanted our love to be CLOSE to where it was when Jill married Abraham in 1968, I could never remind her of the soldier she had been around for the two years following my induction. That was the harsh choice I was willing to make, for that was how much I felt I needed to change in order to stay married to her.

The plane stopped on the tarmac, and we descended by the use of stairs. The airport terminal was still a good 100-150 feet from our aircraft. Since it was a warm day and not hot, several of us got down on our hands and knees and kissed the ground. We gathered our duffle bags and an elderly sergeant walked up to us and told us to follow him. He told us we would have to walk through the terminal a little ways, and then exit the building where two busses were waiting. The transportation would then take us to Ft. Lewis, Washington. We were all excited, and I was right behind the old sergeant when we entered the building.

Instantly I heard the obnoxious chants of 'murderers,' and 'baby killers,' coming from a group of people standing just inside the door we entered. There were about twelve to fifteen protestors of the Vietnam War yelling at us. They each were displaying a derogatory sign, and as we started to move down the hall, they began walking right beside us. Some of them were pretending to spit on the ground at our feet. I was in shock, as I`m sure were several other soldiers in our group. Shock turned to anger rather quickly, and I started to see those jerks as my enemy. The old sergeant turned and prodded us to stay together and keep moving forward. I wanted to tell those assholes that I was a survivor of the war, and that I chose to serve my country rather than leave it or go to jail. I had never seen that much venom and hate from one American to another, and I wanted to grab any one of them and shake him until he came to his senses. Before I could react to my thought, however, I heard the sergeant say loudly, "Here we are. Let`s move quickly, now. We don`t have time to lose," and he opened a door near me, which lead outside.

There was a sign just outside the exit door which indicated we were in a military loading zone, and any protestors trespassing in the area would be prosecuted. I was still in shock, and full of anger when I walked toward the first bus. I thought about how much Jill hated the military, and I wondered how many other people I knew were anti-war. I glanced to my right, and saw a small alleyway. There appeared to be a large garbage container, a dumpster, if you will, sitting to the side of the alley. Without really thinking about what I was doing, I moved to that dumpster, opened my duffle bag, and started dumping the contents in with the rest of the garbage. I had decided that I didn`t want ANYONE back home to know that I had ever been in the army, let alone that I was returning from Vietnam! I was FILLED with confusion and rage.

When I felt I had emptied the whole bag, I just stood there. I was feeling absolutely stunned by the whole situation. Suddenly, there was a hand tapping me on the back of my shoulder. It was the old sergeant, so I turned to face him. He said, in an apologetic voice, "Sergeant, I am so sorry about what happened inside. There is nothing that can be done to stop the protests, unfortunately. I am REALLY sorry you decided to purge your duffle bag. There were probably things in there you may, some day, wish that you had kept. But they are gone now, and that`s a fact. It is the same with the war. You are back in America, so the war is now in your past. Just remember this, you can NEVER change what has happened in your past. What is done, is done, and it CAN`T be undone. The only advice I can give you now is something that has worked for me, lo, these many years....live for today....and look toward the future." After he paused for a few seconds, he patted my shoulder and said, "I also know that the mess here at the airport is over for you, too, so come on, we have to get the busses moving."

I looked at the aging soldier and nodded my head. He walked me back to one of the busses. Then he shook my hand, gave me a slight smile, and said, "Just remember what I told you, and good luck to you." I went inside the bus, walked to the rear where I sat down, closed my eyes, and thought about what that old soldier had just said to me.

I must interject a personal thought here….quite simply, the impact of the sergeant`s words on my life, from that moment until today, has been paramount in shaping who I have become. In 1970 it was becoming a habit of mine to mentally and emotionally punish myself for events that had gone wrong in my life. I was being cruel to myself night after night after night. I would torture my mind to the point where I felt like I was losing my personality. Guilt over losing my friends….things I said to Jill….I wanted to go back in time and change it all. But, no matter how many different ways I corrected the outcomes in my mind, no matter how many times I thought of a better result, I would end up getting furious with myself knowing I COULDN`T change the past. It was like the sergeant said, 'what is done is done.' There was NO way I could have undone one single thing that I said or did….still can`t today.

I also don`t remember receiving any formal assimilation treatments when I moved from the military way of life to a civilian life. I just got out of the service and went home, and that was it. If I hadn`t heard the sergeant`s words, and actually LISTENED to what he said to me, I don`t know HOW I would have ended up handling my nightmares. His words 'live for today, and look toward the future' had become my mantra in everyday life. Whenever I mishandled any stressful crisis, instead of ranting and raving for days on end, I would just repeat the old sergeant`s words. I would then force myself to come to grips with the errors I committed, tried to figure out if there were some things I could have and should have done better in the failed situation, then I would vow to make wiser choices in my future. I do the same process in my life today. I am convinced that his short counseling session that day has helped me, any number of times, move from explosive feelings I begin having inside, to a calmer demeanor, done in a relatively short period of time. That old sergeant was there when I needed something or someone to help me get my head on straight, so if that fellow is alive today, I want to say thank-you.

By the time the short ride to Ft. Lewis was finished, I had calmed down a great deal. I went through my discharge procedure rather quickly, and before I knew it I was on an airplane headed to Cedar Rapids, Iowa to become a true civilian once again. I didn`t LOOK like a civilian, however, since the only traveling clothing I had was the dress uniform the army gave me, and it had all the medals I had received on it, too. I did take home my partially-filled duffle bag, and WAS upset that I had dumped most of my souvenirs at the Washington airport. I may have embellished the story a bit when I stated that I dumped EVERYTHING into the dumpster. I actually gave it two or three good shakes, and most things dropped into the garbage….including my diary. Ironically, all my medals had been on the bottom of the bag, along with a couple pair of olive drab undershirts, underpants and socks, but that was about all that was saved.

As we approached the Iowa airport, I wondered if I would be facing demonstrators there. I hadn`t on previous landings, but I also knew there would be no 'thank-you for serving' comments from anyone either, like sometimes happens to troops today in some airports.

We touched down and taxied a short while. I spotted Jill and my mom right away, as they were waiting by the outside gate I was scheduled to enter. While I was happy to see both of them there to greet me, I was shocked by my mother`s appearance. I knew I hadn`t seen her in over ten months, but she looked much older than what I expected a 47-year-old woman to look like. She looked much thinner than I remember her being, her hair had turned completely grey, and the large black circles under her eyes made her look extremely tired. I should have known that even though I never told her about any of the dangerous situations I had encountered in Vietnam, she was an instinctive veteran of WWII, so she knew I was not on any vacation. I wanted to run to her, hug her, and triumphantly announce that her little boy was home safe and sound.

As I got to within twenty feet of the gate, Jill broke through the gate and raced straight at me with her arms wide open. She had a huge smile on her face, and then she jumped into MY arms. Even though I was wearing a full-dress army uniform she kissed me hard on the lips. She then looked me in the eyes and said, "I love you, and I missed you so much."

Believe me, I was VERY happy when all those things happened. It was like a dream come true. Still, I couldn`t believe that this was the same woman with whom I fought for a week in Hawaii. The woman who only wrote me two letters during my last three months in Nam, and said she wasn`t sure she even loved me anymore. The woman who told me there wasn`t ANYTHING about the army that she didn`t hate, and there I was wearing the gaudiest army coat imaginable. Yes, I had prepared to be greeted by the cold shoulder from Jill, so the kiss took me completely by surprise, but I was more than happy to kiss her right back.

Sadly, it was during the intense hug and kiss, that I first smelled the distinct aroma of marijuana on Jill. It was emanating rather significantly from her hair and clothes. She was high as a kite. I looked at my mom, who kept a smile on her face while she watched us kissing, but I felt certain she was well aware of Jill`s condition.

When she was dropped off at her home, my mother asked if I could 'come inside a minute, so you can get you some strudel I baked today.' I told my wife I would be right back, and followed my mom inside. I grabbed the container filled with her baked goods, gave my mom a big hug, then SHE said, "I`m so glad you`re home, and I think Jill is, too. Please, Abe, you must work hard to heal whatever wounds this war has given you two. I really like her, and I know you love her. She is going to need a lot of understanding from you." She touched my ribbons and nodded. That was a true indication to me that she was aware of the fact that I hadn`t been entirely truthful in my letters about what I did in Vietnam. My mother, like the old sergeant at Ft. Lewis, was giving me sage advice on how to acclimate to my return from a war zone. I thanked her for the strudel and supportive advice, then went to be with my wife.

Jill talked during the entire car ride to our trailer. She talked about her apartment and how well she and her roommate got along. She mentioned several new friends she made, and how much they meant to her. She talked about how school was going for her, and let me know she had just one more semester before she would graduate as a teacher. She talked most about a family she had met, and couldn`t wait for me to meet them. Robert and Cindy were the parents, and they had two delightful young children, whose names I can`t remember. For my part, I nodded approval at everything she said, throwing in a 'that`s great,' or 'I`m proud of you' at appropriate moments. In fact, she talked 100% about herself and what she was going through. I was expecting her to ask a question of me....perhaps, how I felt about being out of the army and a civilian again. She never asked me anything. I was hoping she could tell me she loved me or missed me, phrases like I heard when she greeted me at the airport. She just never got around to that, either. Our journey was twenty minutes long, and like I said, she rambled in her self-absorbed monologue the entire trip. I did count one good thing during that time, however, she didn`t sound the least bit angry about anything, including being upset with me.

Unfortunately, that ride home was the highlight of my first night out of the army. Once we got inside the trailer, the mood changed immediately. The first thing I saw was a six or seven-month old kitten sitting in my chair. Jill raced to the animal, scooped it up, hugged it, and said, "There`s my baby. Did you miss me?" Apparently, my asking Jill to wait until I got home, so we could discuss getting a pet, fell on deaf ears. I won`t go into detail about the discussion we had, but it lasted a very long time. The gist of it was that I mentioned having allergies and how I was tired of her desire to hurt me. For her part, Jill mentioned WANTING to hurt me, especially after the way I treated her in Hawaii, and she kept telling me 'to grow up.' I`m still not sure what she meant by that. After all, I had just returned from being in a war zone, and I felt I grew up there. Jill just wanted to push all the buttons she could find on me, I guess.

We once again talked about the little amount of money we had in the bank, but that was just a re-hash of the arguments we had during R&R. Bottom line, I expected twenty thousand to be there for us, she said we had less than fifteen hundred. That button was pushed hard.

Then something REALLY bad happened. We were talking about give and take, lies and truth, when she said, "OK, Abe, you want the truth? You say that you want to make this marriage work, but only if you have the truth about everything? While you were gone, I had a few lovers."

Suddenly, I was enraged. I couldn`t say a word. It was after nine at night, but I rose from my chair and headed to the door. Jill moved quickly and placed herself between me and the exit. I looked at her and somehow calmly said, "I turned down a sexy prostitute on a beautiful beach because I told her I was married, and that married men don`t cheat on their wives."

"Abe, where are you going?" she said while grabbing both my arms at the wrists.

I continued, "You told me you had a FEW lovers while I was away. In the military, we call those bastards Jody. We HATE Jody! I hate Jody! I am going to deal with them the best way I know how. I am going to go out, buy a gun, and shoot those bastards` balls off! That`s where I am going."

At that point, Jill started to say whatever she could to keep me from leaving. She told me she wished I would have been with the prostitute, especially if I felt I needed to have sexual release. She told me the guys she had didn`t mean a thing to her, that SHE had needs, and they were only acting like prostitutes for HER.

By that time I had thought about how embarrassed my mom would be if I created a big shooting incident, and I never wanted to hurt my mom. What Jill said intrigued me, so I said. "All right, I won`t shoot anybody. But I need you to tell me who they are, and I will go give them each $20. That`s the rate for prostitution in Vietnam."

Jill looked shocked by the thought that I would ever do anything like that. Suddenly, she said something that made me stop dead in my tracks. "Abe, all that shit is over. I just used them because I was thinking about you, and missed having sex with you. They meant NOTHING to me. When I was with them, I made believe they were you….and THAT`S the truth." I didn`t believe her when she said she was thinking of me before, during, or after sex with those guys, but some of her words rang true.

I returned to my chair, sat down, and thought back on the old sergeant`s words….not being able to undo what had been done. Then my mom`s words, about understanding and trying everything I could to make my marriage work, rushed into my head. I ended up NOT leaving the trailer. We stayed up very late, however, and we ESPECIALLY talked for a long time about her one-night stands. She told me there were five guys.

Most of them were athletes, and she bedded them because they reminded her of MY athletic prowess. OK, what she said was really bullshit. I mean, come on, they reminded her of me because of our similar athletic proclivities? Two of them WERE athletes, both of them were Black athletes at Iowa on some kind of athletic scholarship….basketball, Ithink. I was a wrestler at heart, and warmed the bench for my school basketball team. A Black basketball star I wasn`t. Jill DID confide in me that the third guy wasn`t athletic at all. He was a druggie, and probably didn`t know a football from a catchers mitt. The last two guys played chess, if I remember correctly. Reminded her of me and my athleticism, huh? Still, she tried to sound convincing, and I really wanted to believe her infidelity could actually be at an end since I was home to stay. I believed it when she told me in a sincere-sounding way that she still loved me, and she really WANTED to make the marriage work. Sleep that first night was nearly non-existent for me, not only because I hashed over everything we talked about, and also because that damn cat kept trying to sleep on my face. Jill defended the beast by explaining to me that it was cold inside our trailer, and the cat was just trying to stay warm by sleeping near my hot breath. I had to throw that cat off my face three times before it learned to stay off.

We both went to school that winter, and Jill graduated. We spent a lot of time with Robert, Cindy, and their kids, but I wasn`t interested in meeting her other friends. I never talked to anyone about being in the military. When spring came, however, I convinced Jill that I had to move away from Iowa City. I told her I hated the rain, due to the monsoons in Nam. I hated the Iowa cold, and wanted to move someplace where it is warmer in the winters (we got snow-bound in our Iowa City trailer for two days without much food to eat) I finally confided in Jill that I was uncomfortable living in the same town where her romantic companions still lived, and that if she REALLY wanted to make our marriage go, we needed to get a fresh start somewhere new for both of us. I hated to leave my mom, but she understood why I wanted to move. We moved to Arizona in the summer of 1971.

Epilogue

After four more years of being married to Jill, I divorced her. She remained spoiled, and I continued to allow her to torture me. For instance, one night, after a particularly brutal disagreement, she confessed to having a four-month long affair with our Iowa City friend Robert. She even told me they had sex the night before I was to get home from Ft. Lewis.

I remember going back to Iowa City the summer after I divorced Jill, and I went to Robert`s house. He knew Jill spilled the beans about their romance as soon as he opened the door and saw the look on my face. He begged me not to tell Cindy about the affair, and I didn`t....not because I didn`t want to get back at him, but because his children were still quite young and impressionable, and they shouldn`t have to find out how weak their dad was. However, I am pretty sure I walked away leaving that cheating bastard worried.

I told him I wasn`t going to tell Cindy right then, and that I was going to wait until the right moment. When he asked what I meant by that, I just said, "Cindy deserves the truth, and you will for SURE know when I finally tell her." Robert had tears in his eyes when I left him at the door.

The final straw to our marriage came at my school`s year-ending party, which was held on a Saturday at the house of one of the district administrators. (yep, I graduated as a teacher) Jill got drunk and refused to leave the party with me. She got back to our apartment at 5:00 a.m. Sunday, and told me she had slept with that administrator, even though she knew he was a married man. He was a drunken sot anyway, and when I confronted HIM, he claimed he didn`t know what he was doing because of his drunken stupor. He begged me not to hurt him, either physically or professionally. Instead, I thanked the rotten bastard. Told him he did me a favor. His wife found out, somehow, and divorced him within the year.

The favor I alluded to was that his act of stupidity finally convinced me to put an end to my nightmare marriage. In fact, the day after Jill told me of her indiscretion, I went to the court house and got a no-fault divorce packet. I gave Jill everything she wanted, and more. I just wanted to NOT be married to her anymore. The divorce was finalized within the month.

Eight years passed. Then, on one particularly great 'blind date,' I found the true love of my life. Her name is Katherine, and we have been together for thirty, mostly happy, years. (hey, all couples have little spats from time to time) I was lucky to find her, and hope we have another thirty years together.

I have gotten together with several of my platoon members, too. Katherine and I visited Walter Peppleman and his wife in California, James Remington and his wife in Florida, and I`m hoping to get together with Paul Randle and his wife in New York one day. He and I are in contact via e-mail right now.

Our biggest reunions, however, have been in Texas. I have visited Tex Foracker at his homestead on a couple of occasions. Just last summer, Katherine and I went to Tex`s and he had Little Dickie Hart and Johnny Middleton there, too. My wife and I were just passing through his neck of the woods, so we could only visit for a few hours. The four of us 'vets' had a wonderful time together, talking military language, and trying to remember different events. (though none of us could remember the same events the same way) It had been over forty years since we were in Nam, and though we were looking 'kinda old,' I`d go to war with those guys again in a heartbeat. Dickie had joined up with Katherine and me in Pennsylvania for a few days in the early 2000`s. He chose to sleep on a rubber mattress on the ground, instead of a comfy bed. To me that was hard core, though he did put air in it. I have to say again that he is the most instinctive soldier I ever worked with, and could probably hold his own in most battlefield scenarios right now. The one guy I have never gotten to see again is Rodney Nelson, but

I still think of him often. And, Rodney, I want you to know that Dickie, Johnny, and I talked kindly about you, and that Tex said he wished he had known you. You`re still loved.

There is something I have to mention before ending these stories. Conversing with my brothers-in-arms, and reminiscing about the 'old days,' does bring a lot of laughs and maybe some tears, too. But sometimes we discuss what is happening in America today. Now I am going to get a little political, so for those of you who don`t want to read about one of my pet peeves, just skip to the last paragraph.... thank-you. I get furious when I hear about people walking all over American flags, not standing for the National Anthem, or any other stupid act done by disrespectful people showing anti-American sentiment. I witnessed stupid acts when I was young, too, but was too naive to know what I was seeing. However, ever since I have served in the army and fought to protect America`s freedoms and values, those kinds of ignorant acts have become like slaps to my face. I also have a hard time believing that ANYONE in uniform today accepts those miserable acts as coming from people who love America. In fact, those horrible acts are disgraceful and an embarrassment to ALL hard-working people across this great nation. To me, personally, when a disrespectful event occurs, it makes me feel like I did when I encountered the protestors in Washington in 1970.... who is my enemy? My thought is simple, to those rabble-rousers and creeps, who would rather create disharmony and turmoil in America, through ignorance or violent actions, it`s time to go to a country where you CAN find happiness. To you young protestors, please work in POSITIVE ways to get your objections across, or join the military and learn what my platoon members and I learned.... America is the greatest country in the world. Loud, boisterous, obnoxious, and immature behaviors are embarrassing to me and many veterans. When you display childish behavior, the rest of the world sees it in the media. They laugh at how stupid Americans are, and if they believe that the idiots misbehaving on television represent the best America has, then we obviously have to be thought of as being a weak country. What is the saying, 'if you aren`t part of the solution, you are part of the problem?'

Finally, to those of you who have worn the uniform, I say thank-you. I know the battles you fought when you were deployed....I fought the same battles during my military time, too. I know the demons you faced when you got out of the service….I faced them. (many days, I still do) You joined the military to help keep American values alive, and I pray that you can reap the benefits of enjoying life now that your service time has come to an end. If, however, times seem too tough to endure, I want to encourage you to seek solutions….don`t EVER give up. There are people out there to help you gain your equilibrium. For each and every one of you, I know there is an old sergeant out there, waiting to tell you what you need to hear, and showing you what you need to do in order to thrive…. keep looking for him.